Praise for Rachel Cusk

"There is nothing blurry or muted about Cusk's literary vision or her prose . . . She is one of the smartest writers alive."

—Heidi Julavits, *The New York Times Book Review*

"[Cusk] has that ability, unique to the great performers in every art form, to hold one rapt from the moment she appears . . . A stark, modern, adamantine new skyscraper on the literary horizon."

—Dwight Garner, *The New York Times*

"In her effort to expose the illusions of both fiction and life, [Cusk] may have discovered the most genuine way to write a novel today."

—Ruth Franklin, *The Atlantic*

"Cusk has glimpsed the central truth of modern life . . . She moves through it as a blasted centre full only of instinct and superhuman hearing and hackles."

—Patricia Lockwood, *London Review of Books*

"Cusk, like the best artists, has renovated her work from its deepest interior—the self—transforming her private crises into an expansive aesthetic vision."

—Meghan O'Gieblyn, *The New York Times Book Review*

"Quietly staggering and intellectually entrancing . . . [Cusk's] writing is silvery and precise, navigated by elegant syntax that steers its speaker toward revelations of great depth."

—Martha Schabas, *The Globe and Mail* (Toronto)

"[The Outline trilogy] can now be appreciated—and will surely be looked back on—as one of the literary masterpieces of our time."

—Sebastian Smee, *The Washington Post*

"[Cusk] commandeers reality . . . An object lesson in rigor, elegance, and fury."

—Merve Emre, *Harper's Magazine*

"Cusk's prose . . . is a tight guitar string or a wire from an espalier. Her descriptions . . . have a bewildering precision, a feeling of painful truthfulness." —Claire Jarvis, *Bookforum*

"Cusk's brilliantly reasoned argument against the false security of narrative continues to hit a nerve." —Megan O'Grady, *Vogue*

"Alienating yet intimate, dreamlike yet grounded, slim yet substantial, delicate but fierce, Cusk's writing feels, exhilaratingly, unlike any other fiction being written these days." —Emily Donaldson, *Toronto Star*

"[Cusk] writes like someone who has been burned and has reacted not with self-censorship but with a doubling-down on clarity. She is blazingly intelligent, a deep, tough-minded thinker . . . at once freewheeling and exquisitely precise." —Heller McAlpin, NPR

Siemon Scamell-Katz

RACHEL CUSK

The Country Life

Rachel Cusk is the author of the Outline trilogy, the memoirs *A Life's Work* and *Aftermath*, and several other works of fiction and nonfiction. She is a Guggenheim Fellow. She lives in Paris.

The Country Life

ALSO BY RACHEL CUSK

FICTION

Second Place

Kudos

Transit

Outline

The Bradshaw Variations

Arlington Park

In the Fold

The Lucky Ones

The Temporary

Saving Agnes

NONFICTION

Coventry

Aftermath: On Marriage and Separation

The Last Supper: A Summer in Italy

A Life's Work: On Becoming a Mother

The Country Life

RACHEL
CUSK

PICADOR
NEW YORK

Picador
120 Broadway, New York 10271

Printed in the United States of America
Originally published in 1997 by Picador, Great Britain
Published in the United States in 1998 by Picador USA
First paperback edition, 2000
Paperback reissue edition, 2021

The Library of Congress has cataloged the Picador USA
hardcover edition as follows:
Cusk, Rachel.
The country life / Rachel Cusk.
p. cm.
ISBN 0-312-19848-5 (hc)
ISBN 0-312-25280-3 (pbk)
I. Title.
[PR6053.U825C68 1999]
823'.914—dc21

98-31292
CIP

Picador Paperback ISBN: 978-1-250-82815-6

Our books may be purchased in bulk for promotional, educational, or business use. Please contact your local bookseller or the Macmillan Corporate and Premium Sales Department at 1-800-221-7945, extension 5442, or by email at MacmillanSpecialMarkets@macmillan.com.

For book club information, please visit facebook.com/picadorbookclub or email marketing@picadorusa.com.

picadorusa.com • instagram.com/picador
twitter.com/picadorusa • facebook.com/picadorusa

1 3 5 7 9 10 8 6 4 2

My thanks go to Bridget Lutyens and John Cox of
Slade Farm, Dulverton, for showing me the country life;
to my editor Katie Owen, as always, for the resilience of both
her displeasure and her talents; and to Josh Hillman.

For my parents, with love

What makes the corncrops glad, under which star
To turn the soil, Maecenas, and wed your vines
To elms, the care of cattle, keeping of flocks,
All the experience thrifty bees demand –
Such are the themes of my song.

Virgil, *The Georgics*

The Country Life

Chapter One

I was to take the four o'clock train from Charing Cross to Buckley, a small town some three miles, I had been told, from the village of Hilltop. The short notice at which I was required had left me with little time for more than a glance at the area on a map, where I had learned only that the two names belonged to the lower part of the county of Sussex, and where I had gained the impression of a series of subdivisions eventually resulting in a narrow scribble of road and terminating in the dot of my destination. The prospect of travelling away from London was an unnatural one. Some gravitational principle appeared to be being defied in doing so. Tracing the route with my finger, the distance seemed more unsustainable as it grew, and once beyond the city's edge took on in my mind the resistance of an inhospitable element, as if I were now forging out to sea or tunnelling underground. To me the town of Buckley was as remote an outpost as an Antarctic station, and, still further, the village of Hilltop – represented there by a dot, as I have said – seemed to promise neither oxygen nor human life.

It was normal, of course, that I should feel some anxiety about my departure. Not only was I setting out to a place I had never been before; I was also embarking on a kind of life about which I knew nothing; and what is more, stripping myself of all that was familiar to me into the bargain. We are all, in our journey through life, navigating towards some special, dreamed-of place; and if for some reason we are thrown off course, or the place itself, once reached, is not what we hoped for, then we must strike out at whatever risk to set things right. Not all of these forays need have the drastic flavour of my own leap into the unknown; some are such subtle turnings that it is only afterwards that one looks back and sees what it was all leading to. But to drift, blown this way and that, or for that matter to pursue a wrong course for the sake of fear or pride, costs time; and we none of us have too much of that.

I had been given only three days in which to make my arrangements, and as these were absolute required a consideration at once speedy and measured. Fortunately, I have a keen organizational facility, and am able to marshal a group of factors with speed. Judging the letters to be the most important of my duties, I accorded them first place. The tying up of all affairs concerning my flat had therefore to be put second, although the immediate anxiety caused by this deferral tempted me momentarily to promote it. The packing of my suitcase was relegated to the hours prior to catching my train.

As I had expected, the letters took far more time than was really – given the uncertainty with which I could prophesy their effect – their due. I found myself wretchedly unable to achieve the result I desired, despite the fact that, if I had been honest, I would have admitted that I had been writing such letters secretly in my head ever since I was a child. The problem with the letters, as they stood in my mind, was that the ramblings to which I had given subconscious voice over the years lacked the economy crucial to the rendering on the page of an atmosphere of severance. As one sheet became four – closely written on both sides – I grew increasingly dissatisfied with the confessional, injured tone I had adopted. Such a tone, I realized, was useful only if covertly or otherwise one wanted to continue relations with the person addressed, but must get things off one's chest first. I tore up the letters and began afresh. Now, however, I spurned elaboration too forcefully. The tone was bitter, and the sentiments cruel with abbreviation. I worked late into the night and eventually achieved something which, if far from perfect, at least skirted the neighbouring chasms of self-pity and vitriol with relative composure.

4 Hercules Street
London

Dear Mr Farquarson

I am writing to inform you of my resignation, with immediate effect, from the firm. I do apologize for any inconvenience this may cause.

Yours sincerely
Stella Benson

4 Hercules Street
London

Dear Mother and Father

I know that this letter will come as a surprise, and probably a shock, to you, but I suppose that if we all lived our lives only to avoid worrying our parents nothing much would ever be achieved. The fact is that I have been unhappy for a long time. While I don't exactly blame you for this I still think that it probably has a lot to do with you, so on balance I think it would be better for me if we didn't see each other any more. I am going away, so that should be that. I have told Edward what I am intending to do. Please don't try to find me.

Your daughter
Stella

PS. I know you will be worrying about the flat. Perhaps you should just sell it, as I obviously won't be needing it any more. I've left quite a few things here. You can sell those too. Please don't be angry with me.

4 Hercules Street
London

Dear Edward

I hope you had a good holiday. You will have noticed that I was not around when you got back. That is because I have gone away for good, so don't worry that I've had an accident or anything. I'm not telling you where I'm going, and I'm sure you've got better things to do than try and find out. I'm sorry I can't explain this any better, but I don't think you would understand. I hope you have a good life.

Yours
Stella

PS. I can just see your face while you're reading this!

I sealed these letters, there at the table in the middle of the night, just in case I was tempted to look at them again in the morning and tear them up. This later proved both an insufficient deterrent and an irksome obstacle to my crossing out that postscript in the letter to Edward, which I was driven to do after waking in the night, resealing the envelope with Sellotape.

My letter to my parents at least had the advantage of saving me time in consideration of the problem of my flat. While writing, I had had the opportunity to think things through, and had found that the very action of putting pen to paper had simplified the issue. The flat was not, in the very strictest sense, my responsibility; this sense being that although I had enjoyed unchallenged dominion over it since the day of its purchase, in fact it belonged to my parents. I had intended to rent it out for them, believing, in the way that a small sum of money can repay in the mind debts several times its size, that my remaining time in London was so elastic that it could encompass ambitions which extended far beyond it; but I now saw this intention for what it was, a valedictory gesture designed to solicit the approval of those whose fury was the one certain outcome of my move to the country. It was to avoid precisely this type of intrigue that I was going; and I discharged the whole fraught matter without delay. In doing so I had the sensation of lightness I remembered from Rome, when it had been enough to convince me that I could jump from high up over the city where I stood and would not fall. Feeling it again, I could admit that its absence since had worried me. I had been relying on the memory of it and my memory had become a tattered paper, like the letter which sustains love between people far away from each other.

Of course, I wanted to leave things in as orderly a state as possible, so that when my parents eventually called at the scene they would find nothing to displease them; no trace, in short, of myself. This process gave me a feeling, which increased as the hours laboured by, of being gradually but forcefully expelled, not just from my home but from all that had constituted my life up until that point. So unaccountable, in fact, did I begin to feel that had I not been so busy I would probably have committed some criminal or otherwise irresponsible act. Let me say that the most powerful part of the sensation by far lay in my feeling not of being pushed out, but rather of being drawn irresistibly towards something new. My pristine flat had the still-warm, thronging emptiness of a station after a train has departed elsewhere. I should add here, lest this seems too poetic, that my great clean-out went beyond the merely sanitary and involved what could without exaggeration be called the destruction of all evidence that I had ever existed. The purge was far from easy, for my mementoes – I suppose inevitably – reminded me of forgotten episodes, both good and bad. I had not thought my life to be so large, and occasionally, as I wrestled with it there on the sitting room floor, I felt myself to be engaged in mortal combat with a creature which writhed and bit as I sought to slay it. At other times I felt such a drowsy reluctance infuse my limbs that my resolution wavered in the very midst of its work. In these moments I felt quite outside myself, as if I didn't care whether I stayed or went, nor indeed about anything that might happen to me. Once or twice I came upon something particularly sentimental and was almost drowned in a wave of self-pity and regret, wondering why it was that I felt so keen to give away every vestige of love I had ever earned. Minutes later some article of shame would provide a bitter chaser for my sickened palate, and I would come alive with purpose, working faster to free myself as if from beneath a fallen beam.

Towards evening I unearthed a packet of letters, addressed to me at school, which my father had written to me. They did not come, I should explain, directly from him – my father found emissions of feeling difficult, and any betrayal of fondness was always followed by a pantomime of disownment – but rather via the persona of Bounder, our dog.

Kennel House
Canine Close
Barking

Dear Stella

How are you? Is it raining 'cats and dogs' there like it is here? I've had to repair the woof of my kennel as it keeps leaking. Sometimes, when it's raining, my master lets me come into the house, but my mistress usually finds some excuse to throw me out again. It's a 'dog's life'.

I hope you are working hard. You don't get a second chance with your education. And don't get into trouble – you don't want to in-cur any punishments!

Your faithful friend
Bounder

I was very unhappy at school at this time, and as you can imagine, such letters did little to comfort or cajole me. It might give you a fuller picture of my parents' characters to know that the 'here' and 'there' referred to in Bounder's letter were in fact barely a mile apart. The notion that it could rain in one place and not the other certainly betrays a deep delusion on the part of my parents, who never otherwise hinted that they were anything but convinced of their decision to send me to a boarding school within walking distance of their house. Lest you think that I would have preferred a more far-flung institution, and that they kept me close by them for the sake of affection, let me tell you that I saw no more of my parents than the other girls did of theirs; and further, that I detested every day that I spent in that hellish place and begged to be sent elsewhere.

My predicament was, I now see, the result of my parents' own insecurities. Aspiring to a social position to which they had not been born, they believed it correct to expel their children from the family home and live amongst its empty, echoing bedrooms in miserable solitude. Being also, however, thoroughly provincial in nature, they believed it impossible that any school could be better than those found locally; and that the convenience with which they could visit us and attend school functions, not to mention savings in telephone calls and travel expenses, outweighed both the greater convenience and enormous financial benefit of having us at home.

My brothers were scarcely any better off, and indeed once the tide of my own injury had drawn back and the years neutered its memory somewhat, I was able to feel more aggrieved on their behalf than on my own. Like me, they were sent 'away'. The elder thought himself happy enough within those high and privileged walls; but when finally he returned it became clear that he had left something vital and precious behind. It was probably for his own good that he himself never seemed to notice the loss; and how could he? For it was as if, while maintaining his outward appearance, everything in him had been minced into an undifferentiated mass and then re-formed in a blander, more homogenous shape.

Not fitted to run with the elite, the younger was doomed in one way or another to become its prey. The accident occurred on the school playing fields, which my brother was crossing on his way back from his violin lesson. These lessons were a torment to my brother, who, unbeknownst to his teachers or fellow pupils, suffered from deafness in one ear. It is difficult to comprehend how this disability could have gone unnoticed; and perhaps in a more confident pupil it wouldn't have. My brother, however, scion of the brutal bourgeoisie, carrying the weight of my parents' hopes on his small shoulders, was an accomplice in the matter of his own oppression. He struggled to keep up in the classroom, learned with admirable skill to participate in conversations half of which he did not hear, sawed weekly at his violin, and never once considered that he might be happier were he to free himself from this intolerable burden. Labouring under it, then, as he crossed the grass, he did not notice a javelin competition being held at the other end of the playing field. Witnesses claimed that they shouted at him to duck as the pole came hurtling through the air towards him; and there is no reason, I suppose, not to believe them, when you consider that at least three of them required 'counselling' after the event, which suggests at least that they were, as individuals, less callous than the forms their community took. My brother's deafness, as you will have guessed, made any warning to little avail. The deadly instrument felled him where he stood, impaling his small body on the grass like a bird struck by an arrow. He was thirteen years old, a year younger than me.

Many things came to pass as a result of this dreadful event. I will not go into them now. Of all the questions that were asked, however, of all the enquiries painfully made amidst expressions of regret and grief, one was never ventured: to wit, briefly, what arcane and pointless practice was this that deprived my brother of his life? That my parents never asked it was, to me, a measure of the unforgivable awe with which they still regarded the institution that had been so careless with their son. They didn't dare; as if by questioning the sport they would have betrayed their inferiority, the public discovery of which they feared more than all the private sorrow in the world. It has haunted me through the years, even now that my brother is but a shadow, a ghost that flits, unrestful, about my thoughts.

To return to my clear-out, I disposed of Bounder's correspondence with mingled grief and venom. A similarly sized bundle of letters from my mother – with whose contents, which bored me even at the time, I shall not now detain you – followed it; and so on, until all the messy spoils of the past, accumulated over such stretches of time, won in conflicts both arduous and joyful; the whole long, tiring campaign of my existence was parcelled up into three large bags and put downstairs for the proper authorities to dispose of.

Chapter Two

I stood outside Buckley station, with one suitcase on the ground on either side of me, and waited. I had worried that Mr Madden would, never having met me before, have difficulty recognizing me when I arrived, but the station building and forecourt were more or less empty. As I stood there, however, my suitcases picking me out like quotation marks, I found that my attempt to conduct this simple train of thought in a logical manner was strangely confounded. I saw that the station was deserted, but failed to register the significance of this sight in relation to my anxieties concerning my arrival and recognition. Indeed, my acknowledgement of the emptiness of my surroundings, rather than reassuring me as to the ease with which I would be noticed standing there, lacked all memory of the importance the state of the station had assumed in my thoughts previously. This, it soon became clear, was the fault of an entirely new anxiety, which at the sight of the deserted station – a sight I did not, as I have said, find reassuring in any case – now came to torment me. What surprised me was how quickly this second anxiety had superseded the first. It suggested a certain powerlessness to my position, as if my only existence, my only mental function, was to register with each passing second the uncertain outcome of the next.

My anxiety, naturally enough I suppose, was as to the whereabouts of Mr Madden, whose absence at the scene of my arrival I had not, trapped as I was in this new, contingent, and entirely linear mode of thought, even considered. I wondered whether he could have had an accident on his way; a thought I entertained only briefly and with a distinct lack of concern. I could, and did, as I stood there, admit that Mr Madden's existence was as yet a matter of complete indifference to me; and right up until the very second of his arrival would remain that way. It was interesting to think that, perhaps in five minutes' time, I might care about something for which at the present moment I had no feelings whatever. The fact that I was giving such undue attention to my lack of feelings for Mr Madden began itself to seem rather portentous. I wondered whether some significance were being telegraphed to me from the future; a future in which, for example, I would fall in love with Mr Madden and look back on my former indifference with astonishment; or, if my love were unrequited, with longing. Perhaps, on the other hand, this message was reaching me not from the future but from a different room of the present. Were I to discover that Mr Madden had indeed met with an accident on his way to collect me, would I be glad of my impartiality or sorry for it? Could the very fact that I had thought of him having an accident have brought the accident about? And how would his accident affect my contract of employment with the Maddens? Was it selfish or merely practical to consider this aspect of things at a time like this, my indifference towards Mr Madden having already been established?

All of which took me forward by a few minutes, at which point I noticed that a blue car had drawn up and was crouched on the forecourt some ten yards away from me. I had a feeling of abrupt drainage, as if a plug had been pulled on the pool of some inner world. The car sat for some seconds, like an unexploded bomb, before the door on the right-hand side swung open. A feeling of intense fear rolled heedlessly over me. I realized not only that the man who got out of the car and began to approach me must be Mr Madden, but that I was also to have the first human encounter – discounting dealings with ticket collectors, newsagents and the like – I had had since that last day in Rome.

'Sorry! Sorry!' said Mr Madden, coming towards me with his arms flapping up and down.

He was very tall, and quite large, with black, shiny hair which bounced over his face, which was red, as he walked. He was wearing a shirt with the sleeves rolled up, on which the peculiar motion of his arms revealed glimpses of two hidden islands of sweat. From a distance his face had looked oddly crumpled, but now I saw that he was smiling, a smile so forceful that it required the cooperation of all of his features to sustain it, so that it appeared oddly to be his fixed expression.

'Sorry!' he said again.

He was right beside me now, although he was too large and mobile for me to get a sense of him, as if I were at the wheel of a car and had to concentrate with all my might to stay on the road.

'Have you been waiting ages?'

'No,' I said. It just came out, without my even having decided what to say. 'Only a few minutes.'

In that moment, I knew, everything was set. By 'set', of course, I mean only in the most specific sense; I don't want to imply that Mr Madden's future, for example, was in my hands, nor that the more general pattern of events to come had been fixed by this one trivial exchange. What I am trying to describe is my belief that the first seconds of any encounter are those in which the important decisions are made, the fundamental characteristics established, the structural lines laid down. Had I, for example, produced some witticism in the course of my first exchange with Mr Madden, in place of what I actually did say, things might have turned out very differently between us. As it was, of all the shades of character I might have selected, I chose a kind of diffident reserve. He, as you have seen, presented himself as cheerful, kind and slightly distracted. I am not saying that our relationship did not progress beyond these roles, nor occasionally even move outside them; merely that this moment was the mould into which our fluid first encounter was poured, and that even when later we had gelled to form something firm and free-standing, its basic shape was always held.

I must have assumed a slightly stunned expression, because Mr Madden stood before me with an air of polite expectation, as if waiting for me to come to life.

'Ready?' he said finally.

It was only a second before he said it, but those early seconds, as I have said, seemed long.

'Absolutely!' I replied, even giving a little laugh. I knew that I was trying to escape the mould I had made for myself, and knew too that the attempt was futile.

'I'll take these, shall I?'

He bent down to pick up my suitcases. I was immediately worried by how heavy he would judge them to be, and what he might infer from it. As he bent over, I saw the top of his head. Being so tall, it was evidently not a part of him that many people saw – as its aspect of overgrown neglect testified – and looking at it I felt a curious tenderness for him, as if I had chanced on a secret door to his nature which the maze of social intercourse might have kept hidden from me. He straightened up and began walking with my suitcases to the car. I followed behind and watched as he opened the boot and heaved them in. Then, either out of good manners or because I still appeared somewhat stunned, he came round to my side of the car and opened the door for me.

'You might want to take your coat off before you get in,'

he said. I caught the fugitive glance of his small, bright eyes. 'Pretty stifling in there. It's been sitting baking in the sun all morning.'

'Right,' I said.

For the first time since I had arrived, I noticed that it was indeed very hot, and that I was wearing far too many clothes. A fierce sun blazed overhead and the sky was brilliant blue. I had left London in an iron-grey bustle of turbulent cloud and gusting wind, and the change confused me. I tried to recall when it had happened, and wondered if I had fallen asleep on the train.

'It was cold when I left London,' I added, removing my coat. I was grateful that I seemed to have the possession of at least some of my faculties once more. Mr Madden would now know that I did not habitually dress for a hot day in winter clothes.

'Was it really?' he said, with gratifying astonishment.

He slammed the car door shut (I had sat down in the passenger seat by this time) and proceeded around the front of the car to the other side. I looked at him through the windscreen. The car was quite still for a few muted seconds. Then the door opened and he was in, noise and movement reinstated as abruptly as they had been suspended.

'We're off!' he cheerfully cried, starting the car, putting it into gear and lurching forward in a single movement. 'Sorry again to have been so late.'

I waited, assuming he would want to provide an explanation, although by that time I had forgotten that he had been late at all; and forgotten too, as before, the anxieties attendant on his lateness. He laughed suddenly, a single barking noise which jerked his head back as it exited from his mouth.

'That's it,' he said. 'No excuse, I'm afraid.'

'Perhaps you got stuck behind a herd of cows,' I said, much to my own astonishment.

'Perhaps I did,' he replied, rewarding me with another bark.

I had been going to explain that this was how I might have imagined country life to be, making a joke of my being from London, but to my satisfaction he seemed to have understood my comment without further explanation.

We appeared already to have left Buckley, although I could remember nothing about the town, despite the fact that I had been looking out of the window. The road was now very narrow, and to either side I could see fields and trees which the bright sunshine gave a look of fixity, like a landscape in a painting. I thought of saying this but decided against it. Mr Madden drove very quickly, with a sort of proprietorial confidence which I was in no position to question, giving two sharp hoots of his horn at every sharp bend we approached. It seemed unlikely, given that our car clearly filled the width of the road, that this call would provide adequate warning to whatever might be travelling towards us. I sat rigid in my seat, oscillating between the secure thrill of fairground fear and the terror of real risk; and felt almost relieved when, rounding a corner, a vast, muddy tractor reared up at us on the road ahead. In that panicked, overcrowded second I knew we were going to crash and I must have cried out, for after Mr Madden had swerved unperturbed onto the verge, barely slowing his speed, and delivered us safely back onto the road beyond, he turned his head and looked at me.

'Sorry!' he said. 'Pamela's always telling me I'm a menace. Forgot you weren't used to it.'

'I'm fine,' I shrilled.

A feeling of despondency came over me. I felt as if everything had been ruined by my overreaction. Combined with the mention of Pamela (that being, of course, Mrs Madden), the episode served to remind me that the sunny drive was but a prelude to the immovable and at that moment forbidding fact of my employment with the Maddens, which I had all but forgotten. I had been existing in the temporary heaven of believing that I was the guest, rather than the servant, of this world of which so far I had had such an intriguing glimpse. I saw that my new situation in life would require a more extensive range of adjustments than I had anticipated. Any calculation of happiness or sorrow, satisfaction or complaint, would now have to include the weight of my inferiority. There would be benefits, I did not doubt, in relinquishing my stake in the world – it was with the certainty of collecting them that I was making this journey – but they would come at a price. I could not afford, on this budget, to imagine – as admittedly I had there in the car – that I was a friend of the Maddens invited to stay; and still less to entertain a scenario in which Mr Madden was my husband, bowling with me along these bright country lanes. I couldn't, however, help it; any more than I could avoid fostering an immediate and irrational dislike of Pamela. My premature but thriving hostility worried me. I wondered if the mere thought would 'set' relations with her in the manner I described earlier.

'Do you see these fields now on either side?' said Mr Madden, bellowing over the noise of the engine. 'This is the boundary of Franchise. From here on in, the land belongs to the farm.'

I looked obediently out of the window. I saw the jolting fields, which looked no more sinister than those which had preceded them. The heat and the lulling motion of the car were making me drowsy. I wished the journey could go on for ever.

'How long have you had the farm?' I enquired, in an attempt to wake myself up.

'Hmm?' Mr Madden shot me a look of bright bewilderment. 'Oh, it's Pamela's, really. Been adopted into a long line of gentleman farmers.'

'Oh,' I said. I felt obscurely defeated by this information, as if I had been engaged in some form of competition with Pamela from which her landed superiority had now disqualified me. 'Do you do all the work yourself?'

'Me?' yelped Mr Madden, gripping the wheel. 'I've got a manager.'

'A manager? Like a film star?' I said wittily.

'Eh? That's right!' He guffawed, nodding his head convivially. 'He doesn't manage me. He manages the farm, does the day to day stuff. I just hang about getting in his way. Very good chap, although the girls like to have a joke about him. Look, there's Pamela,' he said suddenly. 'She'll be pleased to see us.'

We were drawing up a straight gravel drive banked on either side by trees which abruptly shaded the car and filled it with a sticky medicinal scent. Directly ahead of us stood a large, imposing house. It was built of grey stone and was very square, with a strict symmetrical aspect and three rows of windows whose glass was dark in the sun. At the front of the house was an elaborate white plaster portico, on either side of which stood a large stone pineapple. The front door was open, and standing on the steps watching our approach with folded arms was Pamela.

Chapter Three

There was a hiatus after Mr Madden stopped the car, like one of those pauses which occur in the theatre, when darkness briefly falls and the actors gather themselves in for a change of scene; surfacing from character for a swift second before plunging back into the drama which must, whether they like it or not, unfold. That second passed, there in the unshielded glare of the driveway. In the sudden silence of the engine I became oddly aware of smells, the waxy smell of Mr Madden's jacket, the doggy odour of the car, the tint his skin gave the enclosure, this latter more of a light pressure than a smell. Then Pamela's footsteps were crunching across the gravel and I saw her midriff, above which her arms remained folded, through the car window. She bent down and there was her face, grinning close to mine through the glass.

'Hi!' she said, or rather sang, the word as radiant as her smile. A tangled, autumnal foliage of brittle brown and blond hair surrounded her face. She opened the door as I sat there and I felt strangely exposed, like a cross-section in a biological diagram. Mr Madden got out of the car on the other side, and with both doors now open I was something of a sitting duck.

'Hi, darling,' said Mr Madden from outside.

'I'll bet you were late, weren't you? Did you have to wait *ages*?' said Pamela, to me. Her eyes glittered with expectation.

'No,' I said, looking up from my seat. I felt that I had missed my cue to get out of the car, and as the imperative to do so grew louder, so my intention of rejoining the stream of events correspondingly curdled into that strange and static indifference to which, I find, politeness can at any moment revert.

'Look at her!' said Pamela, to my horror. 'You've frozen her to her seat with fear, darling. Come on, let's get you inside and we'll revive you with endless cups of tea.'

My cue, therefore, was finally provided, although in a manner far from that I might have wished for. As far as 'setting' things went, Pamela certainly stole the show. In my doughy and rather pliant state, I immediately felt the force of her managerial nature. I knew that I would have to take urgent steps to prevent things from continuing in this vein.

'*That*'s it,' said Pamela encouragingly.

As I got out of the car, I was able to continue with my preliminary assessment of Pamela's appearance. It has been my experience that people of a dramatically different physical 'type' to oneself are harder to get along with than those whose flesh one's own instinctively 'recognizes'. Pamela's physical presence immediately struck me as alien; not only in that she was as different from me as was (excluding, obviously, broader possibilities such as having only one leg) possible; but also in that I couldn't imagine what it would be like *to be her*. In looking at a man, this sensation might well be commonplace; but with a woman the problem becomes somewhat more visceral. It relates to the possession of shared sexual characteristics which, while inviting a superficial assessment of sameness, conceals a deep and, I believe, mutual repulsion. This is not merely the repulsion of a repressed and heterosexual nature for its own kind. In the circumstances I am describing, it is the imagination as well as the body that suspects and rejects its rival, for want of any common ground on which to begin the process of understanding. There was, I could see straight away, no corner or crevice of Pamela's form that shared its secrets with my own; and as such I suppose I identified her as a threat, or at least a mystery. Perhaps you understand what I mean, but then again perhaps my mistake is not in the way I attempt to explain things. Perhaps, rather, it lies in my attempting to explain things as if they are universal, whereas in fact they are merely the defective impressions of my own mind.

In any case, having made so much of Pamela's physical appearance, I am bound to describe it now in a more neutral fashion. She was not, in fact, beautiful, although she was of the age – somewhere in her fifties – at which people would say that she *must have been* very beautiful. I, however, believe that she always looked like that; almost beautiful, that is, or post-beautiful, like the sky at the end of a lovely day, when the sun has disappeared but its aura remains, redolent of things past, a memory more piquant even than the thing remembered. She was quite tall, of slender, almost wiry build, with a skin made leathery by sun, and hair, as I have said, both brittle and profuse. Her face was very attractive, in an extrovert and absolutely unmysterious way, and, not unlike the face of a monkey, was both creased and childish at the same time. This, along with her dynamic and compact form, gave an alluring impression of youth and experience combined, and the whole energetic package was wrapped in a veneer of breeding at once impregnable and careless.

If you have kept in mind the fact that, in appearance, I was as different from Pamela as could be, then you will have gained some impression of me from this description. Unlike Pamela's, mine were not the sort of looks that slapped one in the face when one encountered them. They did not disrupt, nor seek, attention. One could, in the presence of my looks, get on with the matter to hand; something I have not found to be without its advantages, and have learned, on occasion, to turn to my own.

There is one further subject requiring attention before I can proceed, and that is the matter of the forms of address I have so far employed. A discrepancy may have been observed in my calling the husband Mr Madden, while the wife, before I had even met her, became known to me as Pamela. Unlike many people of my generation, I was brought up always to address adults formally; even, in some cases, after they had implored me to use their first names. My parents fortified this practice, as they did many others, with the belief that beyond these apparently fragile social barricades lay a wilderness of unimaginable degenerations from which good manners offered our only protection. They were even known on occasion bravely to erect a missionary outpost in the savagery beyond, and demand that some over-familiar friend of their children use the more polite form; and were any of us to affront *their* friends in this manner – even, as I say, if asked to – our presumption was regarded without mercy.

I still, therefore, find it unnatural to use the first name of a person older than me, even though I myself am no longer really young. (I am twenty-nine.) I say this lest it seem that I was Mr-ing and Mrs-ing the Maddens through a sense of my own servility or inferiority to them. This was not at all the case. My free use of the name of Pamela now, however, doubly requires explanation. Suffice it to say that I only adopted it *after* Mr Madden – Piers, incidentally – had revealed it to be Mrs Madden's name, and that, moreover, I was using it strictly in my own thoughts. As soon as I was required to, I would verbally address her as Mrs Madden; but being, in those early stages, mentally intrigued only by her role as Mr Madden's wife, and by his feelings for her, it seemed natural to think of her by the same name that he himself did. Once the habit had been acquired – well, I think I've explained myself pretty fully.

To return to the scene in the driveway, my suitcases were retrieved, as they had been stowed, by Mr Madden. Meanwhile, Pamela had taken me by the arm – a gesture of appropriation entirely unnecessary, given that her aura of ownership hung like a great canopy over the very air we were breathing – and was leading me towards the front steps of the house.

'Piers likes to batten down the hatches,' she informed me in a conspiratorial tone. 'So we'll leave him to it, shall we?'

The skin of her bare arm was dry and very warm on mine. I could smell her perfume and beyond that the more general scent of her, which I was dimly aware was arousing muddled feelings of attraction in me. I had a remote sense of some inner derangement, whose faint call I could hear as if momentarily borne on a favourable wind from a great distance.

'All right,' I said.

I glanced behind me and saw that Mr Madden was indeed occupied with locking the car doors one by one, and, from what I could gather, inspecting the battered bodywork. My suitcases stood obediently side by side behind him on the gravel. My connection with him seemed all at once dreamlike, and he was less familiar to me standing there than he had been minutes earlier in the car.

'Now tell me all about your journey,' continued Pamela, guiding me through the open front door and into the cool, dark hall. I had an impression of many pictures and mirrors pressed against the walls in the quiet and capacious gloom. Directly ahead a grand polished staircase swept lavishly upwards. The floor shone darkly: it was made, I saw, of great, gleaming flagstones, on which my shoes made a clicking sound as I walked. Pieces of furniture stood frozen in elegant poses about the shadows, slim-ankled chairs with elaborately carved backs, delicate side tables bearing a vase or lamp. A grandfather clock loomed still and straight as a butler at the far end, its throaty, leisurely tick punctuating the cavernous silence. 'It was so good of you to come at a moment's notice. I feel terribly guilty. Did you have a *dreadful* amount to do?'

At that, I guessed that I was being presented with an

opportunity to speak. I opened my mouth; but just then there was a furious sound of scuttling and panting up ahead, and all at once a great black bolt of fur and flesh flew at us from the end of the long hall. Taken by surprise, I shrieked as the animal charged my legs, describing crazed circles of excitement around me before plunging his drooling muzzle directly between my thighs.

'ROY!' bellowed Pamela. 'Stop that! Get down!'

The dog was sniffing at me feverishly, his nose rooted deep in the folds of my skirt. Finally, Pamela yanked him back by the collar and administered a sharp slap to his heaving, glossy side.

'You're quite *disgusting*!' she cried; addressing Roy. 'Oh, he *is* vile,' she said, to me. 'Did he get gunk all over you?'

'I don't think so.'

'God, what a *madhouse*!' She set off again, still clutching Roy by his collar. His cowed legs slid and scrabbled over the stone floor. 'You must be wondering what you've let yourself in for!'

We passed the staircase and left the hall through a door to the right. After several twists and turns, and by a manoeuvre about which I was not entirely clear, we entered a large and sunny room which I took to be the kitchen.

'Let's get the kettle on, shall we?' said Pamela, releasing Roy, who skulked off into a corner.

'All right,' I said.

'And then you can tell me *everything*.'

She left my side and began busying herself at one of the kitchen counters. The whole room was kitted out in old wood, which is why I had been unsure as to whether it was a kitchen at all. A large, old-fashioned stove – the 'Aga', as I later came to call it – and a vast wooden dining table were the only clues. Otherwise, it was furnished with the sort of elegant cupboards and dressers which most people put in their formal rooms. I thought I had never seen anything so tasteful.

'What exactly was it you did?' said Pamela.

Her grammar, although I am sure it was correct, confused me for a moment.

'Excuse me?'

'Before,' she elaborated. 'In London.'

'Oh, I see. I worked for a law firm. As a secretary.' It proved harder to say than I had thought. 'This is a lovely kitchen. I've never seen one like it.'

'Thank you!' Pamela, who during the above exchange had kept her back to me, turned and gave me that same large smile she had given me earlier. It was a remarkably pleasant smile to receive. She turned away again. 'And had you always done secretarial work? Or was it a stopgap on the way to something else?'

I saw that I had got off lightly with Mr Madden, who had asked me practically nothing about myself.

'I've done various things, but mostly secretarial work. I didn't mind it,' I added, attempting to turn the conversation, 'but I suppose I just got bored. Which is why I'm here.'

Pamela laughed, and I must admit that my reply had been skilful.

'Well, you *certainly* won't be bored here. Exhausted and infuriated perhaps, but never bored. Although' – her fine shoulders twitched, as though she had been about to turn around, but had thought better of it – 'if you're looking for a social life, you might be out of luck. There's the village, for what it's worth, and Buckley isn't far, but we're definitely rather short on nightlife around here.'

I took this as a subtle warning and responded appropriately.

'I won't mind that,' I said. 'One of the reasons I wanted to leave London in the first place was to get away from all of that.'

'And what about boyfriends?' she continued; quite pleasantly, but still with her back to me, which added to my feeling of being, albeit subtly, interrogated. For the second time – my account of my inglorious secretarial career had been the first – I had the dizzying sense of chasms of treachery yawning open behind me, forbidding retraction. With every step I took on this vertiginous journey, the possibility of going back grew more remote. There was, of course, a feeling of great liberty aroused by the act of severing oneself from the past; but having stripped myself of so much, I had a panicked sense of my own nakedness and the indignities to which it exposed me.

'I'm not seeing anyone at the moment,' I said, and I think I sounded rather unhappy about it.

'Well, we'll soon see about that,' said Pamela, turning around. She had a large teapot in her hands, which she proceeded to bear to the table. 'Let's see if we can't find a nice rich farmer for you.' She laughed, loudly and spontaneously. I felt I had no choice but to join in. 'You must be thinking, what's the old bat on about now? My children are always telling me that I'm far too interfering, but I can't seem to help it. I just can't bear to think of lovely young people going to waste.'

'It isn't always a waste,' I said, quite sharply. I had realized by now that it was sink or swim with Pamela. 'Some people just prefer to be on their own.'

'*Do* they?' implored Pamela, bringing her eyes – which were an unusual light grey colour, and rather small – to meet mine. We were both seated at the table by this time, the teapot between us. 'Or do they only *say* they do, because there isn't anybody on the scene?'

'Perhaps a bit of both,' I said politely.

At that moment Mr Madden entered the room. I was very pleased to see him, concerned as I was that the conversation was straying into deep water. Unfortunately, my pleasure must have announced itself too boldly in my face; for I felt Pamela's eyes prick me from across the table.

'Darling!' she said, smile aloft. 'Is everything shipshape? I've been quizzing poor Stella dreadfully, so she's probably very relieved that you've come to rescue her.'

Mr Madden looked from one to the other of us and back again, an expression of bright vacancy on his rosy face. His response is hard for me to capture, being a sort of grunt or whinny – 'brrr!' would best describe it – which I soon learned was his habitual reaction to Pamela's episodes of sharpness. I myself was mortified by her comment, which penetrated my ears and exited through my cheeks in a matter of seconds with a furious blush.

'Is that tea?' said Mr Madden, nodding at the teapot.

'There's plenty left. Go and get yourself a cup,' said Pamela.

'I'll get it!' I interjected, leaping from my chair; Heaven only knows why. It was a sort of reflex action, I suppose. I had begun to feel uncomfortable with my situation, not because it was particularly unpleasant; on the contrary, it was far more pleasant than I had imagined my welcome would be – I had wondered, for example, if I might be put to work immediately on arrival – although of course there is no reason why I should have been able to imagine it accurately. What did I know of the Maddens and their kind? No, by leaping up in that unexpected manner, I was attempting to place myself in the menial role which must, in one way or another, be assigned to me before much more time passed. I suspected, moreover, that when Mr Madden had mentioned tea Pamela had considered asking me to fetch the cup herself. I have a keen instinct for this type of nuance; and even at this early stage had become alerted to the presence of a certain caprice in Pamela's nature, which suggested that she might not consider the precise articulation of her commands to have undue effect on their speedy and correct enaction.

'That's very kind!' she said approvingly.

'Don't be silly,' said Mr Madden. 'I'll get it myself.'

'She may as well learn where things are kept,' said Pamela meaningfully, fixing him where he stood with her eyes. 'She'll feel more at home once she knows her way around.'

'I'm quite happy to do it,' I said, anxious that my offer was becoming tarnished in this tug-of-war. 'Just tell me where you keep the cups.'

'In the cupboard directly in front of you,' said Pamela. 'That's the one! That's right.'

I opened the cupboard and there indeed were the cups; not, incidentally, aligned in orderly rows, but stacked in a jumble of conflicting shapes and patterns. I selected one painted a cheerful red.

'Thomas been yet?' said Mr Madden behind me. 'I want to tell him about that gate. Bloody nuisance.'

'He telephoned earlier. He's had to drive his wife to the dentist.' Pamela laughed, and began to speak in a voluble country brogue. '*Mrs Ma-adde? The wife's been taken poorly with 'er tooth. She's in turrible pain.*'

'Well, did he say when he'd be over?' said Mr Madden.

'Mr Thomas is our gardener,' said Pamela, turning to me. 'He's a very dear old chap, but he does find things like telephones rather difficult. It scares the living daylights out of you. *That you, Mrs Ma-adde?*' she said, doing her deafening imitation again, in spite of the scant encouragement she'd received for it. 'He said he'd be over later, darling, so do stop worrying.'

We were all seated around the table by this time, Mr Madden with his tea now in front of him. I could not prevent myself from being intrigued by what I had seen of the Maddens' relationship to each other, and the part in it which I had so far played. There was something almost combative in the way they behaved, and by my playing a part I only mean that the presence of a third person appeared to have set their game in motion, as a net would a tennis match or a pitch a bout of football. I noticed – not without some satisfaction, I'm afraid – that Mr Madden had seemed far happier in the car with me than he did in the presence of Pamela. Indeed, he looked rather sullen, staring down at his tea like an adolescent, his black hair flopping over his eyes, his large frame recumbent with that limpness slightly menacing in men, as if at any moment they could explode.

'Jolly good,' he said.

'I think Stella would probably like some time to just regroup,' said Pamela after a pause. She said it brightly, looking at Mr Madden. 'Shall I take her over and settle her in?'

Mr Madden, still slumped in his chair, took in a large quantity of air and held it in his lungs so that his cheeks puffed out. He nodded vigorously, and then expelled the air slowly through his nostrils.

'Right!' Pamela stood up and grinned at me slightly wildly. 'Shall we go?'

I stood up obediently and began immediately to make my way to the door. Behind me, Pamela lingered.

'Darling, you won't forget to dig up some potatoes and things for dinner, will you? And if there are any gooseberries left you could get those too and I'll make a pie.'

There was a brief silence.

'Right,' said Mr Madden. I heard his chair scrape across the floor. 'I'll go and do that now.'

Pamela's footsteps came behind me, and I moved forwards through the doorway. Ahead of me was a small and very dark hallway which I did not remember, with three doors, all of them closed. I stopped, confused, and felt Pamela crowd behind me.

'It's the one on the left,' she said. 'That's it.'

We entered a long, narrow corridor, with white walls and a low ceiling.

'Right down to the end,' said Pamela from behind.

I proceeded to the end of the corridor, which lay around a bend, where I found a door. There being no other option, I opened it, and was surprised when a bank of sunlight and a haze of bushy greenery burst upon me. I could hear the sounds of birds, and the faint, throaty noise of an engine far away. My feet crunched on gravel, and I felt the sun pound on the top of my head.

'We've put you over in the cottage,' said Pamela, taking the lead. We were following a gravel path leading away from the house, on either side of which was a tall, perfectly squared hedge. Surreptitiously I ran a hand along the green wall, half expecting it to be solid, and was surprised by its prickly give. 'It's tiny but very sweet, and I thought you'd want your privacy. If you get lonely you can always bolt back to the house and we'll sign over one of the spare rooms.'

It took me some time to absorb this information. Naturally, I had assumed that I would be living at close quarters with the Maddens, and having abandoned all thoughts of privacy or independence in my new life I greeted their unexpected return with ambivalence. It struck me then that the cottage arrangement could, on the contrary, entail privations more dire than those of which I just been relieved; namely that I would in all probability be sharing it with another of the Maddens' dependants, perhaps Mr Thomas and his ailing wife. I did not relish this prospect, and yet it seemed impossible that I would have a cottage all to myself. Not wishing to appear grasping or ungrateful, I felt unable to quiz Pamela on the subject, which taunted me along the path with alternating delight and dread.

We rounded a bend in the path and there, suddenly upon us, was a vision. It was an old white cottage, built on a single storey, with a thick thatched roof which slanted so low over the front that it resembled a long fringe with two eyes and a nose – the windows and door – beneath it. From the top protruded a chimney, and to the side, I could just see, was a tiny window in the angle of the roof. It was so small that one could take it all in from a single standing position. There was a wrought-iron gate in front of us, beyond which a narrow path led up to the door. On either side of the path was a square of garden, and the whole thing was surrounded by a tall, thick tangle of hedgerows and trees which gave it an atmosphere of shady secrecy. The garden itself was unruly, with sprays of wild flowers and some kind of fruit tree in the middle. On the front of the cottage was a splash of vines, as if the garden had risen up like a large wave and crashed against it.

'Mrs Barker's been in to tidy up, but Heaven knows what kind of state it's in,' said Pamela, opening the gate. 'Our last girl was not the most responsible creature in the world. You're free to brighten it up with anything you can find, and Thomas will come and do battle with the grass for you every couple of weeks.'

At this I deduced, with a cautious pirouette of glee, that I was to have sole command of this vision. We were standing in the buzzing garden now, in the sun, and the heat fused with the birdsong to form a single, pulsing note which thrilled in my heart. The cottage seemed to me to be the loveliest thing I had ever seen. It was in my mouth to ask Pamela why she herself did not live here, before I remembered that of course they had the big house, and that my rhapsodies were those of scale and expectation. Like a child in a room of adults, I had sought out only what was in my line of vision, what represented my own proportions; and consequently found more to please me in this miniature place than I had in its grander neighbour.

'So what do you think?' said Pamela coyly, turning to me with her hands on her hips. Her eyes were wrinkled in the sun.

'Oh, it's lovely!' I said. 'I didn't expect anything like this at all.'

'Well, it *is* rather useful,' said she, with evident satisfaction. 'These arrangements can be tricky, and this just makes everyone feel a bit more their own person.'

She led the way to the front door and wrenched it open.

'You've got to give it a good shove,' she said.

I followed her inside and immediately felt the stony coolness which is a feature of older buildings. The front door gave immediately on to a small sitting room – there being no hallway – with a low ceiling boned with dark beams and the two windows on the other side of which we had been seconds earlier. I had never been in a place with so insubstantial a threshold between inside and out. At one end of the room was a fireplace with another beam above it, and in front of that were a sofa and armchair covered in flowered material with a low table between them. There were several faded, brown-spotted pictures on the wall. They looked like maps, although the lines were so faint that it was impossible to see what they might represent.

'I know it's awful to think of it now in this heat, but you can light a fire here in winter. The whole place gets pretty cosy. The kitchen's through here,' said Pamela, leading the way through a door on the far side of the room. 'It's all fairly basic, I'm afraid, but you can always gallop over to us for a bit of television and comfort in the evenings.'

Pamela, I realized, spoke a language of energetic emergency, in which problems were approached as violently as they were escaped from. We entered the kitchen, which was exiguous, and contained one or two old-fashioned cupboards and a stove such as I remembered from kitchens when I was a child. It had a similar smell, a vague and not unpleasant scent of gas and vinyl. There was a wooden table, two chairs, and a rickety little window which looked directly out from the back of the cottage onto a green wall of hedgerow.

'It's not ideal for dinner parties,' said Pamela. She was not, it appeared, joking. 'But there's no reason why you shouldn't have someone to stay now and again.'

By 'someone' I guessed that she meant a relative or friend. I felt again the momentary, putative shadow of her disapproval, which swam deep beneath her conversation like a predatory fish. She opened a door to the right and proceeded into a tiny hallway. There were stairs up one side of it, and I realized that contrary to my original assessment there was in fact an upper floor.

'The bathroom,' she said, briskly opening a door beyond

which I glimpsed a slightly cramped arrangement of bath, toilet and sink, with a squinting window sharing the same view as the kitchen. She shut the door again. 'Up we go.'

The wooden staircase creaked as we ascended it, and Pamela bowed her head beneath the low ceiling.

'And this is your bedroom,' she said. 'I think it's rather sweet, don't you?'

We had entered a low doorway and were now in a room to the side of the cottage with a slanted ceiling. I recognized the window as that which I had seen from outside. It was quite a light room, with beams similar to those downstairs and a floor which canted steeply downwards to the outer wall. In it there was a double bed with a flowered eiderdown, a wooden bedside table on which sat a lamp, a dark, polished wardrobe which leaned sideways with the floor, and a bookshelf with books on it.

'It's lovely,' I said, proceeding to the window. When I looked through it, I received a shock. Although at an angle, the back of the big house and much of its garden was clearly visible. I had failed to orientate myself during our walk, and had thought the cottage much further away. I saw, as if by design, Mr Madden walking slowly across the lawn with a spade in his hand, thinking himself unobserved.

'Look, there's Mr Madden,' I confessed.

'You certainly can spy on us from here,' said Pamela, crowding at the window behind me and looking out. She laughed. 'It's a pity we're so terribly dull.'

After a few minutes we turned and proceeded carefully back down the narrow staircase, and seeing it all for the second time I was filled with a pleasantly proprietorial feeling. I opened the front door for Pamela and stood hospitably on the threshold while she took her leave.

'Why don't you take an hour or two just to feel your way around,' she said, stepping out into the garden. 'And then come over to the house for a drink at about six. Martin will be back from the centre by then, so we can all have a good chat before dinner.'

'Fine,' I nodded, accepting the plan with the mechanisms of a whole new system, which worked around me now like so many ropes and levers and pulleys.

'See you later!' said Pamela, and with a wave of the hand trod lightly off in the sun down the path. I watched her go from my front door, until she disappeared around the corner into the trees.

Chapter Four

I will not go deeply into the state of my mind at this point, nor my feelings as I watched Pamela disappear from view and found myself alone. Indeed, it was not so very long – perhaps no more than an hour in all – since my solitude had been interrupted there at the train station, and returning to this element, made familiar to me over the past few days, I was surprised to notice that I felt more or less the same, despite the violent change in scenery, as I had in London. The brief and brilliant novelty of arriving at Franchise Farm seemed to be no more than a detour on the long, featureless road of my loneliness. Taking the first opportunity to examine myself, I had expected to discover that my metamorphosis had already taken place, or at least was exhibiting sure signs of being in progress. My disappointment when I found that nothing, as yet, had happened to me was intense; but personal change, I now know, is a long and slow process of attrition, its many meticulous blows invisible to the naked eye. My first encounter with the Maddens, though I didn't see it at the time, was but a wave crashing against a stony flank of rock, whose wet glister dries and fades within seconds in the sun. It would take many, many repetitions for this effervescence to erode hard and stubborn stone; but it would. It had motion on its side, and the moon. There was, of course, a darker destiny written within my metaphor if one cared to look for it; for at the end of it all, these ancient tides would remain unchanged, while I would be diminished.

As it happened, I did not have much time to reflect on this or any other matter. I had closed the door and begun to wander slowly about the downstairs rooms, engaging in the subtle wrestling for dominion which more usually characterizes the first encounter between two humans, urging my surroundings to submit to familiarity and liking. I had begun, rather primitively, I am afraid, to open the kitchen cupboards and pry inside them, when a loud knock came upon the door. In so small a cottage, with the fragile barrier between inside and out which I mentioned earlier, a knock on the door can be a rather threatening thing. In a larger house, a knock or ring is a plea for entrance; in a small place such as my own, it is a demand. I hesitated. The knock came again. I realized then that I had been frightened by the unexpected noise, rather than the identity of the knocker; for who could it be but one of the Maddens, or perhaps dear old Thomas, the gardener? Hurrying now, I skipped through the sitting room and opened the door. There, indeed, stood Mr Madden, tall and rather out of place in my quaint and miniature garden. A blast of heat came in around him.

'Settling in?' he enquired. His face was very red, and he was wet. His shirt was sticking to his chest at the front, forming a long, damp delta between his ribs. At first I thought that he must have fallen into a body of water on his way, but soon realized that he was merely sweating profusely. 'I've brought over your cases.'

'Oh, thank you,' I said. I wondered whether I should invite him in, knowing that my decision would 'set' all future policy for visits between the two properties. 'It's terribly hot, isn't it?'

'Going to be a heatwave,' puffed Mr Madden, wiping his brow. 'Good news for us, of course.'

He turned and looked at the bright, twittering garden.

'Well, I'll let you get on,' he said finally. He picked up the suitcases and heaved them past me just inside the front door, withdrawing immediately from the threshold. 'You're coming over later, are you?'

'Pamela said to come at six.'

'Righty-ho.'

I saw that our early intimacy was struggling to survive, and that we were now speaking through Pamela, as if on telephones linked by her exchange. Unfortunately, I could think of nothing to say which would rescue our nascent friendship. Mr Madden turned with a sort of lurch, and trod heavily off down the path, raising his hand behind him in farewell.

Not wishing to shut the door rudely on his retreating form, I strayed out into the garden after him, vaguely imagining that I could busy myself there. I walked around a little, shielding my eyes from the sun, but my botanical illiteracy – as opposed to the domestic fluency with which I was finding my way around the cottage – set me rather at odds with my surroundings. I don't wish to give the impression that the garden displeased me in any way. It was simply that it seemed far less mine than the house, and I was very glad to recall that Mr Thomas was to take responsibility for subduing it. Still, I stood my ground for several minutes there on the grass, until something large and buzzing swam up before my eyes and collided with my forehead. I recoiled, crying out, although there was no pain. It was then, as my heart thumped with the shock, that I became aware of a menacing edge to the heat of the day, as if the sun had boiled over or burst its confines in some way. All at once I could bear it no longer, and hurried back into the cottage.

The two hours passed there quite quickly. Desperate suddenly to cool myself down, I ran a cold bath in the narrow tub, and lay in it for a while. The intimate sight of my naked body was oddly embarrassing in the foreign bathroom. It was difficult to relax while so exposed in a new place, the timbre of whose interruptions and emergencies were still unfamiliar to me. I was anxiously braced for another knock at the door, or for a face to appear at the tiny window beside me. As I rose, dripping, I realized to my dismay that I had brought no towel with me from London. I cast about, looking for something with which to dry myself, and finding nothing was forced to run, huddled and wet, up the stairs to the bedroom, leaving a dark trail behind me. There I was no luckier. I stood naked in the centre of the room, immobilized by frustration, as when one is unable to accept that a solution to a ridiculous and unforeseen problem does not lie close to hand. Eventually, ashamed and filled with self-doubt, I began to dry myself inefficiently with the papery, flowered edge of the eiderdown on the bed. As I did so, I was reminded of a time when, as a very small child, I had been caught on the lavatory with no paper, and had sat there casting about in a similar manner. Eventually, I had been driven to dab myself with a bath towel. (The very thing which now, of course, I lacked; the thought that I had had one surplus then, and had used it in such a wasteful manner, doubled my frustration.) My parents, although I could not remember how, had found out about my secret gaffe, and standing in the sloping bedroom I was beset by a painful memory of their – quite unjust, in my view – fury.

In the event, the force of the sun streaming through the bedroom window was such that I dried quickly enough. Opening my suitcases, which I had so hastily packed, I was unfortunately reminded that I had brought with me very little appropriate for the hot weather. I am often crippled by dislike of my own clothes, and am possessed by the conviction that for every situation in which I find myself, there is some perfect outfit which I do not own; an outfit, moreover, in which I would best the situation in a manner entirely out of character.

Sensing that I stood on the brink of an abyss of self-consciousness – a void into which I often fall, rendering me unable, even over several hours, to dress myself – I dug deeper into the cases and was surprised to find a summer dress I did not remember packing. It seemed imperative that having made this discovery I activate it immediately and with determination, before my first, faint protests – that it was, for example, too smart; that, conversely, it was also rather crumpled – gained any ground. I looked for a mirror and found one on the inside of the wardrobe door; an old and obscure mirror, which gave back so faint a reflection of myself that it was as if the glass were reluctant to admit that I was there. Averting my eyes from the dress so as not to provoke a crisis, I combed my hair, and boldly put on some lipstick.

Finally, after this absorbing interlude, I strode through the garden in my finery, finding to my relief that the heat had levelled off into a more plangent strain of evening. I retraced the route I had taken with Pamela; a more impressive figure, I felt, than had made the outward journey. I twisted and turned along the tall hedges, the gravel sharp and pleasantly noisy beneath my feet, and came out by the big house at what seemed to be the spot at which we had left it. Standing there, I considered the propriety of my entering by the back door unaccompanied. The alternative – ringing or knocking at the front door – seemed, however, too formal. I tried, therefore, the handle of the back door but found to my surprise that it was locked. I tugged at it quite fiercely, to no avail. Now that I looked at it closely, however, the door did not in fact seem to be the same one through which Pamela and I had left the house. Looking about, I saw that there was another door a few paces further along. I hurried towards it and pulled it open, finding myself seconds later in what appeared to be a woodshed, a dark and musty enclosure which smelt of earth and sawdust. My presence in this inelegant place seemed to constitute some deliberate mockery of my attire. I retreated immediately and returned to the gravel path. Now, looking about, I could not even decipher the way around to the front of the house. The path was blocked by a hedge to my left as I faced out, and treading gingerly to my right and peering around the corner, I saw an unfamiliar flank of the building which seemed to be at the back. I stood quite still, having in effect no alternative, and just at that moment heard the crunch of footsteps behind me.

'Coming in?' said Mr Madden, stopping at the woodshed door several yards away from me with his hand on the handle. His face was friendly.

'Oh yes, thank you,' I said, hurrying towards him. 'I got a bit lost.'

He opened the door and disappeared. Following through behind him, I saw that I was in the long, narrow corridor I had gone along with Pamela. I closed the door behind me.

'Easy to lose yourself in a place like this if you're not used to it,' said Mr Madden from up ahead. 'But you'll soon find your way around.'

'Oh, I'm sure I will.'

'I think we're in the drawing room.'

He opened a door to the left and, following him, I found myself in the great front hall. I heard voices, Pamela's voice and another, male, voice.

'How *hysterical,*' said Pamela, a long, light peal of laughter drifting out through the open door.

Mr Madden stopped at the doorway and stood back, his hand out.

'After you,' he said.

I entered a very large room painted a dramatic dark red, with two huge windows draped by long, heavy curtains in a gold material looking out onto the front drive. I noticed the ceiling immediately, which was very ornate and covered in leaflike mouldings with a type of flower, a sunflower by the looks of it, at its centre. There was a vast marble fireplace with a mirror above it, and in front of that a richly coloured rug. The room seemed to contain a great deal of furniture, and I had an impression of gleaming, finely carved wood, the delicate legs of velvet sofas and side tables. There were several paintings on the walls, large and dark with carved gold frames. Pamela sat on one of the sofas near the fireplace, her legs tucked by her side, with a glass in her hand. I noticed immediately that she was wearing the same clothes as she had done earlier, a faded shirt and a pair of worn, closely fitting jeans. Opposite her sat a young boy, with shining black hair, like Mr Madden's.

'Here they are!' said Pamela, turning and smiling at us from what appeared to be a great distance. 'Come in, Stella. Goodness, you look very smart! Piers, would you get Stella a drink?'

'What will you have?' said Mr Madden.

'We're on G-and-Ts,' said Pamela helpfully, raising her glass.

'Or you could have wine,' interposed Mr Madden, 'or vodka, or sherry. What would you like?'

'G-and-T will be fine,' I said hurriedly.

'Come over here,' said Pamela, patting the sofa beside her. She laughed, the residue of the hilarity I had overheard. 'Martin's just been telling me *such* a funny story.'

I looked at Martin. He was looking at Pamela. He had a very large mouth, and a bad complexion. Curled beside him in a glossy black heap was Roy; an alliance, I felt, to be feared. I hesitated before sitting down, wondering whether Pamela would introduce us formally, and if so, whether I would be expected to get up again. I felt she had behaved slightly improperly in not introducing us, and so with the boldness which an unknown situation can sometimes grant instead of shyness, I held out my hand.

'I'm Stella,' I said.

He turned his face rather menacingly towards me. With a frenzied pang it occurred to me that perhaps he did not have the use of his arms. Eventually, though, after long seconds, he reached up easily and took my hand. I was surprised at finding the dry, warm vastness of his hand at the end of his thin, tentacle-like limb. Slowly, again, he turned his head away from me and resumed looking at Pamela. I felt as if I had committed a social misdemeanour, and sat down awkwardly.

'I think you two will get along very well,' said Pamela. 'Perhaps some of Stella's good manners will rub off on you, Martin.'

Everything was very quiet suddenly.

'Oh, fuck off,' said Martin finally; quite casually, I tell you, his large chin jutting out from his shrunken, compacted chest, which appeared to be directly joined to his head without any neck. I glanced down secretly and saw his legs, which hung thin and tapered like roots from the tuber of his small body. His head, and facial features, were out of proportion with the rest of him; much bigger, that is, like the great lolling wooden head of a puppet on a stick of body. His exaggerated features made his face very expressive, like that of a cartoon character. The only other part of him which seemed to have any life were his long arms.

'How did you get on?' said Pamela, turning away from him.

'Oh, fine,' I said, too loudly. I was straining to penetrate the atmosphere of tension in the room.

'Here we are,' said Mr Madden, striding through the door with a tray. He handed me a heavy glass, made of carved crystal. 'Get that down you, m'girl.'

He sat down heavily on the sofa opposite ours.

'How are you, old chap?' he said, leaning over and ruffling Martin's dark hair.

'All right,' said Martin. His voice was sullen, but his lips flapped open, showing a sudden gap. His mouth was very dark inside. He shook his head slightly after Mr Madden's petting.

'He was very rude to Stella,' said Pamela.

'Oh, I'm sure he didn't mean it,' said Mr Madden cheerfully. 'Did you, old chap?'

'No,' said Martin, loudly. 'Can we just drop it?'

'No, we can't just bloody drop it,' said Pamela. Her voice bolted with anger from her throat so suddenly that it made me jump. I could feel the sofa begin to vibrate beneath us. 'Stella's been very kind and left everything to come all this way just for you, and you can jolly well give her a proper welcome.'

'Brrr!' said Mr Madden, looking at the ceiling.

Martin had put his hands on the wheels of his chair and begun to rock himself back and forth.

'You will damn well apologize to Stella!' said Pamela.

Martin continued to rock, his head buried in his chest and his hair flopping to and fro over his face.

'Go on!' said Pamela. 'Or it's supper on a tray in your room! I'm not having this sort of behaviour in my house. I've got a good mind to send you back to the centre and you can bloody well stay there overnight.'

'It's fine,' I interjected; I was, as you can imagine, extremely uncomfortable.

'No it's not fine!' snapped Pamela, turning her angry, wrinkled face towards me.

'Darling,' said Mr Madden hopefully.

'*Sorry, Stella,*' said Martin loudly. The words came from his chest, so low was his head bowed. 'All right?'

'Thank you,' said Pamela.

Martin muttered something.

'What was that?' said Pamela.

'Nothing,' said Martin.

'I heard you!' said Pamela, her body rigid beside mine on the sofa. 'Go on, say it out loud, you coward!'

Martin raised his head slowly and looked at her. His eyes were positively frightening.

'Silly cow,' he enunciated clearly.

There was a terrible moment of silence. Then, to my astonishment, Pamela burst out into loud laughter. Martin's eyes, which had been dark and narrow, dilated with humour as he looked at her and his mouth split like a wooden mouth into a huge smile. The two of them looked at each other, laughing.

'When's dinner?' said Mr Madden.

'In a minute,' said Pamela, still laughing. She leaned over and pulled Martin's hair affectionately. 'You *are* a bloody nuisance.'

'Bloody bloody,' said Martin.

I had become very nervous during this exchange, and was gripping my drink and sipping from it as if it offered some refuge from the inappropriateness of my presence at a family quarrel. It was a great relief to me when Pamela rose and summoned us all to dinner. I left my glass on a side table, as the others had done, and turned to file out after Pamela. Martin, however, unnoticed by me, had spun his wheelchair around the back of the sofa as a short cut and emerged from behind it in my path. Fearing a collision, I stopped and let him go first. He didn't look at me, but sped off into the hall, with Roy trotting heavily behind him. Looking over my shoulder, I saw Mr Madden dutifully gathering the discarded glasses onto his tray.

'Do you want a hand?' I said, in an attempt to ally myself with him.

'What?' He looked up, surprised, as if he had thought himself alone. 'No, no, just go ahead, I'll be along in a minute.'

In the hall, there was no sign of Pamela and Martin, and my solitary steps were loud as I headed for a doorway at the end. Again, however, I seemed to have become lost. The door opened only on to a cupboard, filled with umbrellas and coats and the ends of hockey sticks. I returned to the hall, and as I could see no other door but that leading to the drawing room, had no choice but to await Mr Madden. After long minutes, during which I stood agonized in the hall, he appeared with the tray, and I thought I saw in his expression a slight exasperation at the sight of me.

'Lost again,' I said quickly, with a laugh.

'We'll have to draw you a map, won't we?' he replied, really quite cheerfully. 'We're eating in the kitchen tonight, I think. It's through here.'

I concentrated closely, not wishing to be so foolish again. Mr Madden pushed with his shoulder against the wall on the right, and as he did so I saw my mistake. Part of the wall was in fact a door, panelled with dark wood like the rest of the wall and thus camouflaged from view. Also, it had no handle, being a swinging door, which was why Mr Madden had been able to open it by pressure from his shoulder. I followed him through it and it swung shut behind me. We were now in a dark antechamber. Mr Madden opened the door directly in front of him, and there we were in the bright kitchen. Pamela and Martin were at one end of it, close together as if they had been talking. They were not talking now. Pamela looked around and smiled. There was something in her smile, taking in both of us as it did, which unnerved me.

'Oh, *there* you are,' she said.

We ate at the large kitchen table, myself and Mr Madden on one side, Pamela and Martin, who ate with his wheelchair drawn up to the table, on the other. The food was excellent – country food, I suppose you would call it, in that it was quite plain – and with it we drank red wine. I cannot tell you how much I drank, for Mr Madden seemed to be refilling my glass without my really taking account of it, but after a while I felt less nervous and rather remote. I wondered whether I would always eat with the Maddens, and decided straight away that I would not – my cottage had its own kitchen, after all, and I remembered something Pamela had said about coming over in the evening and watching television if I wanted to, which sounded more like the exception than the rule. It then occurred to me that the meal might be docked from my wages, and I experienced considerable anxiety attempting to estimate its value. I realized then that the Maddens hadn't made my position quite clear to me. In my mind I recalled the advertisement anew – I could remember it word for word – and found it interesting to notice how different the few lines I had scanned so closely for clues seemed to me now that I was actually here.

> **WANTED**: Kind, intelligent and considerate girl to help parents with their disabled son. A good companion is mainly required, but there will also be some menial duties. Aptitude for the country life an advantage. Driving licence essential. Accommodation and small salary provided, as well as one free day per week.

We had progressed to the gooseberry pie by now, and seeing the advertisement as if before my eyes I began to choke on a mouthful of it. I had, unfortunately, received a shock at the very moment when a large piece of pastry was making its way down my throat, and with the surprise it lodged there, causing me to cough loudly. There was a clatter as the assembled company laid down their spoons.

'Goodness!' said Pamela.

'Hold still!' said Mr Madden, grabbing my arm firmly.

'Give her a good slap,' said Pamela.

Mr Madden administered a firm pat to my back and the piece of pastry flew into my mouth. I closed my lips tightly to prevent it from travelling out onto the table, and managed awkwardly to swallow it.

'All right?' said Mr Madden.

'I'm fine,' I said, coughing slightly. My eyes were watering. The imprint of Mr Madden's fingers remained warm on my arm. 'Thank you.'

As you can imagine, I was mortified by my performance, even though the Maddens had been very kind; except for Martin, whose eyes I had felt unmoved upon me as I choked. There was something malevolent in his gaze which turned even the smallest and most natural gesture into a false act. There was a flutter around the table, nevertheless, as a result of my accident, and in these distracted seconds I was able to return undetected to my contemplation of what had precipitated it. The fact was that I had no driving licence. Of course, it occurred to me that I might have misremembered the advertisement, for my ability to drive had not actually been mentioned by the Maddens in my dealings with them thus far; but in my heart, I was sure that the words I had recalled were correct. I found it hard to picture my original reading of the fatal fact; or rather, I remembered it glancingly, like something casually and unconsciously witnessed which later becomes crucial evidence. I shook and dredged my memory, wanting more from it than it seemed to contain. I had just, I supposed, trodden the requirement underfoot in my great hurry for the job; and the Maddens had, of course, assumed that I wouldn't be applying for it at all had I not possessed the specification which was, though 'essential', too mundane to mention.

Horror upon horror unfolded in my thoughts as I considered the consequences, and had the Maddens not now been engaged in a lively conversation on another matter, I believe I would have confessed my deception there and then. As I have often found to be the case, however, having missed my moment I found myself less and less able as every second passed to hold on to the courage necessary to an act of assertion. This first compromise with falsehood led to others, and as one minute became ten I found my revulsion for untruth slowly settle into a sly accommodation with it. I was already thinking how I could get around the obstacle without actually declaring it, and as my mind was working in this devious manner Pamela looked at her watch.

'Bedtime for you, young man,' she said. She stood up and began piling plates on top of one another. Roy, perhaps with the hope of availing himself of the meal's detritus, issued from his basket and drew sniffing to the table.

'Why?' wailed Martin, fondling his muzzle. 'It's still early!'

'I'll take him up,' said Mr Madden, stretching his large frame and yawning. He got up and, pushing back his chair and walking round to the other side of the table, grasped the handles of Martin's wheelchair. From my seat I could see them both, father and son, and although Martin appeared to submit willingly to the prospect of his removal, this sudden vision of his dependence aroused my pity. For a moment I forgot my troubles, feeling nothing but shame for my early dislike of the boy. His eyes met mine, and seeing as Pamela was distracted by the clearing of plates I risked giving him as kind a smile as I could summon. After the smile had been there for some time, I saw that he was not going to smile back. Then, to my dismay, he put out his tongue; quite slowly, and not at all secretively, as if he didn't care who saw him do it. His tongue was long and thick, like a dog's, and I found it difficult to dislodge the memory of it even after he had replaced it in his mouth.

'Goodnight, darling,' said Pamela, bending down from behind him to deposit a kiss upon his head. An unpleasant smirk appeared on Martin's face. Mr Madden began wheeling him towards the door. 'Say goodnight to Stella, you rascal!' cried Pamela.

'Goodnight, Stella!' called Martin mockingly from the door, without turning his head.

I stood up and began clearing plates from the table. I was desperate to be away from the house and on my own; parched of my own company, I felt as if I could drink down hour after hour of solitude. To my disgust, I saw that Roy had risen on his hind legs and was licking the insides of the dishes on the sideboard.

'Oh, you revolting creature,' said Pamela genially, apparently with no intention of stopping him. 'Don't worry about Martin,' she added, to me. I saw that she liked to think of herself as being able to read other people's minds. 'He's a little monkey.

He likes to give everyone a real going-over before he lets them anywhere near him. He'll be devoted to you before long, I promise you.'

'I liked him,' I said, weakly.

'That's very sweet of you,' said Pamela. 'He's a dear boy. He can be very rewarding.' She turned around abruptly and caught me leaning against the table. 'Poor Stella, you must be exhausted after an evening in this madhouse. Why don't you just turn in?'

'I ought to help,' I said, hoping that she would refuse.

'Don't be silly. Piers loves fussing about down here late into the night. He contemplates the meaning of life and all that. We'll just put everything in the sink for him.'

Almost resentfully, I resumed my clearing. Seeing my opportunity, however, I decided that this might be the time to approach Pamela about my duties.

'What time shall I be here tomorrow?' I said.

'Tomorrow?' Pamela looked surprised. 'We aren't expecting you tomorrow. It's your day off on Sunday.'

'Oh,' I said, overwhelmed by relief.

'Of course, you're free to wander over. We'll be having people for lunch, but you can come and go as you please. You'll probably want a day to yourself just to get your bearings.'

'All right.'

'On Monday we'll start properly. Martin's usually raring to go by about eight thirty. Poor Stella!' she said. Pamela was remarkably self-sufficient in conversation, and seemed to require few prompts from her interlocutor. 'We haven't really explained anything to you, have we? It's all been such a rush, I can't quite keep track of things.'

'Don't worry,' I said. Hearing my own voice, I was shocked by how terribly dull I sounded. 'It'll all work itself out.'

'But it won't!' said Pamela sharply. 'Don't you see that with a boy like Martin, things can't just be left to work themselves out? It all has to be carefully planned and considered. He's quite helpless without us, and he needs his routines, so don't think that we can just muddle along somehow, or work it out, as you say, as we go along.'

Things had suddenly, and without my quite knowing how, taken a turn. I felt my heart begin to pound again with embarrassment and anxiety. Pamela did not appear to be entirely in control of herself.

'I'm sorry,' I said. 'I didn't mean it like that.'

'Well,' said Pamela, unkindly. 'Just so long as we understand one another.'

'If you could just tell me,' I continued, close to tears, 'what exactly his routines are, then I'll find things much easier.'

This comment was clearly spoken in my own defence, making it evident to Pamela that it was through her fault, not mine, that my sense of my own duties was muddled. I had judged her to be a good-natured woman, but whether through tiredness or simply the wearing off of her initial veneer of politeness, I now saw that she had somehow become committed to a brittle and ill-tempered mood which my very presence was guaranteed to inflame. Even her figure seemed to have taken on sharp edges and angles, and as she spoke she gestured quite violently with her thin hands.

'Stella, I really didn't expect to have to mollycoddle you and lead you by the hand every minute of the day. We need to have someone here to help us, not double the load. If you don't think you're going to be up to it, and be able to take responsibility, then you'd better tell me now rather than later.'

'Mrs Madden,' I said. The evening had taken on a surreal character. I was unable even to gauge my own mood, and just then had no idea of what I might do. We had both, I remembered, been drinking, and I for one felt no confidence in my ability to keep my temper. 'I think you might be getting things a bit out of proportion.'

It really seemed possible, in that moment, that I might have a fight with Pamela. The lateness of the hour, the featureless darkness outside the kitchen windows, the despoilt table and blur of food and drink; all this, as well as our unfamiliarity with each other, seemed to permit anything. She wouldn't look at me, and was furiously busying herself at the sink. 'I don't see how I can take responsibility if you haven't explained what you expect of me. Perhaps,' I said, 'we had better both just go to bed, and talk it all through in the morning.'

Pamela did not reply.

'Would that be all right?' I persisted.

'Look,' she barked suddenly, her back still to me. She stopped what she was doing and leaned with both her hands on the kitchen counter, her head down. Her shoulders were rigid. 'Just be here at eight thirty on Monday. Do you think you can manage that?'

'Yes,' I said. I was both furious and upset. I could not understand how all this had taken place. 'Goodnight.'

She said nothing, and did not turn around. I hurriedly left the kitchen, and through some stroke of instinct or good luck found myself immediately outside on the gravel path. I ran along beside the hedges in the dark, my heart jammed against my ribs, my breath heaving in my mouth, my head awash with confusion. The black mass of trees flew by me and suddenly I was at the cottage gate and then through it, and then thudding up the path to the door. I opened the door and slammed it behind me and tore up the narrow stairs, without switching on the light, to my bedroom. There, in the dark, I threw myself upon the bed and wept.

Chapter Five

Some time later – perhaps only three or four hours, I thought, as it was still dark (it was late July and the mornings came early) – I woke up. I was very confused when I opened my eyes. I did not recognize my surroundings; partly because they were unfamiliar to me, and partly because the darkness of the countryside is far blacker than that of town. Indeed, for a few moments I was quite terrified, for when my eyes opened I appeared to see nothing more than when they had been shut. I opened and shut them a few times, unable to transcend my need to apprehend the physical world. I was lodged so deeply inside myself that my consciousness was in that moment but a simple junction of the senses, like that of an animal. I thought at first that I had gone blind, and then that I was dead and in my own grave. Presently I heard a faint rustling of leaves outside my window, and from this single clue was able slowly to piece together my circumstances.

This process was arduous, and as each block was put in place I felt as if I were struggling beneath an increasing burden, like a packhorse being loaded up with cargo. I began with the fact that I was lying in a strange bed wearing my nightdress. Struggling to remember changing into this nightdress, I came instead on a recollection of lying crying on the bed, and with a contraction of the heart plunged anew into the terrible scene with Pamela, which was webbed in my thoughts with the viscous confusion of a dream. It took me some time to disentangle its reality, but finally I possessed it in all its terrible clarity. Like an awful jewel, I worked it into the setting of the day before, the arrival at Franchise Farm, my first meeting with the Maddens, the cottage where now I lay. Monumental as all this already seemed, it lacked, I felt, the sinister adhesive of truth. There was more to my misery; but unable to bear the thought of being roused further from the anaesthetic of confusion, I attempted to coax myself back into ignorance and sleep. The face of the boy, Martin, sprang upon me, however, like that of a ghoul. My eyes snapped open again, and the tide of an irresistible alertness rose in my stomach.

Now that I was really awake, I became aware of something else, something throbbing and sublimated which had borne me from sleep into consciousness. Slowly I groped towards the source of this other discomfort and soon discovered that it was a physical pain. The skin on my body – mainly across my arms, legs and back – felt as if it were burning, and as I considered the sensation, my lethargic nerves conveyed to me the information that I was sleepily scratching myself, and had indeed been doing so before I even awoke. Suddenly alive, I ran my fingertips across the inflamed tracts of skin and found them raised into what felt like a series of long, narrow ridges. I sat up, alarmed, and after some fumbling succeeded in switching on the bedside lamp. Seeing the room illuminated around me I received a secondary tremor of unfamiliarity, as the scene of my swimming thoughts was drained of darkness, leaving close, unfriendly walls and suspicious lumps of furniture. I examined my arms, and to my dismay saw that they were a furious red, cross-hatched with hundreds of thick, raised white lines, as if I had worms embedded beneath my skin. Crying out, I flung back the eiderdown. My legs were similarly inflamed, and leaping from my bed and rushing to the wardrobe mirror, I lifted my nightdress and strained to see my back. The skin there was the worst of all, and seeing it I heard myself make a series of catlike mewlings.

For a few seconds I scratched, tearing at my nightdress like a maniac, and then understood that I was going to lose control of myself if I continued in this fashion. I sat, hot and exhausted, on the corner of the bed, my head in my hands. My skin tingled and itched now that my fingers were not attending to it. I bridled my urge to scratch, forcing my hands into my mouth. My back felt unbearably hot. Around me the night was shrunken and dense, like the pupil of an eye contracted to a pinprick. I was stranded on an island of time from which the only escape was sleep. Reluctantly I got back into bed. Seconds later I sat up again and removed my nightdress over my head, knowing that I would have to make some concession to the inflammation before it would permit me to sleep. Lying down again, the bedclothes felt slightly cooler, and aware that this novelty would last but seconds and could be followed by a rebellion even more severe than the first, I turned off the light, closed my eyes, and forced myself, as one would force the head of a man beneath water to drown him, into sleep.

When I woke up again, the room was brilliant with sunlight. The window was a square of deep blue, and beyond it I could hear the twitter of morning and, further off, the buzz of a lawnmower. I lay for a moment, adrift in that formless, unaccountable ether that swirls just beyond sleep, before all the tallies of self are presented. The daylight was cheerful, and in it my nocturnal activities, which presently I remembered in a more or less complete fashion, seemed sharp and reduced, like the small, shiny negative of a photograph. So preposterous, to the common sense of morning, did my argument with Pamela appear that I felt it was barely required of me to be troubled by it; as if it had disqualified itself, through exaggeration, from inclusion in the normal course of things. I was aware that this process of denial was a form of submission to what I clearly knew to be wrong; but it was good to have been relieved so painlessly of my grievance against Pamela, which was admittedly an inopportune burden to have acquired at such an early stage of my life in the country. Having persuaded myself to pardon one injustice, I found myself tempted to forget every qualm which had haunted me in the depths of the night; and thus I was coaxed, as one would lure a horse into harnesses, back into a state of contentment.

My skin bore no trace of the night's rash, and there being no cause or purpose to thinking more about it, I dismissed it from my mind. Longing to be out in the sun, I got out of bed and dressed quickly. I made the bed, tidied the room a little, and was about to start unpacking my suitcases and hanging things in the wardrobe when a lack of conviction, or perhaps certainty, stopped me. Instead I folded my things there where they lay in the suitcases, and pushed the cases with my foot neatly against the wall.

My first thought was to go outside into the garden, and indeed when I flung open the front door and breathed deeply of the country air, it was a lovely prospect. Feeling in a luxurious mood, I decided that it would be nice to make myself some breakfast and eat it out in the sun. I returned to the kitchen and continued my investigation of the cupboards where I had left off the previous afternoon. The sun was to the front of the house at that point, and the kitchen was rather more dingy in the shade than I had remembered it. The cupboards were very shabby, and several of the linoleum tiles covering the floor had begun to curl up at their edges. Two or three flies were swimming in a dreamy, pointless circle at the centre of the low ceiling and I brushed at them briskly with my hand. They dispersed silently, but seconds later had drifted back again. Aside from a set of old-fashioned blue crockery – two of everything – the cupboards were more or less empty. I noticed a jar of instant coffee in one, however, and took it down, along with a cup and saucer. Beside the oven stood a small, yellowed fridge, and opening it I found a fresh pint of milk. Knowing that Pamela must have placed it there, or ordered it to be placed at least, the carton struck me as both a kindness and a reproof. There was nothing else in the fridge.

I deliberated for several moments, trying to decide what to do. The idea of making coffee, and then sitting and drinking it in the sun, was appealing. The day, however, being my own, held no promise of nourishment other than what I might procure for myself. It was out of the question to call at the big house and ask for supplies to tide me over; indeed, I had already decided to dedicate myself to avoiding any encounter with the Maddens whatsoever during the course of the day. Consequently, I could not apply to them for information about where I might do my shopping; but having no means of transport, I was in any case in no doubt that the answer lay in the village of Hilltop. I had not seen the village, but I knew it to be nearby, and remembering the road along which I had driven with Mr Madden, deduced that the village would probably be found in the other direction. I was quite hungry by this time, and feeling this pang decided that I would attempt the walk first, leaving me with the rest of the day to enjoy the garden.

I returned to my bedroom and found my purse. To my dismay, looking inside it I saw that I had very little money. I counted the coins, aware as I did so that the chances of getting to a bank, considering the transport problems described earlier, were slim. I remembered then that it was in any case Sunday, and at the same time realized that I could always pay for things by cheque. Even as I began to search for my chequebook in this optimistic flurry, however, some deeper instinct told me that it was hopeless. I tried to remember why, and then recalled that I had thrown it out with everything else, believing that I would have no use for it. I cursed my short-sightedness, and the recklessness with which I had effectively cut off all escape routes. The scene with Pamela rose up in my mind, rattling its chains. I counted the coins again and tried to think clearly. How much food would I need to get me through a day? Surely I could survive until Monday, when I would be able to ask the Maddens for an advance on my salary? I had shelter, after all, and water from the tap; and coffee, which now seemed a great luxury. The very simplicity of these thoughts pleased me, even in my distress. Before long the money began to appear quite ample; and putting it in my pocket, I returned downstairs and prepared myself for my walk. Sensibly, I drank a large quantity of water before setting out, aware that in the heat I might become very thirsty and would not want to waste my funds on a drink. Such practicalities were exciting to me. I closed the cottage door and, noticing for the first time a large key protruding from it, turned the lock and put the key in my pocket alongside the purse.

I strode off across the garden; but although it was still quite early, I had not reached the gate before I became aware of the menacing edge to the sun's heat I had remarked the day before. So forcefully did its rays hammer on the top of my head that I had only been outside a few seconds when it occurred to me to turn around and go back inside again. I ignored this urge – at my peril – and continued resolutely along the gravel path towards the big house. Reaching the end I turned left, even as I did so remembering how I had found the route to the front of the house blocked the previous day. From a closer angle, however, I saw that the hedge, which I had imagined from further away to extend all the way across the path, in fact afforded a small gap through which I was able to slip. Once on the other side of it, I found myself in an area of dense undergrowth. Pushing through it the sharp, narrow claws of branches scraped against my legs. Within minutes, to my satisfaction, I had emerged into the driveway, and could see from the sleepy front of the house that all was still quiet there. I made my way quickly down the drive, stepping gingerly over the gravel so as not to make any noise, and soon found myself in the long avenue of greenery I remembered from my drive with Mr Madden.

It was immediately apparent that the road was much further away than I had thought; but it was pleasant to be in the shade and I was still uplifted by the ease with which I had escaped the farm without attracting notice. After a while, though, I began to feel slightly anxious at the endless quality of the avenue. I have good eyesight, and the avenue extended in a straight line in front of me for as far as I could see. I trudged on for some time with no change and, not being accustomed to walking, soon became fatigued. I could not for the life of me remember for how long the avenue persisted before it met the road, and cursed myself for not having paid closer attention in the car. Just as my steps were slowing with the temptation of turning back, I saw a large pair of gates ahead of me. I did not remember these at all, but they clearly represented the boundary of the house's grounds. I hurried towards them and on reaching them found the narrow tarmacked road along which Mr Madden and I had driven. We had approached, I judged, from the right as I stood, and having already made the decision to continue along the road from where we had turned off it, I veered to the left without hesitation.

The tarmac was rather less pleasant beneath my feet than the gravel had been, and it was certainly much hotter there than in the avenue, but it was enough of a novelty for me to have reached a second stage in my journey, and indeed to walk along a road that contained no cars, so I was for the time being content. The view from the road was very attractive in the sun. To my right as I walked I could see a marvellous stretch of countryside billowing out beneath me in a kind of mist towards the horizon. Scattered over it were small groups of trees and one or two houses, so miniature that I might have been seeing them from a great height. This surprised me, for I was not, as far as I could make out, climbing a hill. To my left was a tall bank of hedgerows, which I took to be the continuing boundary of the grounds.

Oriented now, and with no further work to do for the time being, I allowed my mind to focus upon other things. The road, and my memories of my journey with Mr Madden, naturally brought the issue of my inability to drive to the forefront of my thoughts. My deception was still of the greatest concern, but I considered it quite calmly. Now that my arrival at Franchise Farm had been somewhat soured, I was, oddly, relieved of the desire for everything in my new life to be perfect. I had, I suppose, excluded what I can only describe as the human element from my calculations. Although I was disappointed that things had gone wrong at such an early stage of my adventures, still I could see that a measure of imperfection was admissible in, and perhaps essential to, any human situation. You will perhaps find it laughable when I say that I had imagined it possible to exist in a state of no complexity whatever; but a person has a right to their dreams, and this was mine. It had soon proved unsustainable; but I do not regret having had it. Indeed, I find it hard to see how I could be judged harshly, when my willingness to modify my ambitions was so evident. Many people, in the face of such a disappointment, would, I believe, have scrapped the whole thing straight away.

To return to the problem of my driving, I made, as I walked, several plans. This practical side of my nature often comes in handy. It was this very quality, in fact, which had allowed me to list among my attributes, although it was not in the strictest sense true, the 'aptitude for the country life' specified by the Maddens in their advertisement. What I meant was that I possessed the aptitude for any kind of life, country or otherwise. To continue, my several plans were designed to cater for the 'human element' I had now detected in my situation, and would, singly, variously, or in numbers, be adopted according to which way the wind was blowing. The first and least favourable plan was to confess fully to the Maddens if and when the opportunity arose. The second plan, a more subtle version of the first, was to construct, quite carefully, an atmosphere of reluctance around the issue of driving. I could, for example, say that I had not driven for a long time and was nervous. From this atmosphere, one of two things could emanate: either the Maddens would dismiss me from my driving duties; or they would teach me – or remind me, in their eyes – how to drive themselves. Neither outcome was particularly satisfactory, not least because even if I learned to muddle through behind the wheel, this still did not procure me a driving licence. Within minutes I had put together a corollary to the latter half of this plan. While muddling through behind the wheel during the week, I could, on my day off, take proper driving lessons. This plan was expensive, and its detail burdensome, but it was at least feasible.

My remaining plans were rather more drastic. I could feign an injury, such as a broken leg or pulled tendon, which would excuse me from driving. Alternatively I could say nothing at all, and merely drive, come what may. I could adopt a mixture of all these plans; put off driving, say, on the pretext of a broken leg, while secretly learning how to drive on my day off, and then assume my driving duties as soon as I possessed a modicum of skill, taking my test later.

By this time I had come quite a long way along the road. I was extremely hot, but no longer so tired. Indeed, after that first bout of lethargy I had felt new life spring into my limbs, and now was walking with considerable energy. The road was sloping very slightly downhill, and I swung my arms by my sides with a feeling of great physical suppleness. I had noticed some time before a definite settlement ahead of me, but not wishing to disappoint myself I held off from the certainty that it was the village of Hilltop. I had begun to understand that things were invariably much further away in the country than one imagined them to be. My scheme paid off, for within minutes I had entered the village, passing a small sign reading 'Hilltop' for good measure, and was delighted and surprised to have reached my destination so quickly.

The village was very pretty, and quite full of life. It was arranged mainly along the road, which became a sort of quaint high street at its centre, and consisted of a collection of very old houses – mostly red-brick or painted white – many of which had lovely baskets of flowers hanging around their doorways or in pots adorning their window sills. My first thought on seeing these pots and baskets was to smash them. I have no explanation for this impulse, other than that my thoughts were still, at this early stage, essentially urban in nature. In London, I was probably thinking, these pots would almost certainly have been smashed, and perhaps I was, while imagining such an act of vandalism, assuming part of the vandal's character in the process.

At the centre of the village I found a small post office, which was of course closed, it being Sunday, and a very attractive pub with tables and benches outside at which one or two people were already sitting. Quite a few people were also walking about, mainly children and people of about the Maddens' age or older. Several of the children had bicycles and were describing carefree circles on the road. I stopped for a moment, enjoying the sun on my face and the quiet contentment of the place, before remembering that I had come to find food and could as yet see nowhere to buy any. I walked along the road a bit further, and just then had a curious sensation of confidence; confidence, I suppose, in the village being such a charming place that it would provide me with what I required as if by magic; but confidence also in myself, as if my very desire was transformative and would create what it needed to satisfy it. Just as this confidence rose up in me, a small and evidently busy shop appeared on the road ahead. I accept that this was merely a happy coincidence. As I caught sight of this shop, however, I had a strange vision – strange because I could not imagine from where it had come – a vision, I repeat, of the shop door tinkling with a little bell as I entered. This bell would mark me out as an alien, an intruder, and as it gave out its warning those inside the shop would turn and stare with the blank, unfriendly stares of cows. Before long, I had decided that if I opened the door and heard that tinkle, I would go in some way mad. At the same time, I was filled with a dreadful certainty that all this would in fact come to pass; and, moreover, that the outcome was loaded or symbolic, although I could not tell you of what.

Imagine my relief, then, and also my sense that I had 'won' in some obscure fashion, when I came abreast of the shop and saw that its door was wide open; propped open, in fact, by a kind of news-stand displaying the Sunday papers. Jauntily, I had plucked one of these papers from the stand and was bearing it indoors when I was again assailed by this strange symbolical sense of my own activities. As with the tinkling bell, the buying of a newspaper threatened to invite some indeterminate menace. I replaced it quickly on the stand, attempting a vague pantomime of indecision and then resolution, and entered the shop for a second time.

There were several people inside, all of them with their backs to me, for they were forming a queue at a counter at the end. Behind the counter stood an elderly woman and man, both separately busy, but matched in a way – like a pair of dolls – which made it obvious that they were a married couple. The woman wore a blue housecoat, like a school dinner lady or cleaner. The man was thin, as his wife was correspondingly plump, and had grey hair slicked neatly back from his forehead. From behind, the people in the queue did not look entirely real. They were all very quiet – their silence surprised me, for I had thought that country people were invariably acquainted with one another – and stood patiently, rooted to the spot, the purchases clutched in their arms giving them from behind the appearance of strange, goods-bearing plants: a spray of newspaper here, a box of eggs there, a carton of milk depending from white fingers. Their bodies did not look at all normal – they were all different shapes, as if they had been cut from paper – and gave the impression of being, beneath clothes which again had that 'cut-out' look and came uniformly in shades of dove grey and pale blue, made not of human flesh but of something extraneous: mattress ticking, perhaps, or whale blubber, or cardboard. The woman behind the counter talked fairly continuously, but I could not make out anything that she said. This was not because she possessed an unusual accent; rather, I could not distil the meaning of her words because their subject was unfamiliar to me. I have often found this to be the case when people are talking about other people I don't know, or places to which I have not been.

The shop was long and narrow, and had shelves arranged along the walls to either side. Their contents represented a miniature supermarket, a hurried alphabet of human needs reduced to basic principles. I had passed cleaning fluids, washing powder, and personal hygiene in only one or two steps, and having arrived at foodstuffs gained an immediate impression of the dominion of instant coffee, which, of course, I already possessed. I was, I soon saw, out of luck. It was hard to decipher the spirit in which the goods before me had been selected; aside from the coffee, they appeared to cater neither for emergency nor desire. Almost everything was in tin cans, which had the air of not being for sale; as if they had been there unwanted for so long that they had been adopted, or permitted to stay, like old and infirm people in a home. The overwhelming presence elsewhere in the shop of newspapers, greetings cards, and the cleaning fluids mentioned above threatened the status of this section still further, as if, over time, the boundaries between the shelves had gradually been eroded and their distinctions become a vague matter of packaging rather than content. The day was too hot for even the more acceptable among these rations, such as tinned soup, to have any appeal; and yet I was so hungry that a choice must perforce be made.

I had, by this time, been standing there for so long that the whole human contract underlying the existence of the shop, and distinguishing its customers from its owners, was in danger of collapse. The queue had been processed and dispersed. I was, in fact, alone, with the savage eyes of the woman and her husband trained upon me. Their gaze made me uncomfortable, as if all this time I had in fact been standing in their house, mistaking it for a shop. I doubted that the section of shelf before which I stood had ever received so much attention, and this in itself was enough to arouse their suspicions. They did not, however, address me, although the very air around me seemed to vibrate with the suggestion that they might. They had every right and reason to enquire as to whether I needed any help, and this eventuality, predictably, took on in my mind the menace of the newspaper and bell. Keen, then, to be away before ill luck caught me in its talons, I snatched a tin from the shelf and bore it before me to the counter. Once there, I saw something that I had missed: a rack of various breads wrapped in Cellophane packaging. My heart leaped with relief at the prospect of eating something fresh, and I took a package of rolls and placed it on the counter beside my tin.

The woman examined the two purchases – the man had disappeared by this time, through a doorway hung with a long fringe of plastic, behind which I could just make out a narrow corridor leading to a small room containing a table, at which the man was now sitting reading a newspaper – and began to write laboriously with a plastic pen on a small pad of lined paper in front of her. She was, I saw, doing a sum. Her hair, which was grey and set in a neat, rigid basin of florets, like a brain or a cauliflower, bobbed up and down as she inscribed the figures.

'That'll be two pounds exactly,' she said, still with her head down.

I gave her the money, brushing her dry palm as I did so, and she turned with it to the till. Not requiring any change, I was free to leave, but the transaction appeared to be incomplete. I felt that more was expected of me – or of her – before I could go. She did not seem to agree, however, and was busying herself with her back still to me. Eventually she turned around, and looked surprised to see me still standing there.

'Would you like a bag?' she said.

'Oh yes, thank you!' I cried, aware that she had solved the puzzle.

She produced a small blue plastic bag, and there was a moment of tension – for me, in any case – while I wondered who would do the work, in this now fragile situation of role-play, of putting the food into it. I extended a hand, but she stolidly shook out the bag, subtly fending me off with uninterruptible motions which rolled smoothly one upon another, and placed the rolls and tin carefully in it.

'Thank you very much,' I said, impressed. 'Goodbye!'

'Goodbye,' she said.

I made the walk home quite cheerfully, pleased with the way things had worked out. Several times, as I strode along in the sunshine, I forgot more or less entirely who and where I was: so compelling was the rhythm of my legs going back and forth, and my lungs in and out, that it appeared to drown out my consciousness. Remembering the Maddens, as I did now and then between these phases of oblivion, gave me a slightly unpleasant feeling of temporary, but indefinite, enclosure; not unlike the feeling of being in a doctor's or dentist's waiting room and looking up from a magazine to see unfamiliar walls, briefly forgotten.

Eventually I became quite tired; a profound fatigue, which intensified at the thought that I was near, but not yet arrived at, my destination. It being now late morning, the sun was high and very strong. Up until that point I had imagined that my white skin was being gradually toughened up by its exposure to air and light; but presently I sensed the relationship between sun and skin take a nasty turn, most particularly around the left side of my neck and face, and along my bare left arm, where the heat was most brutally concentrated. The road was without shade, and even twisting my body as I walked, I could not shield the afflicted areas from the direct and now aggravating beams of light. I could see that the gates to the drive were not far off, and with no alternative open to me, was forced to turn around so that the sun shone to my right and approach them walking backwards. This may seem ridiculous – it is easier, in fact, than might be thought – but I have always considered it important to protect one's own body from injury, even at the risk of offending etiquette. From an early age, for example, to my parents' horror, I developed the habit of spitting out food immediately from my mouth if I found it too hot. I am not, however, insensible to embarrassment, and when I heard the sound of a car engine behind me – or in front of me, strictly speaking – had every intention of righting myself momentarily while it passed. Unfortunately it was going too quickly for me to respond to the warning in time, and passed me still striding confidently backwards. Seeing it speed off along the road in front of, or behind, me, I gained the distinct impression that the car had been of a type remarkably similar to the Maddens'. I gave a moan of shame as I considered the possibility that a member of the family had seen my strange promenade, and this prospect, combined with the feeling of rawness down the left side of my body, dampened the sprightly cheer with which, only moments earlier, I had been going about my business.

The gates and avenue passed quickly by – I was walking normally now, being in the shade – as I meditated on this new development, and attempted to devise various explanations which might extricate me from it. Presently I reached the front of the big house, where I saw the Maddens' blue car parked where it had been when I left. Rather than dwelling on my deliverance from shame, however, I found the train of thought which had borne me all the way from the road to the house abruptly derailed by the sight of an unfamiliar car parked in the drive beside the Maddens'. As at the station the day before, I felt the jolt of a collision in my mind where there should have been a smooth transfer from one concern to the next. What had been an entire subterranean network circulating a multifarious cargo of concerns was apparently now a frustratingly parochial arrangement incapable of conveying more than one thought at a time. All interest in the Maddens' car immediately vanished, as I laboured over the meaning of the new arrival. To whom did this car belong? Was it anything to do with me? If so, a second route of questioning opened out: had someone come to look for me? Had I been reported for some instance of deviance? Was I to be arrested? If not, one could safely move on to the assumption that the car belonged to visitors of the Maddens, most probably the lunch guests Pamela had mentioned the night before.

Having no further business there in the drive, I plunged into the undergrowth. After some thrashing about, I emerged, rather breathless, on the path at the side of the house, to find Mr Madden standing a few paces away from me. He was carrying a tray with glasses on it, and had evidently been about to enter the house by the side door when he had heard my scuffling in the hedge.

'What *are* you doing?' he said; not unpleasantly, but with a kind of amused astonishment.

'I didn't want to come through the house,' I panted. 'I saw the car in the drive and thought that you might have guests.'

'Ah!' said Mr Madden, nodding as if he understood. 'You needn't have worried, we're all out in the garden.'

'Oh,' I said.

'Did you know there was a gate?' enquired Mr Madden.

'No, I didn't,' I replied, although I would have thought that was obvious.

'It's just there,' he said, balancing the tray on one hand and pointing with the other. 'It leads directly to the drive. We don't expect you to have to fight your way through the hedge every time you want to go out, you know.'

He gave his peculiar bark.

'That's a relief,' I said, with false cheer.

Just then, I heard footsteps approaching along the gravel path behind Mr Madden.

'Piers!' called Pamela, as she emerged around the corner. She stopped in her tracks at the sight of me. 'What on *earth* has happened to you?' she said; again, not unpleasantly, but with the same humorous dismay as her husband.

'She had a tussle with the hedge,' said Mr Madden.

'Good God,' said Pamela, drawing closer. 'You're all scratched – and look, you've torn your skirt! What *have* you been doing?'

I looked down at my legs and saw that they had indeed been badly scratched. One or two of the scratches were bleeding.

'I came through the hedge,' I repeated miserably. 'I didn't want to disturb you.'

'Gracious, she must think we're utter monsters. We obviously frightened the living daylights out of her yesterday, darling,' said Pamela to her husband.

'No, not at all!' I cried.

'Didn't know about the gate,' interrupted Piers. 'She thought she just had to hack her way through.'

'Is there any damage? You mustn't do that, you know,' said Pamela. 'Mr Thomas will be distraught if his beds have been trampled under foot.'

'I'm sorry,' I said.

'Oh, well,' said Pamela. 'Piers can have a look at it later. You'd better go and get yourself cleaned up. Darling, do you want to get on with the drinks?'

'Righty-ho,' said Mr Madden, opening the door.

'And put some more of those salmon things on a plate, would you?' called Pamela after him.

I moved forward, hoping that I would be able to slip by while her back was turned.

'Stella, don't creep off,' said Pamela, turning around abruptly and stepping into my path. She put her arm around me. Her body felt small and hard beside mine. I could smell her perfume. 'Piers and I very much want you to feel at home here. I know it's been a bit of a madhouse so far, but everything should quieten down tomorrow.'

She tightened her arm and bent her head towards mine in a concerned way. I felt very awkward. My plastic bag was still clutched in my hand.

'OK,' I said.

'You mustn't feel that you have to go sneaking about,' she said. 'Why don't you come over and have a swim later, after everyone's gone? It's so hot, you could probably do with a good cool down. The pool's absolutely lovely at the moment. Go on, it would do you good.'

I hadn't known that the Maddens had a swimming pool, but at that moment, as if to prove it, I heard faint splashing sounds and cries of laughter coming from the back of the house.

'I might do,' I said. 'I've got quite a few things I want to do this afternoon.'

'Well, it's up to you,' said Pamela, releasing her arm.

'If not, I'll see you in the morning,' I added, worried that she was angry with me.

'Right,' said Pamela remotely, looking through the door to the house as if anticipating the appearance of Piers.

'At eight thirty,' I continued.

Pamela glanced at me again, as if she had forgotten I was there.

'Well, come if you feel like it,' she said, turning and crunching off down the path.

I stood for a moment, confused. Had she meant come in the morning if I felt like it, or come swimming? I headed quickly towards the cottage, not wishing still to be standing around when Mr Madden returned.

Chapter Six

The damage I had done to myself during my walk surprised me, for I had been overwhelmed by feelings of good health both on the outward and return journey. Reflected in one of the cottage windows as I came up through the garden, I looked positively wild. What must they have thought of me in the respectable village of Hilltop? Worse still, what impression of myself could I have given the Maddens? My legs were the worst, particularly about the calves and ankles, which were raw and cross-hatched with a pattern of scratches. I had also been bitten by insects in various places, and my skin had risen there in a series of small red bumps.

I went to the bathroom, intending to run cold water over my legs. As I took off my shoes, I noticed that they were spotted with patches of a sticky black substance. I touched it lightly and then smelt it, after some time deducing that it was tar. Retracing my steps to the front door, I found that I had tracked tar across the sitting room carpet and kitchen floor. The carpet was quite a pale beige colour, and more or less ruined. For a moment I was bewildered by this scene of destruction. Being very tired, I resisted fiercely the idea of doing anything other than rest, and as I stood there gazing at the floor found myself overcome by feelings of denial and indifference. Even though I was harried by the sight of the damage done to the Maddens' property, and despite the fact that I knew responsibility for erasing it to be mine and mine alone, I could not, in that moment, bring myself to do anything about it. I did, however, work out that the tar must have come from the surface of the road, which had felt remarkably soft beneath my feet in places and must, I now saw, have melted in the heat. I had not known that roads could do that; indeed, never having really walked on one, I had not given roads even the slightest consideration before in my life.

I opened the front door and placed my ruined shoes outside it, and then returned to the bathroom. Looking in the battered little mirror above the sink I was met by a terrible vision. The short walk to the village and back had given me the appearance of a savage. My hair resembled a nest built upon my head, a distressed basket adorned by twigs and leaves, which gave off a light shower of seeds when I shook it above the sink. The sight of my skin – which I had fancifully imagined, during my walk, to be acquiring a healthful burnish – was a considerable shock. The right side of my face was morbid white, and had taken on an unpleasant texture, the pores enlarged, the tone blotchy, a sheen of sweat giving it a resemblance to raw dough. The left side, meanwhile, was badly scorched: the skin, not just over my face but also down the side of my neck and arm, had sprung up a furious red, and was emanating heat as if it were aflame.

My predicament was rapidly approaching the point at which the misery of a situation outweighs the desire to put it right. It seemed incredible that so much could have gone wrong in so short a time; a disappointment made all the more bitter by the high hopes with which I had embarked on my life in the country. It already seemed as botched to me standing there in the bathroom as everything I had left behind; and while, under normal circumstances, the desire to escape is propelled by a dissatisfaction with the world, to feel it in a place of refuge trains the dissatisfaction inwards. Having understood this, I knew that I was trapped and must confront my problems, those being the ruined carpet and shoes, the scratched legs, the tangled hair, the severe burning of one half of my face and body; and on a larger scale, the mean provisions on which I was hoping to survive until Monday; the offer of a swim, which I must turn down on account of having no costume or towel; the hostility which was beginning to characterize relations with the Maddens; the as yet unresolved matter of the driving licence; and the fact that on top of all of this I was far from home, with neither friend nor family to comfort me, and with no means of escape.

The tar stains were impossible to remove entirely from the carpet, but with a knife and the clever rearrangement of some furniture I managed mostly either to reduce or conceal them. I bathed my scratches and rinsed my hair with water, using a teacup from the kitchen. My lack of a towel did not actually trouble me, for I was still so overheated that I was content to let the water dry on my skin. My shoes I elected to throw away when the opportunity arose, and my torn skirt was folded and placed at the bottom of my suitcase to await some future surge of industry. Cleansed and orderly, my sunburn felt rather better, but I daubed it liberally with some lotion I had fortunately brought with me just for good measure.

Clothing myself anew was rather more problematic. With my skirt now out of action, I had only the smart dress and three pairs of trousers from which to choose. I stood in my bedroom, my flaming skin resisting the notion of trousers, and just as I found myself crying out for a pair of shorts was blessed by a remarkably inventive idea. My problem was finding an implement with which to perform the operation, and a brief reconnaissance about the house turned up only a pair of nail scissors from my washbag. I hesitated, deploring the notion of sacrificing with hasty butchery what patience – in the form of a sewing kit perhaps borrowed from Pamela at some point in the friendlier future I hoped for – promised to execute with precision and skill; but I was greedy now for shorts, and seeing in my mind the horrified face of my mother as I murdered a perfectly good pair of trousers, was provoked into action.

For some time I sawed away, not even pausing to stake out the line along which I intended to cut, and when both legs were off held up the amputated stumps to see how I had done. Predictably, the legs, though shorter, were now of drastically different lengths; and finding myself out of breath and awash with sweat, I resumed my cutting slowly and with rather more care. After some time, I had filed away so much of the cloth in pursuit of exactitude that I was left with very little. I tried them on before the wardrobe mirror, already regretting what I had done.

Considering that my alterations had been designed to subtract substance from my appearance rather than add anything to it, the transformation I had wrought with the nail scissors was quite beyond all understanding. I believed, standing there, that I had never looked so good, nor felt so abuzz with a curious power which I could only take to be that of sexual attractiveness. The shorts were very short, even if evenly and equally so, and while I have never been given to gratuitous displays of flesh I had to admit that there was something exciting in this revelation. It suddenly seemed that there was far more to me than I had imagined; that my body, which I had always believed to be immutable or finite in some way, possessed in fact a whole unmined tract of personality, a fresh range of potential to which I had, I now saw, the undeniable right.

I stood, transfixed by the mirror, for some time, accustoming myself to this stranger of whose desires and motives I was not entirely sure. Thoughts of Edward, as faint as the pop and drizzle of distant fireworks, flared sporadically in my mind. I could not match this version of myself with him. He would not, indeed, have recognized me; and my memories of him seemed all at once frustrating and unsatisfactory, as patchy and monochrome as those of childhood or drunkenness, as if the time we had spent together had not been fully lived. I had the brutal desire to be seen through new, less penetrating eyes, to experience a wanton exchange of surfaces. Fulminating with possibilities, my skin seemed all at once to possess a frightening autonomy, as if it could crave and consume, could overpower me with its appetites. The world outside my window pulsed with promise and invitation. I felt an inner fainting, a falling away of resistances: the desire for physical contact with another human being began to rage like a headache about my mind, drowning out the sound of other thoughts and finally gathering to itself such shape and purpose that it felt like a great horn protruding from my forehead. With so little about me that I knew, I was virtually unpoliced; and it was in this strange savagery that I began to touch myself in front of the mirror, while the dim protests of my more civilized self went unheeded.

For how long I remained in this curious state, which was half frenzy, half trance, I could not say. Perhaps it was a quarter of an hour, perhaps more; but eventually I came to my senses, and looking about my bedroom, which I had entirely forgotten, had a feeling of intense exposure and shame, as if the severe furniture and disapproving eye of the window had been observing my antics. I left the room quickly and went downstairs. In the kitchen, I set about making preparations to assuage my now quite fierce hunger. My body felt tremulous and weak. My hands shook as I struggled to tear the Cellophane packaging around the rolls, and once or twice I was forced to stop and lean against the kitchen counter until the rapid beating of my heart subsided. I examined the tin can I had bought, which contained something called 'luncheon meat'; a substance widely consumed, I believe, during the last war, from which period the dusty, crepuscular tin appeared to date. Despite having little appetite for the stuff, I was relieved to discover that the tin carried a device for opening itself; but minutes later, searching a drawer for cutlery, I found a tin opener in any case. I assembled my meal, which consisted of two rolls without butter containing pink slabs of luncheon meat and a cup of coffee, and carried it on a plate out into the garden.

It must, at this point, have been early to mid-afternoon, and outside the heat was so searing that it seemed to have blanched the garden of colour. I arranged myself upon a blasted patch of grass, taking care to keep only my right side in the sun, and began to eat. I do not have a particularly weak stomach as far as food is concerned, but the 'luncheon meat' was grotesque in appearance. A more imaginative person than I would doubtless have seen all manner of horrors in the sinister pink mush, and I bolted it down, keen to avoid having this type of thought myself. I had progressed to my coffee, swatting at a gang of wasps and other insects lured by the crumbs on my plate to pester me, when the sound of Pamela's voice caused me to jump.

'Didi, darling, you couldn't fling over my sunglasses, could you?'

I looked around, startled. The voice had seemed to come from nearby, and yet Pamela was nowhere to be seen. For a moment I sat in utter confusion; but when I heard nothing further, began to think that I must have imagined it. Seconds later, however, I clearly heard Pamela's voice again.

'Thanks, darling.'

This time, I felt quite upset. I turned my head this way and that, telling myself that Pamela must be somewhere in the garden, but knowing in the pit of my stomach that she was not. At that moment I heard a laugh, long and low; again, definitely Pamela's. I had heard that laugh in the hall of the big house the night before, and was not likely to forget it, nor anything else about that evening, in a hurry. Hearing the laugh, then, I thought that I would go mad. It was absolutely impossible that Pamela could be more than a few feet away, and in the end I was driven to get up and search for her, peering ridiculously behind the apple tree and to the sides of the cottage. Finding nothing, there was no more for me to do than sit back down again. I waited, electrified, my heart pounding. There was a much longer silence this time, but eventually the voice came again.

'She is, she is,' it said. 'But it's early days yet, you know.'

I was concentrating so hard that I could hear the thud of my own heartbeat in my ears. It was so loud that I was unable to hear anything above its noise, and I slapped the side of my head with my hand to try and make it go away.

'Well, it was so bloody dreadful last time. We were *this* close to just paying out to get someone professional in, you know.'

This time I was able to analyse the sound closely enough to hear a slight echo at the end of each word. Through some freak of the landscape and the exceptional stillness of the hot air, Pamela's voice must be being carried all the way from the back of the house. It was obvious to me now that what I was hearing was one half of a conversation; the 'Didi' referred to evidently being positioned behind some obstacle which prevented her responses from reaching me. In almost the same moment as I solved this bizarre mystery, I realized that it had a considerable – indeed, an unthinkable – bearing on me. Pamela, it was suddenly clear, was discussing me with her friend.

'I don't really know,' she said. 'There wasn't time beforehand, and we've both tried to hold off from interrogating her before she's had time to catch her breath. She *seems* nice enough, though. Rather mousy, you know.'

I had stopped breathing.

'That's right!' Pamela shrieked with laughter. 'I know, I know.'

I was kneeling by this time, my whole body straining in the direction of the house. The sun grated on my sore skin, corrosive and painful.

'Bog-standard middle, I'd say,' said Pamela. 'Well-spoken.

She seems quite intelligent.' Then, minutes later: 'Oh, nothing very interesting. Some sort of secretary.'

For a few minutes I could hear nothing at all. The sounds of the garden were amplified in the silence, and after a while grew so loud that I feared that I was missing something.

'Do you know, I don't think he even notices when we get a new one,' said Pamela then. 'He's such a darling. They all *adore* him. This one's got a *dreadful* crush on him already.' I heard a long, horrifying peal of laughter. 'Of course I haven't. He'd be *mortified*. God, I must be the only woman in the world who doesn't need to worry about her husband having it off with the au pair.'

I cried out in dismay, there in the garden, and swiftly clapped a hand over my mouth as it occurred to me that the strange echo could just as easily work in the other direction. Some time passed, during which I remained kneeling and alert, but no further conversation came my way. I was profoundly upset and disturbed by what I had overheard. I could not even offer myself the obscure consolation of thinking that I had got what I deserved for eavesdropping, seeing as Pamela's comments had been forced upon my inadvertent ears. My hatred for Pamela, which ever since my arrival at Franchise Farm had been struggling to burst the confines of propriety, broke free and coursed boiling about my veins. For a few minutes I was quite demented with anger and shame, and found myself thrashing and writhing on the spot like a wild animal. My thoughts were in havoc, a babble of concerns from which I could wring no sense, and before long I had exhausted myself so entirely that I fell to the grass, panting. Aware, even in the midst of this chaos, of my skin, I managed to heave my weary body onto its side so that the burnt patches were out of the sun; at which point, much to my surprise, I fell asleep.

Chapter Seven

I awoke to find the garden shrouded in the delicate summer gloom of evening. All around was quiet, save for the last, fading strains of birdsong, and in the stillness I felt a profound calm holding me on the brink of sleep; a pause in which neither my mind nor body was properly engaged, and during which I lay, as innocent and unquestioning as a pebble, on the warm grass, with no memory of my capacity for thought or movement. This pause lasted for some time; and then several things happened at once. The dusky garden, whose soft quiescence had minutes earlier been wrapped close about me, drew back with the menace of unfamiliarity. The silence of the looming trees grew sinister. I had not the faintest idea of where I was, and jumped up straight away from the grass. As I did so, every bone in my body cried out in protest. Bolts of cramp shot through my legs, and my skin felt as if it were crackling or crumpling like paper. Just then, a monstrous and unannounced surge of nausea rose up through my stomach to my mouth. I leaned over and vomited copiously where I stood.

That all this should have happened without my really having ascertained who or where I was left me in a state of shock. I stared at the heap of my own vomit in the dim light, and was surprised by its luminous pinkness, strident even in the dusk. The luncheon meat was thus summoned from my memory, and with it the reluctant cavalcade of the day's events, so unexpectedly severed by sleep. I wiped my sticky, wet mouth with the back of my hand and turned to face the cottage. I had left the front door standing wide open and felt a guilty tremor of irresponsibility. I didn't feel like going inside. Its peevish promise of enclosure was as appalling to my spirits as a warm sweater would have been to my sunburn. The garden, now defaced by my regurgitation and growing gloomier by the second, was no more appealing. I wondered how I was expected to entertain myself, with neither television, radio nor human company to fill the void of evening. I considered going over to the big house, but even setting aside the difficulties already thriving in the barely cultivated ground of my relationship with the Maddens, my day alone, and the peculiar activities to which this solitude had given rise, had left me diffuse and shapeless and unconfident of my ability to assume the coherent form necessary to social interaction.

The thought of a bath and an early night, with the remainder of the bread rolls to hand should I require them, was at least tolerable, and I went inside, closing the door behind me. As I crossed the sitting room, something caught my eye; a shadow of movement of some sort, which I had glimpsed but now thought I must have imagined. I continued on my way, but as I did so it came again; the faintest of shades, almost behind my field of vision. I stopped, my heart thudding. I sensed the pressure of another presence in the room, the slight bustle of air. It was clearly, however, nothing concrete, given that I couldn't see it. I wondered, ridiculously, if the cottage was haunted. It surprised me to think this, not being a superstitious person, nor indeed having ever been aware of this dimension in my personal landscape of fears.

As I stood there, I noticed a white streak, about the size of a finger, on the carpet at my feet. My experience with the tar had left me with a more detailed recollection of the carpet than would be considered normal, and I felt sure that this streak had not been there earlier. I noticed another on the flowered back of the sofa, and then another splashed across the small side table. What on earth could it be? I was becoming quite disturbed by now, and felt a membrane of silent tension begin to gather thickly around me. I went to the door and switched on the lights to try and dispel it. The light was momentarily comforting and prophylactic; but then I caught the shadow again, over by the fireplace – as before, more of a feeling than a visual occurrence.

My mounting sense of unreality was becoming unbearable, and was frightening me more than the thing – for I still had no idea of what it was – itself. In an attempt to jolt the course of events back onto its proper rails, I gave a loud shout. This immediately made me feel better, and so I shouted several times, running about the room and thumping on the furniture to rout whatever spirit it was that oppressed me. I reached the fireplace, still shouting; and all at once there was a terrific squawking and beating, and a great bird rose up like a fury from behind the armchair, hurling itself through the air towards me. It reared above my head, its fat, feathered body suspended in a frenzied gyration of wings, its claws outstretched. I felt feathers fan against my cheek and screamed like a banshee, almost insensate with terror, pummelling the air with my fists and jumping up and down to try and repel the horror.

What happened next could only have been the work of a few seconds, although it possessed a startling clarity which, even though I was quite beside myself with fear, impressed itself for ever on my memory. Still suspended in the air, the bird shied away from my flailing fists, a look of affront in its tiny, stupid eyes. It took a great swoop across the room, a sort of leisurely dive; and then hit the far wall with a thud, sliding directly down onto the carpet.

For some time I was unable to move. At first I was braced

for the bird to revive from its knock; but when after a few minutes I heard no sound coming from it, I crept over to the other side of the room to look. It was lying in a heap on the floor, utterly still. I was surprised by its inertia, and by the limpness of its feathered neck lolling to one side. I was relieved, in any case, that it did not appear to be breathing; for I feared that any claim to 'aptitude for the country life' would have to include the ability coolly to put a suffering animal out of its misery. In fact, I could not bring myself to go any nearer to it, let alone touch it, dead as it was. I recognized it as a pigeon, and realized that it must have flown through the open door while I was sleeping, depositing gobbets of its excrement about the room.

Given that I was unwilling to touch the creature and could therefore achieve nothing by just standing about, I presently found myself on my way once more to the bathroom, where I had been headed before the unfortunate incident waylaid me. I ran a bath in the narrow tub and glimpsed my reflection in the small mirror above the sink, being for some minutes gripped by compelling feelings of alienation and concern at the sight of myself. In a sort of dream, I got into the bath. The water was quite hot; and after some time I realized that a painful tingling sensation was coursing down the right side of my body, particularly around the leg and arm. I washed quickly, unable because of this tingling to endure the long, comforting immersion I had imagined, and by the time I had finished was in such pain that I literally sprang from the water, sending great waves of it sloshing over the sides of the bath and onto the floor. Examining myself, still dripping wet, I saw to my dismay that my right arm and leg – I had been wearing the cut-off trousers, as I am sure you will recall – as well as the skin on my right cheek and neck, had turned a violent purple.

I had had no idea, when I lay down on the grass that afternoon, that the sun could be so powerful at that hour. As well as the dreadful pain of this latest discovery, I was aware that it had had a peculiar effect on my appearance. A brief survey turned up the following: right arm and right leg to the upper thigh, severely burnt; left arm burnt; left leg, marble white; left cheek and neck, burnt; right cheek and neck, severely burnt; torso and upper arms, marble white; central panel of face and neck – a strip no more than an inch wide – marble white.

It was by now dark outside, and I thought of going out into the garden so as to cool myself off; but my recollection of the pile of vomit, though vivid, was not so precise that I could be sure of not treading in it in the dark. The sitting room, where the bird still lay in ghoulish state, was no more inviting. In defeat I retreated upstairs to my bedroom. My skin was still wet, and within seconds of leaving the bathroom I became very cold and began to shiver uncontrollably. Upstairs I tried to dry myself, as before, with the edge of the eiderdown, but the crisp fabric felt like sandpaper as I rubbed it over my sore skin. The lotion skidded about on this raw, wet surface when I tried to apply it, and would not be absorbed. Presently I gave up entirely, and lay down whimpering on the bed.

It was difficult not to have the most desolate thoughts about my predicament as I lay there. Determined as I was not to regret my decision to come to the country, the effort of will required to prevent myself plunging into an abyss of despair was considerable. So occupied had I been with damming the pressing flood of my past life that I had been unprepared for assaults up ahead; and it was tempting, oppressed as I now was on all sides, to relinquish my control of the situation entirely. There are moments at which great blocks of life seem to hang on the slenderest of threads; at which whole limbs of future and past pivot on the tiniest of fulcra. I trembled in that moment in just so exiguous a place. Like someone crouching on a lofty window ledge, I sensed that the slightest movement could undo me. I dared not even shift about on the bed, lest it provide the wing-beat of doubt required to topple me.

In the event a twinge of cramp in my empty stomach drove me to flop over onto my side; and it was then that my eyes fell on the bookshelf propped against the wall opposite. I am not a particularly keen reader, but my thirst for distraction was such that I was prepared to labour over this primitive receptacle to wring from it even a few drops. I got up and went to the bookshelf, squatting down beside it. Idly running my eyes over its offerings I saw several titles that I recognized, and some that I had already read. I dithered, pulling out first one then another from the mêlée of battered spines; and was about to make off with quite an exciting-looking detective story when a most curious thing happened.

At the far end of the shelf, tucked in amidst a crowd of rather tawdry romances, was a book that had my name on it. I blinked, thinking that I must be mistaken, and indeed lost it for a second or two; but there it was again. *Stella Benson.* Quivering and somewhat afraid, I drew it from the shelf. It was quite an old book, with a hard, mildew-green cover. In gold script on the front was the title: *The Runaway Bride.* Transfixed, my heart pounding, I sat crouched on the floor with the book in my hands. What could it mean? Was it a joke, or magic, or something more sinister; an inexplicable collision of worlds, a piece of jetsam tossed up by a mocking wave from an inscrutable sea? Opening the cover, I looked at the flyleaf. The mystery accrued substance, became concrete. *The Runaway Bride* by Stella Benson.

Trembling, I began to turn its dry, yellowed pages where I sat. I must have stayed like that for some time, for when I rose, still reading, to lie down on the bed, my legs ached and tingled. In the end it wasn't about me at all, but about people far away; although it was a fine story, and quite sad. The hours passed, there in the dry, dark pit of the night. Eventually I forgot the abrasive shock of the coincidence; or at least settled into a warmer accommodation with it. My namesake had evidently been a woman of some substance, well travelled, independent, compassionate; and kind, too; for she had thought, all those years ago, to set down this interesting tale, so that I would find it in my hour of loneliness and despair and be comforted.

Chapter Eight

It was already hot when I left the cottage at twenty-five minutes past eight the next morning and set off through the garden towards the big house. Above a fading veil of dawn mist the sky gave out its challenge in uncompromising blue; and in the vanguard at the brink of the trees the sun trumpeted a rallying cry and set off on its long, brutal march to dusk. I was in poetic mood. Even the heap of vomit, last seen lying pinkly in the fading light directly by the front door of the cottage, could not derail me; for perhaps an hour earlier, while the dew still trembled on the grass and the sun dozed on, I had gone about the business of clearing away that which I had deposited on the doorstep the night before. Afterwards I conducted a burial for the bird, scooping it queasily from the carpet with a dustpan I had found in the kitchen and bearing it out to a corner of the garden, where I dug a small grave with a spoon.

I had smothered the burnt areas of my skin in lotion and put on a long-sleeved shirt and trousers to cover the worst of it; but my face still bore the strange markings of my exposures – the white strip between two broader patches of differing red, a pattern which would not look amiss on a national flag – and all over I was very sore to the touch. As for my lack of nourishment over the past twenty-four hours, I was oddly not at all hungry. I had made myself a cup of coffee before I left, and it was now sitting in my poor shrunken stomach like a balloon. In fact, I was generally aware of a certain thinness about me. I am, habitually, neither fat nor thin. This does not mean that I did not find this tautness pleasurable; nor that it did not give me a measure of confidence at the thought of meeting Pamela, who, as I think I have mentioned, was lean and febrile in form.

So, thin and particoloured, I reached the front gate; and in stopping to open it was quite overwhelmed by the delicious smell of the garden, a smell given off by the countryside, I now know, only in the early morning and evening as a kind of scented fanfare to the arrival and departure of the day. I mention this smell simply because it has occurred to me that my descriptions of rural scenery might have been found wanting. The smell was, I believe, mainly of grass; but there were also hedges nearby, and a variety of flowers which might have contributed to it.

As I approached the back door of the big house, I recalled the problems I had encountered on the last occasion I tried to use it. Having striven so hard to achieve promptitude and a neat appearance, I fervently desired not to be led astray before the day had even begun. As it happened, the door was standing wide open; an omen, I thought, of a resolution on the part of the Maddens to give a more welcoming impression to me. I entered the house and, once I had reached the end of the long, winding corridor, found myself in the dark antechamber I recalled passing through with Mr Madden. I could hear no sound at all, which surprised me; I had expected the house to be abuzz with activity. Not wishing to intrude much further without having informed someone of my presence, I called out, quite cheerfully. There was no response at all, although as my ears strained for one I heard the stentorian ticking of a clock somewhere nearby. I called out again, more loudly, and when nothing happened called out several times one after the other, the volume of each shout growing correspondingly greater. My throat was becoming sore when a door to my right flew open and a woman I did not recognize stood before me.

'What's all that noise?' she said. 'Why are you making all that noise?'

She appeared to be angry. I had not the faintest notion of who she was; she looked old enough to be Pamela's mother, although there was no physical resemblance between them. Indeed, this harridan who had confronted me so rudely was decidedly ugly. She was very short and wide, like a barrel, with grey hair forged into a steely ridge upon the top of her head. Her face was peculiarly indented, as if she were drowning in her own fat, and only the tip of her nose and mouth were visible before she disappeared in a wave of chin. Her stance was quite aggressive, her small feet planted astride and her arms ready by her sides.

'I wasn't sure if there was anybody home,' I said. 'Mrs Madden is expecting me at half-past eight.'

'Mrs Madden is busy upstairs,' said the woman unpleasantly. 'If she is expecting you, she'll come down soon enough. It would have been better to go and wait quietly in the kitchen, rather than screaming like a banshee out here.'

'I'm sorry,' I said. Despite my dislike of her, I could see that she was right. 'I couldn't find my way to the kitchen. I didn't want to intrude.'

'You'll find it through here,' she said, turning and pushing open the door through which she had come. I followed her through. From behind she looked like a bus.

'Oh, here we are!' I said brightly, for we were now in the familiar kitchen. 'Thank you very much.'

The harridan did not reply, but merely went about her buslike business, manoeuvring around the kitchen with swift, greedy movements and being careful to keep her broad, bossy back to me all the while. I lingered, wondering if she would offer me coffee or food – I had deduced, from the fact that she was cleaning the kitchen, that her position in the house was menial – but my stance soon proved to be impractical. The woman turned, her lips pursed, and made her way grimly across the kitchen. I, unfortunately, had planted myself directly in her trajectory, and when she reached me she stopped and waited, without saying a word; like a bus, if I may repeat myself, fuming at a set of traffic lights. I stepped hastily aside, and she automatically continued on her way. Although she had not said a word, I felt her commanding me to sit; and I did so, on the same chair on which I had sat during dinner on my first evening at Franchise Farm.

Presently I heard the approach of footsteps from beyond the kitchen door, and Pamela came breezing into the room.

'Morning!' she cried, her waving hair bouncing on top of her head and her face alight with a genial smile.

'Morning!' I replied.

She drew to the other woman's side. I wondered if her cheerful greeting had been directed not at me but at my nemesis; and indeed if Pamela had noticed that I was there at all.

'Now, Mrs Barker,' she said. She lay her slender arm along the other woman's broad shoulders. 'I've cleared the way for you upstairs so you can just *forge* through.' She gestured dramatically with her hands and then replaced her arm, as if she were resting it on the back of a sofa. 'Martin has promised to evacuate that room of his by ten o'clock. I've told him that you are mounting a campaign and he's promised to keep out of your way.' She laughed lightly. 'He offered to be your standard-bearer and roll about the house ahead of you. He's a great fan of yours,' she said confidentially.

Mrs Barker made a peculiar noise which I took to be a laugh. It was in fact more of a snuffling smirk.

'He's quite a character, that young man,' she snuffled. 'Do you want me to do the windows, Pam?'

'Oh – let me think, do I?' Pamela put her head to one side, apparently not affronted by Mrs Barker's free use of a nickname. 'No, I don't think so. I think we can just about still see through them. We'll tackle those another day.'

'Right,' said Mrs Barker. 'I'll get on, then.'

'I'll bring you your coffee in a few minutes,' said Pamela. 'I just need to have a word with Stella.' I had, then, been detected. 'Have you met Stella, Mrs Barker?'

'I met her just now,' said Mrs Barker. 'Although she didn't introduce herself. I guessed who she was, though.'

'Jolly good,' said Pamela.

When she had gone, Pamela turned to me and heaved a sigh, as if she were already exhausted.

'And how are you today?' she said. Something in her failure to pronounce my name made the enquiry seem hostile. 'You've been sunbathing, I see.'

'I fell asleep in the garden by mistake,' I confessed. 'I didn't realize how hot it was.'

'I know, wasn't it glorious?' said Pamela. 'You really should have come over for that swim, you know.'

Seeing that she still bore a grudge over this matter, I felt a sense of opportunity, as if I had pinned down the source of her unfriendliness and could now tackle it.

'I didn't bring a swimming costume with me,' I said. 'I didn't know you had a pool. Otherwise, I'd have loved to have come.'

'Why didn't you *say*!' cried Pamela. 'Oh, silly girl! I've got *stacks* of them upstairs, I could easily have lent you one.' It was, I saw, touch and go as to whether she would think me stupid for not confessing earlier, or would be moved to pity by the thought of my shyness. 'And there you were roasting away all afternoon on your own and probably dying for a swim!'

I nodded.

'Oh, poor Stella! We're not ogres here, you know – you must just *shout* the minute you need anything. Look, I'll go and root one out for you later this morning and then we can all go for a swim at lunchtime.'

'Thank you,' I said.

I wondered if I should broach the small matter of breakfast, and then decided against it. A pause ensued. The subject of my duties, over which we had quarrelled so bitterly, was once again with us. There was, indeed, no way of my avoiding the question of what exactly I was supposed to do next; for there was no further business for me in the kitchen.

'Now, shall we just run through today? Have you got a moment?' said Pamela; for all the world as if I might not.

'OK,' I said.

She looked at me closely.

'Are you all right?' she said, as if concerned. I had thought that I had answered her quite cheerfully. I often have to be on my guard against morosity. 'You do look most dreadfully burnt.'

'Oh, I'm fine,' I said, gallantly brushing the subject away with my hand. 'It looks a lot worse than it is.'

'Shall I make coffee while we have our briefing?' she said, apparently having forgotten my sunburn instantly. 'Mrs Barker will be gasping by now.'

'I'll do it,' I said, getting up.

'You're a love,' said Pamela. My heart swelled absurdly at the words. 'You mustn't be afraid of Mrs Barker. She's a dear old thing.'

'Has she worked here for long?' I said, unable to concur.

'Oh, *aeons*,' said Pamela. I put on the kettle. 'Since the Flood. She was here when I was born. She's very precious and I'd hate to lose her.'

There was something accusatory about this comment, as if I might be liable to take Mrs Barker away and then forget where I'd put her.

'I'm sure you would,' I said.

'Shall we start?' said Pamela after a pause.

I wondered what had wrought this change in Pamela's attitude. She was as efficient now as she had been obfuscating before; and I interpreted this, to my satisfaction, as proof that she regretted the harshness with which she had treated me during my first evening in the country.

'Obviously your priority has got to be Martin,' she continued, enunciating her words clearly. 'He's a darling, but he does get bored just sitting around the house all day, so you have to take him out or find things to do with him at home. Now, on Mondays, Wednesdays and Saturdays he goes to the centre for the afternoon. Sometimes Piers or I take him, but usually I'd expect you to do it.'

'Where is the centre?' I said.

'Oh, it isn't far – in Buckley. You'll take him there in the car, and then one of the carers drops him back when he's ready. They're terribly nice there. It's such a boon having it, and Martin loves it.'

I calculated that, it being Monday, my downfall might lie only a few short hours away.

'Actually, on second thoughts I think I'll probably take him down myself this afternoon. I've got some shopping to do,' said Pamela.

My hands, which were bearing the brimming coffee cups to the table, trembled with relief, and some of it slopped to the floor.

'Careful!' said Pamela.

'Sorry,' I said. 'I'll mop it up.'

'Look, do just sit down for a minute while I finish,' said Pamela wearily. 'We can mop it up later.'

'OK,' I said, keen not to aggravate her.

'Now, there are various things Martin can do for himself, such as go to the lavatory, so you needn't worry about that unless he asks you. You might need to be on hand if he's in the bath and gets stuck. The other difficult thing is getting up and down the stairs. He usually just shuffles down himself, but you may need to help him up if he's tired, and you'll need to carry his chair. We did think,' she continued, 'of getting a second chair for downstairs, but they're such beastly things to have about and they do clutter the place up. It's quite light, in any case. Generally, he'll tell you what he wants you to do. He's not shy.' She put her hands around her coffee cup and raised it to her lips. 'The real thing in the mornings is to get behind him to do his homework. He's a lazy bugger. Always trying to talk his way out of it.'

'Homework?' I said. 'What sort of homework does he do?'

'The same as everybody else,' snapped Pamela, flashing her bright eyes at me. 'He's not retarded, Stella. He goes to school just like other children. It's very dangerous to assume things about disabled people, let me tell you.'

I could sense that we were in steep decline.

'I'm sorry,' I said. 'When you said "centre" I didn't realize you meant that it was a school.'

'It isn't!' cried Pamela, banging her hand upon the table. 'It's you who isn't clear, not I! The centre is a day centre for children like Martin to go to during the school holidays.' She punctuated her words with further sharp slaps upon the table. 'And school is school, just the same as for everybody else.'

I had not, of course, realized that it was the school holidays; nor, if I were to be honest, that Martin even went to school.

'Right, so I'll help him with his homework,' I continued quickly, in an attempt to stem the tide against me.

'He won't need help. He just needs to be told to do it.'

'OK,' I said. 'I'll do that. And what about when he's at the centre? I mean, what do you expect me to do?'

'Well!' Pamela gave a sort of snort. 'Obviously I can't give you a timetable for every spare minute. Personally, I find that I barely have time to catch my breath, but if you think that you're going to be at a loose end then I suppose you can come and find me and I'll give you something to do.'

'Fine,' I said; and regretted it as soon as I heard the unfortunate way in which it had issued from my mouth. I suppose that I had been feeling quite cross at the way Pamela was speaking to me, and some of this resentment had exited inadvertently with my reply. It was impossible that Pamela should not have noticed my tone, and indeed her head shot up at the sound of it and she met me with a steely eye. In her expression, I could see dawning the memory of our exchange in this very kitchen the other night; a sight which surprised me, for I had of course imagined that she had thought a great deal about the scene and made certain resolutions concerning it. It was now apparent to me that she had not given it a moment's consideration; until now.

'I hope we're not going to have trouble with you,' she said; not particularly nastily, although it was not a very pleasant thing to say. 'We've had problems with girls in the past, and we were very much hoping that you were going to be different.'

It was difficult for me to restrain myself from remarking that the 'problems' encountered in the past all had one thing in common – Pamela – and that perhaps she should look to herself if she wanted to solve them. This kind of honesty was not available to me. Still, I could see that Pamela's ill temper, rather than a unique occurrence, was to be a central feature of my dealings with her; a fact which demanded, risky and unpleasant though this prospect was, the immediate formulation of some policy with which to confront it.

'Mrs Madden,' I said boldly. 'I'm sorry if you've had problems in the past. I don't intend to cause you any trouble, and I very much want things to work out well. This kind of life is very new to me, however, and if you remember that this is only my first proper day, then you will understand why I might need my duties to be spelled out for me clearly. It's obviously very important that things go smoothly with Martin,' I continued; ingeniously, I must admit. 'And I don't want to learn by making mistakes. I'd rather know everything I have to know before we start, and that way he will hopefully not be too disrupted.'

This speech was exhausting; and as I delivered it I trembled at what Pamela might be thinking of me. It was impossible to deduce anything from her expression, which was one of open-mouthed astonishment. She seemed to be thinking. Finally, to my relief, she began to nod her head energetically.

'Yes. Yes,' she said. 'I think I see what you mean. Yes, you're quite right, Stella.' She was still nodding. I wondered when she would stop. 'Yes, it *is* better this way, isn't it?'

'I think so,' I said, quite warmly; although I was still panting from my oratory. 'Now,' I continued, pressing my advantage, 'shall I take Mrs Barker her coffee? And then perhaps I can go and find Martin and see what he's doing about that homework.'

'Yes, why don't you?' said Pamela meekly.

'Where will I find him?'

'What? Oh, upstairs in his bedroom, I should think. Mrs Barker will show you the way if you get lost.'

You may be surprised by this evidence of my assertiveness. Perhaps you have assumed that because I was inferior to Mrs Madden – in many ways, and not only because of my position in her house – that I would never find it within myself to stand up to her. My story so far could be regarded, indeed, as a history of oppression, one of those old-fashioned stories in which a poor, plain heroine endures all the misfortunes that social and material disadvantage can devise for her, but lives to be triumphantly rewarded at the last moment for her forbearance. Mrs Madden, for example, might finally meet with a terrible accident, falling beneath the wheels of a tractor or being murdered by Mrs Barker, who would be revealed to be an anarchist working under cover; leaving me to be installed at Franchise Farm as Pamela's successor, Mr Madden having confessed that he hated her all along. I will not pretend that I myself have never entertained daydreams of this type; but one's first duty must always be to reality.

To return to the subject of my unexpected act of self-assertion, I had been in the world; and in the course of my twenty-nine years had encountered all manner of people there. I am not stupid; and as I watched Pamela work herself into a fever of ill temper for the second time was able to observe the phenomenon more closely. I did not do this entirely consciously, of course; I am a sensitive person, and in situations of confrontation find it easier to be emotional than scientific. Let us just say that I was not so disconcerted by Pamela on this occasion; and by remaining calm, that I was able to detect several similarities in the two outbursts which pointed at some kind of pathology on the part of my employer. In order to conduct this experiment, I had, obviously, to be sure that my own position was of the utmost rationality; and I believed that it was. Having established, then, that Pamela had no specific cause to be angry at *me*, I could deduce that the source of her irritation lay elsewhere. Who, indeed, could blame Pamela for being touchy? No matter how much she appeared to dote upon Martin, to have a disabled child is to carry one of life's heavier burdens. Among the feelings which it might provoke, I could identify guilt and resentment in a matter of moments; and who knew what else might be found if one dug deeper?

The second strand of my analysis of Pamela's instability involved separating the reality of Pamela's situation from the manner in which she represented it. I had noticed the frequency with which she resorted to dramatic and exaggerated terminology in general; and to expressions of chaos and overwork in particular. Pamela, according to herself, was busy every minute of the day; the house was a 'madhouse'; she was left with no time even to 'catch her breath'. This, as far as I could see, was far from actually being the case. What, in fact, did Pamela have to do? She had Mrs Barker; she had me. Even Martin, whose helplessness was the cause of my presence here, seemed fairly self-reliant, with his homework and aptitude for shuffling and going to the lavatory alone. When I asked for specific assignments for the afternoons when Martin was absent, Pamela could give me none; and this, being the school holidays, was high season as far as looking after Martin was concerned. What was I supposed to do all day when Martin went back to school? The next question, though cruel, was unavoidable: why couldn't Pamela manage on her own?

In this way, I arrived at the conclusion that Pamela was not the self-possessed and frightening person she seemed. It was this realization that permitted me to stand up to her; but in finding the solution to one of my problems, I created many more. Having discovered Pamela's weakness, I was in a sense electing to carry it, and I had come to the country with the express purpose of avoiding burdens of this type. I did not want to be embroiled in complexity; and it was hard to see how I could continue to use a 'firm hand' with Pamela – for that, I now knew, was the way to tame her – without assuming some responsibility for the consequences. Pamela was unhappy. Should I remain the slave of this unhappiness, and continue to endure the more unfortunate aspects of her treatment of me without complaint, I would, I felt sure, suffer every torment the despotic nature can visit upon the submissive. Things would go from bad to worse. Were I, however, to become its master, I would be accepting a certain amount of power; and with power comes accountability. In other words, if I assumed control of my relationship with Pamela, she would eventually come to expect certain things of me which I was not sure I wanted to provide.

I left the kitchen as speedily as Mrs Barker's laden coffee cup would allow, with Pamela forlorn and subdued at the table. Being rather more familiar now with the route by which the rooms at the back of the house connected with those at the front, I found my way to the hall without too much difficulty. At the far end of it I spied Mrs Barker, who was standing at the front door with her back to me engaged in some extraordinary form of activity. I could not be clear of what exactly she was doing; but whatever it was, she was doing it so energetically that her ample rear portion was vibrating. I was surprised, and somewhat disgusted, to find myself suspecting her of performing there in the hall in broad daylight the act I had carried out in the secrecy of my bedroom the day before. As I drew closer – she was so absorbed in her task that she did not notice my approach – I found myself growing horribly fascinated by her oscillations, and stood for some seconds with my eyes fixed upon her posterior. A moment of some embarrassment was, then, to be mine when finally she sensed my presence behind her and turned from her labours to confront me. I saw that she held in one hand a cloth and in the other a tin of polish; evidence, if any were needed, that she was indulging not in the practice of self-gratification but rather of cleaning the brass doorknob. Her rhinal glare strove to wither me where I stood; but no amount of hostility, not even the threat of actual physical assault which her ready bulk seemed to proffer, can justify the words with which I chose to address her.

'Here's your coffee, you cunt,' I said.

Although I am prepared to admit, and even swear, that I spoke this terrible word, some greater and mysterious force denied it. On the radio they have a button which can be pressed if some indiscretion or obscenity is uttered on air; a ten-second delay, I think it is called. In other words, things are happening, on the radio, ten seconds in the future, by which means the present moment can be cleansed. I have always thought that this would be a useful device to have in life; and on this occasion I seemed to have been provided with it. I am not saying that some kind of magic, scientific or otherwise, came into play in my encounter with Mrs Barker; rather that denial, which after all is the essence of this button, did the work *in extremis* of this ingenious invention. I denied that I had said it; Mrs Barker denied that she had heard it; in short, our situation denied that such a thing could be possible; and *voilà*! It never happened.

'Thank you,' said Mrs Barker. She seemed slightly uncomfortable, as if she knew that something had occurred but couldn't remember what it was, like people in films who are abducted by aliens or go travelling through time, returning to the exact moment at which they left and with only a void or vacuum of memory to show for it.

'Could you direct me to Martin's bedroom?' I politely enquired; tempted to try the trick again but not daring to.

'You'll find it to the left at the top of the stairs,' said Mrs Barker. She hesitated, her fleshy brow still slightly crinkled with confusion, and then turned her attention once more to the doorknob.

Quickly I made my way up the capacious staircase, noting as I climbed the fine, deep carpet which softened my tread and proclaimed the upper realm to be one of comfort and repose. On the landing above, pale walls and delicate framed watercolours continued this theme. A Victorian rocking horse stood beneath the window directly ahead of me, a nursery motif. Pamela really was a dab hand at interior decoration.

Chapter Nine

Turning left at the top of the stairs, I arrived at a closed door which I guessed was the entrance to Martin's bedroom. I stood outside it for a moment in order to collect myself. The abominable rudeness with which Martin had behaved, not only towards me but also towards his mother, on the last occasion we met, returned to my mind and filled me with apprehension.

I summoned up the courage to knock on the door – two swift raps – and was surprised when a cheerful 'Come in!' was relayed to me from the other side. I entered, noticing the well-polished brass doorknob, and found myself in a large room, above whose clutter rose two tall windows which looked out to the front of the house. At the foot of each window was an indented seat, with long panelled shutters on either side folded back like birds' wings. In spite of its elegance, the room was very untidy; so much so, in fact, that for a few seconds I was unable to locate Martin. Bookshelves sagging with their cargo lined an entire wall; adjacent to them was a desk piled high with more of the same. Strewn across the floor was the usual detritus of adolescence: brightly coloured record sleeves littering the carpet as indiscriminately as fallen leaves, knotted items of clothing, ancient, corroded coffee cups. Stray, small shoes, as dejected and heartbreaking as a child's shoe found on a beach, were the only evidence of Martin's abnormality. Mrs Barker would, I felt, take no prisoners here when she stormed the barricades at ten o'clock.

'Oh, it's you,' said Martin. He was sitting in his wheelchair by the bookshelves, as camouflaged as a forest creature in foliage.

'It's me,' I replied, quite sternly; in my moment of contemplation outside the door I had decided on a firm approach.

'Come in.' He wheeled round in his chair and gestured with his long arm. 'Sit down.'

There was a leather armchair beside him and he leaned forward from his chair – so steeply that I feared he might fall out of it – to sweep it free where the tide of jumble had risen over the seat. I weaved my way across the room and sat obediently beside him. The chair was most comfortable. I was aware of the fact that in a matter of seconds any authority I might have possessed had been wrested from me; but curiously, I did not mind. There was something righteous about my charge's presence in this sunny room which his presence in other rooms had so far entirely lacked. I had the feeling that all who entered here abided by his law.

Now directly beside me, Martin was engaged in a close examination of my face. I caught a glimpse of his, the terrible, preternatural spectacle of his features, before I was compelled to look away, embarrassed by my recollection of the sunburn. Immediately I became anxious that he might think me repelled not by my own appearance but by his, and so directed myself to yield to his gaze once more.

'You look nice,' said Martin finally, as if he had arrived at this judgement by a complex means of assessment which I might well have failed.

It is hard to describe the way in which Martin's mouth moved when he laughed or spoke – I have attempted it before – but it was unlike any physiognomical procedure I had witnessed before in my life. His lips incised in parallel almost the entire span of his face, and gave it the odd appearance of being divided into two parts or blocks connected, perhaps, by a hinge at the back of his head; so that one had the feeling, particularly when he opened his mouth wide – which he did frequently – that the upper section of his head could at any moment flip open, revealing his brain sitting like a steaming cauliflower on a platter. Some possible obstruction in his larynx gave his voice a nasal, remote quality; rather like a ventriloquist's dummy, which reiterated the resemblance to a puppet or doll I noted some time ago. His thick tongue, whose unfortunate appearance in the kitchen had left its image firmly engraved on my mind, gave him a slight lisp.

'Thank you,' I said, surprised. Disingenuously, I added: 'So do you.'

'Ha! Ha!' Martin's mouth opened so wide that I genuinely feared the flipping mentioned above. His laughter was loud and I caught a gust of his breath, which was surprisingly sweet. 'Ha! Ha! That's very funny.'

He said this as if he meant it; and I saw, somewhat to my dismay, that he had taken my compliment as an ironical joke; and, what's more, found it amusing.

'Stella,' said Martin abruptly. 'Stel-*la. Stella.*'

'Yes?' I said, trying to sound encouraging, although I was somewhat confused.

'Will you open the windows, Stel-*la*? It's got *rather pongy* in here.'

He said this last comment in a mock-aristocratic voice. I got up, keen for something to do, and threw up first one sash and then the other. The drive below lay deserted in the heat. A faint, warm breeze drifted in.

'Are you happy, Stel-*la*?' he said, when had I sat down again.

'I see no need to continue pronouncing my name in that way,' I replied. I was taken aback by his question, and wondered what mischief he meant by it.

'Are you?' he repeated.

'I suppose so,' I said, settling back in my chair. I was surprised to feel myself on the brink of quite a lengthy reply. 'How would one ever know? I'm as happy as anyone should be, living in a civilized country with no real disadvantages; but whether I am as happy as I could be, I see no way of finding out. I don't happen to think that happiness is the be-all and end-all of everything.'

'Then what is?' said Martin.

'Oh, I don't know. Coming to an accommodation with oneself, I suppose. Not injuring others. Living a good life. Why ask me?'

'Well,' said Martin, putting his large hands on the wheels of his chair and rocking back and forth. 'You did say that you thought happiness wasn't that important. It's an unusual thing to say, Stel-*la*.'

'I didn't say that I thought happiness was unimportant. Merely that it wasn't the most important thing. I happen to believe that the search for happiness is often itself the greatest cause of unhappiness.'

'But if you were happy, you wouldn't be searching,' said Martin.

'I didn't say I was. I was speaking generally. I think it is almost impossible to be happy and to know yourself to be so at one and the same time. People believe that happiness is a goal, as opposed merely to the absence of problems. Looking for happiness is like looking for love. How do you know when you've found it?'

'I always imagined they came together,' said Martin.

'Nonsense. Love makes people more miserable than anything else.'

'Have you been made miserable by love, poor Stel-la?'

'That's none of your business.'

'Oh, go on.' He smiled, and began to rock himself a little faster. 'I won't tell anyone.'

'I should hope not. No.'

'Tell,' he said. 'Tel-la, Stel-la. Tel-la, Stel-la.' He rocked himself to the rhythm of the words. 'Tel-la me-a Stel-la.'

'Stop that immediately,' I said.

'Only if you tel-la me-a—'

'I will not be blackmailed. Please behave yourself.'

At this moment the door flew open, and Mrs Barker, incandescent with sanitary fury, appeared upon the threshold.

'Getting the better of her, are you?' she said, grinning, to Martin.

'Get-ta the bet-ta of Stel-la,' chanted Martin.

'I'll need you both out,' commanded the hag. 'I've got to set this pigsty to rights. Go on, off with you.'

'Keep your hair on, Mrs Barker,' said Martin, while I boiled with anger beside him at the woman's imperious manner. 'Don't get those elephantine bloomers of yours in a twist.'

'You watch your lip,' said Mrs Barker mildly. She positioned herself beside the open door and extended an arm towards the corridor. 'Out.'

Martin rolled dutifully towards the door and I followed. As we passed the bulk of Mrs Barker, he looked up at her and made several loud kissing noises. I kept my head down until we were on the landing. We paused at the precipice of the stairs, and I remembered Martin's disability; a fact which made me feel ashamed for the severity with which I had spoken to him just now.

'Shall I help you down?' I said solicitously.

'Don't be a *vache*,' said Martin. 'Just carry the chair.'

Not being in a position – considering my earlier assault on Mrs Barker – to reprimand him for his language, I said nothing. Martin pulled a lever by the wheels which locked them, and then, with a single, terrifying movement precipitated himself out of the seat and slithered to the ground. For a moment I feared that he had hurt himself, but almost immediately he began to rotate himself with crablike movements upon his long, tensile arms, his shrunken legs dragging on the carpet behind him. As soon as he was positioned facing down the stairs, he began with remarkable alacrity to descend them, twitching his hips and reaching forward with each arm in turn to fling first one immobile limb and then the other ahead of him.

'Come on,' he called.

I picked up the chair – which was not, contrary to Pamela's assertion, particularly light – and began slowly to make my way down behind him. He sat waiting for me at the bottom in a kind of heap, and when I positioned the chair for him in the hall grabbed its handles and levered himself up, like someone emerging from a swimming pool. He disengaged the brake and spun off towards the front door, which he opened dextrously. He sailed through the doorway and then disappeared abruptly from view. Fearing that he had rolled down the front steps, I ran out after him, and to my surprise found him sitting leisurely in his chair on the hot gravel drive.

'How did you get down?' I said.

He pointed to the side of the steps, where I saw a small ramp I had not previously noticed.

'Dumbo,' he said.

'There's no need to be rude,' I said, descending the front steps. 'What shall we do now? Would you like to go for a walk?'

'I can't walk,' he said.

I was beginning to weary of Martin's confrontational style of behaviour. He seemed determined to obstruct me at every turn. Although no longer strictly afraid of him, his volatility made me nervous. I had no idea of what he might do at any given time.

'You know what I mean,' I said tersely. 'You could show me around the grounds. By the time we come back, Mrs Barker will have finished.'

'All right,' he said, affably enough. 'You'll have to push me, though. My arms get tired on uneven surfaces.'

'OK,' I said. I put my hands on the handles of his chair. 'Which way?'

'Through there.' He pointed to a path running from the right of the house into some trees.

We set off. The heat was very fierce at the front of the house and the burnt skin on my face ached. I was relieved when we made it to the trees, which I saw marked the beginning of a small wood. The wheelchair made quite heavy going over the rough path and I began to sweat and lose my breath.

'What do you think of the show so far?' he said from below, in a silly voice.

'Excuse me?'

'What-do-you-think-of-the-show-so-far,' he repeated, this time in the synthesized, unmodulated tones of an automaton.

'Oh, I see. Lovely. *Verdant*,' I hazarded.

'Not *this*. I meant everything.' We trundled over an uneven patch and he gripped the sides of his chair. '*Maman. Papa. Moi*, even.'

'I don't really know yet. I haven't been here long.' I was surprised that he should want to know what I thought of him.

'Oh, come *on*,' he said, tipping back his head so that he could see me, with a smile which suggested that he thought the gesture winning. 'Don't tell me that you haven't already made up your mind down to the last detail. You must think *something*.'

His dwarfish appearance and leering mouth, particularly when seen from above, gave him the look of a sprite or ghoul; not wicked, exactly, but naughty and dedicated to disruption. I decided straight away not to tell him anything. His voice had that same imploring tone that he had used – vainly, I was glad to recall – to extract tales of past romantic disappointments; about which now he seemed to have quite forgotten.

'Why are you so keen to know what I think?' I said, heaving him over a delta of ruts. Seeing that I was not to be so easily seduced, he had given up his gamin gazing and was now looking straight ahead. I was struck, as I pushed the chair through the dark, lovely glade stilled by the profuse calm of summer, by the odd realization that this was exactly how, during those few days in London, I had imagined my life in the country would be. Or was I merely recognizing, in the paradisal picture around me, a kind of mental ideal which, based on what I knew while still in London of the place to which I was going, *might have* constituted such an image? In other words, had I really imagined it like this, or was it just that I had happened on an enclave of time and place so logical in its felicity that it transcended its actual existence to become a kind of paradigm; a vision which, being perfect – and corresponding too to the few things I had known about my future situation – took on the texture of memory, wherein all the flaws and stains of lived events are purged? I have often experienced this feeling of doubt when encountering extreme beauty or happiness.

Martin had not replied to my question, and so I continued: 'After all, it's not as if you know me very well. Why should my opinion matter to you?'

'I don't know,' said Martin sulkily. 'I think it's obvious why. I don't exactly get out much.'

I felt chastened by this remark. I had humiliated him by attributing to prurience or mischief what was in fact a hunger for novelty. Trapped as he was, both now and for the foreseeable future, in the same stale set of circumstances, it was natural that a newcomer should exert more than the usual interest.

'That's true,' I said, keen to made amends. 'But it doesn't alter the fact that I haven't been here long enough to have any view which I could be sure wouldn't change over the next twenty-four hours.'

I was really quite tired out by this point. We had reached a kind of clearing, at the centre of which was a pond. Beside it stood a small, sagging tree – a willow – whose lachrymose branches drooped into the pool below, giving it the appearance of a vast melting candle. The stagnant water was thickly covered by a bright green blanket of algae, above which all manner of creatures circulated in a busy airborne community.

'Shall we stop here for a minute?'

'If you want,' said Martin uncharitably.

I wheeled him round to face the pond and let go of the handles of his chair, intending to sit down on the grass beside him. To my horror, however, his chair began abruptly to roll forwards towards the swampy water. I cried out, lunging for the handles while Martin sat, inert, his small body jolting as the wheels trundled down the slope. Just in time, I managed to grip the back of the leather seat, and dragged the chair back from the brink and up the slope, my chest heaving with panic.

'Oh, my God!' I panted. 'Are you all right?'

'Yes,' said Martin coolly. 'You should always put the brake on before you let go.'

There was a slightly menacing edge to his voice. I remembered having seen him put on the brake himself at the top of the stairs, and suspected, maliciously, I admit, that he had neglected to save himself on this occasion to upset me.

'I'm terribly sorry,' I said. 'Are you sure you're all right?'

I wondered if he would tell Pamela what had happened, and began to think immediately about how I would be able to broach this subject and gain the promise of his discretion before we returned to the house.

'I can't swim,' said Martin. 'I'd have drowned.'

'There's no need to be like that,' I snapped. 'Anyway, I wouldn't have let you drown. I'd have jumped in and saved you.'

'How?' said Martin. 'I'd have sunk like a stone beneath all that muck. You wouldn't have been able to find me.'

'If what you require,' I said imperiously, 'is my assurance that I would have paid with my life to save your own, then you have it. We would have died together.'

'My,' said Martin. 'How romantic.'

'Quite,' said I. 'So if you would be so kind as to accept my apologies, then I should be grateful to hear no more about it.'

'I'm sure you would,' Martin replied, eyes aglint. 'I think my mother might be interested, though.'

'That,' I said firmly, although my heart quavered, 'is up to you.' I applied the brake to his chair and sat down in the shade beside him. 'Obviously I would prefer it if you didn't mention it to her.'

'Perhaps we might strike a bargain,' said Martin, after a pause.

'Really! And what might that be?' I knew full well what the evil dwarf meant.

'You know,' said Martin, folding his arms across his chest.

'I hope,' I replied, 'that you are not trying to blackmail me into giving dubious and ill-formed opinions of your family in return for not telling tales. If you intend to ask me what I think of you under such circumstances, then you will hear nothing flattering. It's up to you.'

Various insects had come to plague me as I sat on the grass, and I swatted at them irritably with my hands. I wished that we had moved ourselves elsewhere, away from the gloomy prospect of the pond, and the near accident to which it testified.

'What makes you think that I care what you think of me?' said Martin presently.

'I asked you the same question not long ago,' I replied. 'Your answer, such as it was, suggested that you did care. If you deny it, then I will call your bluff. As I said before, it's up to you.'

'As a matter of fact, I don't care what you or anyone else thinks of me. It doesn't make any difference. I was only joking, anyway.'

A look of pain collected on Martin's face, like something dense and murky at the bottom of a drain. Seeing the poor, naked savagery of his features, I was moved to feel pity for him. He made a sorry opponent; and I wondered at myself, that I should have been so unkind to him.

'Shall we carry on?' I said then, standing up. I had an awareness of time passing, wasted, untouched. It seemed imperative to me that we continue with our walk.

'All right,' conceded Martin grudgingly. 'Although that was mean, what you just said.'

'I withdraw it,' I said magnanimously.

'Oh, shut up,' muttered Martin, as I wheeled him in a half circle and headed back towards the path. 'You're getting on my nerves. Turn right here.'

We emerged from the wood and before long arrived at a wall, which formed one end of an enclosure. The wall was about six feet high and several yards across, and, being built of apparently very old red brick, over the top of which spilled a froth of vines and flowers of various types, was extremely picturesque. At its centre was a black wrought-iron gate, through which I could make out some form of horticultural splendour within.

'What's this?' I said.

'This,' said Martin, leaning forward in his chair to open the latch, 'is the Elizabethan Rose Garden.'

Having left behind the wood, we were once more exposed to the sun; which, it being now late morning, was astonishingly fierce. I found – and indeed have always found – that the heat exerted a peculiar effect on me. Sunshine can, of course, be very enjoyable, but when it becomes excessively strong, as now it was, I find that I lose sense of myself quite dramatically. I do not mean 'lose my senses', in other words go mad; rather, I am describing a certain loss or interruption of frequency brought about by the dominating presence of an external force. Heavy rain, I find, has precisely the opposite effect; meaning that it enlarges consciousness by waterlogging the other senses. The sun, however, has in my view a blanching, shrivelling influence upon thought; or rather, it seems to make everything the same, and thus melts the boundaries of self.

To continue, I was not feeling quite myself – a dangerous condition, leading to the sort of behaviour people describe as being 'out of character' – as we entered the Elizabethan Rose Garden. This did not, however, blur my impression of the lovely enclave in which I now stood. The garden was quite idyllic; indeed, my amorphous mental state may well have been responsible for the force of my reaction to it. It was rectangular in shape, and consisted in several long rows and wedges of rose bushes with a maze of well-kept gravel paths between, all perfectly symmetrical; a geometrical theme which gave the garden a look of arcane symbolism, like an astrologer's map. Here and there wrought-iron benches were placed; and at the very centre of the garden, standing on a smooth circle etched in gravel, was an old stone sundial. The roses, being in full bloom, were a grand, faded pink and many of them were very large. I reached out to touch one beside me, whose head hung engorged from its stem. To my embarrassment, it disintegrated instantly beneath my fingers in a gentle explosion of velvet petals, falling in a sort of confetti about my feet. I could not help but think, looking at the naked stem, that I had murdered the lovely flower; and I cast about for Martin, hoping that he had not witnessed my act of vandalism.

Fortunately he was nowhere to be seen. Thinking that he must have wheeled off along one of the paths, I set off at no great pace down the nearest avenue to hand to find him. I was, in fact, happy to be alone. The garden was very quiet, its only music the faint, chirruped chords of summer, and in the scented hush I found myself transported back through time to its 'Elizabethan' ancestry, imagining myself there to be an altogether more favoured and elaborately costumed Stella, enjoying privileged seclusion in a world as orderly beyond these walls as within them; a respite of scale rather than substance, furnished by an authority who granted her every whim as systematically as it confounded mine. I often, incidentally, have fantasies of this type. Being essentially happy with myself, my daydreams strive instead to transform my circumstances; usually preferring a more kindly age, offering iron-cast certainties and a less vertiginous view of the future.

I had sat down on a bench beside the sundial by this time and – perhaps, again, due to the peculiar effect of the sun – all at once found that my daydream had delivered me, as if through a secret tunnel bored beneath a fortress wall, to the outermost, unpatrolled reaches of thought where lately I had forbidden myself to wander. The garden faded and then vanished before my eyes, and in the analgesic white light which followed it I was unexpectedly met by a vision. The vision was of a crowded street seen from high above; not an English street, but a narrow, Continental chasm. Everything was very brown and dusty and noisy. From my vantage point I could see the lacy balustrades of balconies depending high up from the elaborate, crumbling fronts of buildings; and then realized that I, too, was standing on a balcony with my fingers gripping the iron railing. I leaned perilously over the edge and saw far, far below trails of tiny, dusty cars beetling along the floor of the ravine. The sun was hot on the back of my head. I was leaning so far over that the rail dug into my stomach. The weight of a solid but indeterminate misery pressed at my back as I leaned, forcing me further over still. The blare of car horns filled my ears. My heart was thrashing in my chest with terror. Then, all of a sudden, I flipped over and fell; but to my surprise, I did not plummet to the pavement. Instead I floated, my weightless body describing elegant arcs like a fluttering leaf, and as I gently descended I looked about. One or two people stood on the balconies opposite and when they saw me they waved. I waved cheerfully back; and it must have been at around this point that I woke up, or came to, and found myself back in the rose garden.

Perhaps less than a minute had passed since I had exited so importunately from the present moment. When I returned the loveliness of the quaint garden, momentarily forgotten, struck me with redoubled force. In this instant of recognition – whose constituent parts, memory and perception, were in this case particularly charged – I experienced the magical, elusive flash of certain happiness: something I had not felt for some time and which, arising as it did from a rapid modulation of fear to safety, provided the substance for my first, indelible identification of Franchise Farm as home.

'What are you doing here, Stel-la?'

Martin was sitting beside me on the gravel path in his chair, his presence so complete and unheralded that it had the flavour of an apparition. His face was screwed into a grimace in the sunlight so that it seemed frozen in an attitude of rigid surprise, as if a door had been slammed on it.

'I'm thinking,' I said. His question, insinuating as it was, demanded a fuller reply. 'I was thinking,' I improvised, 'of how amazing it is that this garden has been here since Elizabethan times. One imagines history to be inorganic, and yet here it is, written into the landscape.'

I was rather proud of this insight, but Martin seemed to find something funny in it.

'Ha, ha!' he brayed, mouth agape. 'Ha, ha!'

'What?'

I fully expected him to repeat my comment, in a voice which would ensure that not one of its nuances was left unmocked. This feeling was not altogether new to me: I find speech a precipitous and exposing business, and often perform it with palpable 'stage fright'; a feeling which, I don't doubt, has resulted over the years in the formality with which now I am unable to avoid expressing myself.

Martin, meanwhile, having prolonged his hilarity beyond all reasonable limits, finally gave me his reply:

'The garden isn't *Elizabethan*, you idiot! It's a breed of rose, the Elizabethan rose. Grumps planted them.'

'Who,' I enquired, 'is Grumps?'

'My grandfather,' said Martin primly, as if he were offended that I hadn't heard of him.

'Well, I can't say I'm not disappointed,' I maintained, after a pause. 'Although he did a good job of it.'

'It's open to the public,' said Martin, still apparently affronted. 'Every Saturday during the summer. It's very well known. People pay to come and look at it.'

I found this information rather surprising, suggesting as it did that the Maddens had been driven by penury to make a going concern of their own garden.

'I think that's sad,' I said.

'Why?'

'Because it's a private place. I liked the thought of it being secret. Knowing that it's an exhibit spoils it.'

'If one is fortunate enough,' pronounced Martin, 'to possess something unique, of more than average worth, one has a duty to share it with one's fellow man.'

'I wouldn't know about that,' I replied. 'But if all this were mine, I don't think I'd want to share it with anyone.'

'There you are.' Martin folded his arms with satisfaction. 'That's why things are better off in our hands. We know how these things ought to be done.'

'Who is "we"?' I enquired.

'The upper classes,' said Martin, his face crumpled and white, like something botched and screwed into a ball. I caught a glimpse of the cavity of his mouth, dark and moist.

'I do apologize,' I said sarcastically. 'I didn't realize that was who you were.'

'Our family,' intoned Martin, 'has lived in this house since the seventeenth century, and in this area since long before that.'

'Does that make you upper class?' I was becoming quite irritated, in a desultory fashion. 'I'd have thought it just makes you *local*. Anyway,' I closed my eyes and leaned back against the elaborate grid of the bench, and as it pressed into my flesh the taste of my vision lingered briefly on my tongue, 'aren't you a bit old to be boasting about your family? There used to be girls who did that at school. If they weren't comparing how much money their parents had, they were droning on about some old relative of theirs in a bearskin who'd got his name in the Domesday Book.'

'My—' Through the crack of my eyelid I saw Martin's mouth, flapping like an open door in the wind. I guessed that he had been about to tell me that his ancestors were in the Domesday Book. 'Bearskins were earlier,' he said finally. 'Don't you know anything?'

I sat up again and opened my eyes. I knew that I had to get out of the sun immediately. My sunburn was proving to be very inconvenient, a form of incontinence. I glimpsed a wedge of shadow on the sundial in front of me, and for no reason other than idle curiosity peered at it more closely. There were numbers engraved all around its circumference, and the shadow fell exactly between a twelve and a one. It then dawned on me that this was the time. I was about to remark on what a clever thing the sundial was when I thought that Martin might laugh at me for it, my logic having a backward flavour.

'Goodness, look at the time!' I exclaimed instead. 'We'd better be getting back.'

'Do we have to?' complained Martin. 'I was having fun.'

'I'll take that as a compliment,' I replied, getting to my feet. My head swam for an instant. 'Personally, I always prefer to quit while I'm ahead. How do we get back to the house?'

I grasped the handles of Martin's chair and wheeled it around on its axis. Much as I pitied him for having to submit, physically at least, to my authority, there were advantages to having him chair-bound. I imagined running around the rose garden trying to catch him as he scampered off on his little legs, and almost laughed aloud. I had certainly been in the sun for far too long.

'That way,' said Martin, pointing directly ahead.

We set off in the opposite direction to that from which we had entered the rose garden and before long came to a gate identical to the first. I tried to work out where this would lead us, and figured that it would be somewhere to the side of the house. Martin leaned forward and opened the latch; and when I propelled him through I was surprised to see that we had entered directly what was evidently the bottom of the back garden. Turning around, I realized that the side wall of the rose garden was also the side boundary of the back garden. To our left was a queue of trees, evergreens, so dense that it was difficult to see what lay beyond them. In front and to our right was a great lawn, at the top of which was the back of the house.

'Come on,' said Martin, jiggling up and down as if he were spurring on a horse.

I braced my back and began to push.

Chapter Ten

The back of the house was quite different from the front; although like a revolving door, some frustration in its design made it impossible to get a sense of both sides at once. Indeed, for some time as we made our slow progress up the lawn I was unable to articulate what constituted this difference, great though it was. The rear of the house seemed far older and more frail, and gave the impression of being ignorant of the monolithic grandeur of its façade, like a rich old aunt tucked out of view. It had a number of flowering vines and other greenery creeping up its walls in patterns of invasion, giving it that sprawling, colonized look which constitutes rusticity: an air of monitored decomposition, as if the house were being held on the brink of an elegant faint before it sank into the garden's arms. At the very centre of the back wall was a glass appendage, like a prosthetic ear, in the shape of a beehive; a conservatory, I soon realized, within which I could discern a muffled profusion of fronds.

The garden which surrounded this fragrant heap consisted mostly of a large expanse of lawn, although to one side I could see the municipal architecture of the swimming pool, its undisturbed, unnatural blue lying flat on the grass like a fallen piece of sky. The lawn itself curiously sported a pattern of stripes – a piece of horticultural frivolity, I guessed, related to the cutting of hedges into the shapes of chickens or dogs – which rolled out towards us in a fan from the distant point of the conservatory. At the far end of the lawn was an arrangement of tables and chairs, upon one of which I could just make out the familiar form of Pamela. On another of the chairs sat a woman I did not recognize. From that distance the scene appeared very small, and the oppressive heat gave it an atmosphere of calcification which reminded me of the little plaster figurines which had populated my doll's house when I was a child. It was odd and not entirely pleasant to remember this object, having not thought about it for years. The feeling that one's own memories have become unfamiliar can give rise to the suspicion that one's identity is malfunctioning and inefficient, like a badly run office. I had a sudden picture of pink plaster hams, and tiny plates to which coloured food was glued. Mr Madden appeared from the side of the house, as elliptical as a butler. Roy trotted heavily behind him. He was carrying a tray and when he reached the table he bent stiffly with it from the waist, distributing glasses which winked in the sunlight.

'Look who's here,' said Martin from below. I was surprised to hear his voice, for although I had been pushing him along all of this time, I had grown so used to the action that the wheelchair, and to some degree Martin's presence, seemed to have become a part of my own physical remit.

'Who?' I said, my voice lower than his, for we were now within fifty yards or so of the group.

'My fucking sister,' Martin volubly replied. 'Come to see her mummy. Can't keep her away.'

'Does she live far?' I enquired, toiling up a slight rise in the lawn.

'Just a stone's throw,' said Martin in a fluting voice. 'She wanted to stay near her *mummy*. I had hoped Dewek would take her away to Papua New Guinea so that they'd both be eaten by savages. Or at least as far as Tonbridge.'

'Who's Derek?'

'Dewek,' amended Martin. 'Dewek is Caroline's damp face flannel of a husband.'

'There's no need to be unkind,' I said.

'What do you know, anyway?' said Martin, drumming his hands abstractedly on the arms of his chair. 'Stel-la.'

Pamela had caught us in her sights and raised her hand in a salute of acknowledgement, using the other hand to shield her eyes, as if we were travellers sighted across a lonely reach of desert.

'Hi-i!' she called from afar, stretching the word in her customary fashion, her face split by a smile.

'Hi!' I called back.

Pamela was wearing a pea-green bikini and a pair of gold sandals. Around her neck glittered a thick gold chain, like a rope. The effect, as she sat glass in hand, was odd, as if she were at a party but had forgetfully come out in her underwear. The other woman – Martin's sister, as I now knew, although she did not resemble him at all – was wearing a dress patterned with vivid tropical flowers. She was fairly plump, not in the dense, landscaped fashion of Mrs Barker, but rather as if she had been filled too full and had spilled over. She had straight fair hair cut in a kind of thatch above her forehead, the colour, if nothing else about her appearance, favouring Pamela. She watched our approach closely through dark glasses, like a secret agent. Even from a distance I took a more or less instant dislike to her. There was something despotic about her solid, suspicious face and bulk. I was beset by an image of her in army uniform, setting about some cringing cadet with a truncheon.

'How did you get on?' said Pamela, as we drew up to the table. The skin about her eyes looked very wrinkled in the sun, and her pupils glinted like tiny jewels kept in a crumpled handkerchief.

'Fine,' I said.

'Mar-Mar?' Pamela leaned forward slightly and concentrated her gaze on Martin. She was not, I decided, speaking in some alien dialect, but rather was deploying, or even inventing, a nickname. I was irritated by her concern, implying as it did a certain untrustworthiness or even outright menace on my part. 'How about you?'

'I'm *fine*,' said Martin crossly, screwing up his face at her. He looked unwell in the strong light, his face as bleached and savage as a piece of rock.

'Hello, Martin,' said Caroline deliberately. Her voice startled me, for despite her looming presence her inertia had caused me to forget her, as one could forget a large mountain. 'How are you? I'm fine, how are you, Caroline? Oh, fine, thank you, kind of you to ask.'

This surprising monologue was rapidly and sarcastically delivered, and rather knocked the stuffing out of any politeness which might have been on the agenda. All eyes turned to Caroline, who remained enigmatic and brutish behind her sunglasses.

'Say hello to your sister, you scoundrel,' said Pamela.

'Hello, sister,' said Martin.

'I'm Caroline,' said Caroline, evidently to me. She precipitated herself forward in her chair and extended her arm. The movement was unexpected, and the unpredictable shifting of her mass caused me instinctively to draw back, as if from the path of a landslide or falling boulder.

'Stella. Nice to meet you,' I added gamely, shaking her hand.

'What will you have to drink, Stella? Martin?' said Pamela. 'We thought we'd have lunch out here, as it's so glorious. If you've had enough of the sun just shout and Piers will put up the umbrella.'

Nobody said anything, and Pamela looked about with the bright, nervous movements of a bird.

'I'll have whatever you're having,' I said awkwardly, indicating their glasses. It sounded rather demanding, as if I were placing an order with a waitress.

'Right!' said Pamela. 'I'll go and rustle up Piers and see what's happening with lunch. You lot just sit here and enjoy the sun.'

She stood up abruptly, as if she were upset, while the rest of us remained guiltily seated. I was surprised by the sight of Pamela's body in her swimming costume. Her skin was brown and shrunken, like dried meat, and running up the pot of her belly was a seam of raised flesh, like a geographical feature on a relief map.

'Do you want a hand, Mummy?' said Caroline.

Martin made a strange noise beside me. When I looked at him, he was mouthing Caroline's offer with an idiotic look on his face, his lips flapping like wings.

'No, no, I don't think so,' said Pamela wearily. She hesitated for a moment, hand to her forehead, as if contemplating a landscape of strictures and duties by which she suddenly realized herself to be surrounded. Eventually she turned and trod lightly off, the soles of her sandals slapping against her feet.

The three of us were set adrift in uncertain silence. Pamela, the focus of our attention, being gone, it was required of us to re-form in a new constellation, and as it soon became evident that neither Martin nor I was equipped to set this orbit in motion, Caroline gathered herself up in her chair and took charge.

'Mummy tells me you're from London,' she said, to me.

'That's right,' I replied. I could see that I was to be interrogated, and felt that no more was required of me at this stage than to give clear and correct answers.

'And you worked as a secretary, is that right?'

'Yes.'

'At a law firm.'

'Yes.'

I should add that while these enquiries were being made,

Caroline was indulging in a shameless inspection of my physical appearance, running the beam of her gaze up and down my body like a minesweeper. Despite keeping my own counsel in so far as I possibly could, I sensed that a deeper, unauthorized method of extraction was at work which I was powerless to prevent. Her appraisal was as penetrating and objective as an X-ray; and yet I felt that I was being sized up as a threat, although to what precisely I could not gather.

'That sounds very respectable. Why did you leave? Did you feel there was no future for you at the firm?'

I deduced from the insinuating, indeed the downright challenging, nature of this question that I was being tested for the weakness of my character, and understood that this was the point at which I must establish my boundary; that if I did not, Caroline would invade and conquer, certain of victory.

'On the contrary.' Caroline's sunglasses were beginning to unnerve me. They appeared to give her an advantage, shielding her from my remarks while at the same time preventing me from monitoring their effect. 'The certainty of my future there was the very thing which enabled me to reject it. I dislike having too clear a view of what lies ahead. It lacks,' I finished rather triumphantly, 'adventure.'

Caroline seemed surprised and, for the moment at least, repelled by my reply. She retracted her interest as an animal would a probing tentacle and appeared to be reconsidering the situation. Martin gave a snort of laughter.

'If adventure is what you want,' she said presently, head held high, 'then you must find things very quiet here. In fact, it is usually for its lack of adventure that people come to the country. We don't really go in for that sort of thing here.'

'Oh, I've had more than my fair share of excitement,' I said. Keeping my eyes fixed on Caroline's sunglasses was proving to be quite a strain. I was beginning to feel very uncomfortable from sitting so still in the heat, and longed to get up from my chair and move around. 'By adventure I mean the unknown, really. I wanted to see a different side of life.'

Caroline snorted, evidently a family trait.

'I'd hardly call Buckley a different side of life. Or Martin, for that matter.'

'Thanks,' said Martin.

'You make it sound so dull here, and yet I find it interesting.' The sun was getting at the side of my neck, and I was forced to unlock my gaze from Caroline's and shift around in my chair. 'I've only been here a day or two, but I feel that I've already learned a lot.'

'Such as?'

Mercifully, at this point I heard the warning rattle of a tray behind me, and turned to see Mr Madden bearing down on us.

'Hello!' he said, looking from Martin to me and back again with stunned cheerfulness. 'How did you two get on?'

'Oh, fine!' I said; a trifle too warmly, perhaps. The sight of Mr Madden, after the tension of my exchange with Caroline, had aroused in me a bounteous, doglike affection for him. 'Martin showed me around. The rose garden is wonderful.'

'Good, good!' said Mr Madden vaguely. He seemed lost in thought for a moment or two. 'Fresh air will have done you the world of good, old chap. Get some colour in your cheeks.'

'I'm amazed you got him out of his room,' chimed Caroline unexpectedly. Her next comment was addressed more generally to the group. 'Mummy says it's an absolute pit in there. It took Mrs Barker the whole morning to set it straight. It's a bit selfish of you, Martin, wasting Mrs Barker's time when there's so much else to do. Why you can't tidy up after yourself I don't know. Mummy's been at it all morning and she's absolutely exhausted.'

It is difficult to convey the speed at which all of this was pronounced. Caroline's diction was high-pitched and rapid, and when she delivered it her mouth moved extraordinarily quickly, as if she were gobbling food. The effect was not very attractive – we were all, I felt, watching it with equal fascination – for her lips were thin and downturned above the piston of her chin, whose motion was so automatic that it seemed possible that it would never stop. I was anticipating, half-gleefully, a vituperative response from Martin, and was surprised to see that he seemed to have fallen asleep in his chair.

'Don't be too hard on him, Caro,' said Mr Madden, laden tray still in hand. 'It's difficult for us chaps to remember to tidy up. We've got other things on our minds, fighting wars and running things and suchlike, what?'

I laughed enthusiastically at this, and was mortified to hear my laughter make its solo flight across the table.

'It just seems unfair on Mummy,' said Caroline sullenly. 'She's got so much to do already, and only Mrs Barker to help her.'

I immediately regretted my rhapsodies about the rose garden, which in retrospect gave substance to the accusation that I was no help at all.

'You're giving me a headache,' said Martin plaintively, opening one eye in a squint.

'Take an aspirin, then,' retorted Caroline.

'Take one yourself,' muttered Martin, sinking his chin into his small, puffy chest. 'Not that it would make you less of a pain.'

'Oh, I'm dying!' said Caroline, melodramatically clutching at her heart with her two plump hands.

'Right!' blustered Mr Madden, intervening with his tray and dealing the drinks one by one. 'That's enough, you two. Lunch'll be ready any minute, so let's clear some space here, shall we, and I'll give Mummy a hand bringing it out.'

I jumped to my feet as if at a starter's pistol and began collecting the empty glasses strewn about the table. I could feel Caroline's eyes on me again behind her sunglasses; or rather, on my body, measuring it as exactly as if she were fitting me for a garment. After a while she folded her arms and looked away across the garden, her lips as pursed as if there were a drawstring threaded through them.

'Shall I take them inside?' I said to Mr Madden.

'No, no,' he replied. 'Just sit down, why don't you?'

I sensed the mildest irritation in his reply, and had an indistinct memory of annoying him before with a similar display of keenness. Searching for this incident, the recollection of Pamela's unfortunate remarks concerning my feelings for Mr Madden – overheard from the cottage garden – returned forcefully to me instead. I snatched my hands away from the table and held them trembling behind my back. I felt myself dangerously capable of directing some obscenity, or even a punch or kick, at Mr Madden, merely to prove my lack of fondness for him. I sat down again; and when I saw the look of affront on Caroline's face felt my situation to be rather miserable. Caroline evidently thought it inappropriate that I, a paid domestic, should sit with her, the daughter of the house, while its owners were scurrying about in the effort to serve us. Mr Madden had, however, spoken; and with the question of my fancy already so publicized, I was not about to confirm it in full view of witnesses by pestering him further.

'What do you do, Caroline?' I sociably enquired instead. My comment had been automatic, an embarrassed reflex, and I was rewarded for my heedlessness by a glacial stare.

'What *do* you mean?' Caroline eventually replied.

'I was asking whether you worked,' I hastily amended. This sounded in some way rude. 'Or whether . . .' For some reason I could think of no alternative, and was compelled to trail off.

'I am a housewife.'

My lips formed the reply 'Oh', but my voice failed to follow it through, leaving us in silence.

'You disapprove of that, do you?' said Caroline. 'Are you one of these feminists?'

'Well,' I began. My skin was now in torment, and I wished

that I had been in a position to ask Mr Madden to hoist the umbrella.

'I personally don't feel the slightest need to compete with my husband,' continued Caroline. 'I am not insecure. Were we desperately short of money, then that would perhaps be different. Of course I would do everything I could, but I would regard it as a misfortune. It would be embarrassing for my friends, and above all for Derek. As it is we are very comfortable.'

'Good,' I said, placing one hand surreptitiously upon my cheek.

'There is a woman, for example, in our village,' said Caroline, entrenching herself deeper in her chair, 'who has been driven by necessity to take a job in some kind of shop, ladies' fashions I believe, in Tonbridge. She used to live in the Rectory with her husband, but then he walked out on her, ran off with his secretary or somesuch, and she had to go it alone. Sold the house, put the children in the local school.'

'That's awful,' I said, sympathetically.

'We've all tried our best to support her, but it is difficult. At one point, Derek and I thought we might buy the Rectory from her to sort of help her out, but she had it on at such a ridiculous price and wouldn't *consider* selling it for less, even to friends. Personally, I think she should have moved right away from the village. We all used to knock about together, you see, but it's harder to invite a single woman to things, and she obviously isn't entertaining any more. I mean that in both senses of the word.' She smiled, surprised at her own unintended cleverness. 'She's so down these days that one ends up just having her to supper in the kitchen, lest she bursts into tears or something. Some of the wives say they won't even have her in the house any more because she gets very aggressive with the men after she's had a drink or two. And of course the children have turned into savages at that dreadful school. The others don't want to play with them.'

'Poor woman!' I cried, my own problems for the time being forgotten.

'I suppose so,' said Caroline after a pause. 'But you shouldn't feel too sorry for her. Things could have gone very differently if she had acted with a little grace. I'm afraid to say that she has behaved – inappropriately. Working in a shop!' She shook her head. 'One or two of the wives went in, not realizing, of course, and said it was quite dreadful when she came from behind the counter. Doing the hard sell, you know.'

'Surely it's not her fault if her husband left her?' I objected. 'What else could she have done?'

'Well, whose fault could it be?' said Caroline, amazed. 'She can't have been doing her duty to him.'

'What do you mean?'

'There are certain things,' said she mysteriously, 'that a woman is expected to do for her husband. You might not always feel like it. But you do it. I don't think Miriam quite saw it like that. She used to say as much. It's no wonder, really, that he went elsewhere in the end.'

I was quite shocked by Caroline's remarks, and by the assurance with which she made them. The fact that her sympathies lay so far from my own was perhaps to be expected, given the evident differences between us; but it was the confidence of her views rather than their substance which disturbed me. It surprised me to feel a strong and in some way reciprocal identification with Miriam, as if we were two lighthouses telegraphing flashes of sympathy to one another across a dark and treacherous sea. This identification did not please me. It suggested that Miriam and I belonged to some form of minority, with its attendant dangers of exclusion and victimization.

'Martin!' called Caroline suddenly. 'Don't just *go off*! We're about to have lunch.'

During our conversation, Martin had been edging his wheelchair further and further away from the table. So subtly had he moved that I had not really been aware of it; but when I looked round, I saw that he had materialized beside a far-off flower bed. He was throwing a stick for Roy, who jogged slowly off to retrieve it, his black belly heaving. He did not return smartly to the table on Caroline's orders, but rather affected not to have heard her, and once Roy had been dispatched seemed engrossed by his inspection of a small bush. To my dismay, all at once Caroline dislodged herself violently from her seat and rose in such precipitate anger that the entire doll's arrangement of table and chairs lurched as she thrashed among them, seeking an exit. She displaced an obstructing chair with one powerful hand, and stormed across the grass towards the inadvertent Martin, whose neck seemed visibly to bristle at her approach behind him. With alarming speed she reached him and, disengaging the brake with her foot, whirled him around so that his hair positively flew and began to propel him back towards the table. I could see her mouth moving, although I could not hear what she was saying.

'Now just stay here!' she panted, bringing him to an abrupt halt at the table and slamming down the brake with her foot. Martin looked so fragile beside her, and so crumpled by his brutal journey, that I genuinely feared for his health; but it was not a good time to be making solicitous enquiries, which would undoubtedly be taken as a form of insurrection by our general. 'You've got all of us running around after you in this heat!' she exclaimed, suitably glistening and red-faced. 'You can't bear not to have all the attention, can you? You can't bear the fact that other people can sit and have a perfectly nice conversation without your help.' I was flattered, but not reassured, by this. 'No, you've got to make everyone stop what they're doing and give all their attention to you. You can't bear it if—'

'Shut up!' said Martin, putting his large hands over his ears.

'No I won't shut up!' shrilled Caroline. 'How dare you speak to me like that? I'll tell Mummy—'

'Just shut up!' shrieked Martin, his small body puffing like a pair of bellows. 'You stupid fat cow! Do you have any idea how your fat voice sounds, nya, nya, nya' – he worked his chin in an admirable imitation – 'Mummy this, Mummy that, it's no wonder Dewek's such a zombie, it must be like living with a *fucking pneumatic drill*!'

'MUMMY!' hollered Caroline in panic, her mouth opened so wide that I could see her pink and trilling tonsils. 'MUMMY!'

'Da-da-da-da,' said Martin, apparently drilling, but in fact sounding, more menacingly, like a machine-gun. 'Da-da-da-da.'

'JUST STOP IT!' she roared, her body writhing.

'What on *earth* is going on out here?' said Pamela, arriving at the scene with the accuracy and effect of a missile, bringing a sudden and deathly silence. 'What can you possibly be thinking of, making all this noise?'

She pushed her way through to the table and stood, to my dismay, glowering at me, hands on her hips. I shrugged and looked at Caroline.

'He's doing it again!' moaned Caroline. Her face was a wreck of emotion, awash with tears. I felt rather sorry for her. 'He's said the most awful things!'

'Oh, for God's sake, Martin.' Pamela put her hand to her forehead. Caroline cried out again in fresh agony. 'Get a grip on yourself, Caroline, for Heaven's sake. What must Stella think?'

All eyes turned to me. At that moment, there was a jostling around my legs beneath the table, and something wet and viscous impressed itself on my knee. I gave a yelp of horror and looked down to see Roy's dripping muzzle nosing between my thighs.

'If you two can't get on, then we shall just have to stop doing things as a family. Do you hear? I won't have it! I won't!'

I forced my thighs together so powerfully that Roy's head jerked back and impacted with a thud on the underside of the table. I wiped the damp flesh of my leg surreptitiously with my hand.

'Sorry,' mumbled Martin, magnanimously.

'Caroline?'

'Well, I really don't see why I should apologize, when—'

'Oh, for fuck's sake,' said Martin.

'Martin! I'm bloody well warning you! *One more word!* Caroline, get on and apologize.'

'*Mummy.*'

'Do it, or you're going home.'

'You'll be sorry for this,' said Caroline, apparently to all of us. Martyred tears streamed down her cheeks. 'Just you wait. You've spoilt everything. This was supposed to be a wonderful day, and now it's all been spoilt.'

'Nonsense,' said Pamela briskly.

'It's not nonsense!' wailed Caroline, stamping her foot upon the grass. 'Oh, you're all so awful, I don't see why I should tell you anyway! I'm just going to go home!'

'Tell us what, darling?' said Pamela, in a more conciliatory tone.

Now that she had recouped some sympathy, Caroline struck an attitude at once sullen and composed, her head hung low.

'I just wanted to tell you all,' she said, generously including me, 'that Derek and I are going to have a baby.'

Pamela shrieked so loudly that I started from my chair, thinking her to be in pain.

'My darling girl!' she cried, flinging her arms around Caroline. Even in that moment of high emotion, I could not help noticing how slim, eager Pamela looked more like Caroline's daughter than her mother. 'Oh, *well done you*! Oh, how absolutely wonderful!'

Thus deluged by appreciation, but still not wanting her injury to be forgotten, Caroline was faced by the difficult task of appearing pleased and hurt at the same time: she achieved this with an attitude of weary vindication, like a plaintiff emerging from a courtroom to a cheering crowd after a long but successful fight against injustice.

'Oh, where's Daddy? Piers! Piers! Come out here!' called Pamela. 'I'm *delighted*, darling! Oh look, *I'm* crying now.' Pamela swiped at one or two crystal beads about her eyes. 'What marvellous news.'

You may think me horribly small-minded, but the fact that Caroline had avoided – albeit in style – making her apology to Martin preyed upon my mind. I found myself watching her, in much the same way as she had observed me earlier, and was rather gratified to see her grow self-conscious beneath my gaze. She turned her head this way and that, and once even placed her hands across her belly and made rubbing motions, as one would rub a lamp to conjure a genie.

'Martin?' she said finally. 'Haven't you got anything to say?'

I was most interested by this development, it being evident to me that Caroline had vowed, as far as she was able, to resist giving any further attention to Martin by eliciting his response to her news. A confrontation would undoubtedly ensue, and Caroline, I saw, had wanted to capitalize on her current sainthood by being seen not to provoke one. She had, however, failed in this resolution, thus proving, to my mind, both that her feelings for Martin were deep and complex, and, perhaps consequently, that she cared more for his opinion than for that of anyone else.

'I'm very pleased for you both,' said Martin, quite the gentleman.

'You don't sound it,' snapped Caroline; giving me, at least, the satisfaction of believing that my diagnosis had been correct.

'It's great news,' said I, heroically. 'I'm sure you'll make an excellent mother.'

'Thank you, Stella,' Caroline replied, nonetheless making it disdainfully clear that her ability at motherhood had never been in doubt.

'Golly!' said Piers, whom Pamela had by now retrieved from

the house. He kissed Caroline on the cheek, smiling so hard that the rest of his features retired in defeat. 'Well done, Caro!'

'Isn't it great?' beamed Pamela. 'Goodness, we haven't even asked you when it's due to land!'

'February,' blushed Caroline.

'Ah!' cried Pamela and Piers, in unison.

'I was born in February,' said I. I had not really considered what I hoped to gain by this announcement, but the fact that I knew Caroline so little made any other kind of contribution difficult. As a coincidence it was not, admittedly, much; and it struck me that by promulgating myself as an advertisement for a February birth, I could be seen to be issuing a threat rather than a consolation. 'It's a good month,' I continued, as the others seemed rather nonplussed. 'You don't get depressed after Christmas because you know there are more presents on the way.'

'True, true,' mused Mr Madden.

'Right!' said Pamela. 'Shall we all drink to Caroline's baby? Has everybody got a glass?'

'And Derek's,' pouted Caroline. 'It's his baby just as much as it is mine.'

'Sorry, darling. Caroline and Derek's baby. Everyone got something to drink? Caroline?'

'I'm not drinking,' said Caroline bashfully, her hand on her stomach again.

We raised our glasses, which had become warm in the sun. Afterwards, nobody seemed to have very much to say. The congratulations having been exhausted, still it seemed rude to change the subject.

'I think I'll bring out the lunch,' said Mr Madden finally.

'Oh, would you?' said Pamela. 'You are a dear. Have you thought of any names, darling? I might be able to suggest one or two if you're stuck.'

'We thought we'd call it Hugh if it was a boy,' said Caroline. I was perplexed, thinking her to have said 'you'. It seemed to me a confusingly renegade feminist stand, considering Caroline's earlier remarks. 'If it's a girl we'll probably call her after Derek's mother. Margaret.'

'That's rather an elderly name for a little girl, isn't it?' said Pamela, after a pause. 'Don't you think?' she coaxed, when Caroline did not answer.

'Obviously we don't,' Caroline coolly replied, 'otherwise we wouldn't have chosen it.'

Tension had entered the scene stealthily and without warning. I wondered if Pamela was offended that the baby was not going to be named for her, and then thought that perhaps Derek's mother had died.

'Well, Maggie will be delighted, anyway,' said Pamela grimly. Derek's mother was evidently still with us. 'Have you told her? About the baby, I mean?'

Caroline hesitated, which of course made what she said next sound like a lie, although whether this was deliberate or not I could not tell.

'No,' she said finally. 'We thought we'd pop down to Hastings this evening.'

'Ah,' said Pamela, nodding energetically. 'Piers!' she called to Mr Madden, who was by now making his laboured progress back across the lawn towards us. 'You couldn't be a darling and put up the umbrella, could you? It's utterly scorching out here.'

Mr Madden nodded heavily and, depositing the tray upon the grass, turned obediently on his heel. I was pleased by this news, for I had been driven by now to place a hand over either cheek, which I was concerned was giving an impression of theatrical dismay. Martin had been so quiet that I had assumed him to be asleep, but when I glanced at him I saw that his eyes were wide open. I had the feeling that he had been staring at me.

'Are you all right?' I said, all at once remembering my role in this family drama. 'Do you want a hat or something?'

Martin shook his head.

'Are you overheating, darling?' intervened Pamela. 'Daddy will have the umbrella up in a minute.'

'I'm *fine*,' said Martin impatiently. A look of resentment was fired off at me. I gathered that Martin, contrary to Caroline's theories, disliked having attention directed towards him.

'Goodness,' said Pamela, looking at her watch. 'You're due at the centre any minute. We'd better get on with lunch.'

The mention of the centre naturally brought the driving issue once more to the foreground, and I wondered if, with the element of change Caroline's announcement had introduced, Pamela's offer to drive Martin herself would still stand. I had a discomfiting sense of having let go of the situation somewhat. I could not remember any of my plans for negotiating the difficulty, and indeed felt that it had regained all of its former complexity and more. Like a child trying to recall how to tie its shoelaces, I found it hard to believe that I had ever mastered the method of this particular deception, having now forgotten so completely how to do so. Were Pamela to ask me now to drive, I would, I knew, undo myself utterly.

'Stella, are you ready to shoot off with him as soon as lunch is over?' said Pamela.

The lawn and sky went briefly out of focus in the ensuing silence.

'Yes,' I said, nodding my head with confidence.

'Actually, I could drop him off on my way home,' said Caroline, whom I thought I would never learn to love. 'I go right through Buckley.'

'He'll need to go straight off,' said Pamela doubtfully. I was tempted to reach across the table and bludgeon her over the head with my heavy crystal glass. 'Don't you want to stay and have a swim?'

'No,' said Caroline, rising ever higher in my estimation. 'No, I've got to get back. I've got such a lot to do. And Martin and I can have a nice chat on the way.'

My betrayal of Martin was regrettable, I can admit; but my

instincts of self-preservation were in this instance too forceful. I risked a glance at the condemned and was met by narrowed eyes. He mouthed something which I could not decipher but which I took to be an explicit promise of revenge. Much as I longed to offer him some apology, under the present circumstances it was impossible. Now committed to a selfish course, I wondered instead whether Pamela would offer me a swim during the afternoon; and if not, how I could tempt such an offer from her.

'Dig in, everybody!' cried Pamela, as Piers discharged his freight of laden bowls and platters upon the table. He produced a large parasol and began to wrestle with it. 'Come on, Stella, don't be shy.' She looked around at us all. 'Oh, what a happy day!'

Chapter Eleven

Some time later, I stood alone in the empty kitchen of the big house. Through the window I could see the deserted scene of our lunch on the lawn, the chairs still pushed back as if in horror or anger from the table where everybody had stood up. Caroline was now safely dispatched, and with her both Martin and the threat of driving duty, my evasion of which was a matter of great but temporary good fortune.

Seeing an opportunity to entrench myself in the family affections, I had undertaken to clear up lunch. My offer had been roundly accepted and the company speedily dispersed in its wake, as if I might be liable to retract it. Pamela was now 'resting' upstairs, and Piers had returned to his indeterminate work on the farm. I had watched him go through the window, his solitary progress – as aimless and slouching as a boy's, discreetly whistling as he ambled off – bespeaking a discomfort with family groupings, from which he was evidently rather glad to get away.

I put the first consignment of dishes in the sink, aware that my solitude in the Maddens' house – a somewhat improper condition, given the fragility of our acquaintance – was beckoning me towards an unwelcome analysis of my situation. I sensed that a clear picture of my predicament lay veiled nearby, like an exam result in an envelope, or a pair of policemen sitting in the next-door room, awaiting my arrival. Although I had already performed several smaller assessments, clods of percipience thrown up by the churning wheels of every passing hour, of how my life in the country appeared to be going, a grander survey required a journey back to all the chaos which had preceded it; and from there, perhaps even an expedition to the permafrost of human unhappiness which lay beyond. Having so recently emigrated from my past, I was not ready to revisit it; yet I felt a swollen, tremulous sorrow, as fragile as a bubble, floating so close in the air around me that it seemed inevitable that at any moment it would touch me and burst, whether I liked it or not. I whistled cheerfully as I ran the gushing taps; and was about to turn them off again and sob uncontrollably at the kitchen table, when I heard the far-off ringing of the telephone.

Telephones, like children, cry out to their owners, and so it was some time before I responded to this shrill summons. Eventually, however, I remembered that Pamela was asleep upstairs, and with a jolt of dismay had an image of her being roused, bad-tempered, from her bed, furious that I had permitted her to be disturbed. This was, of course, an overreaction on my part; but it is the hegemony of an irrational or unpredictable character such as Pamela's that it makes even the most innocent incidents pregnant with the possibility of accusation and blame. I rushed from the sink and through the kitchen door, pausing in the ante-room to locate the sound. For a moment I thought that it had stopped; but then it came again, from the direction of the hall. I flew through the swinging door and ran across the flagstones, my ears filled with the alarm of rings, to where the telephone lay stubbornly plinthed on a small table. The minute I picked it up, however, I felt strongly that I had made a mistake. I saw again, quite clearly, Pamela's anger; but this time it was my presumption rather than my neglect which provoked it. I really had no idea of the correct thing to do. My parents had never relayed guidelines on such matters to me, and I was hard-pressed to see how else I was meant to have studied them.

'Hello?' I said, anxious now that I was incensing the caller, in addition to my unpopularity elsewhere.

'Who's that?' demanded a male voice.

'Stella,' I replied; and was about to give a fuller account of myself when the man interrupted me.

'What are you?' he said.

I was, naturally, taken aback by this question, having never been asked it before. It was difficult to know what sort of information the man required.

'I am a servant,' I said, guessing that he merely wished to know my status in the house – intruder, friend, etc.

'A *servant*?' said he. He sounded younger than I had at first thought. 'What sort of servant? We don't *have* servants!'

'Perhaps servant was the wrong word,' I conceded. I remembered a word Pamela had used, when I had overheard her in the cottage garden. 'I suppose I am a sort of au pair.'

'Oh, you're *Martin's* girl,' said the man. 'You must be new. What happened to Colette?'

'I have no idea,' I said.

'Mummy must have sacked her.' He chuckled to himself. 'Should have seen that coming. Oh well. Listen—' he addressed me again loudly, 'listen, Stella, I'm coming down, all right?' I sensed that he was not asking for my permission, but rather was forcing the message through the undergrowth of my putative stupidity in the hope that it would reach his mother; for I had by now deduced that I was speaking to another of Pamela's brood. 'Later today or tomorrow. Have you got that?'

'Yes.' I heard a telephone burr in the background, and the muffled sound of voices.

'It's a bloody oven. I'm going potty here. Dying for a swim. Tell her that.'

'All right.'

'So I'll see you later, Stella.'

'Yes.'

He rang off without saying goodbye. I put down the telephone and moved back across the hall, assuming an air of puzzlement which felt oddly self-conscious, as if someone were watching me. As I pushed the swinging door I fell still deeper into this distracted performance and by the time I reached the kitchen was moving so slowly that the sight of the gushing taps sending cascades of water over the edge of the sink to form a pool on the kitchen floor did not strike me as a disaster for several seconds. I shrieked aloud and ran to the sink, my feet skidding and my face spattered with foamy spray. Like a wild animal the accident beat off my attempts to control it, but finally I succeeded in turning off the taps.

The silence which followed was terrible, a sepulchral calm punctuated by the cavernous sound of drips. Paralysed by my own ill fortune, I stood for some time while the miniature lake lapped at my feet. Presently I heard the menacing creak of a floorboard above my head. The sound informed me that Pamela must be rising from her bed; and all was now a panicked blur of action as I raced to erase the evidence of my crime.

Grabbing anything I could find which looked capable of absorbing fluid – and scooping up great dripping handfuls of the water and returning them ineffectually to the sink – I laboured to reduce the gleaming reservoir now creeping across the tiled floor. Using tea towels, sponges, even a few chunks of bread left over from lunch, I fought to contain the capricious mass, which dodged and slid away from my every effort to capture it. I succeeded at least in spreading the spillage somewhat, so that although it covered a greater area its level was diminished; and had just gathered up the sodden cloths and screwed them into a ball when the kitchen door opened and Pamela stood before me. She had changed out of her bikini into a pair of jeans and a vest. Her face was still half-closed with sleep, and the cloud of her hair sat unusually high, as if it had attempted to escape her head while she lay unconscious and had been embarrassingly apprehended halfway through.

'Goodness me!' she said huskily, surveying the wreckage. I held the damp clump of towels behind my back and caught my breath. 'You've washed the floor! You *are* kind.'

'I haven't quite finished in here,' I declared in a high-pitched voice. 'I was just about to wash up.'

'Ah!' said Pamela, teetering at the doorway; evidently with the intention of not spoiling my clean floor. 'If you were going to do that, it might have been an idea to wash up first. You've rather hemmed yourself in, haven't you?'

'I suppose I have,' I shrilled. 'But by the time I've finished, it'll be dry.'

'Hmm.' Pamela's face wore a look of puzzlement. 'Oh well, I'll leave you to it.'

I saw that she had been about to discover me, but perhaps because she was not yet alert had wandered past the matter. Unfortunately, at the very moment when it seemed I was to get rid of her, I remembered the telephone message. I wrestled, torn between self-preservation and responsibility.

'Your son rang,' I called out to her retreating back.

'Toby?' Pamela turned around. 'What did he want?'

'He says he's coming down,' I replied. I had spotted a large and incriminating lump of wet bread lying by my foot, and was desperate not to detain her. 'Either tonight or tomorrow morning.'

'Oh, God,' said Pamela. She paused, thinking. 'I wonder what he wants.'

'He said it was like an oven. He wanted a swim.'

'I see. What's that?'

'What?' I innocently replied.

'By your foot.'

'Oh, it's just some – I was about to—'

'I'd better give him a ring. Find out what he's up to. God, I really could have done without Toby this week.'

Miraculously, she went away. I leaned in a sort of swoon against the sink, and felt the warm, filthy water lap against my shirt. An irresistible lethargy had suddenly come over me. I felt as if I could lie down where I stood on the wet floor and fall instantly asleep. The urgency of my half-concealed disaster grew remote and indistinct, and my eyelids were drooping shut when I heard Pamela's voice.

'No I jolly well don't!' she cried. The sound was faint, but I could make out her words clearly enough. 'I've got enough on my plate as it is.'

I moved away from the sink and in the direction of the communicating wall, from beyond which the noise was coming. My back felt chilly and damp where the warm caress of the dishwater had been.

'It isn't that,' said Pamela, after a pause. 'I just feel like it's another thing.'

I was pressed up against the kitchen counters by this time, my ear at the wall. There was quite a long silence now, during which I hazarded that Toby – for it was to him that I guessed Pamela was speaking – was making his case for 'coming down'. My experience in the cottage garden had given me a certain skill at eavesdropping.

'Look, we've got a new girl here, and everything's in utter chaos . . . Stella, that's right . . . Do you mean from your point of view or ours? . . . No, I'm *not* bloody well being oversensitive. You're an absolute menace . . . No I don't trust you, not one bit.'

At this point Pamela broke into a long and complicit laugh.

'You don't waste time, do you?' she chuckled. 'As it happens you're absolutely right. Not your type at all. Oh, damn and blast you, you old charmer, I'm longing for you to come now, God help me. What time shall we expect you?'

Sensing that the conversation was winding down, I began to move stealthily back towards the sink, picking up the sodden piece of bread and depositing it in the rubbish bin as I did so.

'I've got to know because of dinner,' said Pamela plaintively. 'All right. All right. OK. Bye.'

Triggered into action, I began rinsing plates and lining them up in an orderly row on the draining board. Once or twice I slotted one into position so violently that I feared I had chipped the delicate china and was forced to retrieve and inspect it. Returned to a state of emergency, I had no time to meditate on the cause of my fury, which was injured vanity; the price, I had come to realize, of whatever illicit and solitary pleasure I gained from the practice of overhearing conversations not intended for my ears.

'How are you getting on?'

Being accustomed now to my passive role in discussion, it took me a moment to realize that Pamela was in the kitchen and was addressing me directly.

'I'm fine,' I said, nonchalantly. I drew a plate dripping from the water, and placed it gently on the draining board. My stomach was taut with expectation; for in that moment I had devised a way to injure Pamela, and to do so without inviting recrimination. My revenge, however, depended on Pamela entering into some form of exchange with me, and the difficulty lay in trying to initiate a conversation founded on what I had overheard without betraying that I had done so.

'Ahhh,' Pamela sighed, with vexation. I felt her linger behind me and waited to see if she would offer anything further. I heard the scrape of a chair and peered surreptitiously over my shoulder. She was sitting at the table with her head in her hands. 'This was all I needed,' she said.

I took this as a direct cue for manifestations of concern on my part.

'Is he coming down?' I said. The intimacy sounded awkward.

'What?' Pamela lifted her head, confused. 'Oh, yes. Tonight.

I'd better go and make sure that Mrs Barker's changed the sheets on his bed. Piers will have to move his things.' She made this last observation as if to herself. I wondered why Piers should have left a trail in Toby's room, and was so dumbfounded by what this immediately implied that I was almost derailed from my plan. 'God, I'm *exhausted*,' she groaned.

The chair scraped again, signalling that Pamela had stood up and was about to leave. The moment was far from ideal; but I had no choice.

'Was he pleased about Caroline?' I lightly enquired.

There was a profound and menacing silence from behind me. I busied myself nervously at the sink.

'Caroline!' uttered Pamela, in an awed whisper. 'I completely forgot. Oh, God, how *awful* of me!'

My heart gave a little pirouette of glee. So pleased was I, in fact, with my own ingenuity that I had difficulty in restraining myself from rushing from the sink and engaging Pamela in a congratulatory embrace.

'Selfish, selfish cow,' whispered Pamela; not to me, I realized. 'Oh, Stella, how could I have forgotten?'

'You've got a lot on your mind,' I consoled her. 'It's not surprising.'

'I know, I know,' she wailed. 'I've just *got* to get myself sorted out! Oh God, I'd better go and phone him again.' I heard footsteps approaching behind me, and then the light, penitent pressure of Pamela's hand on my back. 'Thank you, Stella. You're very good. Look, why don't you take the rest of the afternoon off, once you've finished here. Martin shouldn't be back until six.'

'Are you sure?' I said.

'No, that should be fine,' she conceded, after a pause. 'I think I can manage. When you come back, we could all go for a swim.'

'Great!' I replied.

She shuffled mournfully from the room, leaving me to celebrate my triumph alone. I ran the taps and even hummed loudly, not wishing to hear anything of Pamela's subsequent conversation from beyond the wall. I realized that I had become somewhat addicted to cunning; but even though I could see that so far I had lost more than I had gained by it, like a gambler this latest victory encouraged me to persist. The normal forms of control over a situation not being available to me, I felt that for the time being I had discovered a more covert way to survive.

Along with the satisfaction I had gained from rattling Pamela, the scene had yielded an additional bonus. Piers's exile could, of course, be explained by a number of factors. My own parents, for example, had increasingly, as they grew older and the rooms became, through death and desertion, available, slept apart. The cause was prosaic – my father's snoring – but there had never been any question of moving personal effects. My mother merely decamped when the noise became intolerable, and returned automatically when it had subsided. Her night-time paddings up and down the dark corridor were a midnight extension of the treadmill of their marriage, a tour of duty undertaken in a spirit of deep and sacrificial secrecy. The cautious creak of the bedsprings bore the imprimatur of love: for despite the glottal riot which had woken her, my mother's own manoeuvres were conducted with pathological quiet.

Piers's predicament, however, emitted the distinct scent of a mystery. I could not imagine the lovely Pamela snoring, although the possibility that she routinely roused Piers from his snores and ejected him, rather than move herself, was a distinct one; but the presence of his 'things' – so many 'things' that they presented an obstruction to Toby's visit – hinted to the devious mind at a disaffection more malignant and incurable. If a falling-out were the reason for the separation, however, why would Pamela have revealed it so unthinkingly? I had certainly caught her at an unguarded moment, with the weighty prospect of a domestic assignment now before her. I had also, apparently engrossed in my washing-up and with my back turned, given the appearance of not listening to what she was saying. It did occur to me that Pamela considered me to be of so little consequence that I was more or less invisible to her; but the frequency with which she seemed to refer to me in her private conversations suggested that this was not the case.

Having pondered this latest development at such length, I found that the washing-up was done and the kitchen returned to its former glory. Judging by the silence from the hall, Pamela had finished her conversation and gone elsewhere. I looked at my watch and found that it was half-past three. Beyond the windows the afternoon simmered, unstirred by breezes. I longed for the postponed swim. There was still the problem of the sodden dishcloths to confront, however, and I decided that this might be the moment to make my escape to the cottage, where I could lay them out to dry in the sun, and think over all that I had learned.

Chapter Twelve

Outside the garden stood still, as if held in a sultry jelly of heat and thick air. I made my way along the path between the twittering hedges to the cottage, feeling within seconds the urgency of getting into the shade. The whining of a lawnmower threaded its way along the path towards me, growing louder and more guttural with my approach. By the time I reached the gate the noise was quite deafening. Entering the garden I saw a man astride what looked like a miniature tractor, driving it bucking and lurching into the dense beard of grass in front of the cottage. Over one half of the garden, stems lay felled on their sides in long executioner's rows. The strong, familiar smell of cut grass, a seasonal memory annually forgotten, flooded up from the lawn. I stood watching the man's progress. He was wearing a large hat which covered most of his face, but as the tensile limpet of his body clung to the thrashing machine I caught glimpses of his neck, brown and knotty as old wood. This, I concluded, was dear old Thomas, mowing the lawn true to his word.

'Good afternoon!' I cried, wading through the grass with my hand shielding my eyes from the light.

Thomas drove roaring on through the stubborn crop, impervious, his skinny shoulders hooked over the handlebars. He was mowing in lengths, and when the machine abutted the cottage wall he turned it in a lumbering circle and began driving back towards me. I waved cheerfully, but when it became evident that he had no intention of stopping was compelled to step aside.

'Good afternoon!' I called again hopefully, as he ploughed furiously past me. I caught a glimpse of the rugged escarpment of his nose, and the blind socket of his mouth.

His truculent back receded to the bottom of the garden, and having been twice slighted I decided to take cover in the cottage before he completed his turn. I have never had much of a touch in such situations. My parents had no gardener or cleaner, nor many visitors either, which may explain my lack of social graces; although I do not want to give the impression that I am using my parents to excuse away everything. They would be furious if they knew even a part of what I ascribe to their influence. Indeed, they have always suspected me of this tendency. 'I suppose that's our fault too!' my mother would remark, if some entirely unrelated misfortune befell me. She would even, no doubt, if she were here, accuse me of blaming them for my habit of blaming them.

I stole away from Thomas, then, looking guiltily over my shoulder lest he should glance up and acknowledge me, and went into the cottage; intending to leave the door open as a further testament to my accessibility, should the need for conversation suddenly overtake him. I had the damp ball of dishcloths in one hand and was about to attend to it when I noticed something lying on the floor in front of me. It was a single slip of paper, and from its position I judged that it had been slid beneath the door while I was out. I picked it up and saw that it was a leaflet of some sort, crudely printed, and bearing the heading, in astonished capitals: 'IT'S MADDENING!'

I dropped the dishcloths into the lap of the armchair and

read it where I stood. Beneath the heading was printed the following message:

> Fancy a walk in the country? Tempted to stroll across the hills and dales of the 'magnificent' Sussex landscape? FORGET IT!! Whether you're down from the big smoke for the day, or just an ordinary local exercising your human rights, you'll have trouble enjoying the simple pleasures of fresh air and scenery. Why? Because a fat cat farmer is out to stop you, that's why! Our public rights of way are being sabotaged by this fascist feline, who has seen fit to make a menace out of an area of natural beauty. Innocent ramblers in the Hilltop area, beware! This farmer has declared war on YOU!! His name? Piers Madden. His game? Protecting his property by *whatever means necessary* from the honest public. YOUR LIVES ARE IN DANGER!! For more information, enquire at the post office.

At the bottom of the leaflet was inscribed the legend *Property is Theft*, with a kind of scroll beneath it. Thomas was now noisily advancing on his mower up the garden behind me, for all the world as if he intended to forge his way through the cottage, and I quickly shut the door, the leaflet still clutched in my hand. It took me several readings to make any sense of it at all. Of what precisely did Mr Madden stand so bitterly accused? What danger could he, mildness incarnate, possibly represent to the lives of the 'honest public'? My unfamiliarity with the countryside and its attendant vocabulary meant that it was some time before I understood 'public rights of way' to mean footpaths; those being, in so far as I could deduce, ordained paths crossing private property along which anybody was permitted to walk. I liked, as I now knew, a walk; but I could not credit the practice, pleasant though it was, with the politics set out before me here, nor imagine their author to be anything other than a lunatic.

My first thought was to take the leaflet and show it to Mr Madden at once. That he was being denounced so liberally, possibly unbeknownst to him, was bad enough; but the thought that his detractor had trespassed deeply on his property, straying far from footpaths to deliver his vitriol, was worse still. It unsettled me to think that an intruder had made it to my door without being apprehended. I wondered if Thomas had seen anything untoward, but decided not to risk another social foray in that direction.

Just as I was about to leave the cottage with the intention of tracking down Mr Madden and reporting the incident to him, another thought struck me. What if, contrary to appearances, Mr Madden was in fact guilty of discouraging ramblers from his property? I did not suspect him of any degree of turpitude, and clearly saw the leaflet for what it was – a cheap patchwork of resentment and agitation designed to rouse the most brutal emotions in those who read it. It was, however, quite possible that Mr Madden had reasons for his hostility, if hostile he was. Perhaps he had had bad experiences with ramblers in the past, or found that they did damage to his land. If the pamphleteer was a fair example of the species, Mr Madden probably had everything to fear from it.

The thought, in any case, that he might be fully aware of the leaflet, and perhaps had suffered from similar attacks before, discouraged me from bringing it to his attention. Were the substance, if not the tone, of the allegations true, he might quite rightly regard it as none of my business. Were it false, he could feel humiliated. Added to this possibility was the delicate subject of my supposed 'feelings' for Mr Madden, and the hint of irritation I caught even when I petitioned him on more trivial matters persuaded me still further against disclosure. The ideal solution, I soon realized, was for him to find out about the leaflet without knowing that the information came from me. The easiest way for this to be done, obviously, was for me to put the leaflet through the front door of the big house unseen. In case anyone did see me, I could carry out this task under the pretence of going for a walk. More convincing yet, I could in fact *go* for a walk; and if in the course of it I found myself at the post office in Hilltop, I could perhaps carry my investigations further.

Having settled on my plan, I hurried to follow it through so as to be back well before six o'clock, the hour of Martin's return. My single remaining problem was the vexing matter of my sunburn. Over the course of the day my skin had become less painful, but where my wrists and neck protruded from my shirt the tide of a violent blush remained high. I dared not look at my face in the mirror. Having no hat, and apparently intent on reconstructing the previous day's activities to the letter, it seemed unlikely that I would avoid a repetition of its misfortunes. The thought of Thomas's hat, capacious and floppy, was tempting; but having failed in the work of charming him, there was little hope of persuading him to lend it to me short of assaulting him in some way.

Being practical by nature, there was only so long that I would permit myself to be paralysed by a question of vanity. The leaflet in my hand was issuing an urgent summons to action; and I challenged myself to deny that the acquisition of aptitude for the country life required some degree of physical toughness. My skin would have to adapt, as my spirit was striving to do. I became aware of a particularly sweet and expansive silence blooming about me and realized that the roar of the mower had ceased. Opening the door I saw the barbered garden lying anaesthetized in the heat, with no sign either of Thomas or his machine. Seizing my moment, I bolted from the cottage, locking the door behind me and putting the key in my pocket.

Mr Madden's mention of a gate leading to the drive lent me more purpose than direction in beginning my journey. I had no idea where this gate might be found, having never glimpsed a diversion from the route I customarily took to the big house. Indeed, it was hard to believe, knowing this route as I now did, that it could surprise me in any way at all. I was confounded, then, by the appearance immediately to my left as I emerged from the cottage garden of what was clearly a path. Given that I would happily have sworn on my life that no such path existed, there was something not a little sinister about its manifestation. I had had this feeling once or twice before since being in the country; a feeling that, as in a dream, the world had become a flaccid structure inflated – like a balloon, or the long, flat tunnel of a sleeve down which a motive human hand snakes – by convenience and will. The thought that perhaps everything was folded in this way, unwrapping itself at the command of my footsteps, was a disturbing one.

Nevertheless I took the path, and found it to lead easily to a small iron gate, on the other side of which lay the pebbled shore of the Maddens' front drive. I cut stealthily across the gravelled expanse, my frame rigid with casual cunning, and made as if I was intending to stroll past the front door and on down the avenue. Just as I drew level with the door, however, I darted to the right, ascending the steps crabwise with all possible haste. Panting, I poked my finger through the heavy silver slot and peered through it, scanning the long, tenebrous tunnel for signs of life and the minatory glare of Roy. Seeing nothing, I fed the leaflet quickly through the gap and heard it fall with a whisper on the other side. Unfortunately, the lid appeared to be sprung in some manner, and despite the careful easing of my finger free, it slammed down with a loud rap as soon as I had released it. I waited, frozen, for the sound of footsteps; for I had decided in that moment that it was too dangerous to run away, given that I might not have time to find a hiding place. I was glad to feel, even in my terror, that my mental processes seemed to be accelerating somewhat. Many people would have fled panicked from the scene as if under fire, and then been run to ground in the open spaces of the front drive.

Fortunately, nobody appeared to have heard the rap, and after a few minutes of waiting I judged that I was free to go. I set off again across the scorched drive and soon gained the shade of the avenue. Feeling that I could now relax, and knowing that I was in for a long walk, I permitted my mind to wander to other things; and was surprised when I reached the road far sooner than I had anticipated. The empty tarmac shone and glinted before me in the sun. I stood on the brink of it, only then remembering what had happened to my shoes when last I had walked on this road. My only other pair was currently on my feet. I cursed myself, hovering at the silent tarmac as if it were a gushing river. If only I had thought to change my shoes! The prospect of trudging back up the avenue to fetch the ruined pair and then down again was uninviting; indeed, I wouldn't have time for it. The only alternative was to go back to the cottage and have my walk another day. I had already, after all, achieved my primary aim, which was the delivery of the leaflet. My desire to enquire at the post office was, however, too strong. Before long I had persuaded myself that the vandalism of my only remaining pair of shoes could be overlooked, and indeed might not happen at all, even though past experience insisted to the contrary. The aggravation of my sunburn, which weighted things still more heavily in favour of abandoning the walk, I regarded with similar insouciance. It might happen, I admitted; but then again it might not.

In committing myself wholeheartedly to a course which was neither savoury, profitable, nor necessary – and could turn out to be downright perilous – I was aware that a certain irrationality seemed temporarily to have taken me in its grip. My experience with the gate, however, had given me a sort of curiosity, a thirst for experimentation which I could see no real reason to deny. What I desired to discover was whether the process which, a few minutes earlier, had manufactured the gate according to my need to use it could in fact be mastered and then employed in reverse. I wanted in other words to see how much my intention of avoiding misfortune in the form of tar and sun – a resolution formed, as I have said, in the very midst of a determination to tempt these misfortunes to their limit – would influence the outcome of my walk.

The heat hammered on my shoulders as I walked along the deserted road, and within minutes I had begun to repent my heedlessness. (My little mental game had, I soon saw, merely led me by a circuitous route to the misfortunes reason had long since visited.) I stopped to look at my shoes, and saw to my disappointment several dark and shiny bruises of tar on the soles. I set off again at a faster pace, yearning for the signal houses which would denote the fringe of the village. Just as I was about to break into a run in order to seek shelter, I heard the rapid approach of a car behind me and I bridled my agony, waiting for it to pass. So quickly was the car travelling that I barely had time to stiffen my aching frame into a simulation of leisure and force my unwilling cheeks into a rictus of enjoyment when it shot by. It was a new car, cast in coruscating silver which gave off lecherous winks in the sun, and its beefy rear was raised to me in a rude salute as it passed. A jet of liquid squirted obscenely onto its back windscreen, which its lazy synthetic tail spread foaming over the glass. I was tempted to make some offensive gesture in its wake, but stopped myself with the thought that even if the car didn't contain one of the Maddens it might be harbouring some acquaintance of theirs who would report the incident back.

The speed with which the brute had passed me, and the knowledge that while I had inched laboriously towards my destination he had doubtlessly attained and surpassed it, redoubled my weariness. My sunburn, however, demanded to be carried with all possible haste to a shady spot, and in the end I was forced to jog feebly along, one hand cupped about my neck and the other reached crosswise over my chest to shield my cheek, until finally I glimpsed the village crouched defensively on the hillside in the glare.

The High Street lay prostrate and almost empty and I flitted unseen from shady doorway to lamp-post towards the post office. There was something disquieting in the silence of the place coupled with the emergency of the heat, as if minutes earlier a siren had sounded ordering evacuation. An old man sat alone at a table outside the pub, one bony knee extended and his hand expansively propped on his walking stick as if he were relating a story to an invisible audience, a cap flat as a coin on his head.

'Good afternoon,' I said to him as I passed.

'Afternoon,' he said, to my surprise, touching his cap. His riddled, crepuscular eyes looked straight ahead, blind with age, abandoned, like the discarded skins of snakes.

The post office was housed behind a squat terraced front, one of a long row of dwarfish red-brick dwellings, each with a single bay window to the street which bulged out like a pot belly or an insect's glassy eye. This window was hung with petitions and advertisements, some typed and some merely scrawled on various cards and slips of paper. I scanned them briefly out there on the searing, narrow pavement, and was able to determine that almost without exception the announcements took one of two forms: that of services required, and that of services rendered. It surprised me to be able to place myself so firmly in the second category, having for so long occupied the first; but I adapted to the change quickly enough. Habits are subtle scales, trained to measure whatever one might choose to put on them; and before long I was cheerfully engrossed in what the ladies of Hilltop were offering for a competent girl such as myself, and even wondering whether a covert few hours a week spent in the employ of Mrs Lascelles or Mrs Gower-Ward was entirely out of the question. My eye was soon, however, caught by a more familiar typescript; and looking up I saw that the same leaflet which had been put beneath my door was boldly occupying a central position towards the top of the display. I propelled myself from the window and through the door, which triggered the shrilling of a little bell when I opened it.

I found the post office – or 'post office' – to be an even more perplexing place than the 'shop' up the road. My first impression was that the pale room whose sepulchral coolness lapped at my burning arms like water contained nothing at all. Its atmosphere was pregnant with lack, and as I stood there I found myself overwhelmed by feelings of need; for food, although there was no reason at all for me to be hungry, having lunched amply with the Maddens; and more pressingly for something to drink. So furious was my thirst that I could look at nothing around me – the empty shelves lining one wall, the yellow Formica countertop leaning against the other, the glass window at the end behind which I could see an old-fashioned till with keys raised high like begging paws – with anything but an eye for its capacity to quench it. Perceiving that I was stranded in a desert of opportunity, my only thought was either to seek out human agency or leave immediately, my greater purpose utterly forgotten. My tongue was as dry as a sock stuffed into my mouth. I scanned the scene once more; and was surprised this time to notice the contours of a human belly tightly encased in a plaid shirt profiled behind the glass screen.

'Excuse me?' I cried, my voice a dramatic croak.

The belly remained intransigent behind the glass.

'Hello?' I cried again.

There was another pause, and then a man's voice issued faintly out to me from the side.

'What can I do for you, dear?'

It was quite a high voice, and heavily accented, but it sounded friendly enough.

'I'm very thirsty,' I said, directing my comments to the belly for want of a more conversational appurtenance. It required the greatest effort for me even to be polite. 'I wondered if you would be so kind as to give me a glass of water.'

Before my eyes, the belly seemed to roll away as if attached to a large rotating wheel lodged behind the scenes, and in its place appeared a grinning human face.

'Glass o' water?' it said – I could now not be sure whether it was a woman or man. Its hair stood up in a frizz above its pocked forehead as if electrified, and confronted with the disastrous, freckled spectacle of its features I felt the thrill of looking at the ugliest human creature I had ever seen. 'It'll cost ya!' it said, grinning wider to show hoary teeth like a jumble of old gravestones.

'But I haven't any money!' I gasped. 'I was merely asking for a drop of human kindness. And besides, as this isn't a restaurant you can't charge me for water. It would be' – I put a hand to my fevered throat – 'unethical.'

The creature looked at me quizzically, its brows – the hairs of which were preternaturally long and curled – furrowed to form a single line, as if a fake moustache had been attached to its forehead.

'I was only joking, girl,' it said, quite sorrowfully. 'If you come round the back, I'll put you right.'

It disappeared abruptly from behind the glass and after some protracted shuffling on the other side of the partition a door slowly opened to my left.

'Come on,' coaxed the creature, beckoning me with a saurian claw. 'Don't hold back, girl.'

It held open the door and I passed through into a narrow enclosure. A further door lay directly ahead of me, and to my right was the scene I had glimpsed through the glass, the old till on the counter with what looked a child's high chair drawn up to it. There was a paperback book lying open on the seat. The space was no bigger than a coffin, and was roughly the same shape.

'Step this way, if you would,' the creature said with sudden formality, as if I had all at once ascended a level in some cryptic hierarchy. I felt it hovering at my elbow, and looking down realized that in height the creature barely rose above my waist.

'Thank you,' said I, moving forward through the second doorway. I was now in a dark corridor which smelt very damp.

'All the way to the end, madam. That's right.'

We entered a room about which, the curtains being drawn to exclude all but a faint white seam of light, I could discern almost nothing.

'Now, let's see, shall we, madam?' murmured the creature, straying from my elbow. I heard the whisper of its feet against the floor, but could not make out in the dark where it had gone.

'It might be easier if you put the light on,' I advised. 'It's pitch black in here.'

'Oh, no need for that, my lady,' it said. 'We'll manage.'

'I think I would prefer it, actually,' I asserted; for I had suddenly become nervous at how I had been lured into this shadowy lair, where no one would ever think of looking for me. 'I insist that you turn on the light!'

There was a pause, there in the dark. I could hear no sound of movement at all and began to feel positively frightened. I was about to turn and flee when a steely grip on my arm pulled me down so that I was bending almost double.

'Are you a sympathizer?' the creature whispered fiercely in my ear. Flecks of spittle rained on my cheek. 'Is that why you came?'

My heart was pounding hard with the surprise, but I was not so cowed that I could not think clearly. Having no idea of what I might be supposed to be sympathetic to, still I could see that it would be a good idea to concur.

'Yes,' I responded, in a loud voice.

'Ssssh! Good. Well, then. You've come to the right place.'

The grip on my arm was released and a moment later the light came on; a naked bulb which depended so far into the room from a length of flex that I felt its heat against my hair. Nothing could have prepared me for what I saw around me. The tiny room was no less than a shrine, a votive chamber dedicated, to my astonishment, to the Maddens.

'Good God!' I exclaimed, my eyes frantically combing the

walls thickly billeted by leaflets and posters, newspaper clippings, photographs, and what looked, more worryingly, like instruments of torture – nooses made from wire, with a chain attached – hanging from nails like commemorative wreaths.

'Impressed?' said the creature, who had been busy meanwhile at a small sink – hardly bigger than a cup – which stood dingy and serene in the corner of the tumult. It crossed the room as coyly as a party host and handed me a large glass of water. 'It's taken me years to get it like this.'

My thirst, forgotten amidst this drama, flamed anew at the sight of the glass. Delicious pearls of liquid trailed down its sides. I took it and raised it trembling to my lips.

'Course it picks up at this time of year,' continued the creature, while I drank. I believe that there is no sensation on earth more pleasurable than the one I was at that moment experiencing. 'We get all sorts down here in the summer, especially round the bank holiday weekend. That's my busy time. Come next week, I'll be flat out.'

'Do you work alone?' I gasped, draining the glass and handing it back. 'Can I have another?'

'Certainly, madam.' It took the empty glass, lost in contemplation of its handiwork. After a moment, and with a last longing look at the noose on the far wall, it shuffled back towards the sink. 'When it started it was just me,' it called, over its shoulder. 'Now there's hundreds, just contacts mostly, but it comes in handy. I'm still the boss, mind. I tell them what to do, and they do it. Day to day, Darren over at the Dog mucks in when he can.'

'Did you put that leaflet under my door?'

'Me?' The creature looked round. 'No fear. I've got a contact at the farm does that kind of thing for me. No, too risky for me over there these days.'

I wondered who the creature's 'contact' could be. Mrs Barker? Thomas? Thomas was the most likely suspect, given his presence at the scene of the crime. From behind I still could find nothing either in the creature's attire nor its physique to determine its sex. Its back and shoulders were round and quite strong, but tapered into bony shanks from which its dirty dark-brown trousers hung in folds. They were too long in the leg, and the hems gathered into frills around a pair of scuffed slippers. It seemed to be taking an inordinate amount of time fetching the water, and with the selfishness of physical need, I resolved to make no further enquiries which might slow the rate of service until I had the glass in my hand. This plan paid off, for the creature, head jerking up slightly at the silence, looked swiftly over its shoulder as if to make sure that I was still there.

'You'll be wanting your water,' it said, nodding. 'Quite a thirst you've got on you.'

I remained silent until the water was safely on its way. When the creature turned around, its swollen belly protruded so distinctly that I wondered if it might be pregnant.

'Thank you very much,' I said graciously, accepting the second glass. Things were less of a blur now that my emergency had been met, and my eyes surveyed the walls more calmly. There were several of the familiar leaflets pinned at intervals around the room, and many others of a similar type duplicated this pattern. Indeed, I soon saw that I had been slightly misled in my first impressions of the place, for the campaign's look of abundance was achieved more by repetition than diversity. The photographs, of which there were some dozen, were blurred Polaroids and I could make out little of what they were supposed to represent; except that all had been taken outdoors and that in each case the photographer appeared to be falling over. A large poster printed on a white background which hung directly in front of me read 'MADDEN KILLS!'. Beneath it was an efficient drawing of a noose identical to those adorning the walls.

'He hasn't really killed anybody, has he?' said I, alarmed.

The creature snapped its head round to look at me,

aggrieved. The cliff of its forehead creased into fleshy ridges and its lower lip protruded, like that of a child about to cry. I wondered then if Mr Madden really had, incredible as it seemed, murdered some close relative or associate of the creature; or at least was suspected of having done so.

'Of course,' nodded the creature, as if to itself. 'You're new around here. You wouldn't have heard, would you?'

'No,' said I. 'But even so, I find it frankly unbelievable that Mr Madden could have hurt anybody.'

The creature looked away sharply, as if in pain.

'Tell that to Geoff!'

'Who is Geoff?' I ventured.

'Was. Was.' It looked down at its slippers and raised a weary hand to the great pale flank of its forehead. It heaved a sigh. 'Geoff,' it said, 'Geoff was my friend. My best friend. And now he's gone.'

'What – what happened to him?'

'Gone!' The creature buried its mouth in its palm. Its shoulders heaved up and down. 'Three years ago this bank holiday Monday! And not a day goes by that I don't think about him!'

'What do you mean, gone?' I cried urgently.

'Dead,' said the creature, matter of factly. 'Murdered.'

This seemed too fantastical to be true.

'Are you sure? Mightn't he just have gone off somewhere without telling you?'

'Ahhh!' The creature let out a long breath and rubbed its eyes with its hands. 'Buried him myself on the Monday night. Just out there in the yard.' It jerked a thumb over its shoulder. 'Shot clean through the head, he was. At least he didn't feel any pain. I found him up on the top field. He loved it up there, used to go chasing rabbits. He could have lain there for days. But I knew something was wrong. When he didn't come back I went out looking for him. Carried him in my arms all the way back to the village. Everyone came out and stood at their doors. You never heard it so quiet.' It swiped a tear or two from its eyes. 'I'll never find another dog like him. Wouldn't want to. He was only a mongrel, you know. But I loved him.'

'How do you know that it was Mr Madden?' I sombrely enquired. 'It could have been someone else. It could have been a mistake.'

'It was no mistake!' said the creature fiercely. 'Trimmer had warned me about Geoff before. Was dying to take a pot-shot at him, he said as much.'

'Who is Trimmer?'

'You not met him yet?' The creature looked at me quizzically. 'No, I suppose you haven't. You've only been up at Franchise since Saturday. Trimmer's the manager. It's him puts those down.' It nodded towards the nooses. 'Fast as I take them away, he replaces them.'

'Well, it was probably Mr Trimmer who killed your dog!' I cried, frustrated at the creature's stupidity.

'Maybe,' admitted the creature stubbornly. It folded its arms and looked at me. 'But it's the institution that should take the blame. You ought to be going, dear. The cripple will be back from Buckley any minute.'

I looked at my watch and saw to my horror that it was a quarter to six.

'Before you go,' said the creature, turning and waddling off, 'I'll give you something to put on that skin of yours. You've had too much sun. You should be more careful. It ages you something terrible.'

'But I've got to go!' I wailed, as it opened a cupboard camouflaged by a crust of leaflets on the far wall. 'I'll get into trouble!'

'Won't take a minute.' The creature took a jar from the top shelf and came back towards me, unscrewing the lid. 'Hold still a jiffy and shut your eyes.'

I closed my eyes and seconds later felt the most astonishing caress upon my cheeks, as if the coolest silk were being gently drawn across the skin. I immediately forgot about the necessity for hurrying back to the farm, and indeed about everything that I had seen and heard during the past hour, longing only for the sensation to continue. It descended to my neck and then beneath the collar of my shirt, and then out again and up my sleeves, up my arms and down again right to my fingertips.

'That's better,' I heard the creature say. 'You can open your eyes now.'

I opened them, feeling as if I had been asleep.

'Thank you,' I said, miraculously cooled. 'You've been very kind.'

'Off you go, then.' The creature jerked its thumb again. 'I'd keep quiet about our little meeting if I was you. I'll be seeing you again, I'm sure. You'll excuse me if I don't show you out.'

I turned and opened the door. As I did so a newspaper clipping pinned beside the frame caught my eye. It bore a grainy picture of Pamela. She was smiling and I could just make out a disembodied arm curled about her shoulders. *Lovers' tiff behind farm attack, say police*, read the headline.

'What's your name?' I cried, turning back.

The creature was screwing the lid back on to the jar. It looked up, surprised amidst the mayhem of paper, and gave me its terrible grin.

'You can call me Al,' it said.

I ran down the dark corridor without looking back, and, crossing the deserted shop floor, stumbled blinking into the glare of the High Street with the bell shrilling in my ears.

Chapter Thirteen

I came up the back passage as quietly as I could – having remembered to remove my tar-stained shoes at the door, my movements were virtually silent – hoping to be able to replace myself in the kitchen, where I had last been sighted by Pamela, unseen. Having no idea of how the Maddens would regard my tardiness – it was by now almost half-past six – my nerves responded to the most exaggerated scenarios imagination could devise. The sound of voices coming from the kitchen froze me outside the door with dread for some time, although eventually I realized that this was merely making my predicament worse.

I opened the door on an idyllic scene; one which filled me with pleasure but also, unexpectedly, with the bitterness of envy and regret. Pamela and Piers were standing side by side beside the 'Aga', their bodies not actually touching but proximate in a way which suggested comfort and fondness. Both were looking with palpable affection at Martin, whose chair was positioned directly in front of them, and who was relating to them some incident which was making them laugh, his hand placed on the glossy head of Roy who sat contentedly beside him. In glimpsing this scene of familial love I also, inevitably, disturbed it. Pamela and Piers looked up in unison at the sound of the door opening, and whatever narrative Martin was embarked on was lost for ever as he twisted round in his chair and gave me his strange, flapping smile.

'Here's Stella!' Pamela cried, as if overjoyed.

'Don't let me disturb you,' I said, filled suddenly with the sorrowful desire to be excluded. 'You all looked so lovely over there,' I continued, unable to stop myself. 'You looked like a proper family.'

'Goodness!' said Pamela. 'That *is* a compliment!'

'Where have you been, Stel-la?' interjected Martin plaintively. 'I've missed you.'

At this I was driven almost to weep, especially given the reasons for my absence, which now I profoundly regretted. Had my skin not still been luxuriating in whatever cream it was that the creature had applied to it, I would have been tempted to believe that the whole interlude at the post office had been a hallucination.

'You look so well!' exclaimed Pamela, continuing in the friendly vein which seemed to have been established. 'Doesn't she, Piers?'

'Marvellous,' said Piers, to my surprise.

'And your skin!' she rhapsodized, raising a hand to her own cheek. 'Oh, to be young, what bliss! Look after it, Stella, please, while you've got the chance. I left it far too late!'

Glad as I was to have escaped a reprimand, I felt that a denial of this fact would push the happy scene over into excess and merely gave her an erubescent smile. It was some time before she removed her hand from her cheek; and seeing her like that, I remembered the newspaper clipping I had seen in the creature's room. What could it have meant? The words 'lovers' tiff' were clear in my mind. They evidently did not, unless I had misunderstood them, refer to the Maddens' own relationship. Could Pamela or Piers have had an affair? It seemed, looking at them now, impossible; and besides, who was there in the countryside with whom to have one? I had seen barely anybody during my time here, except the creature, and the people who ran the 'shop'; unless, of course, you counted Darren over at the Dog, or Mrs Lascelles, for whom I could not vouch. So far, the only people with whom I could consider either of them having an affair were each other.

'Right!' said Mr Madden, brushing some invisible detritus from his trouser leg. 'I'd better get on.'

'OK, darling,' said Pamela radiantly. To my surprise, she even took his arm and walked with him over towards the door. I wondered what had happened in my absence to provoke this marked increase of affection between the Maddens. I soon realized, however, that Pamela had accompanied Piers to the door so that she could talk to him privately; although I am afraid that I could hear every word she said. What she said was: 'You'll sort out that business in the top field, won't you? We don't want any trouble with the police.'

'Yes, yes, all right. Just leave it to me,' Mr Madden mysteriously replied.

I glanced at Martin, but he was occupied ruffling Roy's velveteen ears and did not seem to have heard anything. Pamela, thinking herself unobserved, laid a hand on Mr Madden's cheek and looked at him with an expression I could not fathom.

'Oh, darling,' she said. She withdrew her hand longingly. 'Go on, off you go.'

'What would you like to do now?' I said to Martin in a loud voice as soon as Mr Madden had gone.

'Dunno,' he replied, still engrossed in Roy. 'We could go up to my room and listen to some records if you like.'

'That's a good idea!' said Pamela ingratiatingly, overhearing. She came back across the room and put her arm around me, placing her other hand on Martin's head. We now formed a sort of chain, starting with Roy and ending with me. 'Why don't you two slope off upstairs and have your party, and I'll give you a shout when supper's ready!'

Tiring somewhat, I can admit, of Pamela's jollity, I was relieved when Martin and I had gained the cool sanctuary of the hall.

'Did you have a good afternoon?' I enquired, as he slid from his chair at the bottom of the stairs.

'No,' he panted, inching backwards up towards the first step and lodging his backside on it.

'I thought you liked it there.'

'What do you know?' he said, levering himself on to the second. 'It's crap. How would you like to spend three afternoons a week with a bunch of spastics?'

'That's not very nice,' I said, picking up his chair and plodding after him. 'You don't have to go.'

'Yes I do,' he puffed.

'Why, if you hate it so much?'

'Apparently' – he heaved again – 'I learn things there.'

'What sort of things?'

'I dunno. How to get used to being there, I suppose.'

'What do you mean?'

'Well.' He stopped for a moment, his face red. 'If something happens to them. Mater and Pater, that is. You know.'

He resumed his ascent, his black hair flopping up and down.

'But!' I cried, dumbfounded. 'But you wouldn't – I mean, if something *did* happen – you wouldn't go there!'

'I bloody would. Or somewhere like it.'

'But what about – what about Caroline?'

He stopped again and opened his mouth wide. 'Ha! Ha!'

'I mean,' I extemporized, 'I mean, you might not get on all that well, but she's your sister. She'd be glad to—' I tried to think of a tactful way of putting it: 'she'd be glad to have you live with her, I'm sure!'

'No, she wouldn't.'

'How do you know?'

'Because,' he said firmly, 'she's said so. They all did. Mummy and Daddy sat them all down and asked them. I mean' – he dragged himself onto the landing – 'they didn't say no just like that. But they all made excuses. Even Millie.'

'Who's Millie?'

'My other sister. You haven't met her yet. She's nice.'

I trailed up the stairs, the chair cumbersome in my arms, and deposited it beside him on the landing.

'But why?' I said, or rather wailed.

'Why what?'

'Why won't they have you?'

'Oh, I dunno.' He grasped the handles of the chair and levered himself up. 'Millie was upset about it, I suppose. She just said that she couldn't promise. She didn't know what was going to happen and stuff. I dunno.'

He wheeled past me with a blazing face down the corridor to his room. I lagged behind, my mind alive with curiosity and shame. I had often felt as a child a sense of surprise at how far the machinations of the adult world had progressed beyond my own, while I had been busy cultivating the solipsistic cabbage patch of my own thoughts. My parents had often surprised me with what they knew, the things they had considered and discussed. The reason for my unpreparedness was perhaps because I never saw them do it. To return to the subject of Martin, it had never occurred to me to wonder what might happen to him if Pamela and Piers met with some misfortune. Of course, I could see now that such a discussion, given his age and disability, had been inevitable; but the fact that it hadn't *occurred* to me gave me the perhaps unwonted feeling that Pamela and Piers were more responsible, more *complex* somehow, than I had believed them to be. I have always felt that moments such as this have a peculiarly ageing effect on the mind; and I was to age still further when I arrived at the dreadful subject of Caroline and the others' refusal to accept the guardianship of their poor defenceless brother. My first thought, fired off in disgust, was that I myself would offer to take care of him; but as soon as I had thought it a tempting though unlikely vision of my future life, beckoning me towards footloose adventures in foreign parts and romantic elopements at midnight, came to haunt me.

'Come on!' called Martin from up ahead.

I hurried along after him to his room, which had undergone a transformation since the morning – the fruits, no doubt, of Mrs Barker's campaign – but had already embarked on its return to chaos. One or two items lay abandoned on the pristine carpet, like the first fallen leaves at the end of summer presaging the long but irreversible process by which everything which was lodged orderly on branches would eventually be flung to the ground. Martin was in the corner of the room, leaning far out of his chair to inspect a rank of records which stood in a long rack like hundreds of silvery slivers of toast.

'What sort of music do you like, Stel-la?'

'I don't know. Anything, I suppose. Whatever you like.'

Martin turned around in his chair, as if astonished.

'Don't you like music?' he said.

'Of course I do. I just don't have a favourite sort.'

'Strange girl,' muttered Martin, turning away.

'Edward always used to buy the records,' I added, feeling that I ought to explain myself. 'He had a huge collection. I suppose that's why I don't have any myself. Not that that's any excuse, of course, but if somebody's very passionate about something it tends to mean that you can't be.'

During this colloquy, Martin had been slowly turning around again in his chair.

'Who,' he said, with a gravity which was entirely out of proportion, 'is Edward?'

'He's my – he was just somebody I knew for a long time.'

I turned and looked awkwardly out of the long window. Outside the afternoon was fading, and a strange, floury light hung over the front lawn. Far in the distance a violent red stain, the aftermath of the sun, clung to the rinsing sky; and watching that remote drama I felt suddenly that it held everything from which I had run away; that although for now I was harboured safe in the private splendour of other people's lives, the immanence of that other world, the bloody recrudescence which hung patiently at the horizon, would one day claim me again.

'Where is he now?' said Martin behind me. 'Do you still see him?'

'No,' I said. 'I don't know where he is. Well, I do, he's in London, but I'm not in touch with him.'

Benighted, shameful thoughts stirred like smoking craters in the darkness of the back of my mind.

'Why not?' said Martin, with childish naivety. 'Did you have an argument?'

'Not really. I just had to get away from him.'

'Why? Was he nasty to you?' Martin drew a record from the rack. 'I think we'll have this.'

'Of course he wasn't nasty,' I snapped. 'He was just – wrong for me, I suppose. I don't know. I don't really want to think about it, if you don't mind.'

Just then, the room froze with the sound of the most exquisite music. It was piano music, of such lovely pathos that I experienced it almost as a physical pain. I had been expecting Martin to put on some teenage cacophany; and being taken by surprise, I found myself close to tears again, as I had been in the kitchen, with a kind of alloyed joy.

'What is it?' I said.

'Do you like it? It's the best piece of music ever written. Why don't you sit down, Stel-la? You're making me nervous standing there.'

I sat down in the leather armchair and closed my eyes. I felt very weary suddenly; not physically tired exactly, but shut down as if by some internal device, like an overheated machine. The music was the perfect balm for this condition and I drank it in, wondering why I had spent my life disdaining this free and accessible pleasure when all along it could have been mine.

'Tell me more about yourself, Stel-la,' said Martin. His voice was closer now, and although I had my eyes closed I guessed that he was nearby.

'What do you want to know?'

'What makes you tick.' He made a clicking sound with his tongue, high-low, high-low, like a clock.

'If I knew that,' I said sleepily, 'I wouldn't be here.'

I felt straight away that this last comment had been inappropriate, straying as it did beyond the boundaries of my role at Franchise Farm. I opened my eyes and sat up. Martin was sitting directly in front of me, so close in fact that I could feel his breath on my neck.

'How old are you?' he said.

'Twenty-nine.'

'You're too old for me,' he sighed. 'I'm only seventeen.'

'You'll get over it,' I said lightly, although I was surprised by what he had said, and curiously, both repelled and flattered at the same time. I was surprised, too, by his age, having thought him at least two years younger.

'Did Edward love you?' he enquired, emphasizing the word 'Edward'; for all the world as if his own feelings were now established in the public domain.

'I suppose so.'

'Did you love him?'

'Not really.' It was hard to get the treachery out of my mouth, like expectorating a large and jagged chunk of metal. 'No.'

'Hmm.' He put his hands on the wheels of his chair and began to rock back and forth. There was something slightly lewd in the movement, given our proximity. Seeming to realize this, he stopped. 'How long were you – you know.'

'A long time. Eight years.'

He whistled admiringly.

'Did he ask you to marry him?'

There was a long pause.

'Yes.'

'What did you say?'

'I said yes.'

Martin opened his eyes wide. His jaw was ajar, like a door.

'Are you married, Stel-la?' he said. His voice was confidential. His lips twitched, half gleeful and half dismayed.

'Yes.'

Martin gave a tentative little giggle. As if some small bird were nesting undetected in an internal crevice, I heard an answering trill rise up from my throat. In all the course of my brief but tumultuous acquaintance with the fact of my marriage, among the countless shades of feeling, the range of shame and guilt and regret – and even, once or twice, exultation – with which I had cosseted, fed and bludgeoned it, the spectrum of lights in which I had considered it, of backgrounds against which I had viewed it; in this noisy, crowded jamboree of emotions, it had never even once occurred to me to laugh about it. But that was precisely what Martin and I did now; and the more we tried to stop, the harder we laughed. Our chests heaved, our mouths opened wider to let the torrent out. Occasionally one or other of us would hold out a hand or try to say something; but then a new ascent of mirth unfolded above us, and we would be paralysed by an inarticulate glee which seemed to encompass not merely my revelation, but everything once thought unbearable. With every volley I felt another tract of anguish relieved, and yet sensed that there were reams of it still to come. I knew my laughter, curiously, to be a form of expiation, although I could not comprehend why this might be, or how levity could begin to atone for what I had done.

'Oh dear,' I said finally, wiping my eyes.

'You *are* funny,' said Martin, sounding rather like his mother.

The phrase set off a tremor of retrospective uncertainty in me, suggesting as it did that I had been the object rather than the author of our laughter. 'Imagine not telling us that!'

'You won't tell anybody, will you?' I said. The plea sounded ineffectual. 'I would prefer it,' I rephrased, 'if you kept this strictly between the two of us.'

'OK,' said Martin lightly; too lightly, although I felt it would make things worse to press him further for an assurance. 'Although I don't see what's so bad about it.'

'Just promise me,' I said. I was beginning to regret my honesty; indeed, with every passing minute my revelation seemed more foolhardy.

'I promise,' said Martin.

The record had finished and was spinning silently on the turntable. Martin lingered, as if hoping that I would volunteer more information. When I didn't, he wheeled around and propelled himself to the other side of the room. I wiped my eyes again and sniffed surreptitiously.

'Ahhhh!' he groaned suddenly, bringing himself up short. 'I completely forgot.'

'What?' I said, rather irritable now.

'The dogfucker,' he said, his head tilted back so that he was looking at the ceiling. 'He's supposed to be coming tonight.'

'The who?'

'Toby. The dogfucker. My brother.'

'What a dreadful word!' I exclaimed. 'You can't call him that!'

'What do you know?' said Martin, leaning forward and taking the record off the turntable. 'It suits him, anyway. And he deserves it.'

'Why?'

Martin turned around in his chair with exaggerated portentousness, the record held aloft.

'Why do you think?' he said, grinning horribly.

'I can't imagine,' I retorted primly.

'Oh, come on, Stel-la,' he leered. 'Don't be such a goody-goody.'

'I'm being nothing of the sort. I just don't believe you. It's not possible.'

'Tell that to Roy!'

'If you are insinuating what I think you are, then I have to say that I think you have a depraved mind.'

'But it's true!' He put down the record and wheeled his chair back to mine, his eyes glinting. 'He'd kill me if he knew I'd told anyone. You'll have to promise.'

'I promise,' I said, as though wearily; although in reality I was glad to have exchanged oaths with him.

'It happened years ago – we hadn't had Roy for very long and he was only a puppy. Anyway, one day I couldn't find him, and I was downstairs looking for him and I heard this noise.' He paused suspensefully, and then started to make a whimpering noise. 'Like that, coming from somewhere underneath the stairs. So I called him, *Roy!*, very quietly like that, *Roy! Here, boy!* And the noise just carried on. So I came up *really* quietly, because I'd worked out that it was coming from the cupboard and I thought he'd been shut in and that I'd give him a surprise. And so I threw open the door, *bam!* And there he was.'

'Who?'

'Toby. With Roy.' Martin chewed at his fingernail matter-of-factly.

'What were they doing?' I said finally.

'Well, Toby had his thing out,' resumed Martin conversationally. 'And Roy was kind of squirming and trying to get away.'

'That's disgusting,' I said.

'Oh, he was *desperate*,' said Martin. 'He used to go on about it the whole time. Muff this and snatch that and fucking the other. When I caught him that time he told me that a boy at school had said you could, you know, with a dog. I don't think he did anything, actually, to Roy I mean. But he tried to.'

'Did you tell your parents?'

'Course not!' said Martin scornfully. 'He'd be a complete swine to me if I didn't have something on him.'

There was a faint tap on the door.

'Come in!' called Martin.

The door opened and Pamela stood on the threshold. I could see immediately from her face that the ecstasy of an hour or two ago had begun to fade.

'Darlings, I think we're just going to have to go ahead and eat,' she said, as if in mid-conversation. She looked around, bewildered. 'Where are you both? It's pitch black in here!' She switched on the light, and I realized that the room had indeed been deep in shadow. In the glare Pamela looked small and rather sad. 'Yes, we haven't heard from Toby so I think we might as well just go ahead. Have you been having fun?' She twinkled from one to the other of us with forced brightness. 'I heard you up here in stitches a while ago, and I thought I'd leave you be.'

'What time was he supposed to come?' said Martin.

'Oh, well, he was very vague,' Pamela replied, studying her shoe. 'You know what he's like. He probably left it too late and then got stuck in traffic.'

'What about that pathetic telephone of his? No, he probably hasn't worked out how to use it.'

'Don't start, Martin,' said Pamela, the 'dangerous' edge to her voice. 'It could be broken, for all I know. He could have forgotten to bring it with him. He'll be here soon, anyway, I'm sure.'

A telephone rang faintly from behind her.

'Oh look, that's probably him now. Don't be long.'

She disappeared back down the corridor. I was glad that I was to be included at dinner, for lunch now seemed very far away, and my walk had made me hungry.

Chapter Fourteen

The garden was flooded in moonlight as I made my way back to the cottage later that evening. The moon was vast, pendulous and iridescent as a lamp above the cottage roof, so that it cast a silvery path for me all the way up the lawn. In spite of this, my footing was uncertain. The reason for this was that I was somewhat drunk, Mr Madden having been over-attentive to my glass during the course of a long and not altogether joyous evening. I have a weak head for alcohol, and had probably drunk more of it in the days since my arrival at Franchise Farm than during the entire month which preceded it. In addition, the increasing atmosphere of tension around the table as the prospect of Toby's arrival decamped from the imminent to the distinctly remote, gave the sanctuary of alcohol a temporary but inviting gleam. Pamela grew maudlin, Piers taciturn, and Martin unsettlingly knowing, casting lingering glances at me across the table, silent bulletins which were evidently designed to inform me that should I care to request them, new insights were available from their source into what I had told him earlier.

'I shouldn't think he'll come now,' said Pamela in the end, rising to her feet expectantly as if hoping that the very act of stating a certainty would immediately bring about its refutation.

'Probably not,' concurred Mr Madden, stubbornly lodged at the table amidst the wreckage of dinner.

'Oh, he *is* a wretch!' she cried; and I saw then that she was genuinely hurt, and was trying to disguise it with maternal exclamations of disapproval.

Intriguing as all this was, my eyes were closing; but now, staggering into the cottage and turning on the lights, I rather wished that I had stayed longer; for the cramped, empty sitting room, which admittedly I had done little to make more homely, seemed to look peevishly round as I entered, as if it had spent the evening entertaining a loneliness which I had been appointed to meet but had kept waiting for hours, tapping its fingers and getting in the way. I flung myself into the bony armchair with the cavalier but disturbing thought that I would welcome, were I to possess it, still more to drink. This, for me, was entirely out of character; but so committed did I become to the idea that I was driven to get up again and search the kitchen cupboards to see if a stray bottle lurked there. My compulsion did not strike me as depraved. Rather, I felt frustrated with my circumstances, that I was so ill-equipped as to lack the means of being sociable with myself. I sat for a while in a kind of stupor, unoccupied. Just as it seemed that no barrier remained between me and the misery which lay vertiginously below, I remembered that I could in fact go to bed. This I did, without pausing to do anything other than remove my clothes and fling them to the floor; and once there, I turned out the light immediately and closed my eyes. As soon as I did so, the room took an alarming swoop, as if I were in the hull of a ship. I opened my eyes again, perturbed, and saw the silvered silhouettes of furniture settle. Closing them again, the same thing happened. A feeling of nausea formed itself in my swilling stomach. My eyes grated open like rusty hinges; but I immediately felt so tired that I was forced to close them again.

How long this opening and closing went on for I do not know, but eventually I suppose I must have fallen asleep, for although when I opened my eyes again it was still dark, I could hear the shrill pulse of birdsong outside the window. My first thought on waking was that a foreign body had insinuated itself into my mouth. This proved, on investigation, to be nothing more than my own tongue, which had through dehydration formed a sort of crust which sat snug against my palate. My head, in addition, was clamped in a vice of pain; and I rose automatically from my bed in search of water. Down in the glare of the bathroom, I realized that I was naked; and further, that my body was covered once more in the white cross-hatchings that had tormented me during my first night in the country. All in all I made a pitiful figure; and this gave substance to the first real pang of longing for Edward that I had experienced. This longing was not predicated on the notion that he would have been particularly sympathetic to my plight; merely that he would not have allowed it to happen in the first place. Even that gives an impression of a solicitousness which I cannot in all honesty ascribe to our relationship. Really, the only reason why I even thought of Edward at that moment was because he would have been against my coming to the country at all; and that much only because coming to the country was irrational, and besides, involved going away from Edward.

Unfortunately, the thought of Edward, even in so restrained a context, brought with it the cargo of guilt and anxiety I had tried so hard to shed when I left the flat in London; and I stood in the bathroom for some time, feeling myself blocked by this invidious freight even from returning up the stairs to bed. You will think me very unfeeling when I say that by far the greater part of this consignment of shame concerned money. Everything else relating to the appalling injuries I had inflicted on those closest to me I felt to be in some sense protean; or at least malleable, and tolerant of many different shades of thought. There were times, for example, when I could regard my desertion of Edward with a kind of mournful equanimity, the disappointing of my parents with grudging acceptance; but money never changed. It was as high and hard and intransigent as a wall, and I knew that I could never get over it. So much money had been spent, and it would never be recouped. *So much money*. One doesn't recover from that sort of thing. I knew, standing there in the bathroom, that I wanted to have nothing more to do with money for the rest of my life. Of course, I had felt this subliminally for some time; it was one of the reasons behind my coming to the country in the way that I had. But standing there I *knew* it, as I had known few things before.

Finally I went back to bed, where I slept fitfully until it was light. Whatever cream it was that the creature had applied to my sunburn had worked wonders, for when I got up and looked in the wardrobe mirror I saw that the colour of my skin had completely altered from emergency red to an attractive brown. I had expected, at least, that the mirror would give back a true picture of the previous night's excesses; but the glaze of good health disguised whatever ravages lurked beneath. As before, the strange night rash had left no trace, and I wondered fruitlessly what could be causing it. By this time it was well past eight o'clock, and having no time for a wardrobe debacle I merely picked up the previous day's clothes from the floor and put them on. Downstairs in the bathroom I splashed my face with water, cleaned my teeth and quickly combed my hair. I had time to scrape at the tar on my shoes with a knife, and succeeded in removing the worst of it.

Outside the morning was still gentle with infancy, but behind the dewy innocence of the sky lurked the menace of maturity, and I knew that another day of cruel, triumphal heat lay ahead. I was growing very tired of the sun, and wondered what meteorological force would be strong enough to unseat it; for as yet I had not seen even a lone cloud brave enough to challenge it. I was glad, at least, that my skin no longer singled me out as its victim; indeed, I felt that my tan represented a clear progression in the matter of my aptitude for the country life. With this new armour I might find the courage to confront those problems which remained, being: the issue of driving, although this, it now being Tuesday, was demoted towards the bottom of my immediate agenda; the mysteries pertaining to my encounter with the creature, in which category I placed the 'lovers' tiff' and the cryptic conversation I had overheard between the Maddens in the kitchen; the problem of food, and hence money, which, being relatively straightforward, I resolved to settle before the day was over; and the matter of my conversation with Martin, which had permitted my personal life to escape from its quarantine. I was pleased, at least, to be able to recall that my dealings with Pamela – a subject to which only the day before I would have accorded sovereignty among my problems – were showing distinct signs of improvement; that my sunburn had been cured; and that by scavenging at the Maddens' table so frequently, I had survived my first three days in the country at very little expense to myself.

As on the previous day, the door to the back passage stood open; and entering the corridor I remembered my confrontation with Mrs Barker. Not wishing to repeat it I resolved this time to go and wait in the kitchen until Pamela should appear. Opening the door, I had expected to find Mrs Barker in office, and was surprised instead to see a young man sitting at the table reading a newspaper. His businesslike demeanour gave me the idea at first that he was an associate of Mr Madden's, perhaps Trimmer the manager, but the fact that he was wearing a red silk dressing gown sat strangely with this notion; and I soon realized that this must be the errant Toby, arrived last night – unless he had for some reason travelled in this apparel – after all.

'Hello,' I said, for he hadn't seemed to notice that I had entered the room.

Even after my salutation, he took his time to acknowledge me, and as his eyes taxied slowly off the page in front of him I realized that he had waited to finish whatever it was he had been reading before brooking my interruption.

'Hel-*lo*,' he said presently, having conducted a lightning – but apparently thorough – survey of my appearance. 'You must be Stella.'

He said this as if his deduction came not from the common pool of information but was the fruit of a rarefied and entirely private process of calculation. He pronounced my name with relish and clearly hoped to have some effect by doing so. It required little more to put me on my guard against him; but the insinuating smile he dispatched across the room after it, a gesture as full of the consciousness of his own bounty in doing so as if he had been tossing a jewel or banknote at my feet, cemented my disdain. My dislike of Toby was not, although it may seem so, the work of preconception. I consider myself a fair judge of character, and was not merely acting out of blind obedience to the many factors which insisted that I form an automatic prejudice against him – his depraved treatment of Roy, whose absence from the kitchen was conspicuous; his disregard for his mother's feelings; his own brother's contempt. The truth was that when I entered the kitchen and saw him sitting there, my heart swooned in my chest; for I had never seen such an attractive human being, male or female. It is curious, I suppose, that my reaction to the sight of him should have been so visceral. I didn't 'recognize' him, in the way I described some time ago in relation to Pamela. He might, in fact, have belonged to a different species from my own, so unrelated was his appearance to mine. In these circumstances it is normal to feel an appreciation that is more cultural, as it were, than sexual; a refined, abstract response to beauty, without the hope and hunger which are the features of attraction. My only explanation for this diversion from the norm is that it seemed to have more to do with Toby himself than with me: he radiated concupiscence, and I felt sure that anyone in his region would feel the heat of it, whether they liked it or not.

'I was looking for Mrs Madden,' I said awkwardly; and was rewarded, to my shame, with another smile which clearly communicated to me the fact that he had found as much in my charmless remark to flatter him as if I had flung myself at his feet.

'Ah,' he said.

'Perhaps I should go and look for her,' I continued, when it became evident that he was to say nothing else. There are certain people in whose presence one's own becomes so secondary, so crude, that it seems to require justification. Toby was one of those people. He merely arched his eyebrows at this piece of self-commentary; and with the last precious thread of my novelty snipped, I was powerless to prevent myself from providing him with another. 'Or perhaps,' I trailed miserably on, 'I should just wait here.'

He gave an elegant shrug and his blue eyes hovered above his still spreadeagled newspaper as if on the brink of flight. Were I not to do anything interesting within the next few minutes, this glance informed me, his attention – on which precious commodity a meter appeared to be ticking – would have to be withdrawn.

'You're over in the cottage, aren't you?' he said then, as if my tenancy at least conferred on me a grain of fascination. Something in the way he said it informed me that the cottage bore some special significance for him. I remembered his mention of the name Colette during our telephone conversation, and his mention too of her unexpected dismissal. Unfortunately, I was reminded almost in the same instant of the conversation I had subsequently overheard, in which Pamela had confidently claimed that I was not Toby's 'type'. I felt disproportionately injured by this recollection, and experienced a dangerous desire to disprove it.

'Yes,' I said. 'It's a wonderful place.'

'Isn't it?' He smiled, this time to himself. 'Yes, you're quite tucked away there. I *might*' – he appeared to be dragging this concession reluctantly from the very pit of his stomach – 'I *might* wander over there a bit later, just to take a look at the old place.'

I had no idea whether my presence was a desirable or even necessary feature of this excursion. Fortunately, before this spark of ambiguity could set my thoughts aflame, the door opened behind me and Pamela's quenching presence flooded the room.

'Morning!' she cried, coming through the door with such speed that she was halfway across the kitchen before she ground to a halt. The refulgence of the previous day had, I soon saw, returned; but I sensed something darker beneath it, something secretive and puffy in Pamela's face which I could not explain, but which gave me the distinct impression that she had altered; as if some internal compass had twitched and thrown her off course.

'Morning,' drawled Toby, rustling his newspaper.

He was smiling beneath his hooded eyes, a smile of complicity meant, I saw, for Pamela. She put her hand on his shoulder, which was as finely turned as a banister.

'Coffee?' she said.

'Please,' acceded Toby, his gaze not flickering from the page. Pamela stood for a moment and read over his shoulder, a gesture the least part of whose motivation, I felt sure, was an interest in current affairs. Their bodies were very close, curled like parentheses around some shared but inadmissible aside. My intrusion on this intimate scene was becoming unbearable. Toby's smile was broadening as Pamela stood there behind him, and as if his mirth had insinuated itself up her connecting arm, she too began to smile. Before long, to my bewilderment, the two of them were shaking with silent, private mirth.

'Is Martin upstairs?' I enquired in a clear voice.

'What?' Pamela turned and looked at me, bleary with interruption, her eyes triumphant and annoyed. For a moment, she didn't seem to recognize me. 'Oh, Stella, I *am* sorry!' she said then, after a pause. 'Yes, you'll find him upstairs in his room.'

'Thank you,' I curtly replied.

I walked smartly from the room and closed the door behind me; and as I stood in the dark ante-room was mortified to hear the muted sound of twin laughters burst forth from the other side. My thoughts were so racked with confusion and fury that it was not until I had slammed my way from the cramped vestibule that I was able to give substance to them; but in the empty, polished vault of the vast hall I knew that what I had just seen was not the morning reunion of mother and son, but that of *lovers*. I was astonished, and rather ashamed, at the boldness and vulgarity of my deduction; and yet I knew that I had hacked with this single crude thought right to the heart of the matter. This, I might say, was for me a most unusual experience. I am habitually a person in whose thoughts the insignificant looms large, while the vast and more perilous range of realities forms a dramatic but distant vista, a long and tortuous journey away. I had never even encountered in my life a situation which might have beaten a path to this particular suspicion, nor was I subject in so far as I knew to any tendency – over-imaginativeness, for example – which might have eased its passage. No, the thought was merely a response to what I had seen, and once established it formed a magnet for other things, which adhered themselves to it and gave it weight. Pamela's distracted behaviour the previous evening; her uncontainable disappointment at Toby's lateness; her failure, earlier, to tell him the news of Caroline's pregnancy; even her generally neurotic and overcharged demeanour, her drastic changes of mood, those irrational episodes in which I myself had played a reluctant part: the enormity of the accusation seemed capable of containing all this and more.

Within minutes, however, my exhilarating descent into moral turpitude had come to an abrupt halt. What was I thinking of, harbouring such horrible notions about people who, if occasionally maddening and often incomprehensible to me, were nevertheless decent? I lingered at the foot of the staircase, and in the prospect of its arduous slope saw the long and wearying climb back to reason which was the price of my brief but thrilling speculations. I tried as I slowly ascended the stairs to remember the details of my own mother's behaviour towards my brothers, in the penitent hope that it might mitigate Pamela's. There was certainly nothing of the kind between Edward and his mother either; but then, uncharitably I'll admit, I was unsure whether there was anything of the kind between Edward and anybody. If only in the name of justice, there should surely have been some similar bond between fathers and daughters; but other than Bounder's correspondence – which, if it signalled some special fondness, went both unappreciated and unreturned – I could think of nothing which distinguished my father's treatment of me from that he gave my brothers. I regretted, nevertheless, that I had not treasured these tokens more. Their expulsion to the tundra of London's waste-disposal system filled me both with retrospective guilt and with frustration at the impossibility of scanning them anew for evidence.

I had, at this point, reached the top of the stairs; and remembering that Martin was waiting for me, hurried the final distance along the corridor to his room. His door stood open, and through it I could see him sitting in his chair by the window. He was staring through the glass in deep thought. Seeing him thus, I was struck by how little I knew of his unattended life. The business of looking after him, the work of acquiring familiarity with his needs, permitted the other side of his nature to fall into neglect. I realized – although this may seem obvious – that what to me was employment was life to him; something which in other centuries or places was, I am sure, the grounds for envy and resentment, but here was the cause of feelings of personal good fortune.

'Where have you been, Stel-la?' he said when I presented myself. He was wearing a red T-shirt which drained his skin of colour. 'I've been waiting for you.'

'Sorry,' I said. 'I was in the kitchen. I thought I ought to wait for your mother before I came up.'

'Why?' He screwed up his face.

'It – I don't know. It didn't seem polite just to march through the house.'

'You're so funny.' He paused, as if concentrating. 'On the one hand' – he measured it mathematically with his hand – 'you've got the guts to leave your husband, abandoning everything you know and casting yourself on the kindness of strangers. And on the other, you're scared of coming into someone else's house, even if they're expecting you.'

'I thought,' I said in a steely tone, 'that we had agreed not to discuss that matter any further. As for the business of coming into the house, I did not say that I was scared; merely that I thought it polite to alert your mother to my presence, in case I interrupted something private.'

Given what I had just seen in the kitchen, I didn't have the impression that Pamela was particularly concerned about guarding her own privacy; nor, if I were honest, that she thought my presence important enough to want to conceal things in it.

'We didn't agree not to discuss it,' said Martin. 'I just promised not to tell anyone else about it.' His hands fiddled in his lap and he looked at them sulkily. 'Anyone would think you didn't trust me, Stel-la.'

'I don't trust you,' I said, crossing the room and sitting down in the leather armchair. The sun from the window fell directly on it, and an ache sprung up immediately across my forehead. 'I don't know you well enough to trust you.' This sounded unkind. 'Although I'm sure I will,' I added wearily, 'eventually.'

I was feeling rather unwell, having had no breakfast. Pamela's failure to offer me coffee grated on my memory.

'You look tired,' said Martin sweetly. 'Would you like some coffee?'

'Yes,' I automatically replied. Seconds later I remembered that a trip downstairs would necessitate a further confrontation with the love-birds. 'No, it's too much bother.'

'It isn't. I've got everything up here. I've got biscuits,' he said, leaning forward and whispering the word seductively in my ear, 'which might tempt you.'

I had a strong feeling that I was about to be blackmailed. Unfortunately, so importunate were my hunger and thirst that I was obliged to accept Martin's offer.

'OK,' I grudgingly acceded.

'One lump or two, Stel-la?' said Martin, launching himself off across the room. I saw his pumping arms below his T-shirt as he passed; thin, articulated by muscle, like animals' limbs.

'None.' He reached a cupboard with a slatted door, and when he opened it I saw a neat, minuscule arrangement of sink, fridge and kettle. 'You've got everything!' I exclaimed, surprised.

'Well, I can't go downstairs, silly Stel-la, every time I want something,' he said, in an amplified version of his pantomime whisper. 'Can I? I'd have no *independence.* Would I?'

'I suppose not.'

'You should *think*' – he tapped his forehead exaggeratedly – 'about what it's like to be *me.* No *fun*, Stel-la. No fun at *all.* Nothing to *think*' – again the tapping – 'about except my little *Stel-la* and her *secrets*—'

'Stop that instantly,' I said, sitting up in my chair.

Martin gave a high-pitched giggle and began filling the kettle at the sink.

'I was only joking,' he said, in a more normal voice. 'It's for your own good, Stel-la. It's bad for you to bottle everything up. You'll get cancer.'

'If I get cancer,' I replied, 'it won't be because I have refused to sate your curiosity about my private life. In any case, that was a very tactless thing to say. How do you know my parents didn't die of cancer?'

'Sorry.'

'In fact,' I continued, rather unworthily determining to get my own back on him, 'I was going to tell you a bit more about it. But now that you've said that, I've changed my mind.'

'Oh, *Stel-la*!' Martin wheeled round in his chair, his mouth opened wide in astonishment. 'You can't do that!'

'I can.' The pregnant, silent kettle began to stir behind him. 'You must think me very stupid if you doubt that I can beat you at your own game. And a very silly game it is too, I might say.'

Martin ducked his head and began busying himself with cups.

'You should know by now,' I continued, 'that the best way to find things out is to listen. If people feel they are being tricked or interrogated, they won't tell you anything. If you give them time and silence, they'll come out with it eventually. Either because they're embarrassed or because they're offended at your lack of interest. Most people are fairly selfish. They like to talk about themselves. And the more invisible you are, the more they'll do it.'

The click of the kettle punctuated this soliloquy. Martin said nothing more, although for a while I barely noticed this above the clatter of his preparations. When finally he had loaded everything onto a tray, however, and was bearing it back across the room in his lap, I saw from the compressed seam of his mouth and his too-nonchalant expression that he was implementing my policy in a manner which could soon become infuriating.

'It doesn't work if you make it that obvious,' I remarked. He handed me a cup, and with the other proffered a plate of biscuits. I glimpsed his imploring eyes. 'What on earth could you want to know?' I said. 'It can't be that interesting.'

He nodded energetically. I took one of the biscuits. I was rather impressed by Martin's hospitality. It was, I had to admit, more pleasant being in his room than in any other room in the house. I shifted around slightly so that I was out of the sun and raised the biscuit to my mouth. As I did so, I caught Martin's eye. He was watching me so intently that it was impossible for me to eat it. Instead I took a sip of coffee. He tipped his head back slightly, miming my action, and swallowed air.

'What?' I said finally, in exasperation. He shook his head mutely. 'I met your brother just now,' I continued conversationally, in the hope that it would jolt him from this irritating course. 'In the kitchen.'

'The *kitchen*?' mouthed Martin silently, raising his eyebrows in mockery and putting a fluttering hand to his lips.

'If you don't desist from this unreasonable behaviour, I am going to leave you to do your homework.'

There was a long pause, during which I could not restrain myself from putting the biscuit in my mouth and chewing it as unobtrusively as I was able. Its sweetness was unimaginable, delicious.

'What did you think of him, then?' enquired Martin eventually. His face was sullen. 'Did you *fancy* him? Everybody *fancies* him.'

'He is very handsome.'

'More handsome than *Edward*?'

'Yes.'

'Girls are so stupid.'

'I was merely stating a fact.'

'Did he try and *get off* with you?'

'Oh, for goodness' sake! Of course he didn't. Anyway,' I added incautiously, 'I'm not his type.'

'How do you know?'

'I just do.'

'Was *Edward* your type?'

I saw instantly Martin's latest tactic, which was to lead me by a ladder of association to the precipice of self-revelation.

'I suppose he must have been. I don't know.'

'You're my type,' he said then, sitting back firmly in his chair and folding his arms.

'Don't be silly.'

'It's true! What's wrong with me, anyway?'

'You're too young.' I wondered what this self-deluding boldness signified. 'And besides, I work for you. This kind of conversation is inappropriate.'

'I think it's romantic,' said Martin dreamily. 'So what was wrong with Edward? You're very fussy, Stel-la.'

'If I was fussy I wouldn't have married him,' I said smartly, before I could stop myself.

'That's not very nice.'

'Sorry. I didn't mean it like that. He had – he had many good qualities.'

'Like what?'

'Well, he was clever.' I tried to think of something else to say about him. 'He was pleased with himself, I suppose. Yes, that probably describes him best.'

'Were you *in love* with him? I can't imagine you *in love*.'

'I don't see why not,' I crossly replied. I was troubled by this remark, coming as it did so close to what I had often suspected was the truth. 'Anyway, you've asked me that before. I don't know what love means. If it's just a feeling, then it can stop. I don't see the point of trying so hard to preserve it.'

There was a pause. I knew that Martin was looking at me, although I didn't meet his eye. I was beginning to feel rather upset, and sensed strongly that I should bring a stop to the conversation.

'So why did you marry him?'

'I made a mistake.'

'That's a pretty big mistake, Stel-la.'

'I know.'

'How long?'

'How long what?'

'How long were you married?'

I trembled on the brink of surrendering this final piece of information; for I feared what would happen when the slope of Martin's curiosity came to an end. What I was handing over to him was of so much more worth to me than to he himself; and while I could neither decipher nor control the impulse that had made me do so, still I flinched from the possibility that he was, after all, unworthy of my confidence, and that the very part of me which had most sought release would be the part most injured by it. Any form of confession, I now realize, is a process beset by this type of risk. Even when one's secrets are as besieged as mine were by Martin, the act of divulging them is by necessity selfish, and by implication weak. Revelation requires consent, in however disguised a form; and as such there is no case in which the confessional act can be free from retribution or blame.

'A week,' I said.

The starkness of my admission was mitigated somewhat by the fact that Martin did not spring back in triumph or horror at it. I half expected him to burst out laughing as he had done the last time we had discussed this subject, while fearing that he would be shocked and disappointed, and would judge me harshly. He looked surprised, certainly; his expressive, malleable face could not disguise it.

'What happened?'

'Oh, I don't know.' I looked out of the window, embarrassed. 'I just had to get away. I felt as if I was dying.' This seemed rather melodramatic, even in my turbulent state. 'I expected, I suppose, to feel as if my life had begun,' I qualified. 'And instead I knew it had ended. It was as if we'd been tricked and only found out afterwards, when it was too late. That we'd thought, you know, that getting married meant one thing and in fact it meant another. It felt as if we'd been disabled, and that even though the rest of life was ruined we had each other, and couldn't get away from each other, and even if we did we'd still be disabled.' There was a pause. 'Sorry. I didn't mean it like that. Anyway, we were on honeymoon, and I just came home. I tried to tell Edward, but he didn't really understand. And then various things happened, and then I left.'

'On your own?'

'Yes.'

'But what did he say when he got back?' He leaned closer to me and I glimpsed his eyes, shining and perplexed. 'Was he angry?'

'I don't know. Probably. I mean, I didn't talk to him. I haven't seen him since then.'

I felt the tremor of something precarious between us, and knew that our fragile acquaintance was being overloaded with information. My own discomfort with the facts I was relating had undoubtedly contributed to this atmosphere of strain; for had I known them better, or even shared them previously with someone else, I might have worn them more easily. As it was I could make no more sense of my own actions than Martin evidently could.

'Was this – recent?' he said, slightly awkwardly.

'Just before I came here. Last week.'

To my surprise, I felt a furtive pressure on my hand. I looked down and realized that Martin had taken it in his own.

'Poor Stella,' he said.

I cannot explain why the feeling of human flesh was so unbearable to me in that moment. It was not, I think, embarrassment that caused me to recoil, nor distaste at the pity the gesture conveyed. Rather, it was the loneliness it underscored, the reminder it provided that while I might have found a temporary palliative in company, my unhappiness was my own. Up until that point I had not had an urgent sense of this fact. By keeping myself in a form of oblivion, I had certainly, as Martin pointed out, 'bottled things up'; but while my problems lay beneath this anaesthetic, I had at least had the advantage of not feeling them. Now, as they awoke and unfurled themselves, they sent out latent shafts of pain, on which the presence of Martin's hand seemed to be acting as a conductor. I willed myself to keep it there, knowing that I would offend him if I flinched; and yet it was as if I were asking myself to keep my hand in an electric socket.

'Please!' I cried eventually, freeing myself from his grasp. I saw him look at me for a moment in horror, as the quiet room echoed with the violence of this action. His rejected hand hung, half-withdrawn, in the air. His face was startled. 'Don't ask me any more! I just don't want to think about it!' I said, rather too furiously; I thought that my physical reaction would be less conspicuous if backed up by an equally extreme verbal one. 'Do you understand?'

I must admit that he was very good about it. If he was hurt, he barely showed it, and shortly afterwards we went out to sit in the garden.

Chapter Fifteen

We established ourselves beneath a phalanx of trees towards the bottom of the garden, which sent down the occasional light hail of fragrant missiles from the branches above, and in the rustling, deciduous shade I felt an exquisite languor; a sense of almost *historical* leisure which belonged, I knew, not to me but to the house itself. Martin had brought with him some schoolwork, a battered volume across whose yellowed pages moved a miniature army of arcane symbols; manoeuvres which he appeared to be interpreting with a pencil stub on a pad of white paper in his lap.

'What's that?' I said oafishly, raising myself up on my elbow; for I had assumed a shamelessly horizontal position on the warm grass and had been staring up at the fluttering tracery of leaves against the brilliant blue sky with a mind as scrubbed of thought as a bone.

'Greek. Translation.'

'Oh. Is it difficult?'

'Quite. I suppose I could cheat. Everybody else does. I like it, though.'

'What's your school like?'

'It's OK.' A breeze ruffled the pages of his book and he

clamped his hand over it. His face was secretive, shifty. 'It's normal, I suppose. Better than the centre, anyhow.'

'Is it a boarding school?'

'Mostly. There's a few like me. Day bugs, that is. They're all complete pillocks. The parentals wanted me to board, but it was too difficult.'

I tried to imagine him in a classroom, amidst the riotous, scruffy jumble of his peers. I knew these boys from my brothers' childhood, their fluting, patrician voices, their faces hewn of stone above the regulation *déshabillé* of their uniforms; all that casual, careless perfection incubating in the draughty chambers of a dream.

'Why did they want you to board?'

'Dunno.' He shrugged. 'Family stuff. We always have. And the journey's a pain, I suppose.'

'How long does it take?'

'Hour and a half each way.'

'But that's ridiculous!'

'What's the alternative? They didn't want to send me anywhere else. It isn't for much longer, anyhow. This'll be my last year. And besides, there'd have been no point moving me. They'd already paid for all the facilities and stuff.'

'What facilities?'

'You know, cripple stuff. Ramps and things.'

'Your parents *paid* for them?'

'Yup.' He nodded. 'And a swimming pool. That was a kind of present for the school. Well, it was more of a bribe, actually. They'll take all the other stuff down once I'm gone.'

'Why?'

'Spoils the look of the school. It's crap anyway. Just tacky crap.'

'What if someone else wanted to use it, though?'

'Like who?' He looked at me with adolescent contempt. 'To be quite frank, I don't think you'd find another set of parents prepared to send someone like me to a school like that.'

I remembered my parents' own inexplicable determination to send my partly deaf young brother to one of these privative institutions. In the spirit of refutation, I considered sharing this coincidence with Martin, but having already revealed so much about myself had no more appetite for confidences.

'So why did they?'

'I told you. We always have. The dogfucker. Grumps. Great-Grumps. Everyone.'

He didn't seem particularly put out by the presence of these corroded manacles around the tender, fleeting flesh of his own life. I realized then that, rather than resent his parents' decision, he was grateful for it. At times like these I felt our differences so strongly that our moments of intimacy receded, their once-pungent reality framed and reduced, like holiday photographs.

'I hated school,' I said, collapsing my elbow beneath me so that I lay once more on my back.

'You hate everything.'

I found this comment excessively spiteful, particularly given that I had provoked it with an observation more passing than pointed; and one, too, which deserved if not sympathy then at least the lesser balm of politeness. I sensed in this bitterness the residue of our earlier conversation, which Martin's sensibility had evidently been too undeveloped fully to digest. I wondered whether perhaps he was offended that I had come to him on the hoof, as it were, a fugitive from larger dilemmas in whose shade he was inevitably dwarfed; or whether, more realistically, he was still sore at my rejection of his comforting hand, a gesture which can't have been easy for a boy of his age to make, and which I had rewarded with a reaction indistinguishable from revulsion. I searched, in any case, for some grounds on which to disagree with him, and to my perturbation was unable instantly to find any. As seemed to have become my habit, the longer I delayed making any answer the less I could seem to separate Martin's accusation from the truth; and by the time I had thought through the reasons for his disaffection with me, the two had become inextricably melded. Was it true that I hated everything? It was certainly the case that I could think of little immediately that I loved; but it was for this very reason, I reminded myself, that I had sought to change my circumstances so dramatically. What I had said to Martin about feeling that I had, after my marriage, reached the end of my life was more or less true. Having up until that moment believed that I had hardly begun it, this was quite a leap. What I felt, more exactly, was that I had missed the substance, the filling between these two states, which I felt sure would have contained the meat of love; indeed, the essence of life itself.

I made, then, no reply to Martin as we sat there beneath the trees; and as he had during my silence turned unhappily back to his book, we were stranded far from conversation for some time, before an indistinct shout from the house caused us both to turn.

'Lunch,' said Martin decisively, slamming his book shut, although I had been able to make no sense of the sound.

I was grateful for the distraction; and grateful too for the work of pushing Martin back up the lawn to the house, which gave our relationship a clarity our conversations frequently lacked. The heat was very fierce as we made our way over the long, striped perspective of the grass, but although I soon felt the familiar grind of it on the top of my head, it no longer had the character of an assault. Indeed, I felt almost flippant at the speed with which I had adapted to this new element, and walked through it as proudly as if I had sprouted gills or grown wings. Ahead of us I could see the dormant arrangement of garden furniture being activated by Mr Madden, who went about the business of removing the chairs from where they lay doubled up over the table top and setting them in an orderly circle with the bored efficiency of a factory assembly line worker. His demeanour was not particularly abject, and yet I found myself wondering as I watched him whether he was happy. Seeing him so obedient in solitude, I had the sense that he was waiting for something, or even waiting something out, although I had no idea what it could be. Mr Madden possessed all the attributes of what could reasonably be described as a happy life – but in that moment I had a flash of identification with him which informed me, in the vaguest possible sense, that like me he did not feel entirely at home here.

Pamela and Toby came jauntily around the side of the house, arm in arm, and when Mr Madden hoisted the umbrella from the centre of the table they quickly took their seats, as if at any moment it might start to revolve like a propeller and lift the whole arrangement into the air. Seconds later we reached the table, and after I had slotted Martin's chair into position I looked up to find Toby's eyes on me.

'You're sweating,' he said, as intimately as if we had been alone; or as if some circuit had already been established between us along which such currents of significance could now flow.

'I'm hot,' I said, not wanting the others to think me rude, although the remark had not seemed to me worth dignifying with a reply.

I was in fact sweating quite profusely, despite my earlier feelings of acclimatization; and I was far from grateful to Toby for pointing this out. There are some men, I have noticed, who are driven continually to make observations of this type; who appear to see no reason why what enters their head should not exit from their mouth.

'Say hello to your brother, you scallywag,' said Pamela to Martin, leaning across the table awkwardly so as to jollify the remark further by ruffling his hair. Martin flinched at the gesture, screwing up his face with a child's distaste.

'Hello, bro,' he said dully.

'Wotcha, Mart-hole,' Toby replied, with a fluting attempt at an accent.

'Why on earth do you call him that?' tinkled Pamela, looking from one to the other of them with charming bewilderment. She was wearing a blue sleeveless dress made of silk, and blue earrings. Her shoulders looked very narrow, and her bare arms brown and taut. The impression was one of doll-like fragility; and she was emanating it so indiscriminately that even I felt tempted to place a protective arm around her tender frame.

'Because he thinks it's *funny*,' said Martin in a loud voice.

'But what does it mean?' persisted Pamela naively. 'It sounds rather rude.'

Toby did not reply, but sat motionless in his chair as if in a trance. The pause dampened conversation, and gradually our attention was drawn to him as his startled blue eyes gazed at some distant vista.

'It *is* rude,' he said finally, as if in wonder. 'It's very, *very* naughty!'

At this he suddenly lunged sideways in his chair with a shout and flung his arms around Pamela, who shrieked with delight as he began to tickle her. I was extremely embarrassed at the spectacle of Pamela writhing in her chair; and more so when Toby's fine, excitable hands found the fleshy tops of her bare arms and began to squeeze them energetically. 'Woah! Woah!' he crowed as he squeezed, an unsettling imitation of a teenaged boy let loose for the first time on the female form.

'Stop! Stop!' cried Pamela.

I stole a glance at Martin, confidently expecting him to be telegraphing his contempt, and was surprised to see him giggling in quiet volleys as he watched them.

'Toby, sir!'

The curious exclamation caused us all to jump; but it was not until I had looked up that I realized it was Mr Madden who had pronounced it. I had never heard him speak with such force, and his face as he towered over the table was plump and red with compressed fury. He had a bottle of wine in one hand, and a wooden board with bread on it in the other.

'*Darling!*' said Pamela coaxingly, laying a hand on his arm. 'It was only a bit of fun!'

Toby was looking up at his father pugnaciously, his chin jutting out.

'He's too old for that sort of thing,' said Mr Madden, ignoring Pamela's intervention just as his arm ignored the presence of her hand.

'And what sort of thing might that be?' said Toby coolly.

'Rough-housing. Playing with your mother. Not in my house, sir.'

Toby sniggered; but despite the admittedly comical sound of the words, he did not have the courage to dispute them. There was a long and awkward silence, during which Mr Madden put the bread and wine on the table, his eyes downcast. He appeared to have forgotten about the incident, but then Toby did a curious thing: he yawned, noisily and provocatively. Mr Madden's head snapped up so suddenly that his black hair flew skywards and I saw that his face had darkened to a violent purple.

'Young man!' he said, lunging over the table and banging his hand hard beside Toby's place to punctuate the words. Everything on the table clattered and shook. Toby drew back in fear. 'Don't imagine that I'm not still capable of taking you out onto the drive and giving you a bloody good hiding! I wouldn't think twice about packing you back off to London, but your mother wants you here. I'd advise you to keep your mouth shut and your hands to yourself so long as you're at my table!'

'Piers, please!' said Pamela weakly. I was surprised to see that she appeared to be as frightened as everybody else.

'I won't have it,' said Mr Madden gruffly, straightening himself up. 'Bloody layabout cheeking me at my own table.'

Mr Madden's table, despite the passionate references it was drawing, was in disarray. The salt cellar lay on its side, disgorging grains. The bread had jumped off its board. Knives and forks, meticulously laid, now formed exclamatory symbols on the tablecloth. I glanced at Toby. A distinct blush stained the expression of scornful superiority he had assumed. I was surprised that he had submitted to his father's authority by remaining at the table. I would, in his position, have absented myself, whether for reasons of fury or dignity. I suspected that it was not fear that kept him tethered to his seat, but laziness. He liked being here, that much was obvious. Indeed, he was the sort of person I could not imagine being anywhere that he did not like; which made his acceptance of his recent humiliation even more perplexing. Looking at him, it suddenly struck me that his parents' munificence, the splendour of their lifestyle, had perhaps cultivated in him an opportunistically tolerant attitude to their company. This notion was utterly alien to me, given that any encounter with my own parents was always accompanied by the necessity for enduring the range of their peculiarities, whether at home or outside it. Going home had always been a trial, the reward for which had been that in the moment of leaving I occupied the point furthest in time from the next occasion on which I would have to return.

Still, I was at a loss as to Mr Madden's reasons for behaving as he had done. I glanced at him repeatedly while we ate, in a near silence punctuated only by a sparse conversation between him and Pamela about affairs at the farm. The colour gradually subsided from his cheeks. He neither spoke to nor looked at his elder son. The first thing which intrigued me was how he felt about the fact that Pamela had so obviously sided with Toby. The second was why, at this late stage in Toby's development, Mr Madden should feel so disturbed by his behaviour with his own mother. If Toby had always behaved like this, why had something not been done about it before? If not, why had Pamela and indeed Martin not reacted to it with more surprise? It had seemed, from my perspective, quite natural to all of them. Had Mr Madden never seen anything of the sort before?

The speed of his response to it suggested that he had. Was I to conclude, then, that Mr Madden's objection was part of an ongoing and unheeded protest against Toby's behaviour with

Pamela, and perhaps Toby in general? It was evident to me that in some terrible, unguessable way, Mr Madden disliked his own son. Why?

'Oh, this heat!' said Pamela, pushing away her plate and leaning back in her chair so that her face protruded beyond the rim of shade cast by the umbrella. 'It's simply *glorious*. I shall be flat on my back by the pool all afternoon. How about you boys?'

'I'm in,' said Toby.

'Darling?' Pamela turned to Mr Madden. 'Why don't you just take the afternoon off? You're absolutely exhausted. It would do you good to put your feet up by the pool for a bit.'

'Hmph,' said Mr Madden.

'Go on, why don't you? The boys would love it. I feel like we haven't spent enough time together as a *family*. If Toby will put the hoops up, we could even have a spot of croquet! Stella?' Pamela's gaze fell uninvitingly on me. 'What are your plans?'

'I thought I might go for a walk,' I improvised, as it was clear that the poolside idyll did not include me. I was aggrieved by this, as I was longing to swim; but I could see that after their earlier contretemps, the family might require some time alone to regroup.

'How *lovely*,' said Pamela approvingly. 'Look, why don't you just shoot off? We can manage the clearing up.'

Summarily dismissed, I rose from my seat.

'I'll see you later,' I said to Martin; although when he did not look at me, I glanced more generally at the others, as if my farewell had been directed at them.

I walked quickly away from the table and across the lawn. So awkwardly did I feel myself to be moving that I almost expected to hear laughter ring out behind me. Once I had made it to the shaded gravel path to the side of the house I slowed down. I felt immediately the relief of being on my own. The strain of being always in the company of people – and their numbers seemed daily to be increasing – whose connection to each other was as profound as their relation to me was tenuous, was greater than I had anticipated. I had imagined, when I had first considered the idea of appending myself to a family, that the organism's self-sufficiency would ensure my own liberty; that being by its very nature exclusive, I would naturally be disqualified from the politics into which I would ultimately and inevitably have been drawn by any other social grouping. It surprised me to realize that the Maddens, contrary to what I had expected, seemed if not to require then at least to have uses for the presence of a third party. It was not that they were 'showing off' in front of me – most of the time, in fact, I felt as if they had forgotten I was there; rather that by providing the necessary opposition to their congruity, by marking so clearly the place where they ended and all else began, I was giving it shape and purpose.

I remembered my father once accusing my mother of not being *proud* of us, her family. He longed, I believe, for us to have a *story*, if that doesn't sound too obscure; and thought that my mother's persistent practicality was the thing stopping us from doing so. She wouldn't have believed it herself, was the inference. Admittedly we weren't much good with strangers. We grew tongue-tied and deflated, while my father tried to coax us into the air like recalcitrant soufflés. By the time our troupe was one member down, my father had his story, although it certainly wasn't the kind of story he'd had in mind; and I dare say my mother secretly wished that she'd gone along with it all while there was still time, so that she'd have had something to repeat to herself after it had all got so quiet.

I reached the fork in the path that led to the cottage and stopped, realizing that in spite of my relief at having been liberated from the society of the back lawn, in fact I had little idea of what I wanted to do. Bearing right I would reach the gate to the front drive. Although I was familiar with the route which led from there to the big house, I had little notion of what would happen if one went in the opposite direction. I decided to investigate; and if in the course of my journey I came across the 'top field' I could perhaps satisfy my curiosity over the conversation I had overheard between the Maddens the previous afternoon.

I set off to the left of the gate and within a few paces had left behind the gravelled area, which gave on to a corridor of rough, loosely cropped grass. To either side were tall hedges, the left flank of which, I calculated, formed the boundary of the cottage garden. Directly ahead, at the end of this corridor, the land seemed to give away, and I felt a looming spaciousness which suggested I might soon arrive at open farmland. I had little idea of how the grounds of Franchise fitted into the larger puzzle of the surrounding countryside. The windows of the cottage looked out only onto various manicured aspects of the garden, and even from the upstairs rooms of the big house I could remember seeing little more. The property appeared to be almost entirely screened from what lay outside it by clever arrangements of trees and hedges; which, although they certainly ensured privacy from it, meant that one had little idea of what might be going on in the world beyond.

I progressed along the corridor, the longer grass cool in the shade beneath my feet. Small birds landed ahead of me and then sprang away as I approached, vanishing, garbled ribbons of song trailing behind them. I went on like this for some fifty paces, the gloom appearing to deepen all the way, until I came to a small gate. I opened it; and quite abruptly, everything changed. I found myself flung from the verdant enclosure of the garden into a boundless blast of heat and light, a molten, flattened plain which unfolded as suddenly as if the tall hedges had collapsed like pieces of cardboard scenery to reveal it. I stopped, my eyes, which had grown briefly accustomed to the shade, shrinking from the radiant sea of gold which seemed to rise and fall before me in a warm tide. The vastness of the panorama, which stretched uninterrupted for as far as I could see, stunned me; and I thought that I had never seen something so brutal and lovely as this long embrace of sky and land, breast to breast. I stood there for some time entirely emptied of thought or even the slightest awareness of myself, the sun hot on my face and my eyes filled with colour. My sense of wonder was acute, if inarticulate. (I could not, for example, have told you precisely what it was that grew before my eyes in such a mass of blond and slender wands – some variety of grain, I supposed.) The randomness with which I had stumbled on the silent, swaying field and caught it in this gratuitous display of beauty appeared to me as a benediction of sorts. I felt comforted by it, and at the same time diminished; by which I mean that the feeling of insignificance was in itself a consolation.

Eventually I felt compelled to move, though I didn't want to; some deeper impulse insisted on it. I felt sure that Mr Madden would not appreciate my walking through the field, much as I would have liked to do so. I decided instead to skirt its boundaries, and as there was a generous margin of dry, crusty soil between the field itself and the fence which hemmed it, it seemed I would be able to walk without difficulty. I set off, glad of the breeze which ruffled the great golden pelt of the land and then lifted past me to stir the heavy branches of the trees beyond. It is difficult to convey the contentment I felt in the presence of these sights and sounds. It was as if a certain roughness, a grubby layer of matted, misbegotten aims, was being sloughed from me; as if in this deluge of simplicity I were being absolved of some nameless, primordial confusion. I did not ascribe any more specific meaning to this feeling. I did not, for example, immediately fall on it as a vindication of my move to the country, nor evidence that I had arrived at, or even embarked on, some form of recovery.

Working my way across the top of the field, I saw that I was approaching a wooden fence whose trajectory extended across my path and away to the right for as far as I could see. I had imagined, from further off, that I would either have to climb over it or change direction; but from nearer I could see that a quaint arrangement of steps had been built directly ahead of me over the fence. These did not conform to any image I might have had of a 'stile'; they more resembled a chunky wooden ladder secured astride the fence, so that one could almost have walked up and over them without slowing one's pace. I took the presence of this clever construction as a direct approbation of my walking where I had been, and an encouragement to continue. A small yellow arrow affixed to the fence beside the ladder and pointing directly ahead confirmed this impression; and thus egged on, I was about to vault energetically over the fence when it struck me that the presence of these inducements hinted at a wider specification than my own incidental use of the route. My encounter with the creature rallied from memory; and I realized that I was standing not on the untried terrain of discovery and adventure, but on a public footpath.

My idyll having met with unexpected foreclosure, I stood rooted beside the fence for some time. It was hard to suppress the memory of the leaflet slipped beneath my door, and still more the menacing armoury of the creature's room; all of which suggested that I had wandered into a zone of personal danger from which at any moment some undreamed-of assault might come. Too alarmed now even to take another step, I pivoted myself about from the waist to examine the ground at my feet, swaying unsteadily with the attempt not to move. I was mindful of the nooses I remembered from the creature's room; but tried to be alert also to any other form of trap which might have replaced them. The sky was a hard, hot enamel of blue overhead; and as the wind rolled off the field the shifting ocean of gold sent up wordless whispers to my terrified ears. Eventually I knew myself to be at an impasse; for having found nothing specifically of which to be afraid, the whole landscape entered into the collusion. One way or another, I would have to journey through risk and conjecture to get home. Having understood this I felt rather more courageous; and with courage came the retrospective notion that I had been rather too craven in my fears. The dangers which moments earlier had paralysed me now seemed like no more than superstitions; and before long I had decided to continue with my walk as if nothing had happened; which, of course, nothing had.

I had turned and placed my foot on the first, broad step of the ladder when I heard a shout. I stopped immediately and looked about. The cry had sounded far off, and I wondered if it had been an echo from the house or road, for I could see no one in the vicinity. It came a second time, and I looked about again. At first I could see nothing; but then a distant shape snagged my gaze, moving quickly between the two planes of field and sky. It was a man, and he was waving his arms and coming rapidly towards me through the field, leaving a dark furrow of flattened stems behind him. He had something in his right hand which I understood, surprisingly calmly, to be a gun. I remained exactly where I was, with one foot on the step, which I felt was the most sensible thing to do. In fact, there was nothing else I could have done, for despite having no real consciousness of fear, at the first sight of the man I had experienced a rapid sensation of drainage, as if everything warm and pulsing in me had been voided through a trapdoor. I was no more animate standing there than a lamp-post, and no more capable of running away.

'Stop!' shouted the man – rather unnecessarily – quite close to me now. My first impression of him, being entirely dedicated to assessing his potential for harming me, was blurred. He was young – in his thirties, I thought – and if not big then fairly square. In those panicked seconds I was surprised to notice the burly movement of his thighs as he ran, like two large hams beneath the rippling cloth of his trousers. His face, if I were to be honest, did not look like it bore the intention of murdering me; in fact, as he waded from the field and jogged to a halt in front of me, I was almost distracted from my terror by the curious look of him. His was unlike any face I had ever seen; but its peculiar aspect was characterized more by lack than by the presence of anything unusual. Some dimension appeared to be missing from it, although it was hard in those moments to get a sense of what it was. He had by now been standing in front of me for some time, catching his breath. The gun, I was glad to notice, was held behind his back.

'What do you want?' I finally enquired, impatient at his failure to state his intentions. I felt a surge of valour in the wake of my earlier cowardice, as if I had strained my capacity for self-protection and now didn't care what happened to me.

'What are you doing?' he said finally, still breathless. He looked me in the eye, and it was then that I saw how the two sides of his face seemed to meet in a point or ridge at the centre, as if he had two profiles but no head-on aspect. His eyes were very close together and turned slightly inward; a physiognomical misfortune, giving the bizarre impression that he was looking at himself. Otherwise he was not unattractive. He looked healthy, at least, and had a generous head of brown curly hair.

'I am going for a walk,' I replied. 'As this is a public footpath, I don't see that it is any of your business.'

It was backhanded of me to use as my vindication the very thing I had bemoaned minutes earlier; but as I still had no idea of who the man was, I was forced to defend myself in any way I could.

'I wouldn't walk over that if I were you,' he said presently, nodding at the ladder. He had quite a broad accent, of the sort I had already heard in the village. 'It's broken, see?'

He lunged purposefully towards me and I drew back. In the event it was only so that he could demonstrate a fault in the step on which I had been about to place my weight. It had come almost entirely away from its bracket. Had I stepped on it, I would almost certainly have injured myself.

'How could they leave it like that?' I cried; before remembering that 'they' was in fact Mr Madden, whom I had defended against the creature's accusations so passionately only the day before. 'This is a public right of way!' The man's expression was impassive, which inflamed me further. 'If you knew about it,' I added, 'why didn't you inform somebody?'

This, I felt, was a pertinent enough question; but you would not have guessed from the man's face that I had asked him one. Indeed, he seemed to be waiting for me to say something more.

'Why didn't you tell somebody?' I repeated. I wondered if he was in some way backward. His head cocked from one side to the other at hearing the question again, with the beady, rigid stupidity of a chicken.

'You like walking, then?' he said finally.

'Yes I do,' I briskly replied. I had been about to pose my question for the third time; but the apparent futility of the whole encounter stopped me. It irritated me to see that the man's obtuseness had triumphed over my own rationality. With curious clarity, I quickly understood that my ideas about how the conversation should proceed, and indeed about everything that had happened in the past few minutes, were entirely misplaced; not because they were wrong, exactly, but because they belonged elsewhere. The fact that the man and I did not appear to be communicating clearly seemed, in this light, to be more my fault than his. In my mind I went over what had happened and realized that he had come bounding over the field in such an alarming fashion solely to alert me to the broken step; and what is more, that he had found my ingratitude, as opposed to the admission of irresponsibility towards which I had vainly been trying to direct him, something of an affront. I began to regret the confrontational style of my approach; and at the same time became aware of news of an indisposition being telegraphed to me from several regions of my body at once.

'I've seen you about,' said the man, fixing me with the single beam of his misaligned eyes.

'Have you?' I vaguely replied. Suddenly I was not feeling at all well. My head had grown heavy and a strange prickling sensation coursed about my nose and eyes and down my throat. I tried to focus on the man, and concentrate on what he was saying, but with the mounting turbulence in all my senses he seemed remote. I felt a wave rise between my ears and I sneezed three times in quick succession.

'You've not been here long,' I heard him say. 'But you've been busy.'

I rubbed my eyes, which had swollen so rapidly that I feared they might shut altogether. Dimly I realized that the man would not be capable of acknowledging my sudden decline, nor of encompassing it in whatever plans he might have had for this social encounter. Were my eyes really to seal themselves shut, I might even have to ask him to lead me back to the cottage. It was essential that I escaped immediately, and I summoned every reserve of will I possessed to detach myself as quickly and politely as possible.

'I'm terribly sorry,' I said thickly, 'but I've just remembered that I'm late for something. I have to go.'

I glimpsed his face as I turned on my heel, and the image of it stayed in my mind as I fled streaming through the heat along the top of the field, through the gate, and back along the shady corridor towards the house.

Chapter Sixteen

Pamela and Martin both looked slightly startled when I burst into the kitchen, their heads jerking up in unison and their eyes wide with enquiry. I was now so besieged by allergy that it felt as if a great swarm of bees were milling around my face. Even so, I was dimly surprised to find the two of them indoors, having thought they were to spend the afternoon *en famille* by the pool. Pamela was sitting at the table reading a newspaper laid out flat in front of her like a bolt of cloth, a pair of glasses balanced on her elegant nose. Opposite her, Martin sat with his chair drawn up, absorbed in the same loving transfer of information from book to pad which I had overseen on the lawn that morning. Seen from the side their heads were barely six inches apart; and at my entrance they sprang away from each other, as if I had caught them at some guilty pursuit, like cheating or espionage.

'What's *happened* to you?' cried Pamela; a cry, if I were to be honest, expressive of a dangerously threadbare concern.

'I don't know,' I slurred. 'It started in the field. I think I must be allergic to something.'

I was beginning to feel quite dizzy, and I pulled out a chair and sat down beside Martin.

'Which? The top field?' said Pamela.

'The gold one.' I sneezed. 'Beautiful.'

'The top field. It must be hay fever.'

She nodded firmly. I wondered if she intended to do anything about it. In spite of my distress, I was becoming acutely aware of some fast approaching limit on Pamela's kindness. Martin was looking from one to the other of us, as if he were watching a play.

'Let me think,' said Pamela presently. I understood from this comment that she had, in the period since her last remark, been considering my plight rather than ignoring it. 'What have I got? Oh, I know. Have a look in that cupboard over there beside the door. See if there's a packet of something called Zortek or Zartek. Something like that.'

I realized that she was speaking to me, rather than some other factotum, and felt slightly injured that she should not be sufficiently moved by my condition to get the packet herself. Permitting myself a pathetic sigh, I got heavily to my feet and went to investigate the cupboard.

'See it?' called Pamela unhelpfully from behind me.

I found the packet and went directly to the sink for a glass of water. I had to admit that Pamela's diagnosis had been accurate; for only a few minutes after I had taken the pill and sat down again, I felt the inflammation of my eyes and nose begin miraculously to subside.

'What were you doing in the top field?' Pamela lightly enquired.

'Walking,' I replied, somewhat belligerently. 'There's a public footpath.' My conversion to the whole business of footpaths, though opportunistic, was proving profound. 'I met a man.'

'A man?'

I nodded.

'Well, what sort of man?' said Pamela finally. She appeared exasperated. 'Didn't you ask who he was?'

'I don't see that I had the right to ask,' I said. 'It was a public footpath, as I said.' This was not, I suddenly remembered, strictly true – the man had approached me right over the field. 'He pointed out,' I continued, mounting a new offensive, 'that a step had broken on the ladder over the fence. I had been about to stand on it and he wanted to prevent me hurting myself. That was all.'

'What did he look like?' persisted Pamela. I should probably have noticed that her interest in him was unnatural; but the fact that I myself wanted to know who he was gave Pamela's curiosity the illusion of being merely an extension of my own.

'Very odd,' I said. I couldn't think how to describe him, so instead I placed both hands over my face so that they formed a sort of vertical roof. 'Like that.'

'Oh, that was Mr Trimmer,' said Pamela quickly. She sounded relieved. After a moment she smiled. 'I should watch out if I were you. He's probably taken a fancy to you. He's absolutely notorious. Of course, he's terribly sweet, but simply *desperate* for a girlfriend. I shouldn't think there's a woman in a twenty-mile radius that hasn't been asked out by Mr Trimmer.'

I was beginning to feel rather offended that Mr Trimmer hadn't in fact asked me out, and then remembered that I'd run off before he'd had the chance. It irritated me, nonetheless, that Pamela was so keen to ridicule the notion of someone taking an interest in me. I realized that I had felt flattered by Mr Trimmer's heroic run across the top field, which now had been diminished to public comedy.

'I thought he was nice,' I said. 'He looks peculiar, but there must be plenty of people who don't mind that.'

Martin's head shot up disconcertingly at this remark.

'Oh, he's *terribly* nice,' intervened Pamela. She did not, I sensed, wish to be thought unkind; although I had the feeling that this was for reasons more of vanity than conscience. 'No, he's an absolute *darling*. The problem is with his mother.'

'His mother?'

'Yes, he lives with his mother,' said Pamela, in a confidential tone. 'Mrs Trimmer. Dora. She's a real old battleaxe. She's got poor Jack utterly under her thumb and scares off anyone who comes near him. She thinks they're after his money.'

'Has he got any?'

'Oh, not really. They live in this *wonderful* house, though. It's an absolute pit inside, but it must be worth a *fortune*. Jack's father left it to him when he died, and Dora's worried that if he marries, his wife will boot her out. So she tells him the most *dreadful* things about everyone he meets – simply makes things up!'

'What sort of things?'

'Oh, you know, that they've all got horrible diseases, that sort of thing. She got into terrible trouble once' – Pamela lowered her voice, as if someone might be eavesdropping – 'for saying that a girl in the village was a convicted thief. Poor Jack had been quite taken by her, so he stuck his neck out and brought her round for tea anyway. Afterwards Dora said that some silver had gone missing from the house, so what did he do but go marching over there in the middle of the night to demand it back!' Pamela shrieked with laughter. 'There was the most *terrible* set-to with her father, right out in Hilltop High Street!'

Martin yawned conspicuously. I saw the moist, red cavern of his mouth.

'He's Mr Madden's manager, isn't he?' I said, only then remembering why his name was familiar to me. The creature had mentioned him in connection with the shooting of Geoff.

'That's right. Piers *adores* him. Couldn't do without him. And Dora has given us her seal of approval, so there's no trouble from her. Old George Trimmer, her husband, worked here for years.'

There was a pause. The house ticked and creaked around us. Outside, through the window, shadows surreptitiously advanced across the lawn in the cooling afternoon.

'Right!' said Pamela briskly, standing up. I wondered if she was offended that she had not been implored to continue with her narrative. 'I'd better get on. Can you two amuse yourselves until supper?'

'I – yes,' I said firmly. I had been about to say 'I think so', before remembering Pamela's aversion to qualified statements. 'What would you like to do?' I said, to Martin.

'Dunno,' he ungraciously replied.

'Well,' said Pamela tersely. 'If you don't mind, I'll get on.'

I realized that, having achieved the first steep slope of novelty with regard to looking after Martin, I had slackened off slightly in the efforts I was making to fill his time. It is one of the difficulties of change that the work of one's own accommodation with it can obscure any real assessment of success or failure; and of unhappiness that improvements or otherwise in spirit become the focus, and dictate the sense of outcome, of a day's work. Suffering from both, I had neglected Martin in favour of tending myself; and I saw another ascent rise before me as I acknowledged within the triumph of my own survival the inadequacy of its accomplishments.

'How about a walk?' I said. I tried to sound enthusiastic, but my eyes still itched a little, and my throat was thick. 'Or do you want to carry on with that?'

I was intensely aware of Pamela, who was now busying herself with her back to us at one of the kitchen counters. I could tell from the tense set of her shoulders that she was listening, and willed Martin to respond in an obliging fashion.

'No, I've done enough,' he said, his manner all at once remarkably pleasant. 'Let's go out while it's still light.'

Once outside, Martin's amiability persisted.

'Are you feeling better?' he enquired.

'Yes, thank you,' I said. 'I've never been allergic to anything before. I don't know why it should have happened just then.'

'Maybe you were allergic to Trimmer.'

'As I said, I thought he was nice.'

It was now early evening, and as I pushed Martin along the gravel path at the side of the house, I was struck by how lovely the hot days were in retreat. The air was as thick and soft as the faded petals of the rose garden, and induced a feeling of wistful calm; a curiously alloyed sense of contentment, as if through the sudden stillness the noise of distant troubles could all at once be heard.

I had for some time been shamefully mindful of Toby's supposed visit to the cottage; an intention so vague that I felt I would have to spread my net wide to catch it. Since my return from my walk, a worm of anxiety had been gradually working its way across my thoughts, as events had trespassed further and further into the swath of time with which I had hoped to surround the possibility; and now I began to search deviously for a means of luring Martin to the cottage garden so that I would be able to take up my vigil. I was not fully conscious of the development of this matter in my mind from the seed of suggestion to full-blown expectation; indeed, it was probably for this reason that it had been permitted to grow unchecked. Once or twice I had examined its deleterious progress and hacked it back, appalled; but as soon as I turned my thoughts to other things it would continue its subtle creep through my heart. I did not really like Toby; and if I had dug at the soil beneath these wild hopes I would probably have found the desire for them not to be fulfilled. His attraction was all in the moment, like the taste of something sweet on the tongue.

'Where would you like to go?' I said to Martin, pausing at the junction where the path to the cottage snaked away between the hedges. 'We could go and sit in my garden if you like. It gets the sun in the evenings.'

I waited, my heart suspended in hope.

'OK,' said Martin innocently. I felt immediate guilt at the effortlessness with which I had tricked him. It was, I realized, remarkably easy to husband motives in the presence of those who had none. 'Have you got anything to drink?'

'Like what?'

'Booze,' said Martin, to my surprise.

'Of course not,' I replied. 'Where would I get that from?'

'How should I know? Wherever other people get it from. A shop. I was only asking.'

'I don't have the money for that sort of thing,' said I. By and large I had felt a sense of relief at my own poverty since being in the country, but just then, for the first time, the notion of tiring of it insinuated itself among my thoughts. Like someone on whom the grip of religious fervour momentarily loosens, I caught a glimpse of a route by which one day I might wander out of my conviction; a route which could lead me eventually to regret everything I now felt so keenly.

'I'll tell you what,' said Martin. 'Why don't you go back into the house and get a bottle, and then we can go and sit in the garden.'

'What do you mean, get?' He had made his suggestion as if he were striking a bargain with me; and I wondered if he had guessed at the tawdry aim on which our cottage expedition was founded. 'Are you suggesting that I steal a bottle from your parents?'

'It wouldn't be stealing,' said Martin obstinately. 'It's just getting, like I said.' He put his head back and looked up at me craftily. 'No booze, no cottage garden.'

At that I was sure that he knew of my deceit. In the heat of blackmail I completely forgot that my gracious reception of Toby could have easily been forgone. I was conscious in that moment only of my own guilt, a feeling which invariably looms large in the mind, and which thus appeared to have cornered me in a position from which the only escape was an extreme, if criminal, act of penitence.

'All right,' I said. 'But only if you're sure your parents won't mind.'

'Oh, they won't,' said Martin lightly. 'Just make sure they don't catch you.'

'Where should I go?'

'There's a cupboard in the kitchen. There's usually some stuff in there. It's right by the door.'

I turned on my heel and walked quickly back down the path with a feeling of obstruction in my throat. My mind was a blank of panic and as I opened the back door and entered the quiet house everything seemed to list before my eyes. I trod noiselessly up the corridor and opened the kitchen door. The room was empty; and knowing that I had to act quickly, I went directly to the first cupboard. It was the same cupboard in which I had found the pills, and opening it for the second time I realized that if anyone had apprehended me at that moment, I could have given the excuse for my intrusion that I had come to take another. Sure enough, on one of the lower shelves I saw a rank of bottles; and grabbing the nearest, I shut the cupboard door and fled back down the corridor. Once outside on the dusky path I bent over and gasped several times. My heart was thrashing in my chest. I realized that I had not taken a single breath during the entire operation. My immediate feeling of relief was soon superseded by an overwhelming sense of triumph. I could scarcely believe my own daring; and as I skipped back up the path to where Martin sat waiting in his chair, I found myself starting to laugh.

'Da-da!' I said, waving the bottle gleefully before him.

'I can't believe you did that,' he said. 'I was only joking.'

'No, you weren't!' I said, horrified at his cruelty.

'Yes, I was. Why don't you go and put it back?'

'I can't!'

'Never mind.' He stretched out a hand for the bottle. 'It's done now. What did you get?'

'I don't know,' I miserably replied, giving it to him. 'I didn't look.'

'Gin,' he said, examining it. 'Didn't you get any tonic?'

'That was really mean of you.' I turned his chair around on the gravel and began pushing him up the path towards the cottage. 'I would never have done something like that if you hadn't asked me.'

'Yes, you would,' said Martin. 'If it hadn't been in your nature, nothing would have made you do it. As it was you were off as soon as I'd mentioned it. Was it exciting, Stel-la?'

'I suppose so,' I admitted, my exhilaration punctured. 'It seemed so at the time. I can't believe I did it now.'

'That's what they all say,' Martin replied.

We reached the garden and Martin leaned forward to open the gate, clutching the bottle against his lap. I propelled him up the path and then onto the grass, depositing him beside the apple tree.

'I'll go and get some glasses,' I said sullenly, walking off.

'Don't be angry with me, Stel-la!' called out Martin over his shoulder.

Inside, the cottage was cool with desertion. A smell of damp and neglect hung in the air. I went to the kitchen and found two smudged glasses in one of the cupboards. As I was about to carry them outside, it struck me that I had not looked in a mirror for some time, and that my appearance might require some attention in view of the impression of unstudied charm I hoped to give were Toby to 'wander over', as he had put it. Once I had thought of this aspect of things, it was hard to limit the exertions I was prepared to apply to it; my only constraint being that it was essential that no effort should appear to have been made. I put down the glasses and ran up the stairs to my room, aware that Martin was waiting for me outside; and it was probably the precipitateness his presence forced on my cosmetic interlude that caused me to seize from my suitcase – without the calm consideration that was their due – the cut-off trousers. Frantically I tore off my skirt and put them on, rushing to the mirror with my comb. My reflection was more or less what it had been the last time I had worn them; but what I forgot, as I hurriedly took this pleasing image away with me down the stairs and out into the garden, was that my delight on that previous occasion had been private. I had little idea of what others might think of this display of flesh. Its effect on Toby was uncertain; and on anyone else, unwanted.

'Sorry I took so long,' I said to Martin as I came out of the cottage door and approached him across the grass. 'I was a bit hot, so I got changed.'

I was talking, I knew, to conceal my embarrassment; for Martin's eyes had attached themselves to me, and were travelling unsparingly up my legs as I walked. He looked, frankly, astonished by my appearance; and it was hard to sustain the carelessness with which I was attempting to set about the business of preparing the drinks while so blatantly under examination.

'What,' he said finally, 'are you wearing?'

'Hmm?' I looked up from where I had sat down beside him on the lawn. 'Shorts. What does it look like?'

I had meant the remark to be a reproach.

'It looks sexy,' said Martin.

'Thank you,' I replied.

It occurred to me then that Martin might think I had put the shorts on for his benefit; and all in all, before long I was fervently wishing that I had remained dressed as I was, or could find an excuse to go back into the house and change again without looking idiotic.

'Why did you get changed?'

'I told you, I was hot.'

'I don't believe you, Stel-la.'

'I just felt like it.' I handed him a glass in which there was a small measure of gin. 'Can we change the subject, please?'

'Are you expecting someone?' he said, taking the bottle from me and placing it furtively behind his chair.

I was about to reply adamantly that I was not, when I saw from the direction of his gaze that the question had been more innocent than it sounded. He was looking towards the bottom of the garden, from where there came the sound of footsteps approaching along the gravel path beyond. I realized that he had put the gin behind his chair to hide it, thinking that one of his parents might be coming; a gesture which suggested that I had been slightly misled concerning the seriousness of its theft. I was glad, in any case, that he had concealed it. Combined with the cut-off trousers, it might have given Toby – for they were his footsteps, I was certain, that we heard – an impression of dissolution. The figure of a man came into view, and for a brief moment everything in me seemed to rise to its feet in anticipation; until I saw that my visitor was not Toby, but the man I had met earlier on in the field, the unfortunate Mr Trimmer.

At the sight of us sitting there his expression did not change; indeed, it was hard to know whether he had seen us or not, and if so whether our presence there was a necessary, expected or unwelcome feature of his intrusion. He opened the gate and began toiling towards us up the garden. In the wake of a disappointment, even the most well-intentioned approaches can seem a pest; and at the sight of Mr Trimmer's curiously compacted face, and the diffident set of his clumsy body as he drew near, an unrestrainable irritation took hold of me.

'Hello?' I called out imperiously, as if to a stranger caught sneaking about my property.

'Afternoon,' said Mr Trimmer, drawing to an immediate halt at the sound of my voice and apparently waiting for permission to complete the final two or three yards to where we sat. He raised a hand as if to touch an invisible hat. As he lowered it, his eyes fell upon my exposed legs.

'Hello, Jack,' said Martin affably, grinning at him in an evil manner. He waved an arm in encouragement. 'Come on over. Have you come to see Stella?'

There was a considerable pause.

'I met her,' said Mr Trimmer, planting himself in front of us where we sat, with his eyes averted and his hands clasped before him, like a man about to sing the national anthem, 'in the top field.'

'Ah,' said Martin.

I felt that Mr Trimmer had been intending to enlarge on his description of our meeting, but that Martin's peremptory assent had cut the thread of his discourse. He fell silent, his face working in a peculiar sideways motion, apparently recovering from the interruption. His eyes strayed to my legs and then darted away. Presently he seemed to have gathered his momentum once more, and opened his mouth to speak.

'She was taken ill,' he said. 'I came to see if she was better.'

'I'm much better, thank you,' I said. I found that I too was speaking slowly. My face was burning. I caught Martin looking at me out of the corner of my eye. 'It was very kind of you to come.'

Despite my lugubrious diction, that fact that I was speaking directly to him seemed to hit Mr Trimmer like a strong jet of water. His face wore a crumpled expression of heroic resistance, as if at any moment he might fall over.

'I was going to mend that step,' he said. 'I was on my way to do it when I saw you.'

My complaint had evidently been festering in his thoughts all afternoon; and touched by his avowal, I refrained from enquiring as to how he had thought he would mend the step with a gun rather than a hammer and nails.

'I realized that you probably were,' I said, anxious that my reply sounded more complex than it actually was. 'Afterwards. I would have hurt myself if you hadn't stopped me.'

Martin was watching this tortured exchange with unconcealed fascination, an unpleasant smile on his face.

'Thank you for coming,' I said, nodding enthusiastically in the hope of drawing our interview to a close.

Mr Trimmer stood on, plinthed on the grass by his large, leather-booted feet.

'Would you consider,' he finally pronounced, while Martin's head wagged up and down below him at every word, 'coming out with me one evening?'

'Oh!' I said, horrified. I laughed shrilly. 'That's very kind of you. I don't know if I can, though. I'm usually quite busy over at the house in the evenings.'

'No, you're not,' declared Martin. 'She'd love to come out with you, Jack. She can come tomorrow.'

'Tomorrow?' said Mr Trimmer to Martin, as if he were responsible for the transaction. Seeming to realize that this was incorrect, he turned back to me. 'Would that be all right?'

'I suppose so,' I said, defeated.

'I'll call here at eight, then.'

'That would be lovely,' I rallied. 'I'll see you then. Goodbye.'

Mr Trimmer seemed surprised at being so abruptly dismissed, but he took it well enough, and bidding goodbye to both of us turned and made his way back down the garden, his elbows flying out to either side as if he were in a hurry.

'Thanks,' I said to Martin.

'It serves you right.' He raised his glass to his lips. 'Besides, you said you liked him.'

I lay on my back on the grass. 'What on earth are we going to talk about for an entire evening? And where will we go?'

Martin did not reply, and when I looked at him I saw that he was watching me with a peculiar expression on his face.

'You've got nice legs,' he said in a strangled voice.

Chapter Seventeen

Some time later, Martin and I moved uncertainly through the penumbral gloom of the garden back to the house. We had drunk the better part of the bottle of gin, the remainder of which I had hidden at the back of one of the kitchen cupboards. My theft of the bottle had seemed more and more extraordinary to me as the evening progressed, particularly under the increasing influence of its contents. Martin's behaviour with Mr Trimmer, and the underhand manner in which he had contrived my assignation with him, as well as the assignation itself, took on similarly absurd proportions. In fact, only my inebriation remained real, along with thoughts of what the Maddens would do if they discovered it.

The effect of the gin on Martin was even more worrying. He had grown boisterous and red-faced, and by the time I had wheeled him to the back door and up the corridor was singing a raucous medley of unidentifiable songs, accompanying himself with writhing motions on an invisible guitar in his lap.

'Calm down!' I whispered fiercely in his ear as we manoeuvred our way through the annexe and into the hall. 'You've caused enough trouble.'

'Oh, Stel-la!' he whined, lolling back in his chair. 'Don't be so cross all the time. You're *always . . . cross*.'

His head fell forward, as if he were asleep. At this I was genuinely alarmed and I stopped the chair and knelt beside him.

'Martin? Are you all right?'

His head shot up so suddenly that I leaped back in fright.

'I'm fine. You're the one that should be worried.'

'Why?'

'You look weird.'

'What do you mean?'

'I dunno. It's your eyes or something. They look weird. And you're still wearing your shorts. My mummy won't like those. Not at dinner.'

Withered by this unexpected blast of acuity, I stood paralysed in the hall. In the evening's confusion, I had entirely forgotten the inappropriateness of my outfit.

'Stay here,' I said. 'I'm going to go and change.'

At that moment, Pamela's voice issued faintly from the drawing room.

'Stella? Martin? Is that you?'

'Yes!' bellowed Martin.

'Where've you *been*? We've been waiting for you for *hours*!'

'Too late,' he said. 'Come on, it doesn't matter. They won't even notice.'

Why I accepted this pabulum of reassurance I can't imagine. In the dreaminess of drink I had forgotten the sharp prick of the social misdemeanour; but I felt it in all its steely agony as we entered the drawing room and the assembled company's eyes lighted as one on my cut-off trousers.

'Good God!' said Pamela, a menacing smile on her face. 'Those are very saucy!'

'Wheeew,' whistled Toby, lounging contentedly on a sofa at the far side of the room.

'Drinks?' said Mr Madden, rising dutifully from his chair.

'No, thank you,' I said.

'Yes, please,' said Martin. 'Leave her alone,' he added, directing his remark at Toby, who was still whistling away on the sofa.

'It was *intended* as a compliment,' drawled Toby. I realized that only in that moment had the idea of me entered his head; and that he was entertaining it, moreover, idly, for want of anything better to do. The tangled skein of my wasted, thought-racked afternoon rose up before me in all its monstrous fantasy.

'She doesn't need your compliments,' said Martin haughtily. 'She's embarrassed, and I don't blame her. Those were the only clean things she had to change into. I assured her that none of you would be rude, and you have been. I'm ashamed of you all.'

This final touch, trespassing as it did into excess, threatened to topple the heroic structure of Martin's speech; but to my surprise it held.

'Sor-*ry*,' said Toby ironically.

'I think she looks charming,' added Pamela. 'Why not, if you've got the figure for it? That's what I say.'

I forgave Martin instantly for the transgressions of the afternoon. Pamela I regarded as having levelled her score. Toby was now reassuringly lodged deep in my contempt; and thus set to rights, I felt rather more in the mood for another drink.

'Actually, I will have something,' I said confidentially to Mr Madden, as he passed with his tray. He bent his head towards me and I caught a gust of his breath.

'G-and-T?'

'Lovely.'

'We were just talking about Friday,' said Pamela, in her 'hostess' voice. 'I think it's going to be a real hoot. Mark and Millie are coming down for the night, and Derek and Caroline, and then there'll be all of us—'

'What's Friday?' said Martin, wheeling himself towards the fireplace.

'Honestly, Martin, you are the end,' said Pamela crossly. She looked over her shoulder. Mr Madden was safely from the room. 'It's your father's birthday, in case you have forgotten. Sometimes I wonder if you ever think about anybody but yourself.'

With my advocate thus cast into disfavour, my cut-off trousers seemed to regain something of their controversy. I sidled to the sofa on which Pamela was sitting and stood behind it.

'Dad's birthday's on Saturday,' said Martin.

'I know, but we're *celebrating* it on Friday. Mark and Millie can't make Saturday. They've got to be back in London for something.'

'Darling!' Mr Madden's voice floated in from the hall. 'Have we run out of gin?'

'Of course not!' Pamela shouted back. 'There's a new bottle in the cupboard in the kitchen.'

'No there isn't,' said Mr Madden, appearing in the doorway and scratching his head.

'There must be!' Pamela turned around on the sofa to look at him. 'I only bought it a couple of days ago. In fact, I saw it there earlier today!'

I tried to catch Martin's eye, but he was watching his parents as they debated the matter with so comically innocent an expression on his face that I prayed they wouldn't look at him. I myself, surprisingly, did not panic. After Mr Madden's first mention of the gin, I had checked internally my capacity to lie, as someone going down a steep hill in a car would check their brakes, and found it to be intact. I had no doubt that if questioned, I would deny all knowledge of the theft. Of my accomplice I was not so sure.

'Well, it isn't there now,' said Mr Madden.

'Are you sure you really looked?' persisted Pamela, putting

her hand on the arm of the sofa as though she were about to get up.

'Of course I did!' said Mr Madden crossly. 'I'm not an idiot.'

'Well, you do miss things sometimes, darling,' said Pamela condescendingly. 'You know what you're like. It was definitely there this morning.'

'I promise you that it isn't there now.'

There was a moment of silence.

'Well! *How* peculiar!' said Pamela finally. 'I wonder what could have happened to it?'

'Are you sure you bought a new one?' said Martin, to my horror. 'Perhaps you left it in the shop or something.'

'Don't be ridiculous,' snapped Pamela. 'Anyway, as I said, I saw it this morning.'

'Perhaps you only *thought* you did.'

'Why on earth would I think a thing like that if it wasn't true?'

'Well,' said Martin. 'Let's say you *did* buy a bottle but left it in the shop; your memory of *having bought it* might have created the illusion of it being in the cupboard. You might have created that illusion to reassure yourself that it was there, because subconsciously you remembered leaving it in the shop. Things like that happen all the time,' he added, chewing his finger.

'Are you sure you didn't leave it in the shop, darling?' echoed Mr Madden, evidently converted to this new theory.

'Of course I am!' said Pamela. She put a hand to her head. 'God, I must be going mad.'

'It's Alzheimer's,' said Toby, sniggering. 'What's your name, dear?'

'*Could* I have left it behind?' whispered Pamela, a look of fierce concentration on her face. 'Let me think. I went to the supermarket—'

'What's the date?' continued Toby in a loud voice. '1967? No, you're a bit out, dear. Try again.'

'Shush!' cried Pamela, raising a hand to silence him. He

sniggered again. She sat, evidently deep in thought, and finally raised an astonished face to the room. 'Do you know, I *must* have. How silly of me. I must have left it there. God, do you think I really am going bonkers?'

'Absent-mindedness is a sign of intelligence,' said Martin. 'Apparently.'

'Oh well,' said Mr Madden. 'We'll have to have something else.'

'No, no, let's just get on with dinner,' said Pamela distractedly. 'It's all ready.'

I caught Martin's eye several times as we sat around the dinner table, in the hope of telegraphing to him my approval, but each time he merely looked at me blankly as if he had no idea why I was glancing so significantly at him. I soon, however, forgot about the incident; for with Toby sitting beside me, I found myself once more drawn in to the covert conflict his presence seemed inevitably to set in motion, by which with every proof of stupidity or boorishness issued by his brain the form which enclosed it advanced in loveliness.

It is difficult to explain how it could be that I found myself increasingly attracted to someone of whom my opinion correspondingly descended. I had never experienced such a thing before. It was, I suspected, the very weakness of his personality that gave fatal embellishment to the thought of being physically overpowered by him; for without a rival intelligence to negotiate, without the whole vast and varied territory of taste, intellect and conversation to be explored and cultivated, the sexual domain lay invitingly close by, ripe for momentary plunder. I had no doubt that Toby's charms appeared accessible to everyone he met; but the cheapness of my desire did not make it any less urgent. I wondered that I did not feel more guilty at the thought of Edward, for whom, though I clearly knew him to be the better person, I had not felt this greed; and who, so short a time ago, I had injured so deeply and so wantonly that an entire lifetime of virtue would not have paid for it. I imagined him looking into my thoughts there at the dinner table, but although I felt ashamed, I could not support the opposition for long. I had freed myself from Edward as one would release the hand of someone dangling over a precipice: because my own survival had depended on it. At least, that was how I had seen it at the time. Increasingly, I was coming to regard my action as less catastrophic for all concerned; in other words, that *I* had been the dangling figure, and had let go merely because it had hurt too much, and seemed too hopeless, to hang on; and that when I had had the good fortune to land on something soft and yielding, I had merely neglected to inform Edward of the fact. He, I didn't doubt, was grieving at my disappearance; but at least he would have the chance to recover. Had I stayed with him longer, his portion of blame would have grown larger and larger, his innocence less. My unhappiness would have infected him; an infection he might have passed on to the next person he loved.

As for me, I had rejected an acknowledged life, stamped and certified. I had refused the keys to permanence, left the full cupboard of certainty unopened. I wanted to live by my wits, sleep beneath the stars of solitude, scavenge for scraps: and if in my restless hunger I came across a laden apple tree, no one could blame me for stopping and eating to sustain myself, for who knew when I might next have the chance? Toby was just such a tree; except, of course, that apples rarely disdain to be eaten, as was likely to be the case here.

'Steady on,' he murmured, leaning towards me and nodding at my plate. 'You'll give yourself indigestion.'

For a moment I could not think what he was talking about; but then I saw that I had almost cleared the mound of food in front of me, while the others had scarcely dented theirs. This state of affairs represented a marked change in my eating habits. I am normally a slow and careful eater, having been schooled by my mother in the many social atrocities it is possible unwittingly to commit during the ingestion of food. Since my arrival in the country, I had certainly been hungry; but also, having no independent means, I had quickly developed the opportunistic attitude to food which I have just applied analogously to my feelings for Toby. I realized that over the past few days I had been eating every meal as if it were my last; and I sat for some time in a ferment of retrospective embarrassment, as I wondered whether the Maddens had noticed my gobbling but been too polite to mention it.

'It's the country air,' I said to Toby. I seemed incapable of saying anything to him that was not profoundly dull. 'It makes me hungry.'

'Does it now?' he said, sitting back in his chair. 'I like girls with appetites. It suggests a lust' – he stretched hugely, his arms aloft, and yawned – 'for life.'

Martin, who was sitting opposite us, had been watching this exchange, and now evidently decided to bring it to a halt.

'Stella had a visitor this afternoon,' he said, addressing the whole table.

'Did she?' said Pamela.

'She did. Mr Trimmer came to pay court.'

'Oh, God,' said Toby, whether in sympathy or disgust I could not ascertain.

'*Really?*' Pamela grinned at me. 'I told you he'd take a fancy to you.'

'His gallant behaviour on the footpath earlier,' continued Martin, 'secured him a date with her tomorrow evening.'

'What's this?' said Mr Madden brightly, looking about.

'Better not let Dora find out,' said Pamela.

'No,' chimed Martin, nodding his head solemnly. 'Because if Dora finds out about *Stella* she'll be very cross.' He gave me a menacing look. 'She wouldn't approve *at all*.'

'Oh, I don't know,' said Pamela ingratiatingly. 'She'd come with our guarantee, after all. Jack could do a lot worse than marry Stella.'

I opened my mouth to protest, but Martin interrupted.

'Oh, Dora needn't worry about that,' he said loudly. 'Stella can't *get* married.'

There was silence around the table. I stared at my plate, braced for what seemed certain to come.

'Who would look after me otherwise?' concluded Martin feebly.

'Oh, shut up,' said Toby.

'On that note,' said Pamela, at the same time.

'Bedtime for you,' said Mr Madden.

'I'll take him up,' I furiously declared, pushing back my chair and standing up. I was gratified to see a shadow of fear flit across Martin's face.

'Oh, would you?' said Mr Madden. 'Jolly kind.'

I got Martin out of the room as quickly as I could and stormed up the stairs ahead of him with his chair.

'I can't believe you did that,' I said, from the top, while he scrabbled his way up backwards. 'You're evil.'

'What?' he said.

'I told you that in confidence. I did not expect to be tormented and blackmailed for it. I regret that I ever trusted you.'

'What?' he said, hauling himself into his chair.

'Don't pretend you don't know! I've had just about enough of you!'

'I didn't do anything!' he wailed, following me down the corridor and into his room. 'It was only a joke.'

'It's not a joke if it's not funny. Why do you have to be so *manipulative*?'

'What else is there to do?' He shrugged and wheeled himself to his closet. 'I get bored, that's all. I wasn't going to tell them anything.'

'That's not the point. If you carry on like this, they'll start thinking that I'm hiding something, or that I'm untrustworthy.'

'You did steal their gin,' remarked Martin, pulling his T-shirt over his head. I was surprised by the sight of his chest, which, though very pale and hairless, was extremely muscled. He quickly drew a pyjama top from a drawer in the closet and struggled into it arms first.

'That was not my idea. You said it would be all right.'

Martin wheeled himself to the side of the bed, the pyjama bottoms clutched between his teeth. He levered himself out of his chair and half-threw himself on top of it.

'Do you want some help?' I enquired.

'I can do it. Don't look.'

As I looked away, I glimpsed him beginning to wriggle out of his trousers. I wondered what his legs looked like.

'Ready!' he called.

I turned around and was surprised to see him neatly slotted between the covers. He patted the space next to him and I went and sat down.

'I'm sorry, Stel-la,' he said sweetly. 'Your secret's safe with me.'

'I wish I could believe that,' I replied.

He gazed sombrely at me.

'You like Toby, don't you?' he said.

'No.'

'Don't.'

'Don't what?'

'Don't like him.

'Why not?'

'Because it pains me.'

'I just said I didn't.' I met his eyes and saw that they were indeed inky with some unguessable emotion. 'I find him attractive. That's all.'

'That's bad enough. It's not fair.'

'You've got other things,' I said. 'Anyone can see that.'

He fiddled with the corner of the sheet, his eyes downcast.

'No one will ever love me.'

'Yes, they will. You just have to wait.'

'I have to wait for everything.'

I saw that he was only just beginning to comprehend the range and scale of his exclusion from normal life. I did genuinely believe, however, that what I had said to him was true. Indeed, I felt more confident of his future than my own. His very circumstances dictated a long and difficult journey to loving him; and anyone who made it would by necessity possess more than the average degree of mettle. Out in the milling world, there was no knowing who one might brush up against, nor why they had stopped, nor when they might move on again. Martin, at least, had been saved the endless accounting of mediocrity: the ceaseless, fearful estimating of one's own value, in which those with no claim to the exceptional were forced to engage.

'At least you're different,' I said. 'There's no reason for anybody to choose someone like me.'

'Edward did.'

'He was the same. Sometimes I think that's what brought us together. There was no reason not to, if you see what I mean.'

'That's crap,' said Martin, yawning. 'He probably just made you think that about yourself so that he wouldn't have to worry about you.'

'How do you know?' I said, letting Edward go undefended.

'It's obvious. You're a dangerous woman, Stel-la. The dogfucker was right for once. You've got a lust for life.'

Later that night, I lay awake for some time trying to think about what Martin had said. His remarks had felt true to me – I had heard the clean, clear sound of them as they chimed in my heart – and yet I could not find my way to this truth by any logical process of thought. Confounded, I fell asleep; but some time later sleep spat me out again into the soft palm of the dark. For a moment, when I opened my eyes, I thought that I was to be delivered to this truth for which I had been searching. Within seconds, however, I became conscious of the sound that had woken me, a sort of scrabbling noise coming from outside. I stiffened instantly with fear; and just then heard a light tapping coming from downstairs, like someone knocking at the door. I waited for some time, and when I heard nothing more I got out of bed and felt my way in the dark down the stairs. The sitting room was undisturbed in the shadows. I walked to the window and looked out. A figure I immediately recognized as Toby was making his way down the garden path to the gate. I could see the casual set of his shoulders in the moonlight, and the outline of his hands in his pockets. He opened the gate, looked this way and that, and disappeared.

Chapter Eighteen

I opened my eyes on a day whose prospect was so alarming that it was some time before I could bring myself to get out of bed and begin it. Outside my window the tyrannical sky slyly proffered again its unnatural heat, as if from a never-diminishing wad of banknotes; but I knew that storms were being smuggled in for me beneath its innocent blue. Today was not a day like any other. Today, I felt sure, my luck with regard to the matter of driving would run out; and the whole edifice of my life in the country, which I had begun to believe to be secure, seemed to strain and groan beneath it. In the shadow of this great dread, other smaller concerns lurked: my forthcoming evening with Mr Trimmer; my muddled and inappropriate feelings for Toby, to which his moonlit visit had added an altogether dangerous dimension of fulfilment; and the vague but certain sense I had, which seemed to have been implanted in me while I slept, that despite Martin's efforts I had been judged to have transgressed in wearing the cut-off trousers and would be made to pay for it, whether directly or later as part of a wider tally.

It surprised me that the last and least of these concerns should be the first to flower; but no sooner had I quietly entered the big house by the back door and begun to creep, soberly dressed in a long-sleeved shirt and trousers, up the passage, than the very thing I was hoping to avoid – an encounter with Pamela – rose up in my path.

'Stella!' she said, emerging furtively from the kitchen and closing the door behind her. 'A word.'

She drew to my side in the gloomy corridor. From her air of emergency, I guessed that she had been waiting for me; and from her confidential tone and stern, decided expression that I was to be reprimanded. There are some women on whom authority sits violently, who can use it only as a tool of reward or censure. I had little sense of Pamela's expectations of me between these two extremes, which was probably why I failed so frequently to meet them.

'Forgive me for being bold,' she said in a low, rapid voice. 'But I didn't like to say anything last night in front of the others and I feel I must get this clear.'

I saw that she was becoming agitated, in the way that she often did: like a bottle being shaken hard to stir up what was in itself disposed to settle.

'I know what you're going to say,' I began, in the hope of deflecting her.

'Now I don't mind if we're out by the pool or whatever,' she continued, apparently not having heard me. 'But to dress provocatively in the evening when the men are about really isn't on.'

'I'm sorry,' I interposed.

'If you don't have enough clean things then for God's sake come and see me first and I'll sort you out with something.'

'It won't happen again,' I said.

'It's easy to forget,' she persisted, 'in this day and age that some things are still unacceptable. I know that you don't know us very well, and perhaps that sort of thing is fine where you come from, but with young men in the house I really must ask that it doesn't happen again.'

'It won't,' I said.

'All right?' she finished, meeting my eye. 'I'm sorry to have started the day off on such an unpleasant note, but I felt something had to be said. Let's forget all about it, shall we?'

'Fine,' I weakly agreed.

'Good. Now I think Martin is waiting for you upstairs, so off you go.'

She disappeared back through the kitchen door and shut it after her. Exhausted, I leaned for a moment against the wall, and then made my way heavily through the hall and up the stairs to Martin's room.

'What's the matter?' he said when I came in.

'Nothing,' I gloomily replied. 'What do you want to do?'

Pamela's assault had, I felt, put a fatal imprimatur of misfortune on the day. None of its gambles, after such an opening, could possibly go my way; not only because the theme had been set and the tone determined, but also in that so many of its uncertainties depended for their outcome on my own confidence, a quantity which now lay blighted and forlorn in some shameful corner of my heart. I cursed my own recklessness in my decision to wear the cut-off trousers, and Toby for inciting it. The thrill I felt when I thought of his visit to the cottage the night before was now doubly despicable. Why had he come to see me so late at night? Perhaps, it struck me, he had come so late with the express purpose of *not* seeing me; to visit his memories of the place rather than its new tenant, at an hour when I could be sure not to accost him. This new theory seemed in genuine danger of being accurate; until I remembered that I had distinctly heard him knock at the door, and that besides, even on such brief acquaintance as ours, I could see that he was not a man likely to be given to reminiscence or contemplation. I did not, even in the heat of gratification, believe that Toby really liked me. My earlier disappointment in the cottage garden was still too fresh to permit such an idea. It was the cut-off trousers, I felt sure, which had lured him and lit his path to my door; and having admitted this I found myself in belated and embarrassed agreement with Pamela for her fury.

'Ah!' I said aloud, an exclamation driven to the surface by a surfeit of inner torment.

'*What?*' said Martin plaintively.

'Nothing. I just got off to a bad start today.'

'I don't understand it when people say things like that,' he said; thinking, I didn't doubt, of his mother. 'I never feel that way. They make it sound like they're giving a performance or doing an exam or something. I just decide what mood I'm going to be in and then see what happens.'

'Are you going to the centre today?' I enquired; partly, I'm afraid, to remind him of his misfortunes; but mostly to ascertain whether there was any chance of further avoiding the debacle which, curiously, had grown more insubstantial in my mind with every deferral. I had managed almost entirely to block the driving problem from my thoughts over the past few days; or rather, like a pilot in a small plane, I had been flying just above it, roundly aware of but not feeling the texture of its contours, pulling just in time out of every lurch of fear to skim its menacing peaks. I hoped at least that when the inevitable wall of hard and insurmountable fact rose up before me, my collision with it would be swift and painless; for although I felt that I wanted time to prepare myself for what no amount of meditation could alter, I knew that to be conscious of my fear would be to endure every torment it could devise for me.

'I think so,' said Martin. His vagueness was agony. 'What day is it?'

'Wednesday.'

'Well I am, then. Are you taking me?'

'Yes,' I shrilled.

In moments of greater confidence than this, when I had dared to look down from the height of my denial, I had wondered what could possibly be so difficult about driving a car that the sheer force of my desperation would not overcome.

I had sat beside people in cars often enough; so many times, in fact, throughout my life, that when I tried to recall the various manoeuvres I had, albeit half-consciously, witnessed, I found that I had unwittingly amassed enough images of the driving process to conduct a sort of lesson in my head. Steering was easy enough, a simple matter of instinct and clear vision. Acceleration and braking, once one had determined which levers caused them, could likewise not be hard. It was the gearstick which intimidated me; and the varying styles of using it which I summoned up from my memories of the passenger seat suggested that this, being the zone of personal embellishment, was also the kernel of difficulty. My mother had laboured over it with exaggerated caution; my father had flicked it carelessly from one position to the next; Edward, who drove, unlikely as it may seem, with a sort of epicurean pleasure, had almost *caressed* it in his manipulations. Mr Madden's mastery of the process was the one which most interested me, given that it was his car I was going to drive. He changed gear with a rough confidence which I imagined experts would decry; but what disturbed me were peculiarities in his *handling* of the car which suggested that it was in some sense irascible or untamed, and required not only more than the average degree of skill but also some sort of personal acquaintance to drive it.

'What time will we have to leave?' I enquired, wondering if there was any way that I could slip out to the drive and examine my opponent in advance.

'After lunch some time.' Martin yawned. 'Don't make such a fuss.'

The morning fled by with alarming speed. Every time I looked at my watch, it seemed to have made impossible advances; and in the end my resistance to the passing of time in proportion to its velocity was such that I felt as if I were trapped in some fast downhill ride, with the world a blur around me and the wind buffeting my face, the crowd of my other concerns left far behind at the top. We kept to Martin's room, it having been implicitly understood that the hot spell had endured beyond the point at which it was imperative to go outside to that where it was imperative to stay in. I had instructed him to do his homework, swatting away every attempt he made to engage me instead in conversation, and sat in the window seat in gloomy contemplation and dread. There are few things more unpleasant than the anticipation of some inescapable, solitary trial. What begins as a distant blot can feed on all the intervening hours until it becomes a vast obstacle, in whose shadow it is impossible to feel the warmth of any future consolation. I could not foresee a time when my unhappiness would be over. I knew that at some point I would have driven, and would no longer be driving; but even this certain statement housed a hundred different outcomes, which left no room in it for comfort. The fact that I not only had to endure the interlude, but must give the performance of my life in it, meant that sheer survival was of little use to me. I wished then with all my heart that I had confessed the truth to the Maddens when the opportunity had first arisen; a truth which was now inadmissible, given that it had since gathered to itself so many lies.

'Finished!' said Martin triumphantly, waving a book at me. 'Let's go downstairs. It's lunchtime.'

'We're just having a light scratch lunch in the kitchen,' said Pamela when we presented ourselves. I wondered if her need to give so long and descriptive a title to something whose essence was informality signified a skill at hospitality or a terror of what lay outside it. 'Toby's helping Piers on the farm today, so I gave them sandwiches to take with them.'

'What?' said Martin gleefully, while I tried to work out whether the absence of Toby and Piers improved my situation or worsened it. I had certainly relied on Piers to promote calm during my first and inevitably chaotic manoeuvres on the drive, and on Toby to inspire panic; which left me, I decided, more or less where I had started.

'What's wrong with that?' Pamela was saying sharply. 'I think it was jolly nice of him to offer.'

'I bet he didn't offer,' said Martin.

'Well he certainly didn't refuse,' snapped Pamela.

'I bet he was pissed off.' Martin caught my eye menacingly. 'I bet he envisaged a day of chasing Stella around the swimming pool.'

This, although I suspected he didn't realize it, was the worst thing Martin could possibly have said. Pamela's whole frame tensed at the remark.

'Well, I shouldn't think Stella would have minded too much about that,' she said quietly.

'Whoah!' said Martin, grinning. 'Bitchy!'

Although I was upset by Pamela's comment, and offended by the exchange in general, I did not feel capable of intervening; partly because my anxieties about driving held me in an inescapable clinch, and partly because this type of conversation was so alien to me that I did not know how to enter it. Instead, I did something I rarely do: I bore the affront silently, and with a very apparent air of injury. We sat down at the table, and after she and Martin had made one or two desultory observations on other matters, Pamela turned to me.

'Oh, for God's sake, Stella, don't sulk,' she said, her voice poised between anger and humour. 'It was only a bit of fun.'

This final outrage very nearly provoked me to fury. I remembered what Pamela had said earlier in the corridor about *where I came from*, as if it were, by implication and exclusion, a place of mysterious degenerations which I should, indeed must, concede in favour of the better sphere I now had the good fortune to inhabit; a place which, moreover, located as it was beyond the small circle of her concerns, could have no language of its own but merely an illiteracy in hers. I did not, in fact, think that Pamela regarded me as being beneath her; merely that she accorded such sovereignty to her own ideas about things, and those of people like her, that she took their authority to be a matter of universal agreement. Pamela, I saw, had been reared on the most general notions regarding people unlike herself; and with neither education nor acquaintance to fill in the detail, was possessed of that curious confidence which accompanies ignorance, and which is concerned more with keeping the world at bay than with understanding or even reforming it. Had it occurred under almost any other set of circumstances, she would not have been able to rebuke me for my appearance, nor draw from it the inference she just had; and it was here that her family, her house, and her station in life entered into a fatal collusion with her caprice. Pamela's triumphs were not those of reason, religion, morality, or even etiquette; they were a mere triumph, though she didn't know it, of numbers. She operated by a sort of inverted anomie; by which I mean that although she had rules, and plenty of them, their basis was the ever-shifting ground of what Pamela happened to find pleasing at the time, and their ultimate goal the proper delivery to Pamela of her own way. Where I come from, I wanted to say, we would never be so rude; but the mere thought brought on such a sudden ache of longing for the life I had left behind that I feared I would burst into tears if I articulated it.

'I'm not sulking,' I said instead. 'I'm just thinking about something else.'

Pamela had opened her mouth, ready, I guessed, with some convenient stricture concerning the impropriety of thinking about something else, when Martin intervened.

'Oh, leave her alone, you old bag,' he said with his mouth full. 'She'd tell you to sod off herself if she wasn't so embarrassed.'

'Stella can tell me to sod off if she likes!' said Pamela, with a look of gay amazement. I felt that I would never fathom the process by which personal insult invariably manufactured good humour in her. 'She knows we don't mince our words around here.'

'Sometimes I wish you'd mince them more,' I said daringly, glad that I had managed to fit in some form of retaliation, however belated.

'Oh dear!' Pamela laughed, throwing back her head. 'Do you think we're all *frightfully* rude to each other? I did used to worry about that, but I've got so used to it now. Oh, stop! That's disgusting!' Martin had leaned towards her and was chewing deliberately with his mouth wide open. 'Goodness, look at the time! You two'd better get moving.'

All at once my destiny was upon me. I had almost, in the second before Pamela noticed the time, forgotten what I had now to do; and as it rushed at me once more, I found my terror redoubled.

'Right,' I said, standing up. I was alarmed to notice a feeling of lightness in my legs. Nothing, in that moment, seemed quite real. 'Are you ready?'

'Mm.' Martin stuffed in a last mouthful of food.

'You know the way, don't you?' said Pamela, to me; evidently having been ignorant of the whole silent drama of deferral and relief in which I had been engaged over the past few days. She did not remember, I saw, that I had so far escaped driving Martin to the centre myself.

'I think so,' I said. 'Martin can help if we get lost.'

With no further excuse for lingering in the kitchen, I was forced to grasp the handles of Martin's chair and begin wheeling him to the door. I was profoundly worried by the feeling of physical weakness which had started in my legs and now spread down my arms. I could barely push Martin's chair, and the room seemed to tilt this way and that before my eyes. Once out in the hall, I realized to my horror that Pamela was hovering behind us. I wondered if she intended to see us off, and tried desperately to think of some means of detaching her.

'We'll see you later, then,' I said.

'Have a good time, darling,' she said, still on our trail.

'Fat chance,' said Martin.

'Goodbye,' I said, more firmly, as we reached the door.

'Do you want a hand getting him in?' Pamela persisted, lingering in the doorway as Martin shot off down the ramp.

'No!' I cried. 'We'll be fine.'

I put my hand on the door as if to close it. Pamela stood her ground. Our eyes met.

'Well, I'll leave you to it,' she said finally. She looked at me rather suspiciously; and then, to my relief, turned and made her way back down the hall.

I closed the door firmly after her, and went feebly down the steps to where Martin sat in the sun beside the car.

'Open the door, then,' he said.

I opened the door and he levered himself into the passenger seat. I closed the door after him and made my way round to the other side, feeling as if I were walking on something yielding, like marshmallow.

'You forgot my chair,' he said, when I opened the other door.

'Oh. Sorry.'

I returned to the passenger side, where the chair sat abandoned on the gravel. Martin wound down the window.

'Don't just stand there,' he said.

'I don't know how to collapse it.'

'You put your foot on that thing at the back. That's it.'

The chair folded flat and I carried it to the boot. I had never in my life felt less competent than I did in that moment. I opened the boot and laid the chair in it.

'Get a move on, Stel-la!' cried Martin from the front.

I realized that I had been performing every action in slow motion, so as to delay the moment when I would have to get in the car. The chair now stowed, there was however nothing else that I could do. I went back to the driver's side and got in.

'What's the matter with you?' said Martin plaintively.

Before my eyes was the most alarming panorama I had ever

seen. Across the entire vertical axis of my side of the car extended a vast control panel, a cryptic ridge of dials and switches, knobs and graphs, teeming not merely with numbers but also abbreviations ('m.p.h.', 'k.p.h.', grunts redolent of a prerequisite familiarity), coloured squares, ruled lines, and a whole register of hieroglyphics telling of strange vehicular adventures: a small petrol pump, a group of waving lines like rising steam, three lamps whose beams shone three different ways. From this background rose the mute black circle of the steering wheel, bristling with levers. Pedals lay at my feet like waiting irons. Through the windscreen, beneath the long flank of the bonnet, the engine sat coiled, waiting to burst into life.

'I can't drive,' I said.

There was a long silence. Beside me, Martin sat looking straight ahead.

'Right,' he said, finally.

'If your parents find out,' I continued, 'they'll send me home.'

'Probably.' He nodded. 'They did say driving was essential, Stel-la.'

'I know.'

It seemed futile to explain the process by which, conveniently or otherwise, I had neglected to take notice of this requirement at the time, or to draw this neglect to anyone's attention afterwards. What concerned me in that moment was what Martin intended to do about it. Having confessed to him, I had put myself entirely in his hands. Although I had been aware that our intimacy had gathered strength since the moment of our first meeting, it had never occurred to me to test it. Now I had a sense of my bond with Martin vying with that of his parents; and as he sat beside me in the car, pulled in either direction by these conflicting loyalties, his ruling took on for me an importance beyond the merely expedient. My heart lay hollow, waiting to be filled by his regard; and the thought of his refusing me, and turning me over to be dealt with by the familial authorities while he withdrew into their ranks, was unbearable.

'It can't be that hard,' he observed presently. 'I know how it works. I'll just tell you what to do.'

'All right,' I said recklessly. 'If you're sure you won't be frightened.'

'It would be an honour,' said Martin, 'to die with you, Stel-la. Turn the key.'

I found the key, which was already in the ignition, and turned it. There was a stutter of life from beneath the bonnet, and then the car slowly began to tremble around us.

'Is it on?' I said. I had expected a roar of some kind.

'Of course it's on. Now, there are three pedals at your feet. On the right, the accelerator. Press it.'

I pressed it with my foot, my hands gripping the wheel. The noise of the engine did grow louder, but the car did not move. Thinking this to be because I had not pressed hard enough, I put down my foot until it would not go any further.

'Stop!' shouted Martin, above the scream of the engine.

'Why didn't we move?' I said as it died away.

'Because we're not in gear. I only asked you to press it so that you'd know which one it was. The middle one is the brake. Press that.'

I did so.

'The pedal on your left is the clutch. You press the clutch when you want to change gear.'

'OK.'

'When you press the clutch, you take your foot off the accelerator. Then, when you've changed gear, you put your foot back on the accelerator again.'

'How do you change gear?'

'You just – look, I'll tell you what. I'll change gear for you. I'll just shout *clutch*, and you put your foot on the clutch, OK? You concentrate on steering.'

'OK.'

'OK. Clutch.'

I looked through the windscreen at the remote spectacle of the drive. The car was pointing directly down it, for which I was grateful.

'Clutch, Stel-la.'

'Oh. Sorry.'

I pressed the clutch and Martin manoeuvred the gearstick beside me with his left hand.

'Good. Now, keep your foot on the clutch for the time being. Release the brake.'

'I'm not touching the brake,' I said, bemused.

'No, the *hand*brake. It's beside you. You press the front bit and it goes down.'

'Like that?'

'Fine. Now, hands on the wheel, Stel-la. Put your foot on the accelerator, and *very slowly* take your foot off the clutch.'

I pressed the accelerator and the noise of the engine mounted.

'Not that much!' shouted Martin. 'Just a little bit. That's right. OK, very slowly off the clutch.'

It is difficult for me to convey my surprise, despite the advance warning I had received, at the way in which with the command of my feet the whole world became a blur of noise and motion. Had I been able to drive entirely with my hands, I would probably have applied more natural instincts to the business of pulling away from the house. As it was, the simplicity of Martin's instruction had been profoundly deceptive; for I had no premonition of the chaos my gentle paddling would unleash. I took my foot off the clutch and the car bolted forward at such speed that I pressed indiscriminately at the pedals in panic, while the jolting scenery bore down on us and Martin shouted vainly beside me above the roar of the engine. I had no time in this onslaught of events even to think about controlling them. All I could do was to try and recall, with a contrasting lassitude at once terrifying and inalterable, how to stop the car. Very slowly, my mind dimly remembered that ceasing to press the accelerator would have some effect on the speed at which we were travelling. Even slower, my foot responded; against its will, I should add, because instinct told it to press harder the faster we went. The car veered off the gravel drive and chugged across the grass. It heaved once, twice, and died.

'Not bad,' said Martin in a high voice. 'Let's try again.'

'I don't know if I can.' Now that we had come to a blessed halt, I found that I was shaking with terror and relief. 'I'm terrible at it. I should just accept that I'll never be able to drive.'

'Don't be silly. No one can just *drive*. You have to learn.'

Looking around, I was surprised to see that we had only come a few yards. The house stood patient and contemptuous behind us.

'I can't.'

'You have to, Stel-la. Besides, if you don't get a move on, my mother will be out to investigate.'

This proved the greatest spur to action yet. I turned the key again.

'Now go a bit faster this time,' advised Martin. 'Then you won't stall.'

'I was going fast!' I cried.

'You were going about five miles an hour. Clutch.'

My second attempt proved rather more successful than my first. Less afraid now of the accelerator, I was able to focus on the steering wheel as the guiding principle of the exercise. I directed us back onto the gravel, and with a thrill of confidence realized that I was able to propel the car in a straight line down the drive.

'Clutch!' shouted Martin.

Stabbing about with my foot, I found the pedal. As I pressed it, the engine reared with a horrible shriek.

'Take your foot off the accelerator, stupid! OK, now let go of the clutch and put the accelerator back on.'

The car lurched forward as the engine began to sing in a new key.

'We changed gear!' cried Martin.

Alarmingly quickly, the gates at the bottom of the drive loomed into view.

'What do I do now?'

'Foot on the clutch. Other foot on the brake.'

I put my foot on the brake, and the car stopped so suddenly that both Martin and I were thrown forward.

'Do it gently! OK, we're turning right here. Clutch.'

One way or another, before long we were out on the tarmacked road. My feelings were a curious mixture of the drunken excitement of achievement combined with the more sober consciousness of how fragile my control of the situation really was. Like someone walking a wire, I sensed that the moment in which I became aware of my feat would be the moment I ceased to accomplish it. I wasn't quite sure, in other words, *how* I was driving the car. All I knew was that everything depended on my continuing to do so.

'Clutch,' said Martin.

I was fortunate, at least, in that the remoteness of the narrow roads meant that there was little chance of meeting anybody else travelling along them. This did not particularly strike me at first – I was interested only in my own progress, and had not considered the fact that the realm I had entered was communal and open to invasion by others – but when after some time the fringes of Buckley came into view, replete with obstacles, I felt the force of my presumption in taking the wheel.

'We've got to stop.'

'Now just stay calm,' said Martin anxiously. 'It's not far to go now.'

'I can't,' I said. At the sight of houses and other cars, I had surrendered my authority over the car. I took my feet off the pedals.

'Stella!' shouted Martin. 'We're in the middle of the road! You can't just stop!'

The car slowed down and then shuddered violently to a halt. I could hear the whirr of a fan in the silence.

'OK,' said Martin, more gently. 'Turn the key.'

'No.'

'You have to. We can't stay here. Turn the key.'

My sudden consciousness of my own incompetence, and my retrospective astonishment at the fact that I had driven the car almost to Buckley, was effecting a sort of paralysis in my limbs. I had lost, I knew, the nerve on whose buoyancy I had delivered us to this inconvenient place. I had also experienced an abrupt attack of amnesia, and could not remember anything at all that Martin had told me about how the car worked.

'Look, there's someone coming behind us. Turn the key.'

Wildly I turned the key, against every internal protest. We were facing directly into the sun, and it beat down on my face through the windscreen. In the thick glare, the road beyond was a group of indistinct shapes.

'I can't see anything.'

'Fuck. Hang on.' He reached across me and flipped down the sun shield. 'Is that better?'

'A bit.'

'Right. Clutch.'

'Which one's the clutch?'

'On the left!'

The car surged forward and I clung to the wheel, steering this way and that while Martin shouted indistinct warnings beside me. Several times as we entered the town I closed my eyes and gasped, for the body of the car seemed so broad to me that an intake of breath was required to get it through apertures of impossible narrowness.

'Slow down a bit,' said Martin shrilly. 'That's right. We're going to turn left in a minute.'

The astonished faces of passers-by flashed past me in a blur of houses and shopfronts and parked cars. I had no sense whatever of my own control over what was happening.

'*Left!*' yelled Martin, gesturing wildly with his arms.

My body responded only to the direction of the command rather than the proper procedure for executing it. I slewed the wheel automatically to the left, without slowing down, and there was a tremendous shrieking all around us as we shot into what was evidently a car park and came to a timely, if unintentional, halt.

'Jesus Christ,' said Martin.

'Sorry.'

I felt drained of all life and could only sit limply behind the steering wheel. Martin, when I looked at him, wore a blanched expression of exhaustion.

'You'd better get me out,' he said. 'I'm late.'

When I opened the car door and stepped out, my knees gave way beneath me and I staggered, almost falling over. Clinging to the car, I inched my way round to the boot and opened it.

'Stella,' called Martin from the front. 'How are you going to get home?'

I had not given any consideration to this question, but it was immediately obvious to me that I could not drive the car alone.

'You'll have to stay,' continued Martin, who had evidently reached the same conclusion.

'Stay here? What will I do?'

'I dunno. Help out or something. Meet my interesting friends.'

'What about Pamela?' I heaved the chair unsteadily out of the boot. 'She'll be expecting me back.'

'There's a remarkable invention,' said Martin, 'called the telephone.'

I got Martin into his chair and then, my hands shaking, locked the car. On the far side of the car park was a low modern building made of red brick. Releasing the brake with my trembling foot, I began slowly to wheel him towards it.

Chapter Nineteen

We entered a reception area, with plastic chairs in a row against one wall and a long desk along the other. Both walls were almost entirely covered with drawings held there by drawing pins. Some were very childish; others quite accomplished. My attention was caught by a portrait of a woman drawn in bold pencil. She was sitting rather self-consciously, with her hand beneath her chin, and a slightly tense, impatient smile on her lips. I immediately recognized her as Pamela.

'Did you do that?' I said to Martin.

'Yes. She hates it. She thinks it makes her look old.'

I could not comprehend how Pamela could fail to be pleased by Martin's evident talent for drawing; but looking at it again, I saw how her vanity might have overpowered her delight. Martin had certainly caught her likeness in a manner which foreshadowed what was to come, rather than reflected past glories; but there was something ineffably more real to the picture also, which could only be the work of intimacy and which revealed things about Pamela that I suspected but could never properly have expressed. He had captured her self-regard – a form of insolence which surprised me – and a certain affectation of manner too. Most tellingly, he had included in his picture the fact that its subject did not like being examined; that she regarded his scrutiny as presumptuous and threatening, and the act of drawing itself as rather suspect. It was difficult not to wonder, with his animadversion so publicly displayed before me, what else Martin thought about Pamela.

'Afternoon, Martin!' said a cheerful voice.

'Hello, Mary,' Martin replied. 'This is my friend Stella.'

A woman had emerged from a door at the far end of the room, and now took up a position behind the desk. She was quite elderly, with grey hair set in waves. I was momentarily confused, thinking that I recognized her.

'Stella, is it?' she said, to me. 'Nice to have you here, love.'

I realized that she resembled the woman who ran the village shop in Hilltop.

'Thank you,' I said.

'You'd better hurry in,' she said. 'I think they've started without you.'

'Started what?' I said, following Martin through a doorway at the end of the reception area and down a long corridor.

'Discussion,' he said. 'That's how they kick off. You're not supposed to miss it.'

The corridor, like the reception area, was hung with drawings. From the far end, I could hear a growing rabble of voices. Although it didn't particularly resemble mine, the place reminded me unpleasantly of school. I was conscious, strangely, of my physical size, and of the freedom of my own clothes as I walked. We reached the end of the corridor, and Martin pushed open a door directly ahead which stood slightly ajar. The noise I had heard from the corridor was abruptly silenced. I followed behind him, and as the door swung shut I was confronted by an extraordinary scene. The room was large and very light, with windows all along one wall; and in the centre of it, the sun glancing off them in blinding flashes of steel, was a throng of wheelchairs.

'Well, look who's here!' said a woman's voice.

For a moment I could not work out which among the blank, mute faces which stared at us from within the vast metallic tangle of apparatus had spoken. Looking up, my eyes met a pair level with my own, and I realized that the woman who stood at the centre of this curious circle must be the teacher.

'Hello,' I said, addressing myself to her. 'I'm Stella.'

'Hello, Stella!' she replied; not, I felt, entirely convinced by my attempt to communicate with her as one adult to another. She looked down at her brood. 'Say hello to Stella, everybody!'

There was a dissonant chorus of 'Hello, Stella,' which began as a rumbling groundswell and tailed off into fluting chirps of welcome. Martin wheeled himself towards the group and took up a position on its fringes. His face was sullen. I lingered awkwardly, looking around for a chair.

'Stella, why don't you sit over there?' said the woman, pointing to a chair by the wall.

'OK,' I said.

'Why can't she sit with us?' interposed a boy's voice gruffly. The words were slightly slurred.

'Yes! Yes!' chorused some of the others in agreement.

'*I* see.' The woman laughed ingratiatingly. I sensed that she was not pleased by this minor uprising. 'Who thinks Stella should come and join our group?'

There was an immediate bristling of raised arms and straining torsos.

'OK,' she said, looking around the group with an expression of concentration, as if conducting a serious calculation of votes. 'Well, it looks as if you're very popular today, Stella! Do you want to draw your chair up just there? *That's* it.'

I moved my chair and sat down again. Raising my eyes, I saw that every face was turned towards me and I smiled stiffly. From where I sat, I could only see Martin's shoulder and the side of his head.

'Martin!' said the woman, raising her eyebrows and opening her eyes wide. 'Would you like to tell us why you were late again?'

She spoke very clearly, as if there was some danger that he wouldn't understand what she said. The portion of Martin I could see didn't move.

'Sorry,' he mumbled.

'We talked about this last week, didn't we? I think we all felt that your lateness was a problem, and that the others felt undermined by it. I think you said that you were going to make an effort to be on time, didn't you?'

'It was my fault!' I interrupted, horrified by the woman's remarks.

'Stella says it was her fault,' said the woman after a pause, never taking her eyes from Martin. 'Is that true?'

'I was supposed to drive him and I got delayed,' I insisted.

At this the woman turned to look at me. Her expression was steely.

'We like to let the children speak for themselves here, Stella,' she said. 'Is that true, Martin?'

'I suppose so,' said Martin.

Trying to distract myself from the extreme dislike I was taking to this woman, I looked around at the group. There were about thirty of them, in roughly equal numbers of boys and girls. Most of them seemed considerably younger than Martin; several were barely more than children. It was very odd to see in replica the features I had come to associate with Martin's singularity. In numbers they took on the look of a species; and realizing this, I am afraid to say that I found myself in strong disagreement with the whole character of this convention, and not merely with its leader. The notion that Martin's misfortune should be promoted to the status of a characteristic struck me as wrong. It did not now surprise me, given the indignity of his qualification to attend it, that he disliked the centre so intensely.

'I think some of the others feel that by being late you're giving out strong messages that you don't want to be part of the group,' persisted the woman. 'I think you felt that, Marie, didn't you?'

Her wide eyes described a significant arc, landing on a girl of about Martin's age sitting opposite me on the other side of the room.

'Yeah,' said Marie. Her voice was high-pitched. She had long, fair hair and a tragic expression.

'I think you felt that Martin was trying to seek attention, didn't you?' said the woman presently, when it became clear that Marie was to say nothing more.

'Yeah,' said Marie.

'What do you say to that, Martin?'

'It's crap,' said Martin.

One or two people sniggered.

'Miss!' said a younger boy with a thick basin of dark hair, his arm shooting up. 'He said *crap*!'

'I know he did, Stephen,' sighed the teacher. 'Don't you remember that we agreed Martin could sometimes use that sort of language, because that's how they speak at home? Do you remember that?'

'It's true,' I assented, nodding.

'Martin, do you see now how distracting your late entrances are? Do you see why the others might think you're attention-seeking?'

'I suppose so.'

'Good. So will you be making more of an effort in future?'

'*Yes*,' said Martin irritably.

'OK!' said the woman brightly, the musical cadence of the word signalling a change of subject. 'Let's begin our discussion, shall we? This week I wanted to talk about *feelings*.'

'Feelings,' repeated the group. There was something incantatory in the woman's tone which made the response automatic.

'Now,' she continued. 'Who can tell me what *feelings* are?'

Hands shot up into the air.

'Let's see.' The woman pursed her lips and made a selecting motion with her hand, as if she were choosing a sweet. 'Elizabeth.'

'They're emotions,' said Elizabeth, an unfortunate-looking redhead.

'Ye-es,' said the woman coaxingly, implying that the answer had been insufficient. 'What *sort* of emotions?'

'All sorts,' said Elizabeth quizzically.

'That's right. Good and bad. Who can tell me a good feeling? Stephen.'

Stephen was straining again with his arm aloft.

'Eating chocolate!' he cried.

'Ye-*es*,' said the woman, even more doubtfully. 'But that's more of a *sensation*, isn't it?'

'When your team wins at football!' said another boy.

'Good!' beamed the woman.

'When your friend comes to see you!'

'*Good!*'

I was edging back in my chair in the attempt to catch sight of Martin. He was sitting with his head erect and his eyes closed, with an aspect of almost mystical contemplation. As I was looking, he opened his eyes and gazed at me.

'Now,' said the teacher, when the volley of positives had subsided. 'What about *bad* feelings?'

I sensed that of the two subjects, this one interested her more; and that she would not be so easily pleased by the children's answers concerning it.

'What about *bad* feelings?' she said again, giving the word every nuance that facial expression and intonation could muster.

'When you're sad,' chirped a little girl beside me.

'When you're *sad*,' repeated the woman triumphantly, looking around at the group. 'What makes you sad?'

There was a fidgeting silence.

'Martin,' she said presently. 'What makes *you* sad?'

'Take your pick,' said Martin, shrugging.

'Stephen, what about you?'

'Dunno,' said Stephen in a small voice.

I had my eye on Elizabeth, being more articulate but less defensive, to supply the correct answer; and sure enough, when her forays among the male contingent had proved unproductive, the woman's gaze settled confidently on the girl.

'Elizabeth?'

'When people don't treat you as normal,' said Elizabeth reliably, her fleshy white face barely moving.

'*When people don't treat you as normal,*' echoed the teacher, distributing the phrase with her eyes over the whole group. 'And how does that make you feel?'

'Sad,' said Elizabeth, nonplussed.

Now that I was settled in my chair, and had more or less got the measure of my new situation, the frantic pressure which had been pounding in my chest all day began slowly to subside. My drive to Buckley underwent in my mind the miraculous reduction which time can effect on an unpleasant past event, while other anxieties, emerging from its shadow, grew correspondingly larger. While I had certainly succeeded in conveying myself and Martin to the centre without injury, my accomplishment accrued in my mind a debt to luck which I had not attributed to it at the time. Concerned only with the immediate problem of getting to Buckley that afternoon, I had failed to take into account a future regularly punctuated by these journeys; a future which must, given my reliance on chance rather than skill in the matter of driving, contain down one of its dark trajectories a horrible accident by which I would repay all that I had borrowed from fortune. Despite Martin's willingness to enter into my deception, I knew that by continuing to drive in this manner I would be taking unacceptable risks with his life; and yet his compliance was so tempting, given the consequences of an admission of truth to the Maddens, that I found myself as I sat there without the clear intention of confessing the problem to them at the next opportunity. How could I confess to the Maddens, now that I had exposed not only their car but also their son to danger? Seen in this light, it seemed incredible that I had not been honest when honesty had come at a more reasonable price; but I was beginning to realize that no amount of calculation could cure what probity would have prevented.

'Now just *calm down* everybody,' said the teacher, making leavening motions with her hands.

I realized, surfacing from my reverie, that some kind of argument had broken out around me. Its centre appeared to be Marie, the piercing register of whose voice rose in indeterminate squawks and exclamations above the waves of commentary sweeping the group. The teacher's face was a medley of triumph and fear, as if she were savouring the perils of her job and tasting her own competence as she negotiated them.

'I've got the right to my own opinion,' complained Marie.

'Marie's got the right to her own opinion,' confirmed the teacher above the noise.

'That's like saying I've got the right to pick my nose,' said Martin clearly from the back of the group. 'Everybody would prefer it if I didn't do it in front of them.'

Martin's comment detonated explosions of laughter all across the room.

'I really don't think—' said the teacher amidst the pandemonium.

'That's *typical*!' shrieked Marie. 'That's *typical*!'

'—that sort of remark is what we're all about here, Martin.'

Martin did not reply. A brief hush fell over the room. Then a boy with an oafish face and untidy hair put up his hand.

'I support Martin!' he said loudly, looking to his hero for approval. 'Marie talks too much. She's always complaining.'

'Yeah! Yeah!' chimed a choir of variously pitched male voices.

'Oh, for *Christ's sake*,' wailed Marie.

'Now look.' The teacher's expression of bland geniality was momentarily dislodged by a flash of anger. I saw that her patience with the group was the result of some effort, and that a narrow margin separated it from her loathing. 'Now look,' she said, more calmly. A thread of hysteria ran through her voice. 'Let's all just *cool off*, shall we? This space is meant for discussion only. If you can't all discuss things without arguing' – she looked nervously around the group. I sensed that recourse to a more authoritarian style of leadership was imminent – 'then we'll have to abandon these sessions. Is that clear?' Silence reigned. 'Is that clear?' A grumble of assent rose sheepishly from the wheelchairs. The teacher surveyed the group at a level just above their heads, as if ascertaining the efficiency of their suppression. She wore a slightly vengeful expression as she guarded her painstakingly constructed democracy. 'Now I think we'll end here. You can all go and find your drawings and carry on where you left off on Monday. Quietly!' she commanded, stemming an outbreak of chatter as the group broke up and its constituents began turning on their axes and spinning away to the far end of the room.

I was surprised to hear that more drawing was on the agenda, as from what I had seen so far the building already seemed replete with the group's artistic efforts. I immediately saw in the occupation the slender pretext of distracting the group with minimal effort on behalf of the teacher; a motive I was beginning to suspect underlay the whole character of the 'sessions'. Now that the others had dispersed, I was left rather isolated on my plastic chair; and eventually I stood up and, having nothing else to do, busied myself with replacing the chair where I had found it.

'Stella!'

I turned around and saw the teacher bearing down on me, her arm extended and her face transfixed by a sociable smile.

'Karen Miller,' she said, grasping my hand and shaking it. Having already told her my name, I was somewhat lost as to the correct response to this greeting. 'It's great to have you here,' she continued. 'I always think it's very positive for carers to see the kind of thing we do here.' She laughed ruefully. 'Although I'm afraid they weren't on their best behaviour today. I wouldn't want you to think that it was always like that. Most of the time we have really useful discussions.'

'I'm sure you do,' I said, nodding. I saw that she required some assurance that I would not form a bad opinion of her class, which I might then remove from her jurisdiction and disseminate.

'The discussions are designed to help the children come to terms with their situation,' she continued. Her large eyes pinioned mine, but strangely I did not feel that she was looking at me. 'Our aim here is to enable them to socialize their disability. A lot of them feel very isolated without this sort of contact. Here they can just relax and be themselves. We wanted to create a space above all in which children like these feel *normal*.'

'Right,' I said.

'So.' She leaned back, wedging her backside on the window ledge beside which we stood and folding her arms. 'How are you finding life with Martin?'

Our abrupt arrival at intimacy surprised me. I had found it hard enough to communicate with this curious creature as a professional; but as a woman, she seemed even more alien. At her question, I immediately became aware of her physical appearance. She was shorter than me – although before I would have thought her much taller – and slightly plump beneath loose, silky clothes. Although I could see little of it, I sensed that her flesh was soft and yielding, as if she had no bones. Several silver necklaces circled her throat, and three silver earrings studded one ear. I noticed that she was wearing quite a lot of make-up, which formed creases around her eyes and mouth. Her lips were a moist, lurid red. On her chin rose one or two pimples, at whose peaks her make-up gathered in a sort of volcanic crust. Her short hair was a purplish red, and was elaborately styled in a wispy, feathered cap around her face. She was quite attractive, although whether because or in spite of these cosmetic blandishments it was hard to tell. Her face and hair, held together apparently by great force of will, seemed poised on the brink of chaos.

'Fine,' I said. I sensed an occluded bitterness in her nature, as if she were concealing some complex, self-serving mechanism which any information I gave her might inadvertently nourish. 'I've only been with the family for a few days.'

'Oh, *right*,' she said, nodding as if to herself. Unruly noises were coming from the other end of the room. 'And how are you finding the Maddens?'

She was not interested, I saw, in me; or rather, her interest was indirect, and travelled through me in the hope of reaching the goal of Martin's family. I was surprised that she should be so indiscreet in her curiosity about them.

'I like them,' I curtly replied. 'As I said, I've only been there a few days.'

'Oh, you'll get used to them,' she said, as if I had complained that I had found them uncongenial. 'A lot of people find them a bit stand-offish, you know, but once you get to know them—*Can you keep it down, please?*' She projected her voice powerfully to the other end of the room. The sound startled me; and one or two of the others looked round, their faces white and vacant with surprise. 'Yes,' she continued, 'I've got to know Mrs Madden quite well since Martin's been coming to the centre. She often drops in just for a chat. I think she's a really lovely woman underneath it all. People get very jealous, you know, in a place like this.' She assumed a thoughtful expression. 'They've got nothing better to do than talk. If you're attractive and rich, like she is, then you've got to accept that people are going to gossip about you. And living in that house, as well!

I've only ever seen it from the outside, mind you, when I drop Martin off. Apparently they never ask *anyone* in. What's it like inside?'

'It's very nice,' I reluctantly admitted.

'*He*'s a bit of a dark horse, of course. Nice, apparently, but quite odd. There's been all sorts of rumours about *him*.'

'What sort of rumours?' I could not restrain myself from asking.

'Oh, I shan't dignify them by repeating them, Stella.' She gave me a look designed, I felt, to inform me that she found my curiosity distasteful. 'Besides, I wouldn't want the Maddens thinking that I was passing on gossip.'

There was something not quite right about my conversation with Karen Miller. Although we might have appeared to be communicating, there was no spark of contact between us. This was not merely the customary awkwardness of strangers. It was as if some membrane lay between us which I was unable to penetrate. Our mouths were moving; our words roughly conformed to the principles of verbal exchange; and yet our discourse merely mimicked conversation, in the way a mannequin does a human body.

Looking at her, I found myself wondering what Karen Miller's life outside the centre was like. I tried to imagine her home, her family and friends, and could not. She was not, I hazarded, married: she emanated solitude, boundless and uninterrupted. She did not have the look of one circumscribed by cohabitation. I wondered then if that was what I looked like; if the freedom for which I had given up all restraints and claims was that which I saw before me in Karen Miller.

'I wouldn't repeat it to them,' I indignantly replied. I did not worry about what she might think of my importunity. I did not believe, in any case, that she knew anything about the Maddens that had not been dredged from the common pool of idle speculation. 'I know,' I coaxed, 'that there have been some problems about the public footpaths crossing the farm.'

Karen Miller opened her mouth wide.

'Timothy!' she called. I glimpsed her tongue, moist and plump. 'Give Jenny back her picture! Well,' she continued, after a pause, 'it's mostly just the usual hanky-panky, although people around here have got such tiny minds, I wouldn't be surprised if they get it all from books. You know, the upper classes, at it day and night. As I say, they've got nothing better to think about.'

'I'm sure Mr Madden isn't involved in anything like that,' I said.

'Well, you never know, do you? *She*'s certainly had her fair share.'

'How do you know?'

'Well, it's not exactly top secret, is it? You could probably go and look it up in the public library. I felt quite sorry for her, having her name in the papers and that.'

'What do you mean?'

'*I thought I said to keep it down!* Look, I'd better get on,' she said, all at once brisk. 'Will you be all right over here?'

I assured her that I would. As I watched her walk away, the bossy motion of her legs defined beneath the thin material of her trousers, I had a strange thought. *Nobody loves her.* I don't know why this uncharitable notion occurred to me, and with such certainty. It was something to do with the way she walked. Perhaps it was merely because I did not like the way she walked that I deemed her unlovable. My intuition, however, seemed more subtle to me than that. She did not have the self-consciousness of one who had been singled out. She walked as if no one had ever watched her do so. For the rest of the afternoon, while Karen Miller went about her desultory ministrations, I was unable to prevent myself from embroidering her hapless person with my own insights; and by the time she was commanding the group to finish what they were doing and put away their drawing materials, I had created so monstrous a vision of her future that it was all I could do to stop myself from taking her to one side and pressing my message upon her. Instead I urged her in my thoughts to apply more diligence to the business of securing some affection for herself; to bend, to submit, to deploy whatever wiles were necessary to lure a companion into the dreadful pit of her loneliness. It was imperative, I felt, that she should not be complacent in this matter.

It was for myself, I don't doubt, that I was worrying. After we had bidden goodbye to the group and begun making our way back down the corridor, I was so rapt in the examination of my own deportment that I even forgot the ordeal which awaited me out in the car park. All that mattered, in that moment, was that I should solemnly undertake never to walk like Karen Miller.

Chapter Twenty

Martin and I sat side by side out in the car park. Having had neither the foresight nor the skill to leave the car in the shade, the atmosphere inside it even after we had opened all the windows was oppressive. A strong, unpleasant smell of hot rubber radiated from every surface. The steering wheel was scorching to the touch. To our left, at the entrance to the car park, a long pair of tyre marks described twin arcs across the concrete in the heat, two incriminating fingers pointing at us.

'We can't go on like this,' I said. 'We're going to have to tell your parents everything.'

As soon as I had sat down in the driving seat, my body had gushed all over with sweat. A trickle spouted from my cheek and ran down my neck.

'You're doing fine, Stel-la.'

'I could get us both killed.'

'So could anybody. Cars are dangerous.'

'That's no argument. Your parents wouldn't agree. We've just been lucky so far, that's all. What if I injured you? You could be crippled for life.' There was a pause. I broke out into a fresh volley of sweat. 'Sorry. I wasn't thinking.'

'You might be doing them a favour,' observed Martin.

'Don't be ridiculous.'

'Surely it's up to me? I'm the one taking the risk.'

'That's a very selfish way to look at things.'

'So is your way.'

'No it isn't. I'm sacrificing my job and my reputation for your safety.'

'You're sacrificing my happiness for your guilt, you mean. I'll be depressed if you go. The others have all been awful. Mater doesn't have a clue. Look, it'll be fine. You'll improve in no time. You've just got to practise.'

After a heart-stopping slew out of the car park, we were back on the road. Everything that had happened in the interval took on the texture of a dream. My only reality was this maelstrom of noise and motion, this perilous enclosure in which every second dripped with risk and the world beyond the windscreen was transformed into a hostile adversary, on the elusion of which my life depended. The thing I disliked most about driving was its contingency. To drive was to be in a perpetual state of stress. One could not, while driving, merely stop doing so.

'What did you think of the centre?' said Martin conversationally, once we had left Buckley in a reproachful fanfare of car horns.

'I can't talk.'

'Keep to the left, Stel-la. We're going to change gear. Clutch!'

'Did it work?'

'Yes. So what did you think? Stel-la?'

I was dimly aware that Martin had asked me a question, but the mechanisms required to answer it could not be activated whilst I was in this state of siege.

'*Leemealone!*' I said, unable even to divert the resources necessary to the proper formation of words.

'OK. Slow down a bit. We're almost there. Keep to the left. That's it.'

Miraculously – particularly seeing as my instinct was to steer towards any object which came within my sights – we did not meet a single car during the entire journey from Buckley to Franchise. By the time we had reached the gates at the bottom of the drive, my exhaustion and terror were such that our safe arrival was an inadequate comfort. Of all the feelings I might in the innocence of my pre-driving projections have imagined for myself in the wake of a successful return voyage from Buckley, the terrible, infantile self-pity which welled up in me as we chugged to a halt in front of the house was the furthest from my expectation. It was as if I had experienced some primal violation. I felt the novelty of a desire for my mother; proof, if confirmation were needed, that the whole business of driving was unnatural and that to be inured to it would be to acquire an inhuman range of attributes.

'I was beginning to wonder where you two had got to!' said Pamela, when we presented ourselves, wan and subdued, in the kitchen. 'I suddenly realized after you'd gone, Stella, that Piers forgot to insure you to drive the car. And then when you didn't come back I got dreadfully worried that something had happened to you.'

'Oh!' I put my hand over my mouth, as something was peeled up off the trampled floor of my memory. 'I meant to ring you and say that I was staying at the centre for the afternoon! I completely forgot.'

'Don't worry,' said Pamela genially. 'I phoned and they told me you were there. It was fine. No, we're the batty ones, forgetting that insurance. Thank God you didn't have a crash.'

With Pamela being so kind, I was tempted to fall upon her with a weeping confession; but her mention of the insurance had set my mind once more to cunning. I wondered if she and Piers could be encouraged to keep forgetting it, only to be reminded too late each time Martin required ferrying to Buckley.

'So what did you make of it down there?' she enquired, putting on the kettle. 'Was Mrs Miller at the helm?'

'Mrs Miller?'

'Karen. Red hair. Rather tarty, in a hippyish way.'

'Oh. Yes.' With a rush of shame I remembered the afternoon's speculations concerning Karen Miller. 'I didn't realize she was married.'

'Oh, goodness yes. Her husband's a local cheese. Councillor. Frightful bore called Roger. She's pretty frightful too, actually. Martin's got some noise he makes for her.' Martin, his face bright with approval, made a series of loud, lowing noises. Pamela laughed. '*That's* it. I suppose we're being horribly unkind. She means well. And she really does such good work.'

The centre, I could see, was the object of one of Pamela's unshakeable loyalties. It required little more for me to keep my opinions of the place to myself.

'I'll tell you something about *her*, though,' said Pamela, then, drawing to the table with the empty teapot held distractedly in her hands. 'Martin, you're not listening, are you?'

'No,' said Martin.

'*Apparently*,' said Pamela in a confidential tone, 'she and Roger are involved in some extraordinary club in Buckley. You'd never think it to look at them in a million years, but somebody told me it's true.'

'What sort of club?'

'Oh, you know, the ones where a group of friends get together once a week and swap.'

'Swap what?'

'*Wives*,' whispered Pamela. 'It's got a funny name.'

'Swinging,' said Martin.

'That's right. Swinging. What they do is all get together at one of their houses, and the men put their car keys down on the table and the women pick them up. And off they go.'

'Where to?'

'What? Oh, they don't go anywhere in the *car*!' Pamela gave a peal of laughter. 'They go to one of the bedrooms and have it off.'

It could just have been the albeit minor car element, but I found the notion of what Pamela had described absolutely nauseating.

'That's disgusting,' I said.

'Isn't it?' said Pamela delightedly. 'Some horrible little semi in Buckley just *shaking*. Apparently it's frightfully common.'

It took me some time to realize that she meant widespread rather than vulgar.

'In a way, you can see why they do it, though,' continued Pamela. 'In many ways it's safer than having affairs. Everybody's equal and it's all out in the open. As long as there wasn't somebody you *dreaded* getting. I suppose they couldn't be that fussy. Or perhaps they learn to recognize the car keys. They all have to agree to keep frightfully mum about it, though.'

'In case the police find out?'

'It's not against the *law*, darling,' said Pamela, giving me a look of amazement. 'No, it's just so that they don't get jealous. The men start having punch-ups, apparently. It all sounds absolutely *exhausting* to me.'

I remembered then what Karen Miller had said about Pamela having 'had her fair share'. A whole new dimension, a subterranean realm of operations of which I had been unaware, was revealing itself to me.

'Where are the others?' said Martin.

'Over at the field. They'll be back before long and then we'll have supper. Do you two want to go and amuse yourselves until then?'

'I won't be staying to supper,' I falteringly interjected.

'Why ever not?' said Pamela.

'I'm – busy.'

Martin made several kissing noises. Pamela looked at me slightly oddly. Suddenly a smile dawned across her face.

'Oh, it's your *date*!' she said. '*How* wonderful. Although I shouldn't go on an empty stomach if I were you. Jack will have had his tea on the dot of half-past six. He won't be wining and dining you. In fact, you'll probably be lucky if you get a packet of beer nuts out of him. He's *notoriously* tight.'

At Pamela's words something started to plague me. I reached for it, trying to remember what it was, but it hovered tantalizingly just beyond my compass.

'Well, I'd better go,' I said.

'Good luck!' cried Pamela.

'See you,' mumbled Martin, an injured expression on his face; for all the world as if my assignation were a betrayal of him, rather than the reverse.

Back at the cottage I entrenched myself in the bedroom, sensing that a long and bitter sartorial struggle lay ahead. Ploughing through my suitcases, I realized that most of my clothes were dirty, although I had barely worn them. The extreme heat had rendered my things limp and odiferous, mostly after only a single outing. I wondered how I was expected to do my washing, and whether Pamela would bring the subject up or wait until I was driven by desperation to do so myself. I was keen to give a more decorous impression to Mr Trimmer, after the shameful episode of the cut-off trousers; not because I cared particularly what he thought of me, but because I wanted firmly to retrieve any undesirable notions they might have introduced into his head. In the event, I had no choice in the matter: my smart dress was the only thing clean enough to withstand public scrutiny, although as I put it on I felt that it gave unwanted and wholly inaccurate prominence to an entirely different range of motives; namely that in it I gave the impression of having made an effort. I was bewildered, after I had done up the buttons, by the fact that the material hung about me in great folds. Finding no other explanation, I realized that I appeared to have shrunk quite drastically. That this should have happened in the few days since I had last worn the dress, without cause and without my really noticing, was profoundly disturbing. It was as if I were disappearing; or rather, as if the space I was entitled to occupy were being gradually withdrawn. The change made me nervous, as if without weight I might be overlooked or swept away.

At ten minutes to eight I heard the crunch of footsteps on the gravel path and I hurried downstairs, eschewing lipstick in the hope of offsetting the excessive glamour of my attire. A thunderous knock shook the cottage door, and I opened it to find Mr Trimmer standing legs astride and arms held rigidly by his sides in the falling dusk. I was surprised to see that despite the warmth of the evening he was wearing a sweater. It was blue with a red stripe around the V of its neck; the sort of thing that might be worn as a school uniform.

'Good evening,' I said stiffly.

'Land Rover's over in the drive,' he replied. He seemed embarrassed. 'We'll have to walk there first.'

He turned abruptly and set off. I followed, my chest hollow with dread and disappointment. The evening, I felt sure, was going to be far worse than I had anticipated. From behind, Mr Trimmer had an unusual appearance. His hips were low-slung and his backside so broad that his legs splayed slightly beneath it. He waddled as he walked, like an overfed bird. I ran to catch up with him, so that I would not be left to the contemplation of this view; but the path was narrow, and it was impossible to walk beside him without drawing too close. I fell behind again. He trod heavily and silently ahead of me, as if I were a prisoner being led to a cell. The noise of our footsteps and the tall, oppressive hedges on either side put me in a strange trance. For a moment I forgot entirely where I was, and what phase of my life I was occupying. Presently we emerged on the front drive and I saw a battered pale-green Land Rover parked beside the Maddens' car. Silently, Mr Trimmer opened the door and got in. As I progressed around the front of the vehicle to the other side, I saw him through the window sitting and staring straight ahead. As soon as I had passed him, he started the engine.

'We're off!' I said with false cheer, once I had climbed up to my seat. The inside of the Land Rover smelt of straw and animals. On the floor at my feet was a single, mud-encrusted shoe. Mr Trimmer did not reply to my observation. He seemed to be having some trouble getting the vehicle into gear. The controls were very widely spaced, and as he stamped on the pedals with his outstretched feet and thrashed the far-flung gearstick, his strange body stiffened on a diagonal plane above his seat.

'Come on, you cow!' he broadly exclaimed, his face grim with exertion.

With a great grinding sound, we shot forwards and began clattering at high speed down the drive. Jostling up and down on my seat, I surreptitiously groped for the seat belt but couldn't find one.

'You won't find it,' bellowed Mr Timmer over the noise of the engine. 'Long gone.'

I worried that he might have interpreted my action as a criticism of his driving, but couldn't think of anything to say which might erase this impression. Lost for words on one count, I then found myself locked into a larger silence. Search as I might, I could find no subject on which even a brief conversation might be built. We reached the bottom of the drive and turned left along the road to Hilltop. Mr Trimmer began to drive at an alarming speed. The engine's roar rose to a scream and the Land Rover rocked this way and that. The darkening road rushed up at us and I gripped the dashboard in front of me and closed my eyes, my heart pounding. For longer than seemed possible, we raced along the knife-blade of certain death; until finally the shriek of the engine descended one key and then another, and I dared to open my eyes. We had arrived, I saw, at Hilltop; and after hurtling some way along the

High Street, Mr Trimmer gave a brutal wrench of the wheel and brought us up short, almost flinging me from my seat, in front of the pub. My immediate reaction to this entirely unnecessary display of bravado was intense anger. So forceful and righteous was my fury, and so overwhelming the dislike for Mr Trimmer it caused to surge up in my mouth, that I felt I would be justified in turning around there and then and marching back to Franchise; a course which had the added advantage of sparing me the gruelling evening to come. It is far easier, however, to entertain these thoughts than to act on them; and seconds later I found myself following him, brimming with the consciousness of how unbearable my situation was, towards the pub.

The chairs and tables outside were all crowded, but I hoped that we would still be able to find a space among them; not because I wanted particularly to enjoy the warm evening, but because the thought of being enclosed with Mr Trimmer threatened to turn my agony to torment. Trailing after him, I was buffeted by strong waves of feeling, from which my relative happiness with the Maddens so far had protected me: homesickness, longing for Edward, self-pity, all the predators of the heart which even a momentary weakening of the spirits can unleash. So miserable, in fact, did I begin to feel that I became careless of my own behaviour. Mr Trimmer's boorishness had given me the impression that he was insensible. As I stood beside him at the bar, I made no effort to disguise my unhappiness, and even attempted, by means of sullen looks and meaningful sighs, to communicate it to him. By doing so, I knew, I was presenting a challenge to his imperviousness; a sort of childish game which, in my state of self-absorption, I had elected to play with myself. I did not, in any case, expect him to respond to my taunts; I imagined, in this infantile mood, that he would not even notice them. He stood at the bar, looking straight ahead, while the chatter of the pub grew louder and louder around us.

'Do you want to go home?' he said suddenly, to my horror. His face was expressionless in profile, and his tone of voice suggested that I might want to go home because I had left something there, or was expected back.

'Of course not!' I exclaimed; although, still in a malevolent humour, I could not prevent my protest from sounding slightly insincere.

'You were doing that,' he observed flatly, in response to what I had no idea. He put out his arm in a clutching motion. I realized that he was referring to my behaviour in the Land Rover.

'I'm a nervous passenger,' I said.

'Do you want something?'

He gave no indication as to what this something might be. Eventually, I realized that he was asking me whether I wanted a drink; and at that moment I remembered the forgetful itch I had experienced in Pamela's kitchen. I had no money; and had been trying, I now knew, to remind myself to ask her for some. I wondered what I should do. Were I to permit Mr Trimmer to buy me a drink, he would surely expect one in return during the course of the evening. Meanwhile, my failure to respond to his offer had caused him to turn and look enquiringly at me. His face really was quite extraordinary. It looked as if a door had been repeatedly slammed on it. Not wishing to offend him further, I decided on a plan.

'I'll get them,' I said, gushingly.

His head gave a perky twitch.

'Very kind,' he said, nodding.

With the exaggerated gestures of a pantomime artist, I began clutching at my hip, as if feeling for a handbag. Not finding one, I looked this way and that, my face displaying carefully calibrated degrees of surprise, disbelief, and then outright panic.

'Oh no!' I cried. 'I've forgotten my handbag!'

It was not the cleverest of ploys, and I am not the best of actresses. Mr Trimmer did not respond enthusiastically to the news. In fact, he looked as if he wished that I had taken him up on his offer of a drive home. At first I feared that he didn't believe me; but then I remembered what Pamela had said about him being 'tight'.

'They're on me, then,' he said.

'I'm terribly sorry,' I added, although it would probably have been sensible to have said nothing more. 'I can't think what came over me. It's not like me at all to be so disorganized.' Mr Trimmer regarded me dumbly. 'Oh,' I said, as I realized that he was waiting for me to tell him what I wanted. 'I'll have a G-and – a gin and tonic, please.'

Mr Trimmer bought a half-pint of beer for himself, and carried it, without consultation, to a small table at the back of the pub. We sat in silence, our drinks untouched between us. The pub itself was very pleasant, although slightly gloomy for a summer evening. With its low ceiling and phalanx of black beams, it was like sitting in the ribcage of some vast animal. Fruit machines pulsed steadily in the shadows.

'Have you been abroad?' said Mr Trimmer presently. He picked up his glass and sipped from it.

'Yes,' I said, unsure whether a fuller confession, listing locations and frequency, was required.

'So you speak Spanish, then.'

'No, I don't, I'm afraid.' I said, bemused. Taking my cue from Mr Trimmer, I picked up my own glass. 'Have *you* ever been abroad?'

'No,' he said, nodding. 'My friend has. He speaks Spanish.'

'Oh.'

'Would you agree,' he enlarged, after a lengthy pause, 'that tourists have a . . . detrimental effect on the local . . . communities?'

'It depends,' I said.

'So you don't agree.'

'It depends on the extent of the tourism, and the type of tourist who goes to a place,' I said. Even as the words were coming from my mouth I had a sense of their futility. I felt as if I were chewing dry bread.

'My friend thinks it does. He says all the locals want to do is get their hands on your money.'

'Because they have so little in comparison?' I hazarded.

'That's right!' Mr Trimmer seemed genuinely pleased by my reply. I had evidently confirmed his friend's opinion, elevating it to the status of a theory.

'But tourism itself can bring money,' I added cautiously. 'So it's not entirely a bad thing.'

Mr Trimmer's enthusiasm was abruptly snuffed out. His eyebrows drew together, creasing his forehead; an alarming expression, as if someone were pressing hard on either side of his face. I noticed that, while I had drunk half my glass, he had barely skimmed his.

'How long have you worked for the Maddens?' I said, feeling that a change of subject was required.

'Five years, about,' muttered Mr Trimmer. His expression had modulated to one of resistance, like a child at whose lips a medicine spoon is probing.

'And do you like it there?'

He did not reply at all to this. I glanced at my watch, and saw to my dismay that barely half an hour had passed.

'Madden,' he said suddenly. 'Mad-den. Mad 'un. Get it?'

'Oh yes!' I trilled.

'Are you mad?'

'I beg your pardon?'

'Women say they are. Are you?'

'Certainly not.'

'That's all right, then.' Another long pause. 'Her, his missus, she's a bad one.'

'Are you talking about Mrs Madden?'

'Mrs Mad 'un.' He nodded. 'I don't like her.'

'Why not?'

I was resolved at any moment to put a stop to this bizarre

conversation; but I could not resist letting Mr Trimmer run on, just to see what he would say. It is hard to convey how alien his manner of speech was to me. I could barely understand what he was saying; not because of his accent, although it was strong, but because his words and the sequence of his ideas, punctuating in addition vast lagoons of silence, did not conform to any pattern I recognized. It struck me that perhaps he didn't talk very much. He was embarked now on another great pause, his mouth and eyebrows labouring as if with the effort of giving birth to a fully formed sound.

'She's a *shagger*,' he pronounced finally.

'A *what*?'

'I know. I've seen her. I see everything that happens. Not just that business.'

'What business?'

'That's what gave him the heebie-jeebies.' He tapped the side of his head. 'He doesn't know it all, though. If he did . . .' His fingers uncurled by his temples to form what I took to be a gun. He gave me an idiotic grin.

'What business?' I repeated.

'Nothing to do with you,' Mr Trimmer curtly replied. 'You don't need to worry yourself. It's married business.'

I had by this time finished my drink. Mr Trimmer was halfway through his. I wondered if he would offer me another, or whether I would have to wait until he finished.

'What do you mean, the heebie-jeebies?' I persisted, hoping that he would be more forthcoming on the subject of Mr Madden.

Mr Trimmer shook his head.

'He's mental,' he said presently. 'He's going to hurt his self one of those days.'

'How?'

'Walk into one of his own traps, won't he? I nearly done it enough times. Came near enough yourself, and all.'

'In the top field?'

He nodded.

'I thought the step was broken?'

Mr Trimmer swelled silently.

'You mean it was supposed to be?'

He folded his arms over his chest.

'Why? To discourage people from using the footpath?'

'*Some* people,' he finally pronounced. '*Some* people.'

'Who?'

'You're nosy.' He tapped his nose and nodded at me. 'You.'

'Not nosy. Curious. So,' I recapped, 'Mr Madden sabotages his own footpaths to keep *some* people off them. It doesn't make any sense. Surely if someone got hurt, they would go to the police and he'd get into trouble?'

'Police come up.' He gave me a crafty grin. 'They don't find anything, though.'

'Why not?'

'Because I fixed it!'

He burst out laughing; a terrible, preternatural sound, which made heads turn towards us.

'So,' I patiently resumed, 'Mr Madden breaks things and you fix them before anybody can get hurt.'

'That's so.' He nodded and tapped his head again.

With the excitement of these discoveries I was becoming thirsty. Mr Trimmer had inched his way down his own glass, which now stood almost empty. I curled my fingers significantly around mine, in the hope that he would take the hint. He didn't.

'But why,' I said, clearing my dry throat, 'why don't you talk to him about it? It seems a bit of a waste of your time, after all.'

Even as I said it, I knew that I had taken a wrong turning; and I was rewarded with what could not have been less than five minutes of impenetrable silence. I fidgeted impatiently with my glass while Mr Trimmer absorbed my mistake. I was becoming exhausted with the effort of extracting information from the dark and tortuous passages of his mind, but I was not about to give up. I felt myself to be apprehending something of great significance. Who was Mr Madden protecting himself from? And was there a genuine reason for his doing so, or merely the fact that he was, as Mr Trimmer had put it, 'mental'? I wondered if the creature and his undercover band of lobbyists had anything to do with it. It seemed unlikely that it was they whom Mr Madden feared. What threat could they possibly present to him? I remembered the nooses nailed to the creature's wall, and felt a dark qualm of fear. Presently I realized that Mr Trimmer was staring at me and I gave him an encouraging smile.

'What you saw was nothing,' he immediately announced.

Horribly, I saw that this was the way to coax from him what he knew.

'You mean the broken step?' I smiled again, this time more broadly.

'That's it.' He nodded. 'There's guns.'

'Guns?' My smile slipped and I hoisted it back, shifting my knee out from under the table and putting it into full view for good measure. 'Where?'

'All over. Everywhere.' He fixed his eyes on my knee as he spoke, as if he were reading from it. 'Some have been there so long he forgot about 'em. I have to watch him. He'll get his self shot up one of these days.'

'But how?'

'Walk in front of 'em.'

'You mean they're loaded?'

He looked at me cross-eyed and made a strange motion with his hands, as if he were threading a needle.

'Trip wires,' he said finally. 'Learned it in the army, he did.'

I sat, dumbfounded, for some time. Mr Trimmer was staring reproachfully at our empty glasses. He shook his head and sighed. Then he looked at his watch, his eyebrows shooting up in an unconvincing expression of surprise when he saw what it said.

'Better be going,' he said finally.

He stood up abruptly and began walking towards the door. I had no choice but to follow him. The inside of the pub was now penumbral, as the evening outside had faded to the point at which electric light seems to deepen rather than illuminate the darkness. Mr Trimmer opened the door and went out into the dusky High Street; but before I could go after him, I heard a familiar voice emerge from the shadows.

'He*llo*,' it said. 'Fancy meeting you here!'

I turned and saw the creature, slumped in a chair at a table in the corner by the door. It smiled at me delightedly.

'Hello,' I said.

'Out with Mr Trimmer, are we? Wonders will never cease.'

'I can't stop. He's taking me home.'

'I'd watch yourself, dear. He can get a bit frisky when he's had a drink.'

'I think I've found out what happened to Geoff.'

'Really?' The creature raised a sarcastic eyebrow. 'I wasn't aware of any – how shall I put it? – *ambiguity* in the matter. Has Mr Trimmer been sweet-talking you? I didn't think the oaf had it in him.'

'It's not what you think. I'll come and see you tomorrow.'

'As you like.' The creature shrugged. 'You know where to find me.'

'Goodbye.'

It raised its skinny arm in a salute.

'Toodle-pip!'

Outside, Mr Trimmer was sitting motionless in the Land Rover. He started the engine when he saw me. My thoughts in turmoil, I barely noticed the fact that he drove considerably more slowly on our return than he had on the voyage out. Indeed, so distracted was I by all that I had learned during the evening that when a few minutes later the Land Rover ground to a halt in the darkness, it took me some time to realize that we were not sitting outside the house but lodged in the shadows at the bottom of the drive. I turned to Mr Trimmer, my arms and mouth open to form a protest, and at this invitation he lunged at me across the seat, chest-first like a diver, and flung his body against my own in an artless collision.

'Oh, baby!' he cried, squirming against me. 'Oh, baby!'

So utterly shocked was I by this turn of events that his wet, inert lips managed to make contact with my own before I succeeded in placing my hands on his straining chest and throwing him off. Disgustedly, I wiped my mouth with the back of my hand.

'*Mr Trimmer!*' I said.

I put my hand on the door, intending to get out and run, but then Mr Trimmer turned the key and started the engine again. He did not look particularly abject. In fact, he looked angry. His lower lip jutted out. From the side, with his eyes flat against his head and his pouting lip, he resembled a fish. He put the Land Rover into gear and accelerated up the drive so quickly that the wheels spun noisily on the gravel. He shrieked to a halt outside the house and sat, his hands gripping the steering wheel, staring straight ahead. He began to mutter to himself, although I could not make out what he was saying.

'I'm sorry,' I said anxiously. 'I had a lovely evening.' Still he did not respond. 'Well, goodbye.'

I got out of the Land Rover and carefully shut the door. I could not prevent myself, as I walked slowly across the drive, from glancing over my shoulder to see if he was looking at me. His dysfunctional glare burned at me through the windscreen in the gloom. As soon as I had made it around the corner and through the gate, I began to run. The night was moonlit, and I found my way up the path easily. At the cottage door, I could still hear the grumble of the engine idling. I stood there, waiting to hear him leave, my heart thudding in my chest. The minutes dragged on. I wondered what on earth he was doing. Finally, I heard the distant grinding of gears, and the noise of the engine grew momentarily louder and then faded into the silence. I went into the cottage and made straight for the cupboard in the kitchen where I had put the gin.

Chapter Twenty-One

'*Stella! . . . Stella!*'

I opened my eyes. The movement generated a wave of pain which gathered momentum as it rolled up my forehead.

'*Stella!* Are you there?'

Sunlight poured onto my face through the bedroom window. Dimly I remembered that I had forgotten to draw the curtains the night before. My body was heavy and lifeless on the bed, like a great anchor to which my bobbing head was attached.

'Are you there?'

Slowly, the vast and far-flung continents of thought, perception and memory, shrouded in the receding mist of sleep, were drawn together into the bright pinprick of consciousness. I bolted up in bed and looked at my watch. It was ten o'clock. I had overslept. Pamela's voice asserted itself, reconstituted in my mind. She must be downstairs, come to find out where I had got to. I threw back the covers and ran to the top of the stairs in my nightdress.

'Stella?'

What happened next could only have been the noisy activity of a few seconds, but for me it possessed the heightened deliberation, the glassy silence, of a dream. I reached the top of the stairs. I looked down the well and saw Pamela's upturned face at the bottom. I opened my mouth to speak, took a step forward, and flew. As I fell, I was struck by how impassive Pamela's expression was, watching me; and even before my back had made its first, brutal contact with the stairs, I had registered the embarrassment of my accident, regretted the foolishness of my facial expression as I had it, considered the social difficulty it would present, and decided on the exertions necessary to the re-establishment of normality in the wake of my unforgivable violation of it. I bumped once, twice, three times, before sliding, stiff and prone as a board, to Pamela's feet; where I lay for some time, gazing up at her, without moving. I was waiting, as one would wait for examination results or a salary, to be informed of the exact quantity of pain my tumble had earned me; quite a lot, I thought, judging by the sound I had made as I hit each of the steps. I tried to prolong that moment of anticipatory numbness; but too soon, a symphonic swell of agony, powerful beyond all my imaginings, rose up in a great chorus from the back of my body.

'Are you all right?' said Pamela sharply.

'I don't know. Shit.' It was unlike me to swear, but the word seemed to offer some appeasement to the pain. 'That really hurt,' I added helplessly.

'Yes, you positively *flew*,' said Pamela. She looked as if she were about to smile. I wondered whether she was going to do anything.

'Shit,' I said again. The ache reached a crescendo and held there. Pamela folded her arms. 'Jesus.'

'Look, take your time, why don't you,' she said eventually. 'Come over to the house when you're ready. I simply came to find out what had happened to you.'

'I overslept,' I said, wild now with pain.

'Well, there's no hurry. Just come when you're ready.'

She turned and trod lightly off, before I had a chance to say anything more or even get up from where I lay on the stairs. Her response to my accident seemed, on the surface, profoundly cruel; but oddly, even though the vulnerability of my position exposed me to feelings of self-pity, I did not believe that Pamela's had been an entirely wanton display of indifference. I had forced on her a moment of intense intimacy by falling down the stairs; an intimacy she was unable, whether through ineptitude or fear, to sustain, and whose attendant demands for sympathy, kindness and practical help she could not meet. She was not maternal; by which I mean that she did not appear to have given up, as so many mothers did, her self-regard. Yet her protection of her independence was so fierce – preventing her, as we have seen, even from offering the most desultory help to someone in need – that it suggested one of two things: either that her hold over it was fragile; or that she felt herself to be so constantly importuned by others, who might commandeer her mind and body, that she drew back from any physical or emotional invitation as if it were a trap. Remembering her inappropriate style of behaviour with Toby, it struck me that perhaps what I had seen was of a significance less dark than I had initially thought. Perhaps the language of sexual allure was the only one Pamela knew; or the only one, at any rate, in which she could communicate.

By this time I had picked myself up and carefully ascended the stairs to my bedroom. Twisting round to look at myself in the mirror, I saw several stunned, white areas on my back which I felt sure would bloom before long into bruises. The skin was so searing to the touch that it took me some time to dress; and even longer, crouched at the top of the stairs, to pluck up the courage to inch my way down them. Finally I managed to stagger along the path in the heat and up the back passage into the big house.

My predicament was not simplified by the fact that I appeared, doubtlessly by virtue of the empty stomach on which I had finished the bottle of gin the night before, to have acquired a hangover. It had seemed necessary at the time to staunch the turmoil of my thoughts with liquor; but the evening was even more confused now in my mind than it had been in its tumultuous aftermath. I had not solved anything by my drinking binge, which was probably in addition to blame for my uncertain footing on the stairs. Filled now with self-disgust, I concluded that I had a drinking problem. Indeed, I had been drunk at the end of almost every evening I had spent in the country. I had gone so far as to *steal* drink to appease my habit. In fact, the only evening on which I had not been drunk was when I had been prevented by poverty from becoming so. Even thinking about drink caused a swill of nausea in my stomach. I laboured up the stairs, bending now forward, now back, undecided as to which of my ailments to favour.

'I think I'm going to be sick,' I announced, bursting into Martin's room.

I was dimly aware, borne along on this rush of necessity, of two startled faces looking up at my entry. The first was Martin's. The second belonged to Mrs Barker; the horror of whose presence I was forced to delay while I sought some outlet for my imminent regurgitation.

'In the sink,' said Martin immediately. 'Over there in the closet.'

He sped along a diagonal trajectory towards the sink, while I approached at an adjacent angle from the door. We met at the closet door; he opened it; I lunged inside; and immediately gave forth a hot stream of bitter bile. Halfway through, Martin placed his hand on my sore back. I shot up with a howl of protest, banging my head on a ledge above the small sink.

'*What?*' he said anxiously.

'Hand!' I sputtered.

He removed his hand and I vomited again, retching hopelessly from my withered, empty stomach. Placing my hands on the sink I hung my head, exhausted.

'What's the matter with her?' I heard Mrs Barker say from behind me.

'I don't know,' said Martin in a low voice.

'Too much to drink last night, I'll be bound,' said Mrs Barker, with horrible accuracy. 'Will you be all right here, young man? I'd better get on. I've lost enough time already this morning thanks to this one.'

Waves of humiliation coursed down my spine. I tried to summon the strength to speak but could not. Instead, I retched again.

'Hmph!' said Mrs Barker triumphantly. 'She's had a bellyful.'

'It's probably a stomach upset,' said Martin. 'Off you go, Mrs Barker. We'll be fine here.'

I stood over the sink for some time after she'd gone. Finally I raised my head and saw myself in the mirror above the sink. My face was bright red and my mouth covered with slime. A white mark stood out on my forehead from where I had banged it against the shelf. Tears of effort shone around my eyes.

'Have you a tissue?'

'Hang on. Here.'

Martin's hand insinuated itself into the compartment, waving a tissue like a flag of surrender. I wiped my face and blew my nose and then turned shamefully around.

'Come on. Why don't you lie on the bed?'

Martin took my hand and wheeled me trembling to the bed. I lay down, curled on my side.

'I fell down the stairs,' I said, closing my eyes. 'This morning.'

'That must have been why you were sick. It's very common if you've taken a knock.'

I felt something cool on my forehead and realized that it was Martin's hand. He began stroking my hair, which had stuck around my face, matted with sweat.

'Poor Stel-la,' he said.

'Mrs Barker. Will she tell your mother?'

'No. She's all right.'

'I don't believe you. I'll get the sack.'

'No you won't. I'll look after you.'

I was becoming uncomfortable with Martin's stroking, which had extended its compass to my neck. I felt myself growing tense beneath his hand, but I could not bring myself to tell him to stop. The only solution was to get up, but I feared for what would happen to my stomach, which had now found an acceptable level in this horizontal mode, if I changed position. The thought that Pamela might come in to investigate and find us thus redoubled my anxiety. Martin's fingers caressed the back of my neck, entwining themselves in my hair.

'Don't,' I said weakly.

'I can't help it.'

'Please.' A terrible tiredness lapped at my eyes. 'It's not a good idea.'

'Let me. Just for a little while. I won't do it again. You're so lovely, Stel-la. Let me just touch you.'

I'm afraid to say that I let him do it. True, I was feeble with pain and sickness, and in need too of comfort and human contact; and in a sensual way, the feeling of Martin's large hand on my skin was pleasurable; but deep inside me, far beneath the swirling ether of semi-consciousness, I had a small, hard sense of wrong. My limbs felt numb and vast, too remote from this tiny impulse to be powered by it; and so I lay, while Martin went about his solitary raptures, and did nothing but fail to reciprocate them. I must have fallen asleep, for some time later when I opened my eyes Martin was sitting by the window on the other side of the room watching me.

'You should have woken me!' I said, sitting up. My stomach felt much better, but my back sounded a chord of agony when I moved.

'You probably needed to sleep,' said Martin. He seemed embarrassed. 'How are you feeling?'

'Better.' I rubbed my eyes and swung my feet off the bed. My shoes, I noticed, were sitting neatly side by side on the floor beside me. 'I'm sorry about all that. Not my most graceful performance.'

I immediately felt that this was the wrong thing to have said. Martin fiddled with his hands, his eyes downcast.

'What would you like to do?' I persisted, slapping my knees enthusiastically. 'We could go out for a walk, or – or we could stay here and do some homework' – at this he gave a faint snort of laughter – 'or— What do you want to do?' I repeated.

'Just – just slow down,' he said finally. His expression was pained.

'What's the matter?' I could not seem to say anything without sounding oafish and insensitive.

'Just let me – God!' He threw his head back with frustration.

Things had, I saw, changed between us as a result of the strange interlude on the bed. My regret at the realization was intense. I could not believe that I had allowed it to happen.

'Martin,' I began.

'Don't say anything!' He held up a forbidding hand. 'Just don't!'

'But—'

'I'll be fine. I just need to think, that's all.'

He sat, accordingly pensive, looking out of the window. I stood awkwardly by the bed. I felt, despite his command, that he did want me to say something; and yet I knew that I was not skilful enough with words to form the delicate phrases he required. Any route from here, however circuitous, led to the denial of what he wanted. There was no step that I could take that would not advance us towards what he did not want to know. With nothing better to offer him than physical proximity, I crossed the room and threw myself into the empty armchair. This, in the event, unexpectedly proved the most direct path out of the tension between us; for when my bruised back made contact with the stiff leather upholstery, I leaped up again with such a scream that Martin involuntarily burst out laughing.

'I know,' he said presently. 'Why don't we have a picnic? We can go and get some stuff and then go off somewhere. You can tell me about last night. How about it?'

'OK.'

We went down to the kitchen to inform Pamela of our plan. Mrs Barker, I was relieved to see, was not in evidence.

'That sounds jolly,' said Pamela, who was sitting at the kitchen table with her glasses on her nose, writing laboriously on a sheet of paper. 'Actually, that would suit me just fine. The men are at the farm again today and I wanted to do some shopping, so I might shoot off now if you two are going to look after yourselves.' She lowered her glasses and looked at me. 'Are you feeling better?'

'Much, thank you.' I wondered whether she was referring to my fall, or had received a report from Mrs Barker on my subsequent behaviour in the bedroom. 'I'll have some pretty bad bruises, but I don't think it's too serious.'

'You ought to be more careful, you know. We don't want you breaking something and stuck in bed for weeks on end. Right!' Her tone informed me that our interview was at a close. 'I'll get away, then. There are things in the fridge. You can pretty much help yourself to anything, except the salmon. That's for dinner.'

'Can we have wine?' said Martin innocently.

'Wine?' Pamela looked at me. It was difficult to know what expression was required in response. I looked blankly back at her. 'Oh, I don't see why not. Just don't take your father's vintage hoard. There's plenty of plonk in the cupboard.'

Having plundered the kitchen, we set off in the sun, taking the path to the right of the house that led towards the rose garden. Martin held the picnic basket in his lap. We passed the pond into which he had nearly fallen on our first day. It was unchanged, forgetful of us, its surface busy through the delicate filter of shade.

'*That* seems a very long time ago,' said Martin from below.

It was very painful wheeling the chair over the uneven ground. I thought of suggesting we stop by the pond, but it seemed too odd somehow to do so, as if it would signify that we were caught in some strange cycle of repetition from which it was impossible to progress. I braced myself, leaning in at an angle to put the strain on my shoulders. Presently we emerged from the wood into a sort of meadow.

'This is my favourite place,' said Martin. 'Shall we sit under that tree?'

The meadow was lovely, overgrown and surprisingly cool. Wild flowers danced amidst the long grass. I ploughed the chair through the dense, resistant stems, my back singing in ever higher keys of agony. By the time we had reached the tree I was sweating. Curiously, what I felt as I laboured behind Martin's chair was not, as I might have expected, irritation with him for carelessly choosing so inaccessible a spot; rather, it was a more sober sense of the sacrifices his company entailed, sacrifices which I regarded separately from the fact that I was employed to make them. It was as if I was sizing him up for some other purpose; a development which I interpreted, with some annoyance, as a symptom of a more complex feeling, which his overtures in the bedroom had implanted in me. He had made me feel a responsibility for him greater than that which I was contracted to bear. I resented this imposition; and yet it felt in some way natural, as if all along I had been waiting for a burden to replace those I had shed by coming to the country in the first place.

'My back hurts,' I said, sitting down in the shade.

'Don't worry. I'll do everything. Just lie flat for a bit.'

I did not want to lie flat, but I conceded that it might be efficacious. I heard Martin slither from his chair and closed my eyes. A warm breeze rolled gently off the meadow, stirring the leaves overhead. Images began to dance about in my mind. With them I felt the essence of myself unstoppered and diluted in my thoughts. Slowly, the partitions of time and place began to dissolve and my memories washed freely and incoherently like a great sea against the shores of the present. The crust of my body was pried loose; and I swam deep amongst flashes of childhood, faces at once strange and familiar, snatches of conversation, pieces of feeling broken off and left to drift far from their recollection; further and further, until finally I was washed up in a dry, hot place where the steady buzz of traffic rose from far below and a foreign sun pressed down hard on my back. Something dug into my stomach. My eyes were closed. I remembered a metal railing, rooted in the crumbling concrete of the balcony floor. Arcs of colour, strangely oleaginous, burst like liquid fireworks behind my eyelids. Blood pounded in my head, as if I were under water. I remembered then that I was upside-down, slung over the railing like a towel hung out to dry. Something curious had happened. I tried to recall what it was. There had been a change. I was no longer, for whatever reason, in the place I had always been. I had made some terrible journey, as if down a chute or across a bridge that had snapped behind me, from which I could not return. I had come to a place of inverse proportions to those which nature had dictated, where despair and darkness had overpowered light. I had a strong sense that I had committed a forbidden act in doing so; not because I had done something wrong, but because I had succumbed to a temptation which ought to have been resisted. Searching for some clearer recollection, I felt instead my sense of the meadow in which I lay grow immanent. My daydream wavered. I felt the grass beneath me, and the pain in my back, which had wandered like an idle guard, jumped smartly back into position. In that instant I remembered a dream I had once had, in which I had been shut in a dark room for hours and hours. Was that what I had been thinking of, as I lay there in the meadow? I had surfaced fully now into consciousness but my eyes remained shut. The memory of the dream was familiar, but it did not seem to fit. The more I thought of it, though, the more intangible the other recollection grew. I tried to grasp it but it dissolved, until I was no longer sure what exactly I was trying to remember.

Chapter Twenty-Two

'Stel-la. Lunch.'

I opened my eyes to see a vast sandwich being projected by Martin's arm through the sunlight towards my face. From the curious angle afforded by my horizontal position the thick lips of bread with their lolling tongue of filling looked gargantuan and rough-hewn, like great slabs of stone. My stomach clenched in resistance.

'Wine?'

A proffered glass joined the sandwich on its airy platform. I sat up painfully and took it, placing the sandwich on the grass beside me. Despite my biliousness, my mouth sought the glass as if it contained some elemental fuel without which the normal course of things could not resume. The wine was strong and potent and prickled against my palate. I felt an immediate and comfortable sense of dissociation, as if I had removed a pinching shoe.

'This is very civilized,' I said, making an effort to speak above the loud but private rhythm of my physical needs.

'This is the country life,' said Martin. He raised his glass. 'Ambrosia in arcadia. How are you feeling, Stel-la?'

'All right.'

'Tell me about last night.'

Complicitly, he shuffled closer over the grass. Out of his wheelchair Martin looked tiny and grotesque. Before I could stop myself, I had permitted a shade of disgust at the memory of him touching me to fleet across my mind.

'What did you and Mr Trimmer talk about?' he persisted.

'Not much. Your family, mostly,' I added unguardedly. 'Everybody seems to want to talk about your family.'

'I know.' He seemed quite proud of the fact. 'Just because we live in an old house they think we walk around with our heads under our arms.'

'Not quite,' I said, surprised by his naivety.

'What, then?' He leaned forward on one arm so that his shoulder joint bulged, and picked up his sandwich. 'Cannibalistic dinner parties? Ritual torture of au pairs? I hope you've not been putting ideas into people's heads, Stel-la.'

'Of course I haven't! Actually, it's more to do with sex.'

'Ha! Ha!' barked Martin, with his mouth full. 'That's funny,' he added.

'Why?'

'It just is. We're a family. What do they think we do? Have sex with *each other*?'

Martin could be very obtuse at times, and oscillated alarmingly between wisdom and immaturity. In this case it was fortunate that he had misunderstood me, given that I now felt myself to have been mistaken in bringing up the subject.

'Of course not,' I said. 'It's just gossip.'

'What gossip?'

'Forget I said anything.'

'Tell me.'

'No!'

'What does Trimmer know, anyway?' said Martin presently. 'He's retarded. Did he try and kiss you?'

'Yes.'

'Did he?' said Martin delightedly. 'What was it like?'

'Revolting.'

'I bet!' He puckered his lips, like a fish. 'It must have been like kissing a piece of raw liver.'

'Don't be disgusting.'

'You're the disgusting one, kissing Mr Trimmer.'

'I didn't kiss him! I fought him off. I think he was angry with me.'

'You should watch out, Stel-la. He's a lunatic. So was his father. There's brothers, too, mad as snakes. That whole family. Inbred. They hate each other. They've got loads of guns. One day someone will go over to that house and find them all laid out flat in a pool of blood in the orchard.'

'He won't hurt me, will he?' I found Martin's image sinister.

'I shouldn't *think* so,' said Martin. 'He'll kill his mother, though. He can't get away from her. He tried to move to Buckley once, took a flat and all that.'

'What happened?'

'He came back after about six months. Very sheepish. I think Dora beats him.'

'How could she? He's enormous!'

'Dunno. I once saw him with his shirt off. He had marks on his back.'

The blowsy meadow, and beyond it the luxurious reaches of the garden, cushioned our solitude. A breeze overhead stirred the trees and a deep rustling, almost like thunder, gathered and rolled across the meadow.

'Do you know the person who runs the post office?' I presently enquired.

'What, that weirdo? Not really. I've seen him around. Why?'

'Just wondering.'

I considered telling Martin about the creature's room and the leaflets, but something stopped me. It was as if, as I summoned the words to my mouth, the images which had seconds earlier been so clear in my mind melted away. I was gripped by feelings of uncertainty; and could no longer be sure whether the leaflet, and my visit to the creature, and indeed all of the things that I had done on my own since being in the country, had been real or were the product of my invention.

'Stel-la,' said Martin, after a while. 'What are you going to do about Edward?'

'What do you mean, do?' I said nervously. 'There's nothing *to* do.'

'Of course there is.' Martin leaned forward with the bottle of wine and sternly administered it. 'You can't just disappear. You'll have to face him some time.'

'I don't see why,' I replied. My voice had the hollow sound which signifies the proximity of some strong emotion. 'What would be the point?'

'You made promises, Stel-la. It's not worthy of you.'

A feeling of panic stirred in my chest.

'It's shaming for him,' persisted Martin. 'What's he supposed to tell people?'

'I wrote him a letter.'

'You disgraced him. In front of all his friends and family. He deserves some explanation.'

'He does not!' I said viciously. I felt suddenly as if my face were wrapped tight in Cellophane, at which I would have to tear like a maniac in order to breathe. I had had this feeling before. The memory flashed across my thoughts, too quickly to see. Other things came too, pieces of recollection which seemed familiar but didn't belong anywhere.

'All right,' said Martin. 'But I do think at least that you should do him the courtesy of telling him where you are.'

'And I think you should mind your own business. What do you know about anything, anyway?'

The wine was making me feel loose in the head, as if stitches were coming undone. My mouth was dry. My heart thudded uncontrollably. I thought of getting up then and there and running, across the meadow and the fields beyond, until I was exhausted beyond thought and far away. I closed my eyes for a moment. When I opened them again, everything seemed so unreal to me that I began to wonder if I had even imagined the exchange I had just had with Martin.

'I just think—'

'Don't you understand?' I cried. 'I don't want to think about it! All I want is to be left alone! All right? I just want to be left alone. Like a pair of eyes in a jar.'

Why I made this last remark I can't imagine, although in my overwrought state I might merely have thought that I said it.

'You can't live like that. Firstly, it's cowardly.' He enumerated using his fingers. 'Secondly, you'll regret it. Thirdly—'

'How dare you lecture me?' I was by this time quite angry. 'What gives you the right to do it? Other people don't judge themselves harshly – your own family least of all! Why should I?'

'What do you mean by that?' sniffed Martin.

'Just because you live a life of luxury,' I snapped, 'you think you're all beyond reproach. But you've got problems! Anyone can see that!'

'Well, of course we do. Nobody said we didn't.'

'At least I've been honest.' I began ripping up handfuls of grass. 'At least I don't sit around hating everything and pretending I don't.'

'*I* don't hate anything,' said Martin, perplexed.

'Yes, you do.'

'Like what?'

'Your mother,' I said cruelly, holding up my fingers as he had done, as if I were about to embark on a list.

'My mother? Why on earth do you think I hate her?'

'I – it's obvious.' I folded my arms.

'No it's not!' he said. His body was rigid with affront and his voice young and anxious. 'What made you think that?'

'The way you talk to her, for a start.' My brief flash of confidence began abruptly to fade, revealing a darker feeling of dread. 'And that picture you drew. The one at the centre.'

'That?' Martin looked genuinely confused. 'That isn't like her at all!'

'It seemed – critical,' I said lamely.

'It's just not very good.'

'Sorry.'

We sat in silence. I found the difficulty of remaining in a normal upright posture considerable.

'It's all right,' said Martin presently. 'I suppose I can see why you might have – well, she's sometimes not the easiest person to get along with. She had a frustrating life, stuck here with the farm and all of us. I think she'd have liked to have a career, and some time on her own. She's sad, too.'

'What about?'

'Oh, something that happened a long time ago.' He tore up a few blades of grass and scattered them. 'Father's not the easiest person in the world to be married to, either.'

'What do you mean?'

'Well, he depends on her for everything these days. He had quite an unhappy childhood himself. His father committed suicide.'

'Why?'

'Dunno. He was an army chap. Couldn't cope when he retired or something. Dad was an only child. His parents were quite elderly. I think his mother went a bit mad after that.'

'In what way?'

'Oh, he won't talk about it. Mum says it was pretty grim. Anyway, he joined the army himself eventually but then he got discharged because he went bonkers. Then he met Mum. She saved his bacon. She'd do anything for him. And for us. She's the one that keeps it all together, Stel-la.'

'Yes.'

'It's no good saying that if people aren't perfect you're not going to love them, Stel-la. That's what families are all about.

They absorb things. They grow round them. They may end up looking all twisted and ugly, but at least they're strong.'

There was a long silence. Martin plucked at the grass. I lay down again on my back and closed my eyes. As I did so, I was all at once transported away from Martin and the meadow by a memory which sprang up in my mind so fully-formed and clear that it seemed to pulse with life. The memory was of my family sitting in the garden of our house. It was before the death of my younger brother, which I mentioned early on in my story, and which cast a long and stifling shadow over everything that came after it. It was the absence of this shadow, rather than any real sense of my own age at the time, which located the memory in my early adolescence. It was distinctly sunlit; and by that I do not mean only that the background was that of summer, but also that the atmosphere contained an element of which I was not of course aware at the time but the chill of whose absence I felt afterwards, when it had drained from our house as suddenly as if a plug had been pulled on it. It wasn't happiness, or even contentment; merely, I suppose, unawareness. We had not yet been singled out by tragedy; and as such could conduct our lives with an anonymity, a lack of self-consciousness, which was later unavailable to us.

In this memory I was lying on a blanket on the lawn. My younger brother was nearby on some forgotten business, a fleeting figure in a striped T-shirt. The other was sitting directly in front of me on a deckchair. He was wearing a pair of shorts, and his sturdy legs, over which crawled a fascination of dark hairs, were planted firmly in a V to either side of me. He was reading something out loud which was making us laugh; for he was a comedian in those days, a talent eroded by the steady, subsequent tides of sad years. My parents were sitting next to him at a small table, playing cards. I had entirely forgotten how much they used to love cards; how we would come downstairs in the mornings and find them already into their second hand of whist or rummy, the house littered with scraps of paper used as scoresheets, covered in my father's exact writing.

I felt the warmth of the sun on my back, heard the sound of my brother's voice and the giggles rumbling up from my squashed stomach. I was happy. I was happy. The memory stayed and stayed; and then gradually it became more muted, immobile, frozen into a single, inaccessible image, like a snapshot.

'What did you say?'

'I said, shall we go?' said Martin.

We packed up our picnic things and Martin hauled himself into his chair. My back was in agony when I stood up.

'I could use a nap,' said Martin, as we set off, 'after all this excitement. Wine makes me sleepy. Would you mind?'

'Not at all,' I said. 'I've got plenty to do.'

I took him back to the house. Pamela was still out, and the rooms were quiet. I deposited him in his bedroom and went back down through the cool, empty hall and out of the front door.

Chapter Twenty-Three

No sooner had I turned away from the house with the intention of setting off down the drive than I caught sight of the figure of Toby advancing from a right angle across the gravel. He was striding from between the hedgerows, naked to the waist, his hair unkempt, stray wands of straw clinging to his jeans. I froze in my tracks at this vision, which had aroused in me an immediate feeling of panic.

'Hal-*lo*!' he cried, waving one hand while the other clutched his shirt. He was extremely red from the sun, the burnish of activity rather than the perilous scarlet of sunburn, and a varnish of sweat glinted across the tantalizing geography of his chest. I deduced that he had just come from his work in the top field: the labour, I felt, suited him far better than his customarily sybaritic demeanour. His face wore an almost joyous expression, although it struck me that it was perhaps in the novelty rather than the virtue of manual work that he had found pleasure. He drew close, grinning and panting; at which his physical presence became so overwhelming and pointed that it took on a distinct embodiment, as if a third person were with us whom it would be impolite, or at least strange, not to acknowledge.

'The sun always makes me horny,' he said presently, grinning wider still. 'Doesn't it you?'

'I suppose so,' I said bravely, after a pause. The words, or at least the sentiment with which they concurred, were unsuited to my voice. So clearly did they mark me out as an impostor in the region of sexual banter that I was certain Toby would expel me from it with a scornful laugh; but he merely stretched luxuriantly, showing me the bearded nooks of his armpits.

'Off for a walk?' he said, stroking his flat belly. I had a curious sensation as I watched his hands touch his own glandless flesh, the sense of some void or lack.

'Yes.'

'Very energetic of you, I must say. I was just going to wallow in the pool for a bit. I've been sweating like a pig all morning.' He surveyed me idly. I wondered if he was going to invite me to wallow with him; but then his attention sauntered away. 'How do I look?' he said, flexing one arm and then the other and looking down at himself. 'I'm turning into a bit of a hunk, don't you think? It's the equivalent of spending all day weightlifting. And you get far browner moving around than you do just lying there.' He ran his fingers over the skin of his arm and peered closely at it, rapt in the science of his own vanity. 'You've gone quite a nice colour,' he added, extending his investigations to me. He held out his forearm, crooked at the elbow, as if offering to partner me in a dance. 'Let's have a look. Yes,' he concluded, when I placed my arm beside his own, 'you see, you probably won't get much darker than that because you're fair-skinned. I'm lucky, I go really black.'

'Apparently it ages you terribly,' I unkindly remarked. 'It can also give you cancer.'

'Oh, you don't believe *that*, do you? People who say that sort of thing just want to stop everyone else from having fun. I didn't have you down as a killjoy, Stella,' he added reproachfully.

'I'm not,' I said quickly, wounded by his judgement. 'Apparently it's true.'

'*Appawently it's twoo!*' he mocked. 'Don't tell me' – he opened his eyes wide and looked exaggeratedly over his shoulder – 'don't tell me, *it's all a conspiracy*.'

'No, I—'

'Oh God, they're all out to get me! They're following me! Help!'

He stopped and doubled over, incapacitated by laughter. Watching him I had a feeling of despondency which made me want to get away from him. Even his physical beauty seemed all at once remote and unsatisfactory. It was a mere spectacle, and one I was weary of watching.

'I'd better go,' I said.

Toby abruptly stopped laughing.

'Enjoy.' He shrugged disdainfully. 'Rather you than me.'

I turned and began to walk away from him down the drive, my posture awkward with the thought that he might be watching me. Before I had got very far, a shout caused my shoulders to stiffen.

'Cheer up!' he cried from behind me. 'It might never happen!'

The walk to the village seemed even more arduous than usual. My irritation with Toby had set my heart pounding, so that it seemed to thump in unison with the angry bang of the sun against the sky. Several times I forgot entirely why it was that I was going to the village at all, and as my motivation wavered my steps frequently slowed to a trudge. My promise to visit the creature was by turns oppressive and insubstantial. I wished that I had not made it; and yet I had a small, worrying consciousness of what it would signify were I to renege. To turn around and return to Franchise Farm would have been a form of submission to the Maddens; although what precisely would have been relinquished by doing so was not clear to me.

'Hello, dear,' said the creature, emerging from the back room just as I staggered in from the street, inadvertently slamming the door so that the bell gave a wild shrill. 'You look all in. You shouldn't go hiking about in this heat without a hat and water. You wouldn't catch a rambler gallivanting in that fashion. What's wrong with your back?'

'I fell down the stairs,' I panted, leaning sideways against the post office counter and clutching at my spine.

'They're not taking very good care of you, are they? You won't last the week at this rate.'

'It's not their fault.'

'Touchy on that subject, are we? At any rate you should mind how you go. You've got to be a bit more careful in the country than you do in town. Got to watch yourself. Can't just go running about as you please and then catch the bus home.'

'I suppose not.'

'Let's have a look at that back, then.'

'It's fine.'

'That's as maybe, although I don't see how you'd know. A back's a tricky thing. You may have chipped a bone, but it's unlikely you'd have got here if you had. Probably just a bit of bruising, for which I have the very thing.'

The creature shuffled across to the door to the back room and held it open commandingly. Obediently I headed down the gloomy corridor, its strong and now familiar smell confusingly assailing me like a memory, and waited at the end while the creature switched on the light.

'Let's have that shirt up,' it said matter-of-factly, crossing the room – which was exactly as I had last seen it, although now it looked shabbier and more pitiful somehow – and opening the cupboard. I took the opportunity of looking more closely at the newspaper clipping by the door which had caught my eye during my last visit. There was the blurred picture of Pamela, with the words 'Lovers' tiff behind farm attack, say police' above. Beneath it was written the following:

The apparently motiveless attack on a local farm, which left several farm buildings and expensive machinery badly damaged, and which is thought to have resulted in a serious fire in one of the barns, may not have been the work of hooligans as was previously thought, Sussex police said last night. Franchise Farm, near Hilltop, was vandalized late on Monday night, in a devastating attack not discovered until the following morning when the farm manager, Mr George Trimmer, arrived for work.

'Them's snuck in, the b****s,' Mr Trimmer told the *Buckley Enquirer*. 'Must've greased their shoes. Never heard a dickey-bird over the big house.'

Police spent several hours at the scene, where damage included extensive graffiti, much of it reportedly obscene, spray-painted on walls, in the hope of finding some trace of the perpetrators, but by Monday night could not even confirm whether the attack had involved more than one person. On Tuesday, however, a telephone call to Buckley police station shed some light on the mystery. The caller, whom police have refused to name, alleged that the attack had been carried out by a spurned lover of the farmer's wife, Mrs Pamela Madden.

'It did seem to make sense,' said one officer, who asked not to be named. 'Many of the expletives were aimed at a specifically female target. It was pretty strong stuff, and all. I had to ask my teenaged son what some of it meant!'

Mrs Madden, who has lived at Franchise Farm all her life and has four children – the youngest of whom, a six-year-old boy, is disabled – refused to comment on the incident and is reportedly very distressed. Police confirmed that they had brought in a man for questioning, but would not comment on speculations that the man was the father of Mrs Madden's youngest son, nor give any clue as to his identity.

'Ancient history,' said the creature, who was by now standing directly behind me. 'They had to let him go in the end. She didn't want to press charges.'

'But was it true?' I said sadly.

'More or less. Not that I'd want to pay that old rag the compliment of saying so. Pack of scandalmongers, if you ask me. It's the only time I've ever felt sorry for Mrs Snooty-Drawers. I dare say she could be forgiven for liking a bit of the rough stuff. But if you play the game like she used to, you can expect some trouble.'

'Used to?'

'Oh, she's good as gold these days. Reformed character, from what I hear. The cripple put paid to all that.'

'What do you mean?'

'Retribution, dear. Thought she was being punished for her sins. Not that God came into it, as far as I can see. People like Pam, they like to think they're lucky, do you follow me? Oh, they may act like they were born to it and all that, but deep down they're frightened. They've got less freedom than you and me. Because if things go wrong for them, they've got nothing to blame it on. They just put up and shut up. They've got nowhere to go, see? No *flexibility*. So when little Pam saw it coming down, she changed her story, turned misfortune to her advantage. These days everyone thinks she's a saint. *Isn't it marvellous the way she looks after that boy herself instead of putting him in a home.* Course she never lifts a finger. That's what you're for. Clever.' The creature tapped the side of its head. 'You couldn't accuse her husband of that, mind you. He should have made tracks. You can't forgive a betrayal like that, not really. It eats you up inside, turns you funny in the head. She made a laughing stock of him. But he's just the same, see? Nowhere to go, nothing without his money and his house and his privilege. So he just shuts it out like they all do, pretends nothing's happened. It's heart cancer, dear. A very middle-class disease.'

'So why do you attack him?' I cried. 'He's got enough problems as it is! He doesn't do it deliberately – he thinks people are after him. That's why he sabotages the footpaths. Mr Trimmer told me. It isn't because he's malicious. The whole business with Geoff only happened because he must have run over one of the trip-wires.'

'Geoff died an honourable death.' The creature paused and looked sombrely at the ceiling. 'Why he does it isn't my concern. Adolf Hitler might be after him for all I care. The point is that innocent people are in danger.'

'But he's obviously not well!'

'In that case he should be put in an institution. But people like that, you see, they don't get put away, do they? They're above the law. Let's see what's under that shirt, dear. Lean on the table there. That's it. No, he's a danger to himself as much as anything. Should never have married that flibbertigibbet. There's a piece of advice for you. Never marry someone you can't be sure of hanging on to. You'll end up thinking the whole world wants to take her away from you. Especially if she's got the money. How does that feel?'

'Much better,' I said, surprised. I had barely felt the creature's fingers on my skin, but a luxurious heat was beginning to penetrate the tender bruises.

'You'll find it'll heal up nicely in no time. You watch yourself in future. You only get one body. And there's not much of yours, at that. Are they feeding you?'

'Yes.'

'They'll have your heart and soul as well if you don't mind out. That's the way they are. I see that young Casanova's already circling. He didn't waste his time getting down here to have a look at you.'

'Toby?'

'The very same. He's another one. If he'd been born where he deserved to be, he'd have been locked up by now. You keep away from him, my girl.'

'He's not that bad.'

'And where have you been all your life? He only got the last one pregnant, didn't he? Got her up the spout and got her the sack. She was a silly enough little thing, but nobody deserves that kind of luck.'

'He's not interested in me.'

'He's interested in anything he can shag, if you'll pardon my French, dear. You keep your knickers on. Off you go now. I've got business to attend to.'

The creature opened the door and stood beside it.

'Thank you,' I said. 'And please don't be too hard on Mr Madden. He's nice really.'

'You're a soft touch, aren't you? We'll see. I've been thinking of getting out of rambling anyway, diversifying a bit. There's interesting things going on in bloodsports at the moment. Take care of yourself.'

'Goodbye.'

'Toodle-pip!'

That evening over dinner, Pamela announced that she and Martin would be away the following day.

'We've been summoned to visit Aunt Lilian in Oxford tomorrow, Stella, so you'll be pretty much at liberty for most of the day.'

'Do we have to?' whined Martin.

'Yes, we bloody well do. The old girl's on her last legs, and if we're to stand a chance of getting anything out of her then we're going to have to sit there and smile if it kills us. Come to think of it, Toby, it wouldn't hurt you to come along too. Can you spare him tomorrow, darling?'

'Yes,' said Mr Madden firmly.

'We should be back by teatime, Stella, so if you could give me a hand with tomorrow evening then I reckon we'll have just about settled the score.'

'All right,' I said.

'Actually, I could use a bit of extra cash at the moment,'

interjected Toby. 'Can't we just slip something into her tea and speed things up?'

'That's *awful*!' shrieked Pamela delightedly. 'Aunt Lilian,' she added, addressing me, 'is a very perverse old lady. She's got *pots* of money, which she's always threatening to leave to some dreadful organization – what is it again?'

'The Animal Liberation Front,' said Martin.

'*That*'s right. So we all have to go rushing up there once or twice a year to try and talk her out of it. I think she does it to get attention. She probably thinks we'd never visit her otherwise.'

'We wouldn't,' said Martin.

'I suppose it's rather sad really,' sighed Pamela. 'She never married, so we're all she's got. She's had quite a lonely life. She *adores* the children, of course, but they were always rather frightened of her.'

'She's a crone,' said Martin. 'She's got these scaly hands and when she pinches your cheeks her nails dig into your skin.'

'*Little boy!*' cackled Toby, leaning across the table and pinching Martin's cheeks so violently that his head flew backwards and forwards. '*Come here, little boy!*'

'Get off!' shouted Martin, pushing him away. His cheeks were scarlet where Toby's fingers had been. 'Just fuck off!'

'Enough of that,' pronounced Mr Madden from the other end of the table, without looking up. He was examining his hands intently and his face was dark.

'I'm simply *longing* for tomorrow evening!' said Pamela brightly. 'It'll be the first time we've all been together as a family since – since when?'

She looked wonderingly about the table.

'Since the last time,' said Martin morosely.

Chapter Twenty-Four

That night I dreamed of Edward; but even the dream itself had the guilty atmosphere of a concession, as if my subconscious was manifesting a concern more dutiful than sincere. The dream took place in Franchise Farm, where I was attempting to show him the house and gardens and tell him about my new life. In the dream I kept forgetting him, like a reluctant promise or some newly acquired but not yet treasured object, and would experience rush after rush of anxiety as I remembered him and went chasing back to where I had left him. The most arduous aspect of this peculiar cycle was that each time I went back to retrieve him, finding him sitting helplessly as a baby in the room in which I had last deposited him, I was forced to explain to him not only what I had been doing, but *how* I had been able to do it. In other words, I was compelled to spell out to him over and over again the principles of will and motion, of which he did not seem to have the faintest idea. Each time he gazed at me with an expression of almost idiotic incomprehension, and I would feel a sense of intolerable pressure or enclosure; and each time, just as I felt this, I would remember something persistently forgotten and look down and see that he was sitting in a wheelchair.

Eventually this dream yielded to a mute, horrible nightmare in which I lay in my bed in the cottage while birds flew about the room, diving and pecking at my body; and I woke sweating and aching, with the sense of some imminent and unavoidable misfortune lying in wait for me. Outside the window the day wore the ripeness of mid-morning, and I could hear faint sounds of industry, the buzz of a farm engine, the distant murmur of cars. A sharp consciousness of time scythed through these languorous apprehensions. I bolted up in panic, the bedclothes flying back, before remembering that Pamela had taken the boys to see Aunt Lilian and that I had the day to myself. There are few things more pleasant than this type of realization. One is acquitted not only of the original crime, but also of the suspicion that one might in fact under other circumstances have committed it and of the consequences of having done so; all of which, in addition, are washed away in a matter of moments by some anticipated pleasure. I have often wished that I could make other problems vanish in a similar way. Subsiding back into the pillows, I considered my twice-granted liberty and wondered what I would do with it. With Mr Madden occupied at the farm, both the day and the rest of the property were mine. In my mind I toured its facilities, inspecting them anew with a proprietary gaze. I was surprised to find myself so shamelessly sizing up what did not belong to me, as if I had merely been awaiting the opportunity to do so. Dimly it struck me that this was a consequence of my disfranchised state. Those aspects of life I would previously have regarded with the mild eye of entitlement now lay tantalizingly under lock and key. With the door to privilege left ajar and unattended, I could no more prevent myself from trespassing beyond it than a pauper could stroll past a banknote lying on a pavement.

Having established what I intended to do, and made my dark commitment to it, I found myself in no hurry to begin. I lay for a further half-hour, only vaguely aware of the fugitive motion of thoughts flitting from beam to window sill; until the sudden consciousness of my empty mind seemed to invite more predatory notions. Quickly I got up to escape them; but crossing the room to find my clothes I glimpsed myself unexpectedly in the wardrobe mirror. Before I could fend it off, the sight had filled me with a sense of my destitution. Not being braced against my reflection, I had caught myself unawares and through this brief gap had seen the thing which presented the unfortunate but irremovable obstacle to my own disappearance. What surprised me was to realize how familiar this sight was. I had seen it on busy London pavements, amidst a throng of faces: one or two whose eyes looked out from their bodies as if from behind bars, as they paid for the crime of permitting their misfortunes to outweigh the space their flesh was entitled to occupy.

Some ten minutes later, I was washed and dressed, in the cut-off trousers – the only item, despite the freight of association they carried, that I did not now regard as a 'uniform' – and a short-sleeved T-shirt. I had become so used by now to the heat that I had stopped expecting it to change – indeed, I had forgotten the cadences of weather entirely. Even so, I was forcibly struck as I opened the cottage door by the charged fury of the day. Something brutal had invaded the air. It rushed at me, unnatural and molten, and as I stepped out into the garden I felt the agony of it on my skin, fighting it into my mouth and lungs. I was becoming frightened of the heat. It was out of control. What if it just kept getting hotter? What were we expected to do? I had a desire for some authority to whom I could report it, and wondered if I should go and tell Mr Madden. It was quite some time before the idiocy of this notion struck me. I set off down the garden in search of some shade. It was by now almost midday, and due to my oversleeping and general languor about the bedroom I had had no breakfast. The thought of food was repellent to me, but I felt this to be a trick of the heat and determined to go over to the house and find myself something to eat.

The back door was unlocked, and as I entered the dark passage its abrupt cool and shade caused my head to spin. For some seconds I was entirely blinded by the change, and I loomed dizzily, bumping against the cold, stony flanks of the walls. I was alert nonetheless for signs of Mrs Barker, for although I was not personally troubled by my intention of scavenging for food in the Maddens' kitchen – given that they had not yet offered to advance me any money with which I might buy some myself, nor indeed appeared to have given the matter of what I was eating for breakfast much thought at all – I recognized it to be rather indefensible – or at least to require an energy to explain it which I did not in that moment possess – to others. The house was quiet, and I deduced from the pungent scent of polish which harnessed the air that Mrs Barker had completed her morning's ministrations and gone home. Reassured, I stole up the passage and into the empty kitchen. The room was immaculate and oddly unwelcoming without its usual occupants. The neat arrangement of chairs and table, the scrubbed surfaces and gleaming floor, had a suspicious, superintendent air, as if they were witnessing my intrusion and would register any betrayal – a stray crumb or fingerprint – of it with disapproval.

With an artificially casual motion I strolled to the refrigerator and opened it. Its contents – carefully sealed dishes of leftovers, leafy fronds of salad, silver bricks of butter, packages of raw, pink meat, a number of expensive-looking jars of relish and suchlike – seemed both horribly private and utterly inaccessible. Any incursions there would, I felt sure, be complex both in execution and concealment. My appetite began to retreat. I made to shut the door again in defeat, but as I did so a large bottle lolled forward from the bottom shelf. Anxious that it would fall, I lunged down and caught it by the neck; at which point there was a terrific explosion which almost knocked me over with fright, and a geyser of foam spurted up from the mouth of the bottle and splattered over my legs. It all happened so quickly that I could not comprehend the nature of the disaster for some seconds. My heart thudded in my chest as the sour smell of wine gave off its terrible clue. I lifted the bottle with a trembling hand. The dark green glass with its elaborate gold label confirmed what I already suspected. It was champagne, of a variety, moreover, which I knew from my previous life to be inordinately expensive. A shred or two of foil clung to the bottle's lip, from where its cork had evidently blasted as a result of my inadvertent agitations. I was surprised to see how much remained: despite my dripping legs, the bottle was still three-quarters full.

My first thought was to retrieve the cork and attempt somehow to stuff it back in. Still holding the bottle, I began a panicked search, which eventually turned up the missing cork, still in its wire cage and cloak of foil, lying on its side beneath the table. I saw immediately that I would not be able to force it back into the bottle unless I pared it down with a knife, for it had fattened into a stubbornly flared shape. Even were I to succeed by this method, I realized, the champagne would still be ruined by the loss of pressure.

Within a short time, I had considered all my options; which were, admittedly, limited. The first was that I succeeded somehow in acquiring a bottle of champagne to replace that which I had ruined. I had, at least, the time to attempt this, but with neither money nor transportation was restricted to the faint hope that this bottle would be available in Hilltop, and available, moreover, in such a way that I would be able to steal it. The second option was that I conserved the remains of the bottle as best I could and confessed everything to Pamela – offering, perhaps, a portion of my wages in recompense – when she returned. The third was that I drank the contents of the bottle and proceeded similarly.

While the first of these two alternatives would undoubtedly result in the champagne being wasted, my response to the crisis would at least constitute an albeit futile attempt at virtue. The other was more pragmatic but easily misconstrued: I could, for example, be accused of inventing the story of the exploding cork – which, when considered in that light, did seem rather incredible – to conceal my craven theft and consumption of the champagne. The former course, though illogical, was evidently preferable. At that moment, however, I had a vision of Pamela's face as I apologetically handed her an almost full bottle of flat champagne. 'Why on earth didn't you just drink it, you silly girl?' she cried.

Being by now familiar with the vicissitudes of Pamela's sense of etiquette, my vision struck me as a likely one. Addled, I thought the matter through again. It grew more and more irresolvable with every approach, until my mind was so knotted that I was forced to sit down at the table with my head in my hands and my eyes closed. As I did so, a notion slyly snipped its way through the tangle. I opened my eyes and regarded it with awe. What if I merely absconded with the champagne and then denied having had any involvement with its disappearance? Pamela had successfully been duped over the bottle of gin. Why should she not be again? In fact, her memory of that episode could be the very thing to undermine any conviction she might have about the champagne having been in the refrigerator when she left the house that morning. The whole affair began to gather significance in my mind, until I became convinced that I had been intended to steal the gin as a sort of foundation for the grander theft I was now designing.

It is difficult to consign any event to mere regret, no matter how unpleasant; and the thought of making simultaneous use of two of the darker episodes in my sojourn in the country in this way gathered more appeal with every moment. What, indeed, could be more pleasant on my day off than to sit in the sun and drink champagne; a plan I would never have conceived myself, but on which fate had now kindly insisted by bringing about the accident in the kitchen?

Borne along on this highly coloured wave of logic, I picked up the bottle of champagne, down whose sides chilly beads of moisture now alluringly ran, and went with it out into the garden. From the cool of the kitchen I had momentarily forgotten the heat outside, and as it bludgeoned me along the gravel path I wavered in my resolve. How pleasant could it be, sitting out in the sun? I would have to force myself to do it; and there was no point in being degenerate if it required an effort to do so. I rounded the corner and emerged on the back lawn, where the garden table and chairs sat displayed in an inviting circle. As I saw them, I had an idea. Placing the champagne on the table, I turned and retraced my steps back up the path. I was looking for the umbrella, which I clearly remembered Mr Madden producing on more than one occasion and slotting into the hole at the centre of the table. He had certainly carried it from the side of the house, but it seemed unlikely to me that such an unwieldy object would be kept inside. I guessed that it was in the shed, the door to which stood just beyond the back door at the end of the path. This process of deduction was far from arduous, but nonetheless I was gratified when I opened the shed door to find the umbrella collapsed and leaning against the wall directly in front of me. It was a clumsy object to carry, and surprisingly heavy, but I succeeded after some manoeuvring in removing it from the shed, whereupon I began to drag it along the path back towards the lawn.

At that moment I heard a faint, rapid patter of footsteps ahead of me. Instinctively I stopped short; but before I could even register the sound, a great dog came hurtling around the corner of the house, and skidded to a halt at the sight of me, planting itself in my path. I say 'a dog'; of course, I knew it to be Roy, but detached from his owners he lost the patina of tameness and reverted to the condition of a beast. He lifted his head menacingly, ears alert. A stone of fear dropped down the well of my body. I could see the white points of his teeth flashing in his drooling muzzle. His black belly heaved surreptitiously beneath his rigid frame. The heat rained down between us.

'Hello, Roy,' I said.

At the sound of my voice, a terrible snarl began to emanate from within the vice of his teeth. He drew back slightly in a tensile crouch, his eyes yellow with suspicion.

'It's all right, Roy,' I shrilled. 'It's only me.'

In a flash he was galloping towards me with a volley of savage barking, moisture flying from his gnashing jaws, his shining, muscled body madly contorted in a frenzy of attack. With the dreaminess of terror I watched him come. He landed in front of me with a giant pounce, his legs splayed, writhing as if swarmed by invisible bees, and seemed to gather himself in for another leap. What happened next was so clearly a matter of instinct rather than calculation that I cannot blame myself for it. As he readied himself to spring on me, I remembered the umbrella in my hand. In sheer self-defence I thrust it forward like a lance, rooting myself behind it. The dog leaped; and as he flew through the air, a chasm of horror and disbelief yawned open between us. I met his eyes, suspended in the moment before his collision, and saw them register the canopied pole, the unavoidability of impact. The seconds slowed to a crawl; and then snapped back with a thud as his forehead hit the metal head of the umbrella. His body gave a great flip, tossing itself high in the air and landing with a smack on the gravel, where it lay inertly on its side.

I stood, unable to move, the umbrella still gripped in my hands, for some time. The black heap at my feet was motionless, gorgeous with glossy fur and plump flesh. Roy did not, in so far as I was able to see, appear to be breathing. My fear of him dead was triple that which I had had of him alive, even during his last, brutal moments. I could not bring myself even to take a step towards him, let alone try to help or resuscitate him. Through this curious, shameful terror I tried to assess the implications of this latest and most unfortunate development. To have murdered Roy, even in self-defence, presented extraordinary, perhaps insurmountable, social difficulties. How could the Maddens comprehend, let alone forgive, it? I felt a constriction in my chest and had a sudden sensation of faintness. My entire body, I realized, was trembling. The sun seared the top of my head. Fresh cascades of sweat erupted from my pores. I had to get into the shade and sit down.

Weakly I hoisted the umbrella onto my hip, and slowly, pressing myself as far into the hedge to my right as I could, began inching my way along the path. As soon as I was past the body, I broke into a crazed, awkward run and heard a preternatural shriek stream from my lips. I scarcely felt the weight of the umbrella as I dragged it, still running, around the corner and on to the back lawn. Somehow I managed to lift it above my head and slot it into its hole. The thud it made as it fell into place provided a ghastly echo of Roy's collision. I wrestled, whimpering, with the sprung mechanism which raised the canopy, and finally collapsed into the white plastic garden chair beside me.

For a while my thoughts thrashed about, trying to find some escape from the unalterable fact of Roy's demise. It was becoming steadily more clear, in the oblique fashion of something profoundly denied, that I was going to be unable to do anything about the situation. My hand sought the bottle of champagne which sat before me on the table. The reminder it provided of the insignificance of my earlier crime was comforting. I drank some of it down. It was warm, having been sitting in the sun, and my empty stomach shifted queasily. After a few mouthfuls I got up again and returned to the corner of the house, where it met the gravel path. Peering around it, I saw to my disappointment that the black heap remained exactly as it had been. So incredible did the episode seem to me, and so forceful was my denial of it, that I had honestly expected to discover that I had imagined it, or at least that it had been negated by some greater and more rational force. I was troubled by the abject appearance of the body. It looked smaller than it had before. Also, something had happened to Roy's fur. It was suddenly all rough and mangy. I wondered if this were an effect of the strong sunlight, and whether I should cover him up lest he actually begin to decompose. I went and sat down again. There was nothing else, marooned as I was in misfortune, that I could do. Tears of frustration filled my eyes and I banged my hand on the table, causing the bottle to leap in the air so that I had to throw myself forward to catch it. I broke into a fresh sweat. My bare thighs slimed grotesquely against one another, and I could feel the lagoons of moisture beneath my arms. I raised the bottle of champagne to my lips and drank thirstily from it.

Just then, the inviting turquoise of the swimming pool on the other side of the lawn caught my eye. It may seem curious that the idea of swimming had not suggested itself until that moment; but the ceaseless postponements to which I had been subject over the course of the past week had instilled their discipline in me. I had become servile; and was by now so used to regarding the pool as a mere feature of the landscape that I had more or less forgotten its purpose. I gave a yelp of joy and rose from my chair. My current dishevelment, combined with all the memories of this longed-for but withheld pleasure that I had accrued, stirred up in me an almost painful feeling of anticipation. My skin prickled and gushed at the thought of its imminent immersion. My scalp burned, yearning for the cool water. Having thought of it, it seemed unbearable that I would have to delay swimming by even one more minute; and given that any expedition in search of a costume would necessitate an encounter with Roy, not to mention trespassing into the mysteries of Pamela's bedroom, I decided to eschew the appropriate attire and swim in my underwear. Who, after all, would see me? And even if they did, it would be with accusations of a far more serious nature than indecency that they would regale me.

With this cavalier thought, I removed the cut-off trousers and T-shirt and streaked across the lawn towards the water. As I hovered for a few seconds on the tiled brink of the pool, my certainty that in a very short time I would be in it drove my longing to such a pitch that I thought I would burst. In that charged interval, every anxiety and regret seemed to rise from viscera to skin with the expectation of being discharged and washed away. A momentary despair, like pain felt through sleep to which one briefly awakes, suffused me; and then I jumped.

How can I convey the glory of that transition from desire to fulfilment that I felt as the water closed over my head? One minute I had been diffuse, soiled, porous; the next I was purged, contained, that which had been widely strewn and trampled folded and zipped back into the bag of my body. I stayed under for a long time, flapping sideways with my arms to prevent myself from floating, until the advancing cold of the water succeeded in quenching me to the core; and then I surfaced, sleek and gasping, to feel the sun brilliant on my wet face. The Maddens' pool was smaller than it looked, unsuited to serious swimming, and so after gliding blissfully to and fro on my side for a while I lay on my back and felt the cool tide lap against my scalp. I glimpsed the deep blue of the sky rearing above me, closed my eyes as the watery cradle bore my weight. The thread of my time in the country seemed all at once to snap, and I drifted away from the closely knitted stump of the past week, up to some higher region from where all the things of life appeared visible but remote, as the swimming-pool floor was to me now.

Presently, as is in the nature of even the most pleasurable experiences, I felt the compulsion to conclude my swim; if only so that I could swim again at some future point. I heaved myself dripping over the side of the pool and made my way back across the lawn. Roy was as I had left him when I went to the side of the house to look. A blackbird was pecking at the gravel beside his body. I felt a sense of frustration at the resilience of this obstacle to my happiness, for again I had entertained the curious hope that the incident would have been erased, and indeed might still be if I waited long enough. Returning to the table, I sat down and drank some more of the warm champagne. The taste of it in my mouth released a memory, which moved elusively around my thoughts, just out of reach. Even in the shade, I was already beginning to get hot again. The sun had moved a considerable way to the left, so that blocks of shadow were advancing across the lawn, but its heat did not appear to have abated. I was dimly aware of my strange appearance, which was mostly owing to the extreme variations in skin colour on different parts of my body, but seemed exacerbated by the peculiar sight of my underwear in such a public setting. Anxieties began to stir and scuttle about my mind. I wondered what time it was and when Pamela would appear, whether I should return the umbrella to the shed immediately so that I would not forget to do so later, what I should do about Roy, how I was to manage the lesser concealment of the champagne; until all in all I began to feel fraught with worry, adding the curdling of my afternoon idyll to my catalogue of problems.

It required a considerable effort of will to drive these concerns from my mind, for their power was merely enhanced by the fact that I recognized the pattern of their invasion from my previous life and regarded it with fear. It was precisely to escape this kind of anxiety that I had come to the country in the first place. I determined to think about nothing whatsoever until I had at least had another swim. Drinking down the last of the champagne, which by now tasted really rather disgusting, I got unsteadily to my feet and made my way across the lawn to the pool. The combination of alcohol and heat immediately had a stunning effect on me, and I stood swaying by the side of the pool for some time, my toes gripping the edge to prevent myself falling in. The sun pounded on my shoulders and the back of my neck. I was beginning to feel distinctly unwell. My eyes sought some object on which to focus, but when I looked up the garden seemed to take a great tilt. I staggered to one side, the blood pounding in my ears, the fuzzy outlines of trees spinning about me, and everything seemed suddenly to rush upwards at an impossible speed as I lost my balance and plunged head-first into the water.

I have very little recollection of what happened next, and believe I must in fact have fainted as I fell. I tumbled down what seemed to be a very long way, and then met with something hard which I dimly understood to be the bottom of the pool. I could only have stayed there a few seconds, but the interlude had the framework of a dream, in which everything real is replaced by an entire and quite illusory memory designed to support the thing experienced. It seemed to me, in other words, that I had always lain at the bottom of the pool: its profound silence was the sound of myself, its lovely columns of watered sunlight utterly familiar. On and on I lay; until suddenly I was rushing upwards, and was jerked forcefully from the water by something clamped painfully around the tops of my arms. I could hear a woman's voice saying 'Oh, my God! Oh, my God!' over and over; but again, in this dream-state, it seemed to me that she had always been saying that.

At the sound of the woman's voice, in any case, something peculiar happened. I was in one way quite aware of it, and yet at the same time it was remote and beyond my control. It was as if I were on a train, watching the landscape fly past; and just as the appearance of houses and telegraph poles might have told me that I was about to arrive at my station, so the woman's voice seemed to signal that I was going to wake up. But although the sound itself was clear, the words immediately sent my train lurching off course; so that suddenly I found myself speeding far away from where I wanted to go, on and on with everything around me a blur, until gradually, after some considerable time, it began to slow down. I felt the heat pulsing on my head and the pressure of something hard pushing against my stomach. Far away I could hear the sound of traffic, its faint cries rising discordantly from the steady buzz. Someone was saying 'Oh my God! Oh my God!'; but it was a man's voice this time, which for a while seemed to have nothing to do with me. Presently I realized that it was Edward's voice, and he kept saying it over and over again; so many times, really, that eventually I wanted to tell him just to be quiet and go away. It was impossible for me to do this, however. My physical predicament would not allow for it. I appeared to be upside-down, and even though I was too frightened to open my eyes my gradual recollection of events, as well as the sound of traffic from far, far below, told me that I was very high up and could fall at any moment.

I remembered that I had been standing on the balcony of our hotel room, looking down at the busy street several storeys below. In my mind I appeared to be standing there again. The noise filled my head like the sound of an argument. The sun hammered on my shoulders. Edward wasn't there. I remembered then that he had gone out on some forgotten business, but my thoughts were dark with the threat of his return. This was my honeymoon, perhaps the third or fourth day of it, and the fact of my marriage still clung to me like an ugly, ill-fitting suit. I had woken each morning with the hope that it would have softened, loosened, accommodated me; but its tight, itchy grip, the shame of it, was unrelenting. I knew myself to be in the wrong place as surely as if I were looking at it on a map; and my head was filled only with panicked thoughts of escape and extrication, which as yet had found no outlet. It was with these thoughts that I leaned over the iron railing of the balcony. The deep, foreign chasm with its indifferent swarm of traffic opened itself to me with the promise of my own insignificance.

I realized that there was nowhere else I wanted to be. It wasn't that I liked it here; merely that at the invitation of this cruel vista I had searched, frenzied, for a sense of my own belonging, for my home, for somewhere I might be wanted more, and found nothing. There was no secret comfort, no lodestar, in my empty heart. I was merely lodged at the inconvenient junction – this small, crumbling balcony – between a past I had been glad to leave and a future whose alien prospect seemed to provide the proof that I would never visit it. It was at this moment, in my high, hot imprisonment, that I wanted to fly; that I knew it, indeed, to be my only course. And it was at this moment that I understood, as if I had conducted a scientific experiment, that the weight of my life would not be enough to stop me.

In the event, the iron railing of the balcony saved what I had become convinced I did not want; for as I stood there, the shock of my discovery combined with the strong sunlight to bring about a sudden giddiness and I appeared briefly to faint. When I came to, with the sound of Edward's monotonous exclamation in my ears, I was collapsed in a kind of V over the balustrade, which, had it given way, would certainly have resulted in my death.

How long this unfortunate recollection endured I could not say. After I had gone through it in my mind, I was awash with strong emotions, which sluiced over me in inarticulate waves. Everything became very confused; but presently I began to come to my senses there in the garden of Franchise Farm. My eyes were closed, but I felt the warm, prickly grass beneath my back and legs and realized that I was lying down.

'She's still unconscious,' said a man's voice. 'I think she'll be all right, though.'

I opened my eyes a crack. The man was crouched beside me. He was wearing a blue T-shirt and was looking away so that I couldn't see his face.

'Are you sure we shouldn't call an ambulance?' said the woman, whom I couldn't see without moving my head. She sounded young and was well-spoken.

'Maybe. I don't know. She vomited a lot of water, which is the main thing.'

I snapped my eyes shut again, fully alert now.

'Perhaps she banged her head.'

'Might have. Doesn't look like it. I'm sure she'll wake up in a minute.'

'God, where on earth is Daddy?' cried the woman impatiently. 'He's never around when you need him! I don't even know who she is or anything.'

'She's probably his mistress,' said the man with a laugh. 'Running around the place in her knickers.'

I felt a blush begin to suffuse my cheeks. Now I dared not open my eyes, and began wondering how long I could reasonably prolong my coma.

'*Mark!*' said the woman reproachfully. I could hear a smile in her voice. 'Thank *God* we were here to pull her out, though. A minute later and she'd have drowned.'

'She was pretty lucky.'

The woman giggled suddenly. 'She does look terribly odd. Look, I'm just going to run back over to the house and make sure he hasn't slipped in the front way.'

'OK.'

There was silence. The man cleared his throat once or twice beside me. I was beginning to feel an uncontrollable desire to move. The sun was burning my face.

'Mark!' shouted the woman just then, from a distance. 'Look at this!'

'Jesus!' he said after a pause. 'That explains that, then. She must have been pissed. No wonder she's out cold.'

'I've just realized,' said the woman, closer now. 'She must be Martin's au pair. What a *scandal*! Mummy'll be furious.'

I opened my eyes. The woman – girl, really – was standing above me to my left. She wore a short red dress with no sleeves.

'Oh look!' she said, meeting my eyes. 'She's waking up! Hel-*lo*.' She knelt down beside me, suddenly solicitous, and put her hand on my arm. 'How are you feeling? You nearly drowned, you know.'

I couldn't take my eyes from her face. She was around my own age and quite beautiful, dark and slender with a mass of black ringlets. Her expression was tender. Around her neck was a delicate gold chain. I don't think I have ever hated anyone in my life as much as I hated this girl in that moment.

'Welcome back!' said the man cheerfully, kneeling down and putting his arm affectionately around her brown shoulders.

As soon as I saw his face, I knew that everything was over. I sat up abruptly and our eyes met.

'*Stella?*' he said.

Chapter Twenty-Five

'So *how* do you know her?' said Pamela again, as if she couldn't take it in.

'From university,' said Mark. 'Actually, I knew Edward better than I did Stella. I haven't seen her for years. I didn't recognize her at first. She looks different.'

'Who is Edward? The ex-boyfriend?'

'No.' Mark sounded surprised. 'He's her husband.'

I was standing behind the door in the dark ante-room, which I had discovered to be an excellent location for eavesdropping on the events of the kitchen.

'Her *husband*!' shrieked Pamela. 'How on earth – why on earth didn't she tell us? Are they divorced?'

'Not so far as I know. They only got married a few weeks ago.'

'Mark was supposed to go to the wedding,' interjected Millie.

'But then that Egyptian trip came up and I couldn't make it.'

'Can you *believe* it?' added Millie.

'Well.' Pamela sighed dramatically. 'I must say I'm absolutely *astonished*.'

'Isn't it a coincidence?' persisted Millie.

'But does he know she's here? I mean, why hasn't he been in touch? Why has she never mentioned that she had a husband squirreled away?'

'I had *heard*,' began Mark doubtfully, 'that something had happened.'

'What sort of something?'

'An accident of some sort. I'm not sure of the details.'

'Don't beat about the bush,' said Pamela briskly. 'What sort of accident?'

'No, really, I only heard the vaguest rumours about it. I couldn't say for sure. I'd hate to get it wrong.'

'Oh, for God's sake,' said Pamela.

'Come on, Mark,' said Millie.

'It happened when they were on honeymoon. That's all I know. I think she had a bit of a fall or something, and that's the last anyone heard of her.'

'What *can* you mean?' cried Pamela. 'What sort of a fall? Do you mean she fell off a cliff and her husband couldn't find her, and the next thing we know is that she's washed up here?'

'Calm down, Mummy.'

'She fell,' resumed Mark, his voice constricted, 'and nearly went over the balcony of their hotel room. In Rome, I think. She wasn't hurt. But she evidently went a bit funny.'

'In the head?' demanded Pamela.

'Possibly. There was a suggestion that it might have been – *deliberate*, if you see what I mean. Don't quote me on that, though. As I say, I've only heard the vaguest rumours. In any case, she came back to London without Edward and then disappeared.'

'Well, perhaps she didn't like Edward. Perhaps that's all there was to it.'

I felt a pang of fondness for Pamela as I stood crushed behind the ante-room door.

'Why would she have married him if she didn't like him?' said Millie.

'Oh, how should I know?' said Pamela irritably. There was a clatter of saucepans. 'Pass me that dish, would you? I really must get on with dinner. It's getting terribly late.'

'I still can't understand what she's doing here,' said Mark after a pause. 'Even if things did go wrong with Edward, it does seem rather extreme to pack in your job and leave London and all that.'

'What job?' said Pamela. 'I thought she was temping.'

'Oh no, I don't think so. She was a solicitor, as far as I remember. Something like that, anyway. She had a degree, for God's sake.'

'I can't see what having a degree, if that's what she's got, has to do with anything. We're not exactly barbarians down here. You may think country people sit around discussing crop rotation, but—'

'*Mummy!*' said Millie.

'I'm merely defending myself against the suggestion that we're some sort of second best. I shouldn't think Stella would say that she's been bored. You'd need a degree to keep up with Martin, for Heaven's sake.'

There was a silence, and more clattering sounds.

'I should call Edward, I suppose,' said Mark. 'He's been going mad, wondering where she is. So've her parents, apparently. And her boss must be furious. I'd say she'll be lucky to get her job back.'

'Frankly, I'll be sorry to lose her,' said Pamela. 'Martin *adores* her, and it's such a trial for him chopping and changing every other day. Quite honestly' – a tearful strain entered her voice – 'I don't see how we're going to begin to cope.'

'Oh, it'll be *fine*,' consoled Millie.

From my shadowy enclosure I began to hear sounds from elsewhere, a sort of scratching noise coming from further along the passage. I stood rigid as a board, not daring to move. The scratching became a scuttling, and then all at once I felt a rush of air and something jostling me about the legs. A shriek of surprise escaped my lips.

'What on earth was that?' said Pamela from the kitchen.

A pair of Satanic eyes glared up at me through the gloom. I heard the familiar sound of panting, the unmistakable bustle of canine chops. Roy, or his ghost, had returned to haunt me.

'*The wind beneath the door!*' Mark was saying in a spectral voice, while Millie trilled with appreciation.

'Don't you start as well,' said Pamela. 'My children think I'm batty enough as it is. Be a dear and go and have a look, would you? Everyone says we're mad still leaving our doors open, but I'd hate to be barricaded in.'

I heard footsteps approaching across the kitchen floor. In a flash I had bolted silently from the ante-room and into the hall, leaving Roy – the miracle of whose resurrection I had not even had time to appreciate – behind as prime suspect for the unexplained noise. Quietly I ascended the stairs to Martin's room and stood outside his door.

I was not relishing the thought of an encounter with Martin, even with the weighty matter of Roy off my conscience. After the incident beside the pool, I had fled back to the cottage, where I had sat in my bedroom crouched out of sight beside the wardrobe for a considerable time. Nobody had come to look for me, even after I had heard Pamela's car pull up in the drive. The absence of a search party had lent weight to my suspicion – confirmed just now by what I had overheard from the kitchen – that Mark and Millie had given an immediate and unsparing account to Pamela of my disgrace, and that I had been outlawed from the society of the family, to be dealt with when the opportunity arose and presumably without mercy. I felt guilty nonetheless that I had been unable to fulfil my promise to Pamela of helping her with the dinner. I had considered the option of presenting myself in the kitchen with this offer as if nothing had happened, and indeed had come over to the house with that aim.

With that expiatory course of action now ruled out, however, I was forced to fall back on the harder truth; namely that my life in the country was to be brought to an abrupt conclusion, and that I was to return to London as soon as possible with few good wishes on the part of those I left behind. I will not go into my feelings concerning this prospect. You may recall the letters I wrote before my departure. I had the sensation, characteristic of the landscape of unrelieved misfortune, that I was rushing very fast downhill, as if through the blackest of tunnels; and that I could neither resist my slide nor indeed feel very much about it at all. There is something almost purifying about this type of loss of control, if one can forget that it will inevitably lead at some point to the most brutal contact with the solid ground of reality.

'Hello,' said Martin, when I entered the room. He was sitting in his chair reading a book.

'Hello,' I replied, seating myself in the leather armchair. It was almost dark now, and in the twilight Martin's face wore an indistinct beauty of suggestion. 'You shouldn't read in the dark.'

'I wasn't reading.'

'How was Aunt Lilian?'

'Old. Aunt-like.'

'When did you get back?'

'Hour ago. Bit more.'

'Sorry. There didn't seem much point in coming over.'

There was a pause.

'What happened, Stel-la?' said Martin gravely, turning his face towards me.

I had admittedly made my apology on the assumption that news of my afternoon's activities had reached him, but nonetheless I experienced a form of grief at hearing this assumption confirmed. I have always, ever since I was a child, disliked being in trouble, and would find the machinations of whatever authority it was I had crossed – the deadly conveyance of information, the steely privacy of consultation, the resultant efficiency of the reprimand – strangely sinister. It aroused in me a primitive fear, and even though I was not strictly afraid of the Maddens, and could indeed if pressed make a good case for not caring what they thought of me in the slightest, I felt it now.

'I could explain it,' I said, 'but you wouldn't believe me.'

'Try.'

I remembered my investigation of the Maddens' fridge that morning, the early and innocent misdemeanour which had subsequently cost me so much. What else had I been supposed to do, abandoned without food and with no means of procuring any?

'I was hungry!' I cried. My still unrelieved inanition flooded forth at the words and I sank weakly back into my chair. 'I haven't eaten anything all day,' I continued, my mouth dry.

'Why ever not?' said Martin. 'You don't need to diet. You're thin.'

'I don't want to be thin!' I wailed. 'I just don't have any money!'

'Well, I know it's not *much*,' said Martin doubtfully. 'But it certainly should be enough to—'

'No,' I said, closing my eyes. 'I mean I *really* don't have any. They – your parents haven't paid me yet.' Summoning my last reserves of energy, I explained the chain of consequence which had led from this simple omission to my discovery, drunk and unconscious, in the swimming pool.

'Oh, I don't think it was just that,' said Martin, with that hint of 'authority' which instilled in me such terror. 'I think they thought you weren't – *happy*.'

'What's that supposed to mean?' I demanded, rallying slightly.

'Never mind,' said Martin. 'Look, I'll talk to them. See if I can sort this business out. There's obviously been a misunderstanding.'

'You won't be able to. They've made up their minds.'

'How do you know?'

'I just do.'

There was a long pause.

'If that's the case,' concluded Martin with a sigh, 'it's probably because they think it's for your own good, Stel-la. And they've got a point. They're used to having a different sort of girl here – you know, someone from abroad who wants to learn English for a year, waifs and strays. You've got a life, for Heaven's sake.'

'But I don't want it!'

A voice could be heard issuing faintly from downstairs.

'Mum's on the warpath,' said Martin. 'We'd better go down. It's supposed to be Dad's birthday dinner, after all. Come on.'

'I can't!'

'Why not?'

'I can't face them all! Mark, and your sister, and your parents—'

'Everyone has to face things. It's the only way. Come on.'

We went out into the corridor, whose unilluminated gloom ushered us along, a reprimand for our lingering upstairs. I paused at the top of the stairs, while waves of conversation drifted up through the empty hall from the open door of the room below. Martin began hurriedly to shuffle down at the sound, evidently recognizing in it the call of his tribe; and for a moment I too longed to be part of this human noise, to feel the ache of singularity eased by other bodies, the strange spikes and curlicues of solitude which protruded from me like invisible horns sanded down by the gladsome, warming rub of society.

'Hurry up,' called Martin over his shoulder. 'They've already gone in to dinner.'

I followed Martin down the stairs, as sombrely as if to the beat of an executioner's drum. I could not believe that I was to be made to face those whose only thought when they saw me could be that I had failed to justify my presence here and was to be sent away. He mounted his chair and span swiftly off to the right, from where the voices were coming. I stood in a void of dread and disbelief outside the door; and then reeled after Martin into the room.

What a lovely sight would have greeted me, if only I had been looking at it through different eyes! We had entered the dining room, a room I had never been in before, its novelty ornamented with the magic of a special occasion. It was lit entirely by candles, whose pale, guttering columns rose from a vast table in the centre, and whose glow in the velvety dark gave every surface the appearance of being heaped with treasure. The light glittered off glasses and cutlery, sparkled on the china rims of plates, flashed over rings and necklaces, and pooled warmly over the circle of faces gathered around the table; faces which to me were but half-familiar and at this point probably hostile, but which to Martin formed the landscape of everything that he loved.

'Finally!'

'Where have you *been*?'

'We've been calling you for *hours*, darling!'

The volley of exclamation caused me to shrink momentarily back into the shadows; but Martin looked over his shoulder as if to bring me to heel, and I reluctantly followed him towards the table. Now that the fog of our arrival had lifted slightly, I could begin to distinguish one face from another. There was Caroline, resplendent in some floral garment with elaborately puffed sleeves, from which the slabs of her arms protruded and rested powerfully on the table. Next to her was a man I did not recognize, with a babyish face and a very pale, oval head, the fringe of whose fair, fuzzy hair clung in a sort of tide mark around the level of his ears. Beside him sat Mark, and beside him Millie. Even in that rushed first assessment of the table, I could not prevent myself from being struck anew by her loveliness. She was wearing the same red dress in which I had seen her earlier, but her mouth glistened darkly with lipstick. Next to her sat Toby, groomed and buffed to perfection in a crisp white shirt and dark jacket; and next to him Pamela, whose impossibly girlish form was encased in a tight black dress. Around her neck was a rope of pearls. Mr Madden beamed combustibly beside her. A double gap remained between him and Caroline, which it took me some time to appreciate constituted my own invitation to dinner. Dimly I was struck by the operation of manners in this foreign, fortunate, sparkling world. It was, I understood then, their law, their discipline, their religion. I may have been scorned, reviled, found wanting; but it had been deemed correct, for reasons which were unclear to me and which I sensed had not even been exhumed for re-examination on this occasion, that I should attend dinner.

'Stella, why don't you sit next to Piers?' said Pamela. 'And Martin can slot in there beside Caroline.'

'Happy birthday,' I said to Mr Madden, seating myself in the high-backed chair beside him. An exquisitely arranged plate, which I understood to be the first course, sat in front of me, bearing a small dish of pâté and several delicate slivers of toast.

'Not yet!' he barked jovially, looking about the table with abrupt, jerking movements, a bewildered, slightly desperate smile on his face, as if he were unsure whether a mistake had been made.

'We know it's not yet, darling,' said Pamela soothingly, placing a hand on his arm. 'We're just sort of seeing it in.'

'A toast!' cried Toby suddenly, raising his glass.

'Oh yes, let's have a toast,' said Pamela.

'To—' Toby looked around the table, making it clear that his toast was not dedicated to any particular cause. His eyes lighted on Caroline. 'To Caroline's baby!'

There was a chorus of approval. Caroline blushed.

'And Derek's,' she asserted over the noise. 'It's Derek's baby too!'

'*Cawo*,' said Derek reprovingly.

'We know it's Derek's baby, darling,' said Pamela.

'Unless there's something you haven't told us!' snorted Toby, casting around the table for more appreciation in the wake of his toast triumph.

'It's just that you're our *daughter*,' continued Pamela. 'Margaret probably feels the same about you, doesn't she, Derek?'

'She's vewy pleased,' nodded Derek.

'I should hope she is!' said Pamela. 'Caroline told us you were going to name the baby after her.'

'Only if it's a girl,' said Derek dubiously.

'*Obviously* only if it's a girl, darling,' said Caroline between her teeth.

'Well, I should be very flattered if I were her,' said Pamela. 'I've obviously abused my children horribly. They'd *die* rather than pay me that sort of a compliment.'

'*Ahhh*,' said Toby, putting his arm around her. 'Poor Mummy.'

'It's true!' protested Pamela. 'When I think of what I went through to bring you four lumps into the world! And never a word of thanks from any of you!'

'I'm not a *lump*,' said Millie to Mark.

'*Mummy!*' shrilled Caroline nervously. 'How can you say that?'

'Thank you for giving birth to us,' intoned Martin solemnly.

'Now, now,' said Mr Madden.

'Thank you for fathering us,' continued Martin, turning to him.

At this a mouthful of pâté, which I had been surreptitiously consuming while the others conversed, lodged in my throat, causing me to choke.

'Goodness!' cried Millie.

'Heave-ho!' said Toby.

'Not *again*,' said Pamela, while Martin slapped me on the back.

'Excuse me,' I spluttered, my eyes watering.

'Are you all right?' said Mark, whom I could feel watching me from the other side of the table.

'I'm fine,' I said, glancingly catching his eye.

There was a pause around the table while my interruption was absorbed. As if by agreement, the assembled company bent their heads to their plates or took up their glasses.

'Mark and I have got an announcement to make,' said Millie presently. She took Mark's hand firmly in her own. Their slender fingers lay entwined on the table.

'What?' said Caroline with her mouth full, looking around as if she had missed something.

'Oh, *darlings*!' cried Pamela, catching her breath and clasping her hands to her chest in anticipation.

'We've decided that we're going to move in together,' beamed Millie.

'You're going to *what*?' said Caroline.

'Oh *darlings*,' said Pamela, more severely. 'Are you sure that's a good idea?'

'What are they saying?' said Mr Madden, casting about confusedly for some translation and eventually turning to me.

'They—' It seemed inappropriate for me to repeat the announcement, and so I sat far back in my chair, passing the responsibility to Martin.

'They're going to move in together,' explained Martin. 'In London.'

'Move *in*?' said Mr Madden. 'Not get married?'

'We don't want to get married, Dad,' said Millie.

'Why ever not? Caroline did.'

At this Caroline's face immediately took on a rigid expression. The compliment had evidently taken her by surprise, but not so much that she was unable to prevent herself from being seen to be glorying in it. She put her hand beneath her chin and looked interestedly at her father.

'Mark's against it,' said Millie.

'*Against* it? How can you be *against* marriage?' Mr Madden guffawed, as if in appreciation of some joke, which he evidently expected to be informed his daughter's remark was.

'His parents are divorced,' said Millie, while Mark looked silently down at his plate. 'He's seen how much damage it can cause.'

This remark, although I couldn't discern why, was evidently judged to have exceeded the boundaries of good taste. There was an immediate chill in the atmosphere of the room. Millie sat with a stricken expression. Caroline touched Derek's arm and quietly asked him to pass her the butter. Pamela stood up.

'Right,' she said brightly. 'I think I'll get the second course in. Would someone mind giving me a hand?'

'I will,' I said.

'Thank you, Stella,' said Pamela. She gave me quite a friendly look. Millie's unpopularity had evidently freed up a quantity of approval which I, by my offer, had been able to claim. 'If you could just stack up some of these plates and bring them out with you, I'll go and get on.'

Obediently I toured the table, collecting the debris of the first course. As I reached over each shoulder to retrieve a plate, I seemed to be dipping briefly into the charged aura of another human being, tasting their incredible autonomy. Millie seemed to shrink from my proximity as I leaned past her, as if she were too delicate and fragile to withstand it. The sturdy, tanned back of Mark's neck visibly prickled when I came to him. Derek was as mild as milk, yielding immediately to the temporary authority of my business.

'Families!' exclaimed Pamela when I reached the kitchen. She was tapping about in her high heels, incongruously glamorous. 'Is your family as noisy as ours, Stella?'

'No,' I said.

'Do you know, I've never even *asked* you about your family!' she shrieked, above the rattling of plates and dishes. 'How many are you?'

'Five. Four,' I said.

'You don't sound very sure,' she remarked.

'I had a brother who died.'

'Oh.' She bent down, hands muffled in oven-gloves, and opened the oven. 'How terribly sad.'

'Yes, it was.'

'You must miss him dreadfully.'

'It was a long time ago. But yes.'

She didn't say anything more. When she straightened up, her face looked pinched and rather annoyed.

'Shall I start taking things through?' I said anxiously.

'You're a darling.' She laid a hand briefly on my arm and I flushed with pleasure. 'I don't know what I'd do without you. I hope that's not too hot.'

She handed me a serving dish full of bright, steaming vegetables. I bore the dish out of the kitchen and into the anteroom. It was in fact very hot, and by the time I reached the hall I was forced to stop and put it down on the floor for a moment to relieve my hands.

In that moment, crouched on the floor beside the steaming dish, I had a most peculiar feeling. It started as a sensation of almost overwhelming unreality, as if I had woken up and found myself there without the faintest idea of how I had come to be so; but then this feeling peaked or crested in some way, and I felt it flood out of me like something boiled over. When it had gone, I became aware of the most remarkable silence; not in the house, but in myself. The roar of the past week had ceased. I was quiet. I was quiet inside. I picked up the serving dish and bore it into the dining room.

'Where on *earth* have all my dishcloths got to?' said Pamela, when I returned to the kitchen for the next consignment. 'I used to have simply masses of them.'

'It's not *fair*!' Millie was wailing when I returned to the dining room. 'I don't see why she's got to act as if everything's a personal injury to her. It's not as if she can stop us. She may as well just be nice about it.'

'Being old-fashioned,' observed Mr Madden, uncharacteristically epigrammatical, 'is hardly an unreasonable quality in a parent. Your mother's entitled to her opinion, as am I. Don't see why we should pretend to be pleased if we're not.'

'Your father's got a point,' nodded Mark diplomatically. His forehead shone with sweat.

'Mummy and Daddy are only being honest,' added Caroline. 'I do think you're being a teensy bit oversensitive, Millie.'

'There's no need to stick your tongue *right* up their arses,' said Martin crudely.

'Daddy!' shrieked Caroline. 'Derek!'

'Steady on,' said Derek, although to whom it was not clear.

'I can see your point, mate,' said Toby, grinning horribly at Mark. 'I'd want to keep my options open too.'

'That's not funny,' said Millie.

'If you really believe that Mummy and Daddy can't stop you,' rallied Caroline, 'then I don't see why you're so upset. It suggests that you *do* care what they think.'

'Of course she cares,' said Martin. 'She just wants their blessing.'

'Exactly,' nodded Millie.

'I heard that,' snapped Caroline, turning on Martin.

'What did he say? What did he say?' implored Toby.

'I won't repeat it. Something very rude, not surprisingly. Our boy genius doesn't seem to have all that much imagination.'

Martin was mouthing something at Toby, who was chortling oafishly, leaning across the table.

'Look, let's just change the subject, can we?' said Mark wearily.

'I hope you're all hungry!' announced Pamela, bearing in a joint of meat on a vast silver platter.

I sat down in my chair as Mr Madden got up and prepared to carve. My hands were resting in my lap; but presently I felt the warm, clammy pressure of another hand, Martin's, taking one of mine. He removed it from my lap and held it under the table. I glimpsed him out of the corner of my eye. He was looking straight ahead, as if nothing unusual had happened. I didn't resist his gesture, which I took to be one of comfort and solidarity. What surprised me more was that I actually seemed to be having some physical response to it. Waves of electricity were passing from his hand up my arm. I did not interpret this as proof of some deeply submerged romantic feeling for Martin on my part. It was merely, I felt sure, that I was not touched very often by another human being. A plate of meat and vegetables arrived in front of me. The pâté had served to awaken rather than satiate my appetite; and at the sight of the plate, saliva began to prickle in my mouth. I wondered how I would be able to eat with Martin gripping my right hand.

'Dig in!' cried Mr Madden cheerfully.

'*Bon appetit!*' said Toby.

'This looks *delicious*,' said Millie.

'Great,' affirmed Mark.

'Mummy's gone to *so* much trouble,' declared Caroline.

'Looks splendid, Mrs M.,' said Derek.

'Happy birthday, darling,' said Pamela, leaning towards her husband and giving him a kiss on the cheek.

'Hmmph!' exclaimed Mr Madden, who evidently felt it was not worth his while pointing out again that it was not yet his birthday.

I picked up my fork face-up in my left hand – it is surprisingly easy to do this, once you accustom yourself to it – and began to eat. The food tasted good. My wineglass sat untouched in front of me. Martin shifted his grip slightly, squeezing my fingers tighter. I squeezed back. We turned our heads and our eyes met; and we both smiled.

Reading Group Guide

Discussion Questions:

1. *The Country Life* could be seen as a modern take on *Jane Eyre*, as well as on a certain popular type of British novel that extolls the virtues of country living. How does Rachel Cusk play with the themes and plot of Charlotte Brontë's classic novel, and with the perceived ideals of a rural existence?

2. What role does Martin play in bringing Stella to a better understanding of herself? How are Martin and Stella alike?

3. Stella tells Martin: "I don't think that happiness is the be-all and end-all of everything....I happen to believe that the search for happiness is often itself the greatest cause for unhappiness." How does the resolution of the novel support or refute Stella's belief? Do you agree with her assertion?

4. Stella finds Pamela Madden puzzling and intimidating, until she is able to separate "the reality of Pamela's situation from the manner in which she represented it." How does this split between reality and appearance manifest itself in the Maddens, in Stella's own life, and in the novel as a whole?

5. What purpose do Stella's visits to the postal clerk serve?

6. When she arrives at Franchise Farm, Stella is almost immediately overtaken by all manner of physical calamity and destruction. What does her misfortune say about her, about her surroundings, and about her decision to embark on this new life?

7. Class is often an issue in British life and British fiction. Stella sees her younger brother as a victim of her parents' social aspirations, while she believes her older brother was made "homogenous" by the same desires. Do the Maddens, and the village, bear out Stella's sense that class has a dangerous power to destroy individuality, whether literally or figuratively?

8. In what ways is *The Country Life* a morality story? A farce?

9. "It's no good saying that if people aren't perfect you're not going to love them. That's what families are all about. They absorb things. They grow round them. They may end up looking all twisted and ugly, but at least they're strong." By the novel's end, do you think Stella would agree with this statement of Martin's?